U0037398

PETER
PAN
EX-LIBRIS
©DEE TEN PUBLISHING CO.

彼得潘
PETER PAN

詹姆斯・馬修・巴利／著
盛世教育／譯

笛藤出版

目次

彼得潘

Content

Peter Pan

第一章

彼得闖了進來

直到彼得潘出現之前，世界上再也
沒有比他們更樸實快樂的家庭了。

除了一個孩子，所有的孩子都會長大。他們很快就會發現這件事，而溫蒂是這樣發現的：她兩歲時，有一天在花園裡玩，她摘了朵花跑向媽媽，我想她的樣子一定非常討人喜歡，因為達林太太把手放在胸口大聲地說：「噢，你要是一直像這樣子該有多好啊！」關於這件事，她們之間只說過這句話。從此，溫蒂就知道自己一定會長大。孩子們總是到了兩歲就會明白這件事。兩歲既是結束也是開始。

他們住在十四號（*他們的房子在大街上的號碼*）。當然，一直到溫蒂出生之前，媽媽都是家中的主角。她是個很有趣的太太，內心充滿幻想，嘴甜甜的，卻愛捉弄人。她充滿幻想的內心，就像是來自神奇東方世界的小盒子，一個裡面還有一個，無論打開多少個，裡面永遠還有另一個。而她那張甜甜的、愛捉弄人的嘴上總是掛著一個吻，一個雖然明顯地掛在右邊嘴角上，溫蒂卻始終都得不到的吻。

達林先生是這樣贏得芳心的：當達林太太還是小女孩時，很多男孩不約而同地喜歡上她，而當他們長大成為紳士之後，都跑去她家求婚，只有達林先生租了輛馬車搶先抵達，就這樣娶走了她。達林先生得到了她的一切，除了她內心最深處的小盒子和那個吻。他從不知道那個小盒子的事，最後也放棄了那個吻。溫蒂認為拿破崙應該可以得到那個吻，不過我能想像拿破崙嘗試之後，也只能氣沖沖地甩門離去。

達林先生常常向溫蒂炫耀，說她的媽媽不僅愛他，還很尊敬他。他學識淵博，懂得股票和股份。當然，沒有人真正了解這些事，不過他看起來很像是知道的，他常常說股票漲了，股份跌了，說得頭頭是道，讓所有女人都尊敬他。

達林太太結婚時穿了一身雪白的婚紗。剛開始，就像玩遊戲一樣，她興高采烈地把家中的帳記得一清二楚，連一顆包心菜都不會漏掉。可是漸漸地，她連整棵花椰菜都漏掉了，取而代之的是一些沒有臉孔的嬰兒畫像。她在應該算帳的時候畫畫，每一幅都是達林太太的想像。

第一個出生的是溫蒂，接著是約翰，最後是麥可。

溫蒂出生後的一、兩個星期，他們懷疑是否能夠留下她，因為又多了一張嘴要吃飯。達林先生對溫蒂的到來十分引以為傲，但他是個體面的人，他坐在達林太太的床邊，一邊握著她的手，一邊計算開銷，達林太太則是用哀求的眼神望著他。不管發生什麼事情，她都想要冒一次險，可是達林先生不想這麼做，他想做的就是拿著筆跟紙計算。如果達林太太提出建議干擾了他，他就會從頭再算一次。

「別再打斷我了。」他懇求。

「我這裡有一鎊十七先令，辦公室裡還有二先令六便士；我可以取消辦公室的咖啡，那樣可以省下十先令，加起來是兩鎊九先令六便士。加上你的十八先令三便士，總共有三鎊九先令七便士，我的支票簿還有五鎊，總共八鎊九先令七便士——是誰在亂動？——八、九、七，小數點進七——別說話，親愛的——還有你借給找上門的男人的一英鎊——安靜點，孩子——小數點進，寶貝——你看，還是被你給打亂了！——我剛才是說九、九、七嗎？沒錯，我說的是九、九、七。問題是，我們能靠九鎊九先令七便士過一年嗎？」

「我們當然可以，喬治。」達林太太大聲說。她偏袒溫蒂，但達林先生才是兩人中比較有分量的人。

「別忘了腮腺炎。」達林先生用近乎威脅的語氣警告她，接著計算下去，「腮腺炎一鎊，我先記下這個數字，但我敢說差不多三十先令——別說話——麻疹一鎊五先令，德國麻疹半幾尼，總共要兩鎊十五先令六便士——別搖晃妳的手指頭——百日咳十五先令。」他就這樣計算著，每次算出來的結果都不一樣。不過最後溫蒂還是熬過來了，腮腺炎減到十二先令六便士，兩種麻疹合併算成一種。

約翰出生時，也發生過同樣的騷動，麥可的遭遇更是驚險，不過這兩個孩子最終都被留下了。不久之後，你就能看見三人排成一排，在保姆的陪伴下，一起去福爾森小姐的幼兒園上學。

達林太太喜歡安於現狀，達林先生卻堅持凡事要和左鄰右舍一樣，所以他們當然也請了保姆。因為他們沒有錢，而且孩子們奶粉錢開銷太大，所以他們家的保姆是一隻端莊的紐芬蘭犬，名叫娜娜。在達林家雇用她之前，她並沒有特定的主人，不過她總是很重視孩子。達林家是在肯辛頓公園認識娜娜的，她花了大部分的閒暇時間窺探著嬰兒車。那些粗心大意的保姆們很討厭她，因為她會跟著她們回家，向她們的女主人打小報告。她確實是個不可多得的保姆。洗澡時，她總是做得一絲不苟；夜裡不管什麼時候，只要她照顧的孩子發出些微的哭聲，她就會一躍而起。想當然，她的狗屋在育嬰房裡。她有一種天賦，知道什麼情況下的咳嗽不能輕忽，什麼時候要在脖子上圍長襪。她始終相信傳統療法，像是用大黃葉治病，並對新流行病菌這類說法嗤之以鼻。看她護送孩子們上學就像上了一堂禮儀課，當孩子們表現得規規矩矩時，她就安靜地走在他們旁邊；當他們亂跑亂動時，她就會用頭把他們頂回隊伍。在約翰要踢足球的日子，她從來不會忘記他的毛衣；她嘴裡經常叼著一把傘，以防下雨。福爾森小姐的幼兒園裡有一間地下室，保姆們都在那裡等著接孩子們放學。她們都坐在長凳上，只有娜娜臥在地板上，不過那是唯一不一樣的地方。她們假裝沒有看見她，認為娜娜配不上她們，其實，娜娜反而很鄙視她們膚淺的閒聊。她不喜歡達林太太的朋友們來參觀育嬰房，可是如果她們真的來了，她會先迅速扯下麥可的圍兜兜，替他換上有藍色花邊的衣服，然後撫平溫蒂的衣裙，再匆忙梳理一下約翰的頭髮。

沒有任何一個保姆比娜娜更稱職了，達林先生非常清楚這一點，但有時還是不安地懷疑鄰居們會不會說閒話。

他必須顧及到他在城中的名聲。

娜娜還有件事讓達林先生很困擾，有時候他會覺得娜娜不夠尊重他。「我知道她非常敬佩你，喬治。」達林太太向他保證，然後暗示孩子們要對爸爸再好一點。然後，她會跳起迷人的舞，而另一位，也是唯一的女僕莉莎偶爾也會被獲准加入。穿著長裙、戴著女僕帽子的莉莎顯得如此嬌小，雖然當初受雇時她發誓自己超過十歲。這群嬉鬧的人多愉快啊！最高興的就是達林太太了，她踮起腳尖瘋狂地旋轉，你能看到的只有她的那個吻。如果這時候衝向她，或許就能得到這個吻。直到彼得潘出現之前，世界上再也沒有比他們更樸實快樂的家庭了。

達林太太第一次聽說彼得這個名字，是在她整理孩子們心事的時候。每個好媽媽晚上都有個習慣：當孩子們睡著以後，徹底檢查他們的心思，把白天散亂的物品放回原位，讓第二天早晨變得井然有序。如果你能醒著不睡著（*當然你肯定做不到*），就能看見你的媽媽在做這些事，你還會發現看著她這麼做很有趣。這很像在整理抽屜，我想你會看見她跪在那裡，津津有味地翻著你腦海裡的東西，很好奇你究竟是從哪裡撿到這些東西的，她會發現有些東西很可愛，有些沒那麼可愛。她會把這樣東西當成可愛的小貓般，貼在她的臉頰上，也會把那樣東西快速地收起來，放在看不見的地方。當你早上醒來，睡前那些淘氣的想法和壞脾氣都被折得小小的，放在你腦海的最底層，而最上層放著的，則是美好清爽的想法，等著你使用。

我不知道你有沒有見過人類心智圖。有時醫生會畫出你身上其他部位，然後你自己的圖像就變得特別有趣。但是當你碰巧看到他們試著畫出孩子的心智圖時，你會發現那張圖不僅雜亂無章，而且始終旋轉不定。上面有彎彎曲曲的線，就像體溫的曲線圖。這些線大概就是島上的道路吧，因為永無島或多或少像個島嶼，灑滿了驚人的色彩。附近的海面上有一片珊瑚礁，漂浮著輕快的小船。島上有侏儒和荒涼的獸穴、大部分是裁縫師的地精、河流穿過的洞穴、有六個哥哥的王子們、一間快要倒塌的小屋，還有一個身材矮小有鷹鉤鼻的老太太。如果只有這些東西，這張圖就好畫多了，但是那裡還有第一天上學、宗教信仰、神父、圓形水池、針線活、謀殺案、絞刑、不及物動詞、巧克力布丁日、穿吊帶褲、數到九十九、獎勵自己動手拔牙的三便士等等。這些東西不是在永無島上，就是在另一幅地圖上，一切都混亂不清，尤其裡面沒有東西是靜止不動的。

當然，每個人的永無島都很不一樣。例如，約翰的永無島上有潟湖，上面飛著許多紅鶴，約翰正要用箭射牠們。麥可年紀還小，他的永無島上也有一隻紅鶴，上面飛著許多湖泊。約翰住在一艘翻倒在沙灘上的船，麥可住在簡陋的棚屋，溫蒂住在一間用樹葉精巧地縫成的房子。約翰沒有朋友，麥可在睡夢中有朋友，溫蒂有一隻被父母遺棄的小狼犬。不過整體說來，他們的永無島還是離不開家庭模式。如果讓他們安靜地站成一排，你大概會說他們的鼻子長得一樣。玩耍的孩子們總是拖著小船登上這些神奇的海灘。我們也到過那個地方，我們到現在還聽得見浪潮聲，雖然我們再也無法上岸了。

在所有令人愉悅的島嶼之中，永無島是最舒適、最緊湊的，島不太大，也不會太分散，從一個冒險到另一個冒險的距離恰到好處，十分緊湊。白天你用椅子和桌巾玩遊戲時，一點也不會感覺到它的存在，但是在你入睡前的兩分鐘，它就變得非常真實，這就是要點夜燈的原因。

有時候達林太太在孩子們的腦海裡漫遊時，會發現一些她想不通的事，其中最讓她困惑的就是「彼得」這個名字。她不認識叫彼得的人，但是他卻出現在約翰和麥可的腦海各處，溫蒂的腦子裡更是塗滿了這個名字。這個名字比別的字還要醒目，當達林太太盯著它看時，覺得這名字有種奇怪的傲氣。

「對，他蠻自大的。」當達林太太問溫蒂時，她遺憾地承認。

「他是誰啊，寶貝？」

「他是彼得潘啊，你知道的，媽媽。」

剛開始達林太太根本就想不起來有這麼一個人，但是當她回想起自己的童年，便想起了有這麼一個名叫彼得潘的人，據說他和仙子們住在一起，還有許多關於他的傳說。例如，當孩子們死了之後，他會陪著他們走一段黃泉路，免得他們害怕。那時候達林太太也很相信他，可是現在她結婚了，懂事了，她非常懷疑是不是真的有這個人。

「而且，即使這個人真的存在，他現在也應該長大了吧。」她告訴溫蒂。

「噢，沒有，他沒長大，」溫蒂很肯定地告訴媽媽，「他跟我一樣大。」溫蒂的意思是，彼得的身高、心智、年齡都和她一樣。她也不清楚自己為什麼知道，反正她就是知道。

對此，達林太太詢問過達林先生的想法，不過達林先生只是不屑地笑了笑。「聽我說，這一定是娜娜灌輸他們的，只有狗才會有這種想法。別管了，自然會被忘記的。」

可是這件事並沒有被忘記，而且很快地，這個難纏的男孩將讓達林太太嚇了一大跳。

孩子們常會有些奇遇，但他們卻絲毫不覺得奇怪。例如，他們可能會在事情發生的一個禮拜後，才提起他們在森林裡遇見了死去的父親，還跟他一起玩。某天早上，溫蒂就是這樣漫不經心地說了一件讓人心神不寧的事。他們發現育嬰房的地板上有幾片樹葉，明明昨天晚上孩子們上床睡覺前不在那裡的。正當達林太太百思不得其解時，溫蒂卻笑嘻嘻地說：

「一定又是那個彼得做的！」

「你在說什麼，溫蒂？」

「他真調皮，玩完了也不打掃乾淨。」溫蒂嘆了口氣說道。她是個愛乾淨的孩子。

她煞有其事的說，有時候彼得會在夜裡來到育嬰房，坐在她的床邊吹笛子給她聽。可惜她從沒醒來過，因此她也不知道自己是如何知道的，反正她就是知道。

「你在胡說些什麼，寶貝！沒敲門誰也進不來的。」

「我覺得他是從窗戶進來的。」溫蒂說。

「親愛的，這裡可是三樓呢！」

「樹葉不就在窗邊嗎，媽媽？」

的確，樹葉就是在離窗子很近的地方被發現的。

達林太太不知道該說什麼，因為這一切在溫蒂看來都是那麼自然，不能隨便說她在做夢，就把這件事含糊帶過。

「我的孩子，你為什麼不早點告訴我呢？」溫蒂的媽媽大聲說。

「我忘了。」溫蒂毫不在意地回答，急忙跑去吃早餐。

啊，她一定是在做夢。

可是另一方面，樹葉的確就在那裡。達林太太仔細檢查了這些樹葉，那是些只剩下葉脈的枯葉，不過可以確定的是，這些樹葉絕不屬於任何英國生長的樹種。她趴在地板上，藉著燭光仔細查看地面，看看是否有陌生人的足跡，又舉起火鉗伸進煙囪裡翻動、敲打牆壁。她從窗戶垂下一條帶子到人行道上，足足有三十英尺，而牆上甚至沒有任何可以攀爬的水管。

溫蒂一定是在做夢。

可是溫蒂並沒有做夢，這件事在隔天晚上就被證實了，孩子們非比尋常的冒險可以說就是從那天晚上開始的。

那天晚上，孩子們和平常一樣上床睡覺。那一晚碰巧娜娜休假。達林太太替他們洗澡，唱歌給他們聽，直到他們一個個鬆開她的手進入夢鄉。

一切都顯得如此安寧舒適，達林太太不禁嘲笑起自己的多慮，於是靜靜地坐在火爐旁縫起衣服。

這是給麥可做的，等他過生日的時候就該換襯衫了。爐火暖洋洋的，育嬰房裡點著三盞夜燈，朦朦朧朧的。沒過多久，針線就掉在了達林太太的腿上，她睡著了，優雅地點著頭。看看這四個人，溫蒂和麥可睡在那邊，約翰睡在這邊，而達林太太睡在火爐旁。本來應該有第四盞夜燈的。

達林太太睡著之後做了一個夢，她在夢中看見永無島離她很近很近，有個陌生的男孩從那裡衝了出來。這男孩並沒有嚇到她，因為她覺得自己曾在一些沒有小孩的女人臉上見過他，也許在一些母親的臉上也可以看到吧。但是在她的夢裡，這個男孩撥開了遮掩著永無島的那一層薄霧，她看到溫蒂、約翰和麥可正藉由那條裂縫窺探著。

這個夢本原本是微不足道的，但就在她做夢時，育嬰房的窗戶被風吹開了，果真有個男孩落在地板上，身旁還有一團不到拳頭大的奇異光芒，在房間裡四處亂竄，像是有生命一樣。

我想肯定是這團光把達林太太驚醒了。

她尖叫著站了起來，發現了那個男孩。不知道為什麼，她立刻知道這個人就是彼得潘。如果當時你我或溫蒂就在那，我們會覺得他像極了達林太太的那個吻。他是一個可愛的男孩，穿著用枯葉脈和樹漿做成的衣服。不過他身上最讓人著迷的地方是他那一口乳牙。當他發現她是大人時，就朝她呲牙裂嘴，露出了小小珍珠般的乳牙。

第二章

影子

她回到育嬰房，發現娜娜嘴裡叼著東西，原來是那男孩的影子。

達林太太尖叫了一聲，房門就像應門似的打開了，傍晚散步回家的娜娜衝了進來，對著男孩咆哮並撲向他，但他卻輕盈地從窗戶跳了出去。達林太太又叫了一聲，這次是因為擔心那個孩子，她以為他摔死了，於是她跑下樓，到街上尋找小小的屍體，但是沒找到。她抬頭仰望漆黑的夜空，除了一點她以為是流星的亮光，什麼也沒看見。

她回到育嬰房，發現娜娜嘴裡叼著東西，原來是那男孩的影子。當他跳出窗戶時，娜娜迅速地關上窗戶，不過動作太慢了，沒能捉住他，可是他的影子來不及逃出去，窗戶「砰」的一聲關上，把影子扯了下來。

你可以肯定達林太太仔細地檢查了那個影子，但只是非常普通的影子。

毫無疑問地，娜娜知道該怎麼處置這個影子。她想把影子掛在窗戶外面，因為她覺得「彼得一定會回來拿，就把影子放在可以輕易取得，又不會驚動孩子們的地方吧。」

可是，達林太太沒辦法把影子掛在窗外，那看起來像在晾衣服，會降低房子的格調。她想把影子給達林先生看，不過達林先生正忙著計算給約翰和麥可買冬季厚大衣的費用，他甚至還在頭上繞了條濕毛巾，用來保持頭腦清醒。這時候去打擾他似乎不太恰當，何況她非常清楚他會說：「這全都是因為找了一條狗來當保姆。」

達林太大決定把這影子捲起來，小心翼翼地放在抽屜裡，等合適的時機告訴丈夫。唉，真是的！

一星期後，機會來了，就在那個永遠無法遺忘的星期五。那天當然是星期五。

「我應該特別小心星期五才對。」事後她經常對丈夫這麼說，娜娜通常會在她的另一側，握著她的手。

「不，不，」達林先生總是這麼說：「所有的事情都是我的責任。都是我，喬治・達林，都是我造成的的。皆吾之過，皆吾之責任。」他曾受過古典文學教育。

他們就這樣坐著，夜夜回想著那個無可挽回的星期五，直到所有細節深深地烙印在他們腦海，穿透至另一面，像劣質錢幣一樣。

「如果我沒答應二十七號的晚宴邀約就好了。」達林太太說。

「如果我沒把我的藥倒進娜娜的碗裡就好了。」達林先生說。

「如果我假裝愛喝那藥水就好了。」娜娜以濕潤的眼眶示意。

「都怪我太愛參加舞會了，喬治。」

「都怪我那天的幽默感，親愛的。」

「都怪我太愛計較了，親愛的主人。」

接著他們會一個個崩潰大哭起來。娜娜心想：「是啊，是啊，他們不該讓一隻狗當保姆。」有好幾次都是達林先生用手帕替娜娜擦眼淚。

「那個惡魔！」達林先生大吼，娜娜吠著附和他，可是達林太太從沒責怪過彼得，因為她右嘴角上似乎有什麼東西不希望他責罵彼得。

他們會坐在空蕩蕩的育嬰房裡，傻傻地回想著那個可怕的夜裡所發生的每一個小細節。一開始，那天晚上就和其他無數個夜晚一樣平凡無奇，娜娜為麥可放洗澡水，然後背他去洗澡。

「我不要睡覺。」麥可喊道，自以為這件事他說了算。「我不睡，我不睡。娜娜，還不到六點。討厭，討厭，我再也不愛妳了，娜娜。我說我不要洗澡，我不要洗嘛，我不要洗嘛！」

這時穿著白色晚禮服的達林太太走了進來。她很早就已經穿戴整齊，因為溫蒂非常喜歡看她穿晚禮服的樣子，她脖子上戴著喬治送給她的項鏈，手臂上戴著溫蒂的手鐲——那是她和溫蒂借的，溫蒂也很願意把手鐲借給媽媽。

達林太太發現老大和老二正在玩扮家家酒，一個扮演她，一個扮演他們的爸爸，演著溫蒂出生那天的情景。她聽見約翰說：

「我很高興地告訴你，達林太太，你當媽媽了。」說得好像達林先生真的在那個場合說過這句話一樣。

溫蒂高興地手舞足蹈，好像真正的達林太太一定這麼跳過舞。

接著約翰出生了，他的神情格外得意，他以為這是因為生了個男孩吧。這時，麥可洗完澡過來，也要求把他生下來，可是約翰殘忍地說，他們不想再生了。

麥可差點哭了出來。「沒人要我。」他說。當然穿晚禮服的那位太太無法坐視不管。

「我要，」她說，「我多想要第三個孩子啊。」

「男孩還是女孩？」麥可不抱期待的問。

「男孩。」

他聽到之後跳進了媽媽的懷裡。現在回想起來，達林夫婦和娜娜都覺得這只是件小事，但如果想到這是麥可在育嬰房的最後一晚，那就不是件小事了。

他們繼續回憶著。

「我就在那時候像一陣旋風闖了進去，對不對？」達林先生自嘲，當時他確實像一陣旋風。

或許他確實情有可原。那時他也正在為舞會穿衣打扮，一切都很順利，直到打領結的時候。這件事說來也確實讓人驚訝，達林先生雖然懂得股票和紅利，卻無法擺平他的領結。有時這玩意會乖乖的屈服於他，但如果有時他能放下自尊，戴上現成的領結，或許會對這個家更好。

這次恰巧就碰上了這種情況。達林先生手裡捏著一條皺巴巴的領結，急急忙忙地衝進了育嬰房。

「怎麼了？發生什麼事了，親愛的爸爸？」

「什麼事！」他大吼，他確實是在大吼。「這個領結繫不上去。」他變得非常尖酸刻薄。「沒辦法繫在脖子上！在床柱上就可以！沒錯，我已經繫在床柱上二十次了，可是沒辦法繫在我的脖子上！噢，不要這樣！求你饒了我吧！」

他覺得達林太太並沒有特別在意他所說的話，於是嚴厲地說：「孩子的媽，我警告你，除非這個領結繫在我的脖子上，不然今晚我們就不去晚宴了，如果今晚我沒去參加宴會，那我就再也不去上班了，如果我不去上班，你和我就會餓死，我們的孩子就會流落街頭。」

即使如此，達林太太還是十分鎮定。「讓我來試試吧，親愛的。」她說。其實這正是達林先生跑來想讓她做的事。達林太太用她那雙靈巧的手替他繫上了領帶，此時孩子們都圍在一旁，等待著他們的命運。她輕而易舉地打好了領帶，有些男人也許會因此生氣，不過達林先生天生寬容大度，並不在意這種小事。他隨口對太太說了聲謝謝，馬上就忘了自己在生氣，轉眼間已經背著麥可在房裡跳起舞來。

達林太太回想起當時的情景：「那時我們玩得多瘋狂啊！」

「那是我們最後一次嬉鬧了！」達林先生嘆息著說。

「噢，喬治！你記不記得有一次麥可突然問我：『你是怎麼認識我的，媽媽？』」

「我記得。」

「那時候他們真是可愛，對不對，喬治？」

「他們曾經是我們的，是我們的，現在他們都不見了。」

那天晚上，一直到娜娜出現，他們才停止嬉鬧玩樂。很不幸的是，達林先生撞在娜娜身上，褲子上黏滿了狗毛，這不僅僅是條新褲子，而且還是達林先生人生中第一條帶花邊的褲子，因此他不得不咬著嘴唇，以免眼淚掉下來。當然，達林太太幫他刷乾淨了。可是他又開始發牢騷，說請一隻狗當保姆真是個錯誤。

「喬治，娜娜是我們的寶貝。」

「這點毫無疑問，但有時我會不太自在，總覺得她把孩子們當小狗看待。」

「不會啊，親愛的，我相信她知道他們是有靈魂的。」

「我懷疑，」達林先生深思熟慮後說道：「我很懷疑。」他的妻子覺得可以趁這個機會把小男孩的事告訴他。剛開始，他對這個故事嗤之以鼻，但是當達林太太拿出影子給他看後，他就變得很關心這件事。

「我不認識這個人。」他邊說邊仔細觀察那個影子。「不過看起來的確像個無賴。」

「你記得嗎？我們還在討論的時候，娜娜帶著麥可的藥進來了。你以後再也不要用嘴去拿藥瓶了，娜娜，這都是我的錯。」達林先生說。

雖然他是個堅強的人，但在吃藥這點，他的確表現得相當愚蠢。

如果他有什麼弱點的話，那就是他自以為他這輩子吃起藥來都很勇敢。因此，當麥可把頭避開娜娜嘴裡銜著藥的湯匙時，他責備道：「像個男子漢，麥可。」

「不要，不要。」麥可調皮地哭喊著。達林太太走出房間給他拿了塊巧克力，達林先生覺得態度要夠堅決。

「孩子的媽，不要太縱容他。」他在達林太太後面喊：「麥可，我像你這麼大的時候，可是一聲不吭就把藥吃下去。我會說：『親愛的爸爸媽媽，謝謝你們給我吃藥，讓我的病快點好起來。』」

麥可信以為真，已經穿上睡衣的溫蒂也相信了，為了鼓勵麥可，她說：「爸爸，你偶爾吃的那種藥比這個還難吃，對不對？」

「難吃多了，」達林先生勇敢地說：「如果我沒有把那瓶藥弄丟的話，麥可，我會立刻示範給你看。」

達林先生並沒有把藥給弄丟，只是在夜深人靜的時候爬上衣櫥，把藥藏在裡面。可是他萬萬沒想到，忠實的僕人莉莎找到了那瓶藥，又把它放回了盥洗台。

「我知道藥在哪裡，爸爸，」溫蒂嚷嚷著，她總是樂意為別人效勞。「我去拿。」達林先生還沒來得及阻止她，她就跑了出去。這時達林先生的心情馬上跌到了谷底。

「約翰，」達林先生打了個寒顫：「那玩意非常噁心，難吃死了，黏黏的，甜得要命。」

「很快就會沒事的，爸爸。」約翰興高采烈地說。這時，溫蒂拿著一杯藥水，匆匆忙忙地跑了進來。

「我已經盡快回來了。」她氣喘吁吁地說。

「你真是出人意料的快啊。」她爸爸彬彬有禮，卻有點賭氣的反駁，但溫蒂完全沒注意到。「麥可，你先吃。」他堅持地說。

「爸爸先吃。」麥可說，他生性多疑。

「吃下去會不舒服的，你知道嗎？」達林先生嚇唬他說。

「快吃吧，爸爸。」約翰說。

「安靜點，約翰。」他爸爸嚴厲地說。

溫蒂感到很困惑：「我還以為你會毫不費力地吃下去，爸爸。」

「這不是重點，」他反駁：「重點是，我這杯子裡的藥比麥可湯匙裡的多很多。」他那顆驕傲的心幾乎要爆炸了。「這不公平，即使我只剩下最後一口氣，我也要說，這不公平。」

「爸爸，我還等著你喝呢。」麥可冷冷地說。

「你等著，你說得倒好，那我也等著。」

「爸爸是膽小鬼。」

「你才是膽小鬼。」

「我才不怕。」

「我也不怕。」

「那好，喝下去。」

「那好，你喝。」

溫蒂想到一個絕妙的點子：「為什麼不兩個人同時喝呢？」

「當然可以，」達林先生說：「你準備好了嗎，麥可？」

溫蒂數著，一、二、三，麥可喝下了他的藥，達林先生卻把藥藏在他背後。

麥可憤怒地大叫著。溫蒂驚叫：「噢，爸爸！」

「『噢，爸爸』是什麼意思？」達林先生質問。「不要吵，麥可。我本來打算要喝的，但是我沒喝到。」

三個孩子盯著達林先生，那種眼神真是可怕，就好像他們不再敬佩他似的。「你們三個，看這裡。」當娜娜一走進浴室，達林先生就懇求他們。「我剛剛想到一個很棒的玩笑，我要把這杯藥倒進娜娜的碗裡，她會以為是牛奶而喝下去！」

藥的顏色確實很像牛奶。不過孩子們並沒有他們爸爸的幽默感，他們用責備的目光看著達林先生把藥倒進娜娜的碗裡。「真是太有趣了。」達林先生沒有把握地說，達林太太和娜娜回到房間以後，孩子們也不敢揭穿他。

「娜娜，乖狗狗，」達林先生拍了拍她說：「我在你的碗裡倒了一點牛奶，娜娜。」

娜娜搖著尾巴跑了過去，舔了舔那碗藥，然後給達林先生一個眼神，那眼神並不是憤怒，而是含著一滴又大又紅的眼淚，這讓我們為這條高貴的狗感到難過。然後她爬回了自己的狗窩。

達林先生感到非常羞愧，可是他並不想讓步。在一陣令人害怕的沉默中，達林太太聞了聞那個碗。「噢，喬治，」她說：「這是你的藥！」

「只是個惡作劇而已。」達林先生大吼，此時達林太太正在安慰兩個男孩，而溫蒂擁抱著娜娜。「很好，」達林先生心酸地說：「我這樣拚死拚活，還不是想讓全家開心。」

溫蒂依舊抱著娜娜。達林先生喊著：「是啊，你們就寵著她吧！都沒有人向著我，一個都沒有！我只不過是個賺錢養家的人，為什麼要討好我呢！為什麼，為什麼，為什麼！」

「喬治，」達林太太懇求他說：「別那麼大聲，傭人們會聽到的。」不知為什麼，他們習慣叫莉莎「傭人們」。

「就讓他們聽見好了，」達林先生毫忌憚地回答：「讓全世界的人都來聽聽吧。但是我不會再讓那條狗在我的育嬰房裡作威作福了，一刻也不行。」

孩子們都哭了，娜娜跑到達林先生面前求情，可是他揮揮手要她走開。他再次覺得自己是個堅強的男子漢。「沒用的，一切都是徒勞，」他喊。「院子比較適合你，到院子裡去，我立刻就把你拴起來。」

「喬治，喬治，」達林太太低聲說：「別忘了我跟你講過關於那男孩的事。」

唉，他聽不進去了。他堅決要看看誰才是這個家的主人。當他的命令無法將娜娜從狗窩裡喚出來時，他就用甜言蜜語引誘她出來，然後粗暴地抓住她，把她拖出育嬰房。他覺得有些慚愧，但他還是這麼做了。這一切都是因為他天生感情豐富，渴望得到崇拜。當他把娜娜拴在後院之後，這個可憐的父親走到前廊坐了下來，用指關節遮住雙眼。

與此同時，達林太太在少有的寂靜中哄著孩子們上床睡覺，點亮了夜燈。他們聽見娜娜的吠聲，約翰啜泣著說：「都是因為爸爸把她拴在院子裡。」可是溫蒂更聰明。

「那不是娜娜傷心時的吠聲，」溫蒂說，並沒有猜到將要發生什麼事，「那是她嗅到危險時的吠聲。」

危險！

「你確定嗎，溫蒂？」

「嗯，確定。」

達林太太打了個寒顫走到窗前。窗戶牢牢地鎖著。她往外看，夜空繁星點點，簇擁著房子，彷彿好奇地想看看屋裡將會發生什麼

事。但是她並沒有注意到這些，也沒有看到有一兩顆小星星正在對她眨眼示意。然而，一股莫名的恐懼感揪住她的心，讓她喊道：「唉，真希望今晚不用去參加宴會！」

即使是半睡半醒睡的麥可也感受到了媽媽的不安，他問：「媽媽，點了夜燈還有什麼東西可以傷害我們嗎？」

「沒有，寶貝，」她說：「夜燈是媽媽們留下來守護孩子們的眼睛。」

達林太太走到每一張床前，給他們唱搖籃曲，小麥可張開雙臂摟著她的脖子。「媽媽，」他說：「我很高興有妳在我身邊。」這是之後很長的時間裡，她聽到小麥可說的最後一句話。

二十七號公館離他們家只有幾步路，不過剛下了點雪，為了不弄髒鞋子，達林夫婦很有技巧地挑著路走。街上只剩下他們倆個人，滿天的繁星都注視著他們。星星很美，但不會主動參與任何事，永遠只能做旁觀者。這是對它們的懲罰，因為很久以前它們犯了錯。由於時間太過久遠，如今已經沒有星星知道到底做錯了什麼事。所以年長的星星就這樣睜著茫然大眼沈默寡言（*眨眼就是星星的語言*），可是小星星們仍舊充滿了好奇心。其實它們和彼得並沒有很要好，因為他十分淘氣，經常偷偷摸摸走到它們背後，想吹熄它們。但是它們太愛玩了，所以今晚都站在他那邊，急著想趕走礙事的大人。當達林夫婦走進二十七號公館，關上了門，天空起了一陣騷動，銀河裡最小的那顆星星高喊：「趁現在，彼得！」

第三章

走啦，走啦！

他們不像彼得飛得那麼優雅，雙腿
會不自覺地踢幾下，不過他們的頭
已經可以碰到天花板，沒有什麼比
那更美妙了。

達林夫婦離開家門之後，那三個孩子床邊的夜燈還一直明亮地照著。那是三盞非常精緻的小夜燈，我們巴不得它們能一直醒著，這樣就可以看見彼得了。但是溫蒂的燈眨了眨眼睛，打了一個大大的哈欠，另外兩盞夜燈也跟著打起了哈欠，打完哈欠的嘴都還沒閉上，三盞燈全都熄滅了。

此時房間裡又出現了一道亮光，比夜燈還要亮一千倍。就在我們說到這裡的時候，那亮光已經翻遍育嬰室裡所有的抽屜，尋找著彼得的影子，它在衣櫃裡到處亂翻，把每件衣服的口袋都徹底翻了過來。其實它並不是亮光，只是因為它飛得太快，看起來就像一道光，當它停下來休息時，你會發現它是一個小仙子，比手掌還要小，不過還在長大。她是個女孩，叫做叮噹，身上裹著枯葉做成的禮服，四方形的領口開得很低，恰到好處地展現了她有點豐滿的身材。

小仙子進來後不久，窗戶被小星星們吹開，彼得跳了進來。他帶著叮噹走了一段路，所以他的手上還沾著許多仙塵。

「叮噹。」他在確定孩子們都睡著後，輕聲呼喚。「叮噹，你在哪？」這時叮噹正在一個罐子裡，她非常喜歡這個地方，因為她以前從沒待在罐子裡。

「噢，快從罐子裡出來，告訴我，你知不知道他們把我的影子藏在哪裡？」

一個極其可愛的叮噹聲回答了他，那聲音就像金色鈴鐺一樣清脆。這是仙子的語言，普通的小孩是永遠聽不到的，但是如果聽到了，你就會知道自己曾經聽到過。

叮噹說影子在大箱子裡，其實她指的是五斗櫃。彼得跳到五斗櫃，用雙手把裡面的東西全都撒在地上，就像國王向人群拋撒半便士硬幣一樣。他很快就找到了自己的影子，高興得把叮噹被關在抽屜裡的事忘了。

如果他動腦筋想想——雖然我不認為他會這麼做——當他和他的影子相互靠近時，就會像兩滴水一樣融合在一起。可是，他們並沒有合在一起，彼得嚇壞了。他試著用浴室裡的肥皂把影子黏上，一樣失敗了。彼得渾身發抖，坐在地板上哭了起來。

彼得的哭聲吵醒了溫蒂，她坐了起來。當她看到一個陌生人坐在育嬰室的地板上哭泣時，她並沒有驚慌，只覺得很好奇。

「男孩，」她親切地說：「你為什麼在哭？」

彼得非常有禮貌，因為他在仙子的慶典上學會了一些優雅的禮儀。他站起來，非常紳士地向溫蒂鞠躬。溫蒂受寵若驚，也在床上優雅地回禮。

「你叫什麼名字？」彼得問。

「溫蒂·莫伊拉·安琪拉·達林。」她頗為得意地回答，「你叫什麼名字？」

「彼得潘。」

溫蒂確定他就是彼得，不過這名字真的有點短。

「只有這樣嗎？」

「對。」彼得尖聲回答。他第一次覺得自己的名字很短。

「我很抱歉。」溫蒂・莫伊拉・安琪拉說。

「沒關係。」彼得強忍著這口氣。

溫蒂問他住在哪。

「第二個路口右轉，」彼得說:「然後一直向前走，直到天亮。」

「好奇怪的地址！」

彼得有點失落。他第一次覺得或許這個地址很奇怪。

「不奇怪。」他說。

溫蒂想起自己是女主人，於是溫柔地說：「我的意思是信封上就這麼寫嗎？」

彼得寧願她沒提起信的事情。

「從來沒收過信。」他輕蔑地說。

「你媽媽也不收信嗎？」

「沒有媽媽。」彼得說。他不但沒有媽媽，而且根本就不想要什麼媽媽。他覺得人們實在太高估了媽媽的角色。然而，溫蒂立刻想到她應該是遭遇了悲慘的事。

「噢，彼得，難怪你會哭。」溫蒂說著跳下床跑到他面前。

「我不是因為媽媽才哭的。」彼得頗為氣憤地說。「我是因為沒辦法把影子黏上才哭的。再說，我沒有哭。」

「影子掉下來了嗎？」

「對。」

這時，溫蒂看到了地板上的影子已經被拖得髒兮兮的，她為彼得感到非常難過。「真糟糕！」她說。可是，當她看到彼得試著用肥皂黏影子時，又情不自禁地笑了，真是個不折不扣的小男孩啊。

幸虧她立刻就想到了辦法。「一定要用針線縫上才行。」她用小大人的口氣說。

「縫？」彼得問。

「你還真是無知。」

「不，才不。」

不過溫蒂就是喜歡他傻傻的。雖然彼得和她一樣高，但她還是說：「小夥伴，我來幫你縫上吧。」然後拿出她的針線盒，把影子縫在彼得腳上。

「我想會有點痛。」她警告彼得。

「噢，我不會哭的。」彼得說，他自以為他這輩子從沒哭過。他咬緊牙關，還真的沒哭，影子很快就被縫好了，不過還有點皺。

「或許我該把它熨一熨。」溫蒂想了想之後說。可是彼得跟別的男孩子一樣，對外表一點都不在乎，此刻他正欣喜若狂的跳著。唉，他早就忘了這都要歸功於溫蒂。他以為影子是他自己黏上去的。「我真聰明，」他興高采烈地大喊著：「噢，最聰明的人就是我！」

雖然有點難為情，但還是得承認，彼得的狂妄自大正是他最有魅力的特色之一。坦白說，從沒有像彼得這樣驕傲自大的男孩。

不過，這時的溫蒂很驚訝。「你這個自大狂，」她語帶嘲諷地說。「當然我沒幫什麼忙！」

「你也是有點貢獻的。」彼得毫不在乎地說，然後繼續跳舞。

「有點！」溫蒂傲慢地說：「就算我什麼都沒做，那我至少可以不理你吧。」她相當優雅地跳上床，用毯子把臉蓋住。

彼得假裝要離開，想吸引溫蒂抬頭，但沒有成功，於是他坐在床尾，用腳輕輕地踢她。「溫蒂。」他說：「別不理我，溫蒂，我只要一高興，就會忍不住歡呼。」溫蒂仍舊沒有抬頭，儘管她非常熱切地聽著。「溫蒂，」彼得用一種沒有女孩能抵抗得了的語氣繼續說：「溫蒂，一個女孩比二十個男孩還管用。」

雖然溫蒂的身高不過幾寸，但是她畢竟是個女孩子，因此還是忍不住從床單底下探出頭來偷看。

「你真的這麼想嗎，彼得？」

「對。」

「我覺得你實在是太可愛了，」溫蒂說：「我現在就起來。」她和彼得並排坐在床邊。她還說如果彼得願意的話，她想給他一個吻，可是彼得不明白她的意思，滿懷期待地伸出雙手。

「你應該知道什麼是一個吻吧？」溫蒂驚訝地問。

「把吻給我，我就知道了。」彼得固執地回答。為了不讓他傷心，溫蒂給了他一枚頂針。

「現在我可以給你一個吻嗎？」彼得說。溫蒂拘謹地回答：「如果你願意，那就請吧。」她迫不及待地把臉頰湊了過去，但他只是把一顆橡實放在她手上，於是溫蒂慢慢地把臉縮了回去，並且親切地說，她要把他的吻串成項鏈戴在脖子上。幸虧她真的把這項鍊帶在脖子上，因為這東西後來救了她一命。

在這個故事裡，人們相互認識之後，總是習慣詢問彼此的年齡，於是一向喜歡做對的事的溫蒂就問了彼得他幾歲。這對彼得來說不是個愉快的問題，感覺就像希望考題是英國歷代國王時，卻拿到了英文文法的考卷。

「我不知道，但我還很小。」彼得不自在地回答。對此他的確一無所知，只是猜想自己很小，可是他胡亂地說：「溫蒂，我在出生的那天就逃跑了。」

溫蒂非常驚訝，可是又覺得有意思。於是她非常有禮貌地碰了碰睡衣，暗示彼得可以坐近一些。

「因為我聽見我的爸媽在談論。」彼得輕聲地解釋。「談論我將來長大以後要成為什麼樣的人。」說到這裡，他變得格外激動。「我不想長大。我要永遠當個小男孩，開開心心的玩。所以我逃到肯辛頓公園，和仙子們一起住了很久很久。」

溫蒂用崇拜的眼神看著他，彼得以為她是在羨慕自己離家出走，不過其實是因為他認識仙子。溫蒂過著平凡的家庭生活，在她看來，能夠認識仙子是件非常新奇有趣的事。她問了一大堆關於仙子的問題，這讓彼得很意外，因為對他來說，仙子很討人厭，老是礙手礙腳，有時他甚至得打他們一頓。不過，整體來說，他還是喜歡他們的。他還跟溫蒂說起了仙子們的由來。

「你知道嗎？溫蒂，當第一個嬰兒第一次發出笑聲時，這個笑聲會碎成一千片，到處跳來跳去，這就是仙子們的由來。」

這個故事很無聊，但整天待在家裡的溫蒂很喜歡。

彼得溫和地繼續說：「所以每個男孩和女孩都應該有一個仙子。」

「應該？實際上沒有嗎？」

「沒有。現在的孩子們懂得太多了，他們很快就不相信仙子。每當有孩子說『我不相信仙子』，某個地方就會有一個仙子墜落死亡。」

其實，此刻彼得覺得關於仙子的話題已經談論得夠多了，而且他忽然想起來叮噹一直沒吭聲。「不知道她去哪裡了。」彼得邊說邊站起來，叫著叮噹的名字，溫蒂的心突然興奮得怦怦跳。

「彼得，」她緊緊抓著他喊：「你該不會要告訴我房間裡有仙子吧？」

「她剛剛還在這裡。」他有點不耐煩地說：「你沒聽到她的聲音吧？」他們倆安靜地聽著。

溫蒂說：「我只聽見叮叮噹噹的鈴聲。」

「沒錯，那就是叮噹，那是仙子的語言。我想我也聽到她的聲音了。」

聲音是從五斗櫃裡傳來的，彼得露出開心的笑容。沒有人像彼得擁有如此燦爛的笑容，最可愛的就是他那咯咯的笑聲。他還保有最初的笑聲。

「溫蒂，」他開心地輕聲說：「我想我肯定把她關在抽屜裡了！」

他把可憐的叮噹從抽屜裡放了出來，叮噹一邊在育嬰室裡到處亂飛，一邊怒氣沖沖地尖叫。「你不該把那些事情說出來的。」彼得不甘示弱的反駁：「我真的很抱歉，可是我怎麼會知道你在抽屜裡？」

溫蒂並沒有注意他說的話。「噢，彼得，」她喊：「要是她能站著不動，讓我看看就好了！」

「她們很難好好站著。」彼得說，但是接下來的瞬間，溫蒂看見那個傳說中的身影停在一座咕咕鐘上。「噢，真的好可愛！」她喊，雖然叮噹早就氣得臉都歪了。

「叮噹，」彼得親切地說:「這位淑女說希望你當她的仙子。」

叮噹非常傲慢無禮地回答。

「她說什麼，彼得？」溫蒂問。

彼得不得不翻譯說:「她不太有禮貌。她說你是巨大的醜八怪，還說她是我的仙子。」

他試著說服叮噹：「叮噹，你知道你不能當我的仙子，因為我是一個紳士，而你是一個淑女。」

對於這番話，叮噹是這樣回答的：「你這個大笨蛋。」說完就飛進浴室裡消失了。「她是個很普通的仙子，」彼得抱歉地解釋。「她之所以叫叮噹，是因為她會修理鍋子和水壺。」

這時他們一起坐在扶手椅上，溫蒂又纏著彼得問了很多問題。

「如果你們現在不住肯辛頓公園—」

「有時還是會住在那。」

「那你現在通常住在哪？」

「跟遺失的男孩住在一起。」

「他們是誰？」

「他們是保姆東張西望時，從嬰兒車裡掉出來的孩子。要是七天之內沒有人認領的話，他們就會被送到遙遠的永無島，用來支付費用。我是隊長。」

「那一定很好玩！」

「對啊，」狡猾的彼得回答：「不過我們非常孤單。我們沒有女的夥伴。」

「孩子們之中沒有女生嗎？」

「噢，沒有。你懂的，女孩子們太聰明了，不會從嬰兒車裡掉出來。」

這段話讓溫蒂十分滿意。「我覺得有關女孩子的事，你說得真是太好了。那個約翰瞧不起我們。」她說。

為了回應溫蒂，彼得站了起來，一腳把約翰連人帶毯踢下床。溫蒂覺得第一次見面就這樣似乎太魯莽了，她對彼得說他不是這個房間裡的隊長。不過約翰仍舊在地板上安安穩穩地睡著，溫蒂也就由著他睡在地上。「我知道你是好意，」溫蒂有些心軟地說：「所以你可以給我一個吻。」

此時溫蒂已經忘記彼得不知道什麼是吻。「我就知道你會把它要回去。」彼得有些難過地說，拿出頂針想要還給她。

「噢，親愛的，」善良的溫蒂說：「我指的不是吻，是頂針。」

「那是什麼？」

「就像這樣。」溫蒂親了他一下。

「真有意思！」彼得莊重地說：「現在我可以給你一個頂針嗎？」

「如果你想的話。」溫蒂說，這次她的頭保持不動。

彼得給了她一個頂針，幾乎就在同時，她尖叫了一聲。

「怎麼了，溫蒂？」

「好像有人拉我的頭髮。」

「一定是叮噹，我從沒見過她這麼頑皮。」

果然是叮噹，她飛來飛去，嘴裡不停地說著難聽的話。

「溫蒂，她說每次我給你一個頂針，她就會這麼對你。」

「為什麼？」

「為什麼，叮噹？」

叮噹再次回答：「你這個大笨蛋。」彼得還是不了解，可是溫蒂明白了。而當彼得承認自己到育嬰室的窗邊並不是來看她，而是來聽故事時，溫蒂有一點失望。

「你知道，我沒聽過故事。遺失的孩子們也從沒聽過故事。」

「那真是糟透了。」溫蒂說。

「你知道燕子為什麼會在屋簷下築巢嗎？」彼得問：「就是為了聽故事。對了，溫蒂，你媽媽說的故事實在太好聽了。」

「哪個故事？」

「就是那個王子找不到穿玻璃鞋的淑女的故事。」

「彼得，」溫蒂興奮地說：「那是灰姑娘，最後王子找到她了，他們從此過著幸福快樂的日子。」

彼得聽了之後高興到從坐著的地方上跳了起來，急忙跑到窗口。「你要去哪裡？」溫蒂疑惑地大聲問道。

「去告訴其他男孩。」

「別走，彼得，」溫蒂央求：「我還知道很多故事。」

她的確是這麼說的，因此，不可否認是她先勾引彼得的。

彼得轉身回來，眼中閃爍著貪心的目光，溫蒂應該要警覺到的，但她沒有。

「噢，我可以說很多故事給那些男孩們聽！」溫蒂喊道。此時彼得拉著她走向窗戶。

「放開我！」溫蒂命令他。

「溫蒂，跟我走吧，去說故事給那些男孩們聽。」

這個要求當然讓溫蒂很高興，可是她說：「噢，親愛的，我不能去。我得替媽媽想想！再說，我又不會飛。」

「我可以教你。」

「噢，會飛真好。」

「我教你如何跳到雲的背上，然後我們就可以飛走了。」

「噢！」溫蒂欣喜若狂地呼喊著。

「溫蒂，溫蒂，何必睡在無聊的床上呢？妳可以和我一起到處飛翔，和星星們說些有趣的事情啊。」

「噢！」

「而且，溫蒂，那裡還有美人魚。」

「美人魚？有尾巴嗎？」

「尾巴有這麼長。」

「噢，」溫蒂叫了起來：「看美人魚！」

彼得狡猾極了：「溫蒂，我們都會非常尊敬你的。」

溫蒂苦惱地扭著身體，看起來好像在努力不讓雙腳離開房間地板上一樣。可是彼得才不會同情她。

「溫蒂，」這個狡猾的傢伙說：「晚上睡覺時候，你可以幫我們蓋被子。」

「噢！」

「從沒有人在晚上替我們蓋被子。」

「噢。」溫蒂張開雙臂伸向彼得。

「你還可以替我們補衣服、縫口袋，我們的衣服都沒有口袋。」

溫蒂怎麼可能抗拒得了。「這一定非常有趣！」她喊：「彼得，你能不能也教約翰和麥可飛呢？」

「你希望的話。」彼得毫不在乎地說。於是溫蒂跑到約翰和麥可床前把他們搖醒。「快起來，」她喊：「彼得潘來了，他要教我們飛。」

約翰揉了揉眼睛說：「那我要起床。」其實他早已經躺在地上了。「哈囉。」他說：「我起來了！」

這時候麥可也起來了，他精神抖擻，就像一把帶六刃一鋸的刀，不過彼得突然暗示大家安靜一點。他們的臉上露出十分狡猾的神情，那是孩子聆聽來自大人世界的聲響時的表情。一切都顯得很平靜。不，等等！一切都不對勁。娜娜一整晚都痛苦地吠著，這時候卻安靜了下來，他們沒聽到娜娜的聲音。

「把燈吹滅！躲起來！快！」約翰喊著。這是整個冒險中他唯一一次發號施令。因此，當莉莎牽著娜娜進來的時候，育嬰室又恢復了原樣，一片漆黑，你甚至會發誓你聽見了三個淘氣的小主人睡覺時發出的天使般的呼吸聲。其實，這聲音是他們躲在窗簾後面巧妙地裝出來的。

莉莎不太高興，因為她正在廚房攪拌聖誕布丁，娜娜荒謬的猜疑讓她不得不丟下布丁，她臉上還黏著一顆葡萄乾。莉莎認為要想得到片刻安寧，最好帶娜娜去育嬰室瞧瞧，不過當然要在她的監視之下。

「好了，你這個多疑的畜牲。」她一點都不同情娜娜丟了臉。「他們都很安全，不是嗎？小天使們都躺在床上睡得正香呢，聽聽他們輕柔的呼吸聲。」

這時麥可受到自己成功的鼓舞，呼吸得更大聲，害他們差點被識破。娜娜認出那種呼吸聲，試圖拖著腳步以掙脫莉莎的掌控。

可是莉莎反應很遲鈍。「不要再鬧了，娜娜。」她嚴厲地呵斥，把娜娜拉出了房間。「我警告你，你再叫的話，我馬上把先生太太從舞會請回來，那時候，哼，先生不把你打一頓才怪。」

她又把這隻不幸的狗拴了起來。可是，你真的覺得娜娜會停止狂吠嗎？把先生太太從舞會上請回家？這正是她求之不得的。只要她照顧的孩子平安無事，你覺得她會在乎挨打嗎？不幸的是，莉莎又回去做她的布丁了。既然不能得到她的幫助，娜娜只好不斷拉扯鏈子，最後終於把鍊子扯斷了。轉眼之間，她就闖進了二十七號公館的餐廳，高舉雙腳在空中猛揮，那是她溝通時最直接的表達方式。達林夫婦立刻明白育嬰室裡發生了嚴重的事，他們來不及跟女主人告別，就衝到了街上。

但是現在距離三個小壞蛋躲在窗簾後面假裝呼吸，已經過了十分鐘，在這十分鐘裡，彼得潘可以做很多事。

我們現在回過頭來講育嬰室裡的事。

「沒事了。」約翰從躲藏的地方走出來。「彼得，你真的會飛嗎？」

彼得懶得回答，而是繞著房間飛了一圈，半途還拿起了壁爐架。

「太棒了！」約翰和麥可說。

「好厲害！」溫蒂喊道。

「對啊，我好厲害，噢，我最厲害了！」彼得又得意忘形了。

飛行看起來好像很容易，他們先在地板上嘗試，接著又在床上試，但是一直往下掉，飛不起來。

「告訴我，你是怎麼做到的？」約翰揉著膝蓋問。他是個很實際的男孩。

「只要想著美好快樂的事，那些念頭會把你抬到空中。」彼得解釋。

彼得又表演了一次。

「太快了，」約翰說：「能不能慢慢地再做一次？」

彼得示範了慢的與快的。「我學會了，溫蒂！」約翰喊道，可是他很快就發現自己並沒有學會。他們沒有一個能飛到一吋，儘管最小的麥可已經在學兩個音節的單字，而彼得連二十六個字母都不認識。

當然，這是彼得是在跟他們開玩笑，沒有人能飛得起來，除非身上沾了仙粉。很幸運的，如同我們前面提過的，彼得有一隻手沾滿了仙粉，於是他往每個人身上吹了一點，起了絕佳的作用。

「現在，像我這樣扭動你們的肩膀，然後放手去飛！」

他們三個都站在床上，勇敢的麥可第一個飛了起來，他原本沒打算飛的，但他做到了，轉眼間就飛遍了整個房間。

「我飛起來了！」他在半空中尖叫了起來。

約翰也飛起來了，在浴室附近和溫蒂會合。

「噢，太美好了！」

「噢，太棒了！」

「快看我！」

「快看我！」

「快看我！」

他們不像彼得飛得那麼優雅，雙腿會不自覺地踢幾下，不過他們的頭已經可以碰到天花板，沒有什麼比那更美妙了。剛開始彼得還會伸手幫溫蒂，但後來不得不收手，因為叮噹氣得要死。

他們上上下下飛了一圈又一圈，依照溫蒂的說法，就好像在天堂。

約翰嚷道：「我說我們為什麼不飛到外面去呢！」

這正是彼得一直想引誘他們做的事。

麥可準備好了，他想知道飛十億英哩要花多少時間。但是溫蒂猶豫了。

「有美人魚噢！」彼得又說了一次。

「噢！」

「還有海盜呢。」

「海盜。」約翰喊著，一邊抓起他星期天戴的帽子。「我們馬上走吧。」

就在此時，達林夫婦帶著娜娜離開二十七號公館，他們衝到街道中央，抬頭看著育嬰室的窗戶，窗戶還緊閉著，但是房裡燈火通明，而最讓人膽顫心驚的是，他們看見三個穿著睡衣的小身影映在窗簾上不停地繞圈圈，不是在地上，而是在半空中。

不是三個人影，是四個！

他們顫抖著推開面向街道的大門。達林先生原本想衝上樓，不過達林太太示意他放慢腳步。她甚至努力讓自己的心跳得輕一點。

他們會及時趕到育嬰室嗎？如果趕上了，他們該多高興啊，我們也可以鬆一口氣，但是這樣就沒有故事可以說了。另一方面，要是他們沒趕上，我鄭重地保證，最後一定有好結局。

要不是那些小星星們監視著他們，他們原本可以及時趕到育嬰室。但星星們再次吹開了窗戶，其中最小的那顆星星大聲喊：

「彼得，小心！」

彼得知道，沒有時間可以浪費了。他霸道地喊：「來！」接著立刻飛進了夜空，約翰、麥可和溫蒂也跟著飛了出去。

達林夫婦和娜娜衝進育嬰室時已經太遲了，鳥兒們已經飛走了。

第四章

飛行

這一路上儘管偶爾有些小爭吵，但大致上來說還是愉快的，他們終於快到永無島了。

「第二個路口右轉，然後一直向前走，直到天亮。」

這是彼得之前告訴溫蒂去永無島的路，但即使是天上的鳥兒帶著地圖，按照上面每一個風角，按照每個指示也無法找到這個地方。你知道，彼得只是想到什麼就隨口說出來。

剛開始時，他的同伴們還對他深信不疑，而且飛行的樂趣如此美妙，以至於他們浪費了不少時間繞著教堂的塔尖，或是繞著沿途中其他有趣而高聳的東西飛行。

約翰和麥可比賽誰飛得快，結果麥可領先。

不久之前，他們才繞著房間飛就覺得自己非常了不起，現在想想還真有點可笑。

但不久之前到底是多久之前呢？當他們飛越一片大海之後，這個問題開始讓溫蒂心神不寧。約翰認為這是他們飛過的第二片大海和第三個夜晚。

有時候天很黑，有時候很亮。有時候很冷，有時候又太熱。有時候也不知道他們是真的餓了，還是假裝餓了，因為彼得用一種非常有趣的方法給他們食物：追逐那些嘴裡叼著人類吃的東西的鳥類，從牠們那裡搶奪食物。然後那些鳥兒就會追上來，又把食物奪回去。他們就這樣開開心心地互相追逐了好幾英里，最後在互相表示友好之後彼此告別。但是善解人意的溫蒂發現，彼得似乎不知道這種覓食的方法有多怪異，也不知道還有其他覓食的辦法。

當然他們不可能裝出睏倦的樣子，他們是真的睏了。在空中睡

覺是很危險的，因為只要一打瞌睡就會掉下去。更可怕的是，彼得居然覺得這挺有意思的。

當麥可突然像塊石頭往下掉時，彼得居然高興地大喊：「他又掉下去了！」

「救他，快救他！」溫蒂喊，驚恐地望著下面那片洶湧的大海。最後，在麥可快要掉進大海的瞬間，彼得從空中俯衝下來，一把抓住麥可。他這身手真是漂亮極了，不過他總要等到最後一秒才救人，你會覺得他只是想要賣弄他敏捷的身手，而不是為了救人。而且他的喜好變幻無常，此時他全神貫注於某種樂趣，但過一會兒他又突然對此失去興趣。因此，下一次你往下掉時，他很有可能就不理你了。

彼得可以在空中睡覺而不往下掉，他只需要仰臥著就能飄浮在半空中。這是因為他的身體太輕了，如果在他身後吹一口氣，他會飄得更快。

當他們在玩「請你跟我這樣做」的遊戲時，溫蒂低聲對約翰說：「對他禮貌點。」

「那你跟他說要他別再炫耀了。」約翰說。

原來在玩「請你跟我這樣做」的時候，彼得貼著水面飛行，又順便摸了摸每條鯊魚的尾巴，就像你走在街上時，用手指滑過一根根鐵欄杆一樣。這一招是他們做不來的，因此，彼得就像在炫耀，特別是當他時不時回過頭來張望，看看他們到底錯過了多少條鯊魚尾巴沒摸到時。

「你們一定得對他好一點，」溫蒂再三叮嚀弟弟們。「如果他丟下我們不管，那我們該怎麼辦？」

「我們可以回家啊。」麥可說。

「沒有他，我們怎麼找到回去的路呢？」

「我們就繼續往前飛。」約翰說。

「其實這才是最糟的，約翰。我們不得不一直往前飛，因為我們根本不知道怎麼停下來。」

這倒是沒錯，彼得忘記告訴他們該怎麼停下來了。

約翰說如果最倒楣的事情真的發生了，他們只要一直往前飛，反正地球是圓的，總有一天他們會飛回自己家的窗戶前。

「那誰替我們找吃的，約翰？」

「我剛剛乾淨俐落地從老鷹嘴裡搶奪了一小塊食物，溫蒂。」

「你嘗試了二十次才成功。」溫蒂提醒他。「就算我們順利找到食物，沒有彼得在身邊，我們會撞上雲朵或其他東西。」

的確，他們不斷撞到東西。現在他們可以飛得很穩了，儘管兩腿還是蹬踢很多次。但是當看到前面有雲朵時，他們越是想躲開，就越是要撞上去。如果娜娜跟著他們，她一定會在麥可的頭上纏一條繃帶。

此刻彼得不在他們身邊，他們覺得在天空中蠻寂寞的。彼得飛得比他們快多了，可以突然消失在眼前來場冒險，這可沒他們的份。他會因為想起和某顆星星說過的有趣笑話而狂笑著俯衝下來，可是他已經忘記是什麼笑話了；有時他又會從海裡飛上來，身上還沾著美人魚的鱗片，可是他又說不上來究竟發生了什麼事。這對那些從沒見過美人魚的孩子們來說，確實讓人生氣。

「如果他那麼快就忘了這些事，」溫蒂說：「我們要怎麼指望他一直記得我們呢？」

是啊，有時候他回來時真的不記得他們了，至少是記不太清楚了。溫蒂確認了這一點，白天在彼得正要超過他們時，她看到他眼裡流露出辨認的神情。有一次，她甚至不得不喊出自己的名字才讓他認出來。

「我是溫蒂。」她焦急地說。

彼得感到非常抱歉。「我說，溫蒂，」他對溫蒂輕聲說：「如果你發現我把你忘了，你只要一直說『我是溫蒂』，我就會想起來了。」

當然，這件事讓他們有點不滿。不過，作為補償，彼得教他們如何平躺在一陣與他們同向的狂風上。這變化是如此令人興奮，所以他們試了好幾次，然後發現這樣就能安穩地睡覺了。其實他們很想多睡一會兒，但彼得很快就不想睡了，然後迅速的用隊長的口吻喊道：「我們要在這裡著陸了。」這一路上儘管偶爾有些小爭吵，但大致上來說還是愉快的，他們終於快到永無島了。經歷了那麼多個月，他們真的飛到了，自始自終他們都是筆直地向前飛行，這倒不完全是因為有彼得或是叮叮鈴的帶領，而是因為那個島正期盼著他們的到來。只有這樣，人們才能看見神奇的海岸。

「就在那。」彼得平靜地說。

「在哪？在哪？」

「所有金箭指的地方。」

真的有一百萬支金箭為孩子們指出島的位置。那些金箭都是他們的好朋友太陽照射出來的。在黑夜來臨前，太陽要讓孩子們認清道路。

溫蒂、約翰還有麥可在空中踮著腳尖，想要看看這座小島。說來奇怪，他們一下子就認出它來了，在還沒害怕之前，他們跟它打了招呼。他們覺得那座島並不像是夢想已久終於看到的東西，反而像是放假回家遇見的老朋友。

「約翰，那邊有潟湖。」

「溫蒂，快看那些往沙堆裡埋蛋的海龜。」

「約翰，我看見你那隻斷腳的火鶴了。」

「看，麥可，那是你的洞穴。」

「約翰，在灌木叢裡的是什麼？」

「是一隻狼，還有牠的小狼。溫蒂，我肯定那就是你的小狼。」

「那是我的小船，約翰，兩邊都破了。」

「不對，那不是你的船。我們早就把你的船燒掉了。」

「不管怎樣，那就是我的船。約翰，我看見從印地安人帳篷裡冒出來的煙了。」

「在哪？指給我看，我可以告訴你，看這些煙怎麼彎曲就能知道他們是不是要打仗了。」

「在那裡，剛好穿過了那條神秘河。」

「我看見了，沒錯，他們正準備出兵打仗呢。」

他們知道得太多讓彼得不太高興。不過，如果他想在他們面前逞威風，那可說是勝利在望，因為，我前面已經說過了，不久之後他們就會籠罩在恐懼之下。

當金箭消失使整座島陷入黑暗時，恐懼也隨之降臨了。

以前在家的時候，每到睡覺時間，永無島就開始變得漆黑恐怖。島上出現了一些未知的荒涼地帶，慢慢擴張開來，黑影穿梭其中，野獸的吼聲聽起來也和從前很不一樣。最重要的是，你失去了取得勝利的信心。當夜燈亮起時，你會非常開心，你甚至很希望聽到娜娜說那只不過是壁爐，永無島只是他們的想像。

在家的時候，永無島當然是想像出來的。但此時此刻它是真實的。這裡沒有夜燈，天色也漸漸暗了，娜娜又在哪呢？

他們本來是各自飛，現在卻都緊靠在彼得身邊。彼得那漠不關心的神情終於不見了，他的眼神閃爍著光芒。每當他們碰到彼得的身體，就感覺到一陣刺激的電流。此刻他們正在那個恐怖島嶼的上空，飛得很低，低到他們的腳時常會擦過樹梢。天空中看不見什麼陰森恐怖的東西，可是他們卻飛得越來越慢，越來越謹慎，就好像要防備什麼敵人。有時他們還會停在半空中，等彼得用拳頭敲打一番，才繼續前進。

「他們不想讓我們著陸。」彼得解釋說。

「他們是誰？」溫蒂顫抖著小聲說。

可是彼得說不上來，或者是他不願意說。叮噹已經在他肩上睡著了，不過又被他叫醒了，讓她在前面飛。

有時候彼得會停在空中，把手放在耳邊，專注地聽著，然後又往下看，那目光亮得就好像要把地面鑽兩個洞似的，之後又繼續向前飛。

彼得的膽量真是驚人。「現在你是想先冒險呢？」他漫不經心地對約翰說：「還是想先吃茶點？」

溫蒂立即回答「先吃茶點」，麥可感激地握了握她的手，可是比較勇敢的約翰猶豫了。

「是怎麼樣的冒險？」他慎重地問。

「在我們下方的這片草原上，有一個海盜睡著了，」彼得對他說：「如果你願意，我們現在就下去殺了他。」

「我看不到他啊。」思考了一會兒後，約翰說。

「我看得到。」

約翰有點沙啞地說：「如果他醒了怎麼辦？」

彼得憤慨地說：「你以為我會趁他睡著的時候殺死他嗎 ？我會先把他叫醒，然後殺了他。我一向都是這麼做的。」

「你殺過很多人嗎？」

「非常多。」

約翰說：「真厲害。」不過他還是決定先吃茶點。他問彼得現在這個島上是不是有很多海盜。彼得說他從沒看過這麼多海盜。

「現在誰是船長？」

「虎克。」彼得回答說，說到這個可憎的名字，他的臉變得嚴肅起來。

「詹姆士‧虎克？」

「對。」

麥可一聽哭了起來，就連約翰也嚇得說話直吞口水，因為他們早已聽說過惡名昭彰的虎克。

「他是個黑鬍子船長。」約翰沙啞地輕聲說。「是這群海盜裡最兇的，沒有人不怕他。」

「就是他。」彼得說。

「他長什麼樣？個子高大嗎？」

「沒有以前那麼魁梧了。」

「什麼意思？」

「我從他身上砍下了一點。」

「你？」

「對，就是我。」彼得厲聲說道。

「我並沒有冒犯的意思。」

「噢，沒關係。」

「話說回來，你砍了他哪兒？」

「他的右手。」

「那他現在不能打架了嗎？」

「照樣能打！」

「用左手嗎？」

「他用一隻鐵鉤代替右手，用鐵鉤來抓人。」

「抓？」

「我說，約翰。」彼得說。

「怎麼？」

「要說『是，是，先生。』」

「是，是，先生。」

「有一件事得告訴你，」彼得繼續說：「凡是在我手下做事的孩子都必須對我發誓，所以你也一樣。」

約翰嚇得臉色蒼白。

「如果我們和虎克公開交戰，一定要把他交給我對付。」

「我保證。」約翰忠誠地說。

這時候他們已經不覺得那麼害怕了，因為有叮噹跟著他們一起飛，在她亮光的照射下，他們可以看見彼此。但不幸的是，她沒辦法飛得和他們一樣慢，因此她得一圈一圈地繞著他們飛，他們就像是在光圈裡行走一樣。溫蒂很喜歡亮光，可是後來彼得指出了亮光的危險。

「叮噹告訴我，」彼得說：「海盜在天黑之前就發現了我們，他們已經把『長腳湯姆』拖了出來。」

「是大炮嗎？」

「沒錯。他們肯定看得見叮噹的亮光，如果他們猜到我們就在亮光附近，一定會攻擊我們。」

「溫蒂！」

「約翰！」

「麥可！」

「快叫叮噹走開，彼得。」三個人異口同聲地喊，但是被拒絕了。

「她以為我們迷路了。」彼得固執地回答。「她嚇壞了。你覺得我會在她害怕的時候把她趕走嗎？」

那亮光突然熄滅了，彼得被充滿愛意地輕輕捏了一下。

「你告訴她，讓她把光給熄滅了。」溫蒂懇求。

「她辦不到。那大概是仙子們唯一做不到的事情。等她睡著的時候，亮光自然會熄滅，跟星星一樣。」

「那就讓她馬上睡覺。」約翰幾乎是在命令他。

「除非她睏了，否則她是睡不著的。這大概又是一件仙子們做不到的事。」

「依我看，這是唯二值得做的事。」約翰抱怨。

話才剛說完，他就被捏了一下，但不是充滿愛意的捏法。

「如果我們誰有一個口袋就好了，」彼得說：「那就可以把她放在口袋裡。」不過，他們出發時太過匆忙，四個人連一個口袋都沒有。

彼得想出一個妙計：約翰的帽子。

叮噹同意待在帽子裡，只要這帽子拿在手裡就行。帽子由約翰拿著，儘管叮噹希望讓彼得來拿。這會兒，溫蒂接過了帽子，因為約翰說他在飛的時候，帽子一直碰到他的膝蓋。這樣一來有好戲看了，因為叮噹討厭接受溫蒂的照顧，不想欠她人情。

亮光完全被黑帽子遮蓋，孩子們繼續靜悄悄地向前飛。這是他們一生中經歷過最安靜的沉寂了。途中被遠方傳來的波濤拍岸聲打斷了一次，彼得說那是野獸在淺灘喝水的聲音。後來又被一種摩擦聲打斷，大概是樹枝在風中相互摩擦的聲音，可是彼得說那是印地安人在磨刀。

現在，就連這些聲音也停止了。對麥可來說，這寂靜太可怕了。「如果有點聲音就好了！」他喊道。

話才剛說完，空中就爆發了一聲他從未聽過的巨響，就像在回答他的請求似的。是海盜們向他們開炮了。

炮聲在山谷中回盪著，那回聲似乎兇猛地嘶喊著：「他們在哪兒？他們在哪兒？他們在哪兒？」

三個恐懼的孩子這才突然意識到，真實的島和想像中的島是多麼不同。

天空終於再次平靜了下來，此時約翰和麥可發現，黑暗之中只剩下他們兩個。約翰機械地踩著空氣，原本不知道如何飄浮的麥可竟然也會飄浮了。

「你被擊中了嗎？」約翰畏懼地低聲問。

「我還不知道。」麥可輕聲回答。

現在我們知道沒有人被大炮擊中。但是，彼得被炮彈引起的狂風遠遠地吹到了海上，溫蒂被吹到了高空之中，只有叮噹在她身旁。

如果那時候溫蒂把帽子扔掉就好了。

不知道叮噹是突然想到，還是在路上早已盤算好，她立刻從帽子裡鑽出來，引誘溫蒂走向厄運。

叮噹並不是真的很壞，或者說，她只是在這一刻心腸惡毒。有時她又變得心地善良。仙子們不是這樣就是那樣，因為她們身體太小，以至於同一時間，她們體內只能容下一種感情。她們可以改變自己的感情，然而，要改就得徹底改。此刻叮噹心裡充滿了對溫蒂的嫉妒。溫蒂聽不懂她發出的可愛叮叮聲，不過我相信有些話一定很難聽，雖然聲音聽起來很親切。她來來回回飛著，很明顯是在告訴溫蒂「跟我來，一切都會沒事的」。

可憐的溫蒂還能做什麼呢？她呼喊著彼得、約翰還有麥可，聽到的只是嘲笑自己的回音。至今她還不知道叮噹就像一個女人一樣狠毒地嫉妒著她。不知所措又搖搖欲墜的溫蒂就這樣跟著叮噹飛向了災難。

第五章

來到了真正的島

所有人都密切注視著前方，可是誰都沒察覺到危險可能從背後偷襲。從這裡就可以看出這座島是多麼真實。

永無島察覺到彼得正在回來的途中便醒了過來。我們應該說它被喚醒了，但是說「醒來」更好，彼得也常常這麼說。

彼得不在的時候，島上通常非常安靜。早上，精靈們會偷懶多睡一小時，野獸們照顧著牠們的孩子，印地安人們大吃大喝整整六天六夜，當海盜和遺失的孩子們相遇時，他們只是咬著大拇指看著對方。但是當討厭死氣沉沉的彼得一回來，他們又全都活躍了起來，如果此時把耳朵貼在地上，就會聽到整個島都在沸騰。

這天傍晚，島上的中堅力量進行著下面這些活動：遺失的孩子們出來尋找彼得，海盜們出來尋找遺失的孩子，印地安人尋找海盜，野獸尋找印地安人。他們一圈又一圈地繞著小島轉，卻沒碰見彼此，因為他們的速度都一樣。

除了那些遺失的孩子，所有人都渴望鮮血。孩子們通常也愛鮮血，但今晚他們是出來迎接隊長的。在這座島上，出於被殺或其他原因，孩子們的數量常常在變。當他們看起來好像在長大一這違反了島上的規矩一彼得就把他們餓死。不過此時，如果把那對孿生兄弟算為兩個人的話，他們總共有六個人。現在假設我們趴在甘蔗林裡，偷看他們排成一列縱隊，每個人手裡拿著匕首。

彼得禁止他們看起來與他有任何相似之處。因此他們穿的是熊皮，那熊還是他們親手殺死的。穿著熊皮的他們圓滾滾、毛茸茸的，跌倒時會在地上打滾。因此他們走起路來非常穩健。

第一個經過的是托托。在這支英勇的隊伍中，他並非最不勇敢，卻最倒楣。他的冒險次數比其他人都少，因為大事總是等他轉彎後才發生。等一切都風平浪靜時，他就趁機去找燒火的柴草，然後等他回來時，別人早已經把血跡打掃乾淨了。這種霉運使得他總是面帶愁容，但是他並沒有因此變壞，反而變得更可愛了，因此他是這些孩子中最謙虛的。可憐又善良的托托，今晚有危險在等著你。千萬要當心，否則冒險的事就要落在你頭上了。如果你接受這個冒險，你就會陷入最為沉痛的悲哀之中。托托，今天晚上叮噹一心想搗亂，正在找人當殺人工具呢，她認為你是這些孩子當中最容易上當的。要提防叮噹啊！

但願托托能聽見我們的話，不過我們並不在島上，他咬著手指頭走了過去。

第二個走過來的是尼布斯，活潑且溫文儒雅，後面跟著斯萊特利，他把樹枝削成哨子，和著自己吹的曲子跳起舞來。斯萊特利是這些孩子中最自以為是的一個，他總認為自己還記得走失前的事，還有那些禮節與習俗，所以他的鼻子總向上翹著，讓人討厭。第四個是捲毛，他是個頑皮鬼。每當彼得厲聲說「這是誰做的，站出來！」時，他總是不得不站出來。因此現在一聽到這個命令，不管有沒有做過，他就會自動站出來。走在最後的是一對雙胞胎，我們無法形容他們，因為我們肯定會把他們兩個搞錯。彼得從不知道什麼叫雙胞胎，而且只要他不知道的事，他的隊員也不許知道。所以，這對雙胞胎也是糊裡糊塗的，他們不得不慚愧地靠在一起，努力讓別人滿意。

孩子們消失在黑暗之中。過了一會兒，不是很長的一段時間，因為島上的事都發生得非常快，一群海盜尾隨他們而來。我們在看到他們之前，就聽到了他們的歌聲，他們總是唱著那首可怕的歌：

繫上纜繩，唷喲，拋錨停船，

我們去搶劫！

即使炮彈將我們打散，

我們註定會在深深的海底重逢！

即便在絞刑台也從未見過一群如此凶狠的海盜。稍稍走在前頭的是帥氣的義大利人伽可，他時不時地把頭貼在地上聽著什麼。他兩條強壯的手臂赤裸著，耳朵上掛著兩枚西班牙古銀幣作為裝飾。在加奧的監獄裡，他曾用刀在監獄長的背上刻下他自己的名字。走在伽可後面的是一名彪悍的黑人，在加若木河沿岸，那些壞心腸的母親仍用他的名字來嚇唬孩子們。自從他拋棄這個名字之後，他又用了很多名字。接著是比爾 · 裘克斯，就是那個渾身上下都是刺青，在海象號船上被弗林特砍了七十二刀才丟下金幣袋的比爾 · 裘克斯；還有庫克森，據說是黑墨菲的弟弟（*不過這點從未被證實*）；還有紳士斯塔奇，他曾是一所公立學校的助教，現在殺起人來依舊文質彬彬；還有「天窗」（*摩根的「天窗」*）；還有愛爾蘭水手長斯密，他是個非常和氣的人，可以說就算他捅別人一刀也不會得罪別人，虎克手下的海盜裡他是唯一不信英國國教的人；還有努德勒，他的手總是放在背後；還有羅伯特・木林斯和阿爾夫・梅森，以及其他許多在西班牙惡名昭彰、人人畏懼的惡棍。

在這群惡貫滿盈的海盜中，最邪惡、最粗暴的當然非詹姆士 · 虎克莫屬。他自己把名字寫成詹・虎克，據說他是唯一能讓海上庫克害怕的人。虎克安逸地躺在一輛簡陋的戰車上，由他的手下推著向前走。虎克沒有右手，而是裝了一隻鐵鉤來代替。他時不時地揮動著鐵鉤，催促他的手下加快速度。這個可憎的傢伙像狗一樣看待他們、使喚他們，而他們也像狗一樣順從他。他長得枯瘦黝黑，頭髮長而捲曲，遠遠看去活像一支黑蠟燭，他俊俏的五官露出一種異常兇狠的神情。他的眼睛像勿忘我花一樣藍，眼神深邃而憂鬱，只有在他用鐵鉤刺進你身體的那一刻，他的雙眼才會閃過熊熊火焰般的紅光。至於行為舉止，他身上還殘留著某種貴族的氣派，因此他那種跋扈的氣勢也能將你撕成碎片。我還聽說他以前出了名地會講故事。他最溫文儒雅的時候，也是他最陰險狠毒的時候，也許這就是他具有貴族血統的最佳證明。即使在他咒罵別人時，那高雅的措辭也和他顯赫的舉止一樣，顯示了他和他的水手們的差異。虎克這個人性格不屈不撓、無所畏懼。據說，唯一讓他懼怕的就是看到自己的血。他的血很濃，顏色與眾不同。說到穿著，他有點像在模仿查理二世。因為在他年輕的時候，他聽別人說自己長得很像那位倒楣的斯圖爾特國王。他的嘴裡叼著一根他自己發明的煙斗，可以同時吸兩支雪茄。不過，毫無疑問地，他身上最令人生畏的正是那隻鐵爪。

現在讓我們拿一個海盜示範，看看虎克是怎麼殺人的，就找斯蓋萊吧。在海盜們行進的時候，斯蓋萊步履蹣跚、笨手笨腳地湊到虎克跟前，摸了摸他那鑲邊的衣領。虎克的鐵鉤嘶地一聲伸了出來，緊接而來的是一聲慘叫，隨後斯蓋萊的屍體被踢到了一邊，海盜們繼續前進。虎克甚至都沒把雪茄從嘴裡拿下來。

彼得潘要面對的就是這麼可怕的人。誰會贏呢？

緊跟在海盜後面，悄無聲無息地行走的是印地安人。對於缺乏經驗的眼睛來說，這條小徑是很難被覺察的，他們個個都把眼睛睜得大大的。手持戰斧和匕首，赤裸的身體上塗滿了油彩，閃閃發亮。身上掛著成串的戰利品，有小孩的，也有海盜的。因為這些印地安人屬於野蠻部落，和那些心腸較好的印地安人大不相同。衝在最前方匍匐前進的是偉大的小黑豹，他是一名驍將，身上掛滿了戰利品，在爬行時，這些東西多少有些阻礙他前進。走在最後，處於最危險位置的便是驕傲地站立著的虎蓮，她生來就是位公主。她是黑人女將中最漂亮的一個，也是部落裡的大美人。她時而妖豔，時而冷酷，時而多情。沒有一個勇士不想娶這位變化無常的公主為妻，但是所有的求婚者都被她那把短斧擋在了門外。讓我們看看他們是如何穿過掉在地上的枝葉而不發出聲響的。唯一能聽到的就是他們粗重的喘息聲，這是因為他們在大快朵頤之後，肚子有些鼓起，不過，慢慢地食物就會消化了。可是目前這是他們主要的危險。

印地安人來無影去無蹤，很快地，他們的位置就被野獸取代了，雜七雜八的一大群。獅子、老虎、熊、還有在前面躲避他們的無數小動物。各式各樣的獸類，特別是所有的食人獸，都在這個得天獨厚的島上雜居並存。牠們的舌頭都伸了出來，今晚牠們都餓了。

野獸過去之後，最後一個角色出場了，一條巨大的鱷魚，待會我們就知道牠到底在找誰了。

鱷魚爬過去了，但是沒過多久孩子們又出現了。因為隊列必須不停地進行下去，直到某一隊停下來，或是改變前進的速度。然後他們很快就會開始互相廝殺。

所有人都密切注視著前方，可是誰都沒察覺到危險可能從背後偷襲。從這裡就可以看出這座島是多麼真實。

最先停止繞圈的是那些孩子們。他們全都躺在離他們地下的家很近的那片草地上。

「真希望彼得能回來啊。」每個人都不安地說道，儘管他們的身高和體型都超過了他們的隊長。

「我是唯一不怕海盜的人。」史萊特利說，那語氣使得他不受大家喜愛。不過大概是遠處的聲響驚動了他，他又慌忙加了一句，「不過我也希望彼得能回來，告訴我們他有沒有聽到仙杜瑞拉的其他故事。」

孩子們談起了仙杜瑞拉。托托確信他媽媽以前一定很像仙杜瑞拉。

只有彼得不在的時候，他們才會提起自己的媽媽，因為彼得覺得這個話題很蠢，於是禁止大家談論。

「我所記得關於媽媽的事，」尼布斯對他們說：「就是她總是對我爸爸說：『噢，真希望我能有自己的支票本。』雖然我不知道支票本是什麼東西，但我很想幫媽媽弄一本。」

聊天的同時，他們聽見遠處傳來的聲音。你我都不是林中的生物，當然聽不見，但是他們聽見了，就是那首可怕的歌：

喲呵，喲呵，海盜人生
骷髏白骨旗飄遙，
一陣歡樂，一條麻繩，
深海閻王共逍遙。

剎那間，那些遺失的孩子們——可是他們都在哪兒？他們已經不在那裡了。連兔子都沒辦法像他們溜得那麼快。

我告訴你們他們在哪，除了尼布斯飛快地跑去探聽敵情之外，其他人全都回到了地底的家，那真是個非常有趣的住處，等一下我會詳細介紹。可是他們是怎麼進去的呢？因為根本看不到入口，連塊大石頭也沒有，如果有一塊大石頭，搬開之後就會露出洞口。不過再仔細看看，就會發現七棵大樹，每個空心的樹幹下面都有一個洞，洞口有孩子的身體那麼大。這就是地底的家的七個入口，這幾個月以來，虎克一直找不到這些入口。今晚他能找到嗎？

隨著海盜的逼近，斯密眼明手快，發現尼布斯消失在樹林中，他立刻掏出手槍，可是一隻鐵鉤緊緊抓住了他的肩膀。

「船長，放開我。」他掙扎著說。

此刻，我們第一次聽見虎克的聲音，那是個邪惡的聲音。「先把槍放回去。」那聲音威脅道。

「那孩子不正是你的宿敵嗎？我本來可以打死他的。」

「是啊，不過槍聲會把虎蓮的印地安人引過來。你是不是不想要你的腦袋了？」

「那我可以去追他嗎，船長？」可憐的斯密問。「我可以用我的強尼鑽搔他癢嗎？」斯密替每樣東西都取了好聽的名字，他的短刀就叫強尼鑽，因為他喜歡拿刀在傷口處旋轉。斯密身上還有很多可愛的特徵。譬如說殺人之後，他總是擦他的眼鏡，而不是他的武器。

「強尼是個非常安靜的夥伴。」他提醒虎克。

「現在還不行，斯密。」虎克威脅說：「才一個人，我想要的是把他們七個全部殺掉。大家分頭去找。」

海盜們在樹林裡消失了，很快就只剩下船長和斯密兩個人。虎克沉重地嘆了口氣。我並不知道他為什麼嘆氣，也許是因為這溫柔美好的夜色吧。不過他忽然心生一念，想把自己一生的故事全講給他忠誠的水手聽。他真誠地講了很久，然而愚蠢的斯密完全不知道他在說什麼。

之後斯密聽到了彼得這個名字。

虎克憤恨地說：「我最想要抓的就是他們的隊長彼得潘。就是他砍掉了我的手臂。」他兇狠地揮舞著那隻鐵鉤。「我等了那麼久，就是想要拿這鐵鉤跟他握個手。噢，我要把他撕成碎片。」

「可是，我常聽你說，這鉤子勝過二十隻手，能梳頭，還能做別的家事。」

「是啊，」船長回答斯密：「如果我是個母親，我一定祈求我的孩子生下來就有這鐵鉤，而不是那隻手。」他得意地看了一眼他那隻鐵腕，又輕蔑地看了另一隻手。接著他又皺起了眉頭。

他畏畏縮縮地說：「彼得把我的手臂扔給了一條碰巧路過的鱷魚。」

斯密說：「我常看到你對鱷魚有一種莫名的恐懼。」

「我並不是怕所有的鱷魚，」虎克糾正說：「唯獨怕那隻鱷魚。」他壓低了嗓音說。「那隻鱷魚很喜歡吃我的手臂，斯密。從那時開始，牠就一直跟著我，飄洋過海地跟著我，舔著牠的舌頭，想吃我身體的其他部位。」

「從某種程度上來說這也是一種讚美。」斯密說。

「我才不要這種讚美。」虎克任性地咆哮。「我要的是彼得潘，是他先讓那畜牲嚐到了我的滋味。」

虎克坐在一顆大蘑菇上，此時他的聲音有些顫抖。「斯密。」他沙啞地說：「其實那條鱷魚早該把我吃掉的，幸虧牠吞下了一個鐘，那個鐘在牠肚子裡滴答滴答作響，因此在牠抓到我之前，我聽到了滴答聲，然後拔腿就跑。」他大笑起來，不過那是一種乾笑。

「可是總有一天，」斯密說：「那鐘會停下來的，到時候鱷魚就會抓住你了。」

虎克舔舔他乾澀的嘴唇。「是啊，」他說:「我怕的就是這個。」

他坐下來後覺得特別熱。「斯密，」他說:「這個座位是熱的。」他跳了起來。「不得了啦，不得了啦，我快要被燒焦了！」

他們仔細檢查了這個蘑菇，一個從未在大陸上見過既大又硬的蘑菇。他們試圖把它拔起來，沒想到一下子就拔了起來，原來這個蘑菇沒有根。更奇怪的是，地上立刻冒出了一股煙。兩個海盜相互對視，並異口同聲地驚呼：「是煙囪！」。

他們真的發現了地底的家的煙囪。當敵人在附近的時候，孩子們就用蘑菇把煙囪蓋上，這是他們的習慣。

煙囪裡不光冒出煙來，還傳出了孩子們的聲音。因為他們都覺得藏在這裡十分安全，所以大家開心地聊著天。海盜冷冷地聽了一會，然後把蘑菇放回原位。他們四處搜尋了一番，發現了七棵樹上的洞穴。

「你有沒有聽見他們說彼得潘不在家？」斯密一邊輕聲地說，一邊擺弄著他的強尼鑽。

虎克點了點頭，站在那裡思索了半天，最後那黝黑的臉龐浮現一絲冷笑。斯密已經整裝待發。「說出你的計畫吧，船長。」斯密急切地說。

「回船上去。」虎克慢慢地從牙縫裡擠出幾個字來。「做一個料多味美的大蛋糕，奶油要厚，還要淋上青糖。那下面應該有一間屋子，因為有一個煙囪。這些愚蠢的『鼴鼠』們竟然不知道他們只需要一個出口，可見他們真的沒有媽媽。我們把蛋糕放在美人魚的潟湖邊，那些小孩經常在那裡游泳，和美人魚嬉鬧。他們會發現這個蛋糕，然後狼吞虎嚥地吃掉。因為他們沒有媽媽，不知道吃料多潮濕的蛋糕有多麼危險。」他突然笑了起來，這次不是乾笑，而是開懷大笑。「哈哈，他們死定了。」

斯密越聽越佩服。

「這是我聽過的最邪惡、最完美的計畫了。」斯密說。兩人得意忘形地又跳又唱：

繫上纜繩，我來了，
他們嚇得魂飛魄散；
虎克鐵鉤一握手，
皮開肉綻剩骨頭。

他們開始唱起這首歌來，不過並沒能把它唱完，因為另一個聲音忽然響起，打斷了他們的歌聲。起初，那聲音很小，樹葉掉下來的聲音都能將那聲音蓋過去，但是隨著牠越靠越近，聲音也就越來越清晰。

滴答，滴答，滴答，滴答……

虎克戰戰兢兢地站著，一隻腳懸在空中。

「是鱷魚。」他氣喘吁吁地大叫一聲，拔腿就跑，身後緊跟著他的水手。

真的是那隻鱷魚，牠已經超過了在追蹤海盜的印地安人。而此時印地安人正在追蹤其他海盜。鱷魚悠哉地跟在虎克身後。

孩子們再次回到了地面上，可是黑夜的危險並沒有結束，因為很快地尼布斯就氣喘吁吁地跑到他們中間，後面跟著一群惡狼，各個吐著舌頭，發出可怕的嚎叫聲。

「救救我，快救救我！」尼布斯呼喊著，跌倒在地上。

「我們該怎麼做？我們該怎麼做？」

在這可怕的時刻，他們都想到了彼得，這應該是對彼得的最高讚譽。

「如果彼得在，他會怎麼做？」他們不約而同地喊道。

他們幾乎異口同聲地說：「彼得會從兩腿中間看著牠們。」

「那我們就用彼得的方法對付牠們吧。」

那真是對付狼群最有效的辦法，他們全都彎下腰，從兩腿中間往後看。接下來的時間顯得有些漫長，可是勝利來得很快，因為孩子們用這種可怕的姿勢向狼逼近時，那群狼全都夾著尾巴逃跑了。

尼布斯從地上爬了起來，依舊目不轉睛地盯著，其他孩子以為他還在看那些狼，可是他看的並不是狼。

「我看見一個更奇怪的東西。」他喊道。其他孩子都急切地團團圍過來。

「有一隻很大的白鳥正朝這邊飛過來。」

「什麼鳥？」

「我不知道，」 尼布斯充滿敬畏地說，「但是牠看起來很疲倦，一邊飛一邊呻吟著『可憐的溫蒂』。」

「可憐的溫蒂？」

「我想起來了，」史萊特利馬上說：「有一種鳥就叫溫蒂。」

「看，牠飛過來了。」捲毛指著空中的溫蒂喊。

溫蒂現在差不多已經飛到他們頭頂上了，孩子們可以聽到她哀傷的聲音。可是聽得更清楚的是叮噹的尖叫聲。這個心懷嫉妒的仙子，此刻已經拋棄了一切友好的偽裝，從四面八方對溫蒂進行攻擊，每次撞到她的身體時，就狠狠地擰她一把。

「叮噹。」那些滿臉疑惑的孩子們喊道。

叮噹回答說：「彼得要你們射死這個溫蒂。」

他們從不懷疑彼得的命令。「彼得吩咐，我們就遵命。」這些單純的孩子嚷嚷著。「快，準備弓箭。」

除了托托，所有人都鑽進了他們的樹洞。托托隨身攜帶著弓箭，叮噹發現了，搓了搓她的小手。

「快，托托，快射她！」叮噹大叫。「彼得會很開心的。」托托激動地拉弓搭箭。「別擋著，叮噹。」他大喊，接著箭就射了出去，溫蒂搖搖晃晃地倒到地上，胸口插著一支箭。

第六章

小房子

「快看，」他說：「箭剛好射中了這東西，這是我送給溫蒂的一個吻，是它救了溫蒂。」

當其他孩子手拿武器從樹洞裡跳出來的時候，笨托托像個勝利者似的站在溫蒂身旁。

「你們來晚了，」他驕傲地喊：「我已經把溫蒂射死了，彼得一定會對我很滿意。」

頭頂上的叮噹大喊了一聲「笨蛋」後就急忙地逃走並躲了起來，其他人都沒聽見她說了什麼。

他們圍在溫蒂身邊盯著她看，林中籠罩著一種可怕的寂靜。如果溫蒂的心還會跳，他們一定聽得到。

史萊特利第一個開口說話了。他驚恐地說：「這不是鳥，我想這一定是一位小姐。」

「小姐？」托托說，心裡打了陣寒顫。

「可是我們已經把她殺死了。」尼布斯沙啞地說。

他們都摘下了帽子。

「現在我明白了，」捲毛說：「是彼得把她帶過來的。」說完便悲傷地倒在地上。

「終於有一位小姐來照顧我們了，」雙胞胎中的一個說：「可是你卻把她殺了。」

他們替托托感到愧疚，更為自己感到難過，托托靠近他們時，他們都轉過身去不理他。

此時托托臉色慘白，可是他的臉上卻浮現了前所未有的尊嚴。

「是我做的，」他反省地說：「以前每當小姐們來到我夢裡時，我總是說：『漂亮媽媽，漂亮媽媽。可是，這次她真的來了，我卻把她射死了。」

說完後他慢慢地走開了。

「別走。」其他人同情地說。

「我非走不可，」托托顫抖地回答：「我非常害怕彼得。」

就在這悲傷的時刻，他們聽到了一個聲音，這讓他們的心都提到了嗓子眼裡，因為那正是彼得的叫喊聲。

「彼得！」他們大喊，彼得每次回來都會發出這樣的信號。

「快把她藏起來。」他們耳語著，匆匆忙忙地把溫蒂圍了起來。只有托托孤零零地站在一邊。

這時又傳來一陣響亮的叫喊聲，彼得落在他們面前。「你們好啊，孩子們！」他大喊，孩子們按照慣例向他行了禮，接著又是一陣沉默。

彼得皺了皺眉頭。

「我回來了，」他激動地說：「你們為什麼不歡呼？」

他們都張開了嘴，卻沒有發出歡呼聲。彼得沒注意到這些，他急著想要告訴他們這個好消息。

「好消息，孩子們，」他喊：「我終於替你們帶來了一位媽媽。」

依舊是一片沉默，只聽見托托撲通一聲跪倒在地上。

「你們沒見到她嗎？」彼得有點不安地問，「她朝這邊飛過來了。」

「唉。」一個聲音嘆息著，另一個聲音說：「唉，真是令人悲傷啊。」

托托站了起來。「彼得，」他平靜地說：「你來看她吧。」其他孩子還想遮掩，托托說：「雙胞胎兄弟，退後，讓彼得看。」

於是他們都往後退，讓彼得看。彼得觀察了一會兒之後，也不知道接下來該怎麼辦。

「她死了，」彼得心神不寧地說：「也許是受到驚嚇而死的。」

彼得想要跳著滑稽的步子離開這裡，直到看不見她，然後再也不回這個地方。如果他真這麼做了，孩子們也會樂意跟著他走的。

可是有支箭很明顯地插在那。他把箭從溫蒂的心上拔了下來，看著自己的隊伍。

「這是誰的箭？」他嚴厲地詢問道。

「是我的，彼得。」托托跪在地上說。

「啊，你這個懦夫！」彼得說著，舉起那支箭，把它當成一把刀想要刺去。

托托沒有絲毫畏縮，敞開胸膛。「刺吧，彼得，」他堅定地說：「用力刺過來吧。」

彼得兩次舉起箭，但兩次都放下了。「我沒辦法刺，」他驚慌地說：「好像有什麼東西拉住了我的手。」

所有人都驚訝地望著他，除了尼布斯，他正盯著溫蒂。

「是她，」尼布斯叫道：「是溫蒂小姐，快看，她的手臂。」

說來奇怪，溫蒂真的舉起了手臂。尼布斯彎下身去，恭敬地聽著她說話。

「我想她好像是在說『可憐的托托』。」他輕輕地說。

「她還活著。」彼得簡短地說。

史萊特利立刻叫道：「溫蒂小姐還活著。」

彼得跪在她的身旁，發現了他那顆橡實。你還記得吧，溫蒂把它串成了項鏈，掛在自己脖子上。

「快看，」他說：「箭剛好射中了這東西，這是我送給溫蒂的吻，是它救了溫蒂。」

「我記得吻的樣子，」史萊特利立刻插嘴說：「讓我看看，沒錯，那是一個吻。」

彼得沒聽到史萊特利在說什麼，他只祈禱溫蒂可以快點康復，好讓自己帶她去看美人魚。當然，溫蒂還沒辦法說話，因為她仍在極度昏迷當中。此時上頭傳來了一陣嚎啕的哭聲。

「聽，是叮噹，」捲毛說：「因為溫蒂還活著，她就哭了。」

於是孩子們不得不告訴彼得叮噹所犯的罪行，他們從沒見過彼得如此嚴肅的神情。

「聽著，叮噹，」他喊道：「我再也不是你的朋友了，走吧，永遠離開我。」

叮噹停在他的肩上，向他求情，但是彼得拒絕了。直到溫蒂再一次舉起她的手臂，他才軟下心來：「好吧，那就不要永遠，一個星期好了。」

你覺得叮噹會因為溫蒂舉起手而感激她嗎？噢，絕對不會，她反而更想狠狠地捏她一把。仙子們確實都很奇怪，彼得最了解她們，因此時常用手打她們。可是現在溫蒂身體那麼虛弱，該怎麼辦呢？

「我們把她抬進屋裡去吧。」捲毛建議。

「沒錯，」史萊特利說：「就該這麼對待一位小姐。」

「不行，不行，」彼得說：「你們不能碰她，那太沒禮貌了。」

「我剛才就是這麼想的。」史萊特利說。

「但如果讓她就這麼躺在這，她會死的。」托托說。

「是啊，她會死的。」史萊特利承認。「但沒有別的辦法了。」

「有了，」彼得喊：「我們圍著她蓋一間小房子吧。」

他們都非常高興。「快，」彼得命令：「把你們最好的東西都給我拿出來。把家裡所有的東西都搬出來，快點。」

頓時他們就像婚禮前夕的裁縫一樣忙碌起來。他們東奔西跑，回家拿被子、出門找木柴。正當大家忙成一團的時候，約翰和麥可來了。他們拖著腳步走過來，站著就睡著了，停住腳步時醒了過來，再走一步又睡著了。

「約翰，約翰，」麥可說：「約翰，快醒醒，娜娜在哪裡？還有媽媽呢？」

接著約翰揉揉眼睛，嘀咕著：「是真的，我們會飛了。」

你可以想像他們再見到彼得時有多欣慰。

「你好，彼得。」他們說。

「你們好。」彼得友善地回答，儘管他已經完全把他們給忘了。此時彼得正忙著用腳測量溫蒂的身高，看看她需要多大的房子。當然，他還預留了放桌椅的地方。約翰和麥可在一旁望著他。

「溫蒂睡著了嗎？」他們問。

「對。」

「約翰，」麥可提議：「我們把她叫醒，讓她替我們做晚飯吧。」正在說話時，他發現很多孩子抱著蓋房子用的樹枝跑了過來。「快看他們！」麥可大喊。

「捲毛，」彼得用隊長的口氣說：「讓這兩個人幫忙蓋房子。」

「是，是，隊長……」

「蓋房子？」約翰驚呼。

「給溫蒂的。」捲毛說。

「給溫蒂？」約翰驚訝地說：「為什麼？她只是個女孩子。」

「就是因為這樣，」捲毛解釋說：「所以我們都是她的僕人。」

「你們？溫蒂的僕人！」

「沒錯，」彼得說：「你們也是，把他們帶走。」

這對吃驚的兄弟被人拉去砍樹運木頭了。「先做椅子和壁爐，」彼得命令：「然後再圍著它們蓋房子。」

「沒錯，」史萊特利說：「房子就是這麼蓋的，我全記起來了。」

彼得想得很周全。「史萊特利，」他喊道：「去請個醫生來。」

「是，是。」史萊特利立刻回答，然後搔著頭皮離開了。他知道彼得的命令必須服從。很快他戴著約翰的帽子回來了，神情很嚴肅。

「請問，先生，」彼得走上前去說：「你是醫生嗎？」

在這種情況下，彼得和其他孩子不同的地方是，他們知道這是假扮的，而對他來說，真的假的都是一樣的。有時這個問題讓他們感到很為難，比如說，他們不得不假裝已經吃過晚飯了。

如果他們停止假裝，彼得就會敲他們的指關節加以斥責。

「是的，小夥子。」史萊特利戰戰兢兢地回答，因為他有些骨頭已經被敲裂了。

「拜託了，醫生。」彼得解釋：「有位小姐病得很重。」

病人就躺在他們的腳旁，可是，史萊特利卻假裝沒看到她。

「嘖，嘖，嘖，」他說：「病人躺在哪兒呢？」

「在那邊的草地上。」

「我要把一個玻璃棒放進她嘴裡。」史萊特利說，並假裝這麼做著，彼得則守在一旁。當史萊特利把玻璃棒從嘴裡拿出來的時候，那真叫人擔心啊。

「她怎麼樣？」彼得問。

「嘖，嘖，」史萊特利說：「這東西已經把她治好了。」

「太好了。」彼得說。

「晚上我還會再來的，」史萊特利說：「用一個有壺嘴的杯子餵她喝點牛肉湯。」但是當他把帽子還給約翰時，他深深地嘆了口氣，這是他逃過難關時的慣性表現。

與此同時，樹林裡傳來一陣陣斧頭聲。一座舒適的房子所需的材料幾乎都已經堆在溫蒂的腳邊了。

一個孩子說：「如果我們知道她喜歡什麼樣的房子就好了。」

「彼得，」另一個孩子喊道：「她睡覺的時候動了一下。」

「她張開嘴巴了，」第三個孩子說著，恭恭敬敬地往她的嘴巴看了看：「啊，好可愛。」

「也許她在夢裡想唱歌，」彼得說：「溫蒂，把你喜歡的房子唱出來吧。」

溫蒂連眼睛都沒有睜開，就立刻唱了起來：

我想要一間漂亮的房子，
從未見過的小巧的房子，
四面都是可愛的小紅牆，
屋頂鋪滿綠油油的苔草。

孩子們聽了，都咯咯笑了起來，他們的運氣真是好極了，那些

砍來的樹枝剛好都黏著紅色液汁，而地上都長滿了青苔。他們蓋房子的時候也唱起歌來：

我們已蓋好小紅牆和屋頂，
還有一扇很可愛的小門，
溫蒂媽媽，請告訴我們，
你還想要什麼呢？

對於這個問題，溫蒂有些貪心地回答：

噢，對，接下來我想要
四周圍繞著明亮的窗户，
玫瑰花從窗口探進來，
小寶寶向外張望。

他們一揮拳頭，就造起了窗戶，黃色的大葉子當窗簾，可是玫瑰花呢？

「玫瑰花！」彼得厲聲喊道。

很快他們就假裝沿著牆壁栽上了可愛的玫瑰花。

小寶寶呢？為了防止彼得要嬰兒，他們趕緊唱道：

玫瑰已在窗口探頭，
小寶寶正在門口等候，
我們無法製造自己，
因為我們已被造出來了。

彼得覺得這主意不錯，就立刻假裝這是他出的主意。房子非常漂亮，毫無疑問，溫蒂住在裡面一定非常舒服，雖然他們已經看不見她了。彼得在房子外面走來走去，安排最後的工作。任何東西都無法逃過他的雙眼。正當房子快要完成時——

「門上還少了門環呢。」彼得說。

孩子們感到很羞愧，不過托托拿起他的鞋底，做出了一個絕妙的門環。

他們想，現在應該完成了吧。

還差得遠了。「沒有煙囪，」彼得說：「一定要有煙囪。」

「當然要有煙囪。」約翰煞有其事地說。這倒讓彼得想到了一個好主意，他一把抓過約翰頭上的帽子，在帽頂上挖個洞，然後把帽子扣在屋頂上。有這麼一個絕妙的煙囪，小房子似乎非常高興，一縷青煙立刻從帽子裡冉冉升起，就像在表達謝意。

現在真的完成了。所有事情都已經做完，就只剩下敲門了。

「把自己打扮得體面些，」彼得警告他們說：「第一印象是十分重要的。」

他很慶幸沒有人問他什麼是第一印象，因為他們都忙著打扮。

彼得很有禮貌地敲了敲門。此刻樹林和孩子們一樣寂靜，除了叮噹發出的聲音之外，聽不到一點聲響。她正坐在樹枝上看著他

們，毫不掩飾地嘲笑著。

孩子們好奇的是，會有人開門嗎？如果是位小姐，她會是什麼樣子呢？

門打開了，一位小姐走了出來，那個人正是溫蒂，孩子們都摘下帽子。

她看起來有些驚訝，這正是他們希望看到的表情。

「我在哪裡？」她問。

第一個回答的當然是史萊特利。「溫蒂小姐，」他迅速地搶話道：「我們為你蓋了這間房子。」

「你喜歡嗎？」尼布斯問。

「好可愛的房子。」溫蒂說，這正是他們希望聽到的話。

「我們是你的孩子。」雙胞胎兄弟說道。

之後他們全都跪下來，張開雙臂叫道：「溫蒂小姐，請你做我們的媽媽吧。」

「我可以嗎？」溫蒂笑容滿面地說：「這一定非常有意思，但你們都看見了，我只是一個小女孩，一點經驗都沒有。」

「沒關係。」彼得說，好像這裡只有他懂這些事情。其實，他是懂最少的。「我們需要的，只是一位像媽媽一樣溫柔的人。」

「哎呀！」溫蒂說：「我覺得我就是這樣的人。」

「沒錯，沒錯，」他們全都喊道：「我們一下子就看出來了。」

「那就好，」溫蒂說：「我一定會盡力當個好媽媽的。快進來吧，你們這些淘氣的孩子。我想你們的腳一定都濕了吧。在我安頓你們上床睡覺之前，應該還有時間講完仙杜瑞拉的故事。」

孩子們進去了。我不知道為什麼這間房子可以容得下那麼多人。不過在永無島，是可以擠得非常緊密的。這是他們與溫蒂一起渡過的第一個快樂夜晚，他們還會渡過很多這樣的夜晚。不久之後，溫蒂把他們安頓在地底的家的大床上。那一晚她自己睡在小屋裡。彼得手拿著出鞘的刀，在屋外守著，因為海盜們還在遠處尋歡作樂，狼群也在四處徘徊覓食。在黑暗中，這座小屋顯得如此舒適安全，窗簾映射出明亮的燈光，煙囪裡冒出縷縷輕煙，還有彼得在外面站崗。過了一會兒，彼得睡著了。一些狂歡後搖搖晃晃回家的仙子們，不得不從他身上爬過去。如果是其他孩子擋住了仙子們的夜歸路，他們一定會惡作劇一番，不過對於彼得，他們只會捏捏他的鼻子，然後走過去。

第七章

地底的家

這是一個很難回答的問題，因為誰也說不出永無島的時間是怎麼算的，在這裡是用月亮和太陽計算，而島上的太陽和月亮比在陸地時多很多。

第二天彼得做的第一件事就是替溫蒂、約翰和麥可量身材，好替他們找合適的空心樹。你應該還記得，虎克曾經為了這些孩子每個人都有一棵空心樹而嘲笑他們，其實虎克才無知。因為除非那棵樹適合你，否則想要爬上爬下是很困難的，再說，孩子的身材也各不相同。如果樹洞大小合身，只要在上面吸一口氣，就能不急不徐地往下滑；要上來時，只要一呼一吸，就能扭動著爬上來了。當然，等你掌握這套動作之後，就能不假思索地自由上下，沒有比這更美的姿態了。

不過，身材和樹洞得完全吻合才行，因此彼得在量身材時，就像量一套衣服一樣仔細。唯一不同的是，衣服是依照你的身材量身訂做，現在則是你必須符合樹洞的大小。通常這是很容易辦到的，只要多穿或少穿幾件衣服就可以了，但如果是在難以處理的地方凹凸不平，或者唯一可用的樹長得奇形怪狀，彼得就得在你身上動手腳，然後就會合身了。一旦合身，就得格外小心地保持。正因為這樣，後來溫蒂高興地發現，全家人都維持著良好的體態。

溫蒂和麥可第一次試的樹洞就很合身，不過約翰的還得稍微改造。

經過幾天練習，他們已經能像井裡的水桶一樣開心地上下自如了。漸漸地他們都瘋狂地愛上了這個地底的家，特別是溫蒂。跟所有的家一樣，這裡也有一間大房間，想釣魚的時候，可以在地板上挖洞，地板上還長著五顏六色的大蘑菇，可以當凳子坐。在房間的中央有一棵奮力生長的永無樹，每天早晨，孩子們都會把樹幹鋸得跟地板面一樣齊平。等到下午茶時間，它又會長到兩英尺高，於是他們把一

塊門板放在樹幹上，變出一張大桌子，等他們吃完茶點，再把樹幹鋸掉，屋子裡又有寬敞的地方可以玩耍了。屋裡還有一個巨大的壁爐，照亮房子的各個角落，溫蒂在壁爐前拉了很多用纖維做的繩子，用來晾洗好的衣物。佔據了將近半間屋子的大床，白天時斜靠在牆邊，到了晚上六點半才放下來，除了麥可，所有孩子都睡在這張床上，像罐頭裡的沙丁魚一樣，一個挨著一個地躺著。嚴格禁止翻身，除非有人發號施令，大家才能一起翻身。麥可原本也應該睡在床上，但溫蒂需要一個嬰兒，而且他最小，你應該也知道女人們的心思。總之，結果就是麥可睡在一個吊籃裡。

這個家很簡陋，如果熊寶寶有個地底的家，應該跟這裡差不多。牆上還有個跟鳥籠差不多大的凹洞是叮噹的房間，其中有一幅小巧的門簾可以將房間與外面隔開來。叮噹是個細心的仙子，不管是穿衣服還是脫衣服，她都會把門簾拉上。沒有一個女人，不管她的身材如何，能擁有這麼一間臥室與起居室相結合的房間。她的臥榻——她總是這麼稱呼她的床，是麥布女王式的，有梅花形的床腳。她的床罩則是隨著不同季節開花的果樹而更換。她的鏡子是穿長靴的貓的那種鏡子，據仙子商人所說，目前這種鏡子市面上只剩下三面沒有破損。臉盆是派皮式的，可以雙面使用。五斗櫃是貨真價實白馬王子六世時期的迷人古董。地毯是糖果屋的產品。還有一盞飾以亮片的大吊燈，但叮噹自己發出的光就足以照亮她的房間。這也難怪叮噹很瞧不起家中的其他地方。雖然她的房間非常漂亮，看起來卻很驕矜，趾高氣昂。

我想，對溫蒂來說，這一切肯定會令她格外陶醉，因為她那些吵鬧的孩子讓她忙個不停。的確，除了某幾晚到上面補襪子之外，整整幾個星期，她都沒有上去地面。說到做飯，可以這樣告訴你，她的鼻子一直沒辦法離開那個鍋子，即使鍋子裡什麼都沒有，或是根本就沒有那個鍋子，她還是得看著它冒煙。但你永遠無法確認他們到底是真的在吃飯還是假裝在吃飯，這都取決於彼得的反覆無常。如果把吃飯當成是遊戲的一部分，他就能吃，而且是真的吃，然而，他不會為了填飽肚子而吃，可是大部分的孩子都很喜歡這麼做。其次就是談論吃的，對彼得來說，假裝吃飯也非常真實，當他假裝吃飯的時候，你可以看到他真的變得越來越胖。當然，假裝吃飽是件折磨人的事，但又不能不服從彼得，如果能向他證明你比樹洞瘦，他就會讓你飽餐一頓。

等他們全都上床睡覺之後，就是溫蒂縫補衣物最好的時間了。據她所說，只有在這個時候，她才有喘息的機會。她利用這段時間為他們做新衣服，還在膝蓋部位縫上兩層，因為他們的褲子差不多都是膝蓋磨損得最厲害。

當溫蒂坐下來看著一整籃腳後跟都有破洞的襪子時，她會伸出手臂驚呼：「哎呀，有時候我還真羨慕那些沒結婚的老小姐。」

她在說這些話時臉上滿是燦爛的笑容。

你們還記得她那隻可愛的寵物小野狼吧。沒錯，牠很快就發現溫蒂來到了島上，而且找到了她。他們奔向彼此相擁。從那之後，牠就形影不離地跟著溫蒂。

隨著時光的消逝，溫蒂會不會很想念被她拋在腦後的親愛的爸媽呢？這是一個很難回答的問題，因為誰也說不出永無島的時間是怎麼算的，在這裡是用月亮和太陽計算，而島上的太陽和月亮比在陸地

時多很多。但恐怕溫蒂沒有非常想念她的爸媽，她完全相信他們一定會一直開著窗戶，等著她飛回去。因此，她覺得非常安心。有時候讓她感到有點不安的是，約翰只是依稀地記得爸媽，就像是他曾經認識的人；麥可則是非常樂意相信溫蒂真的就是媽媽。這些事都讓她有些害怕，於是她義無反顧地承擔起姐姐的責任。她用考試的方法，就像她過去在學校裡做的試卷一樣，試著喚起他們心中對過去的記憶。其他孩子都覺得這非常有趣，堅持要參加考試，他們還自己準備了石板，溫蒂用另一塊石板寫下問題，讓他們傳閱。他們圍坐在桌邊，努力地思考並回答非常普通的問題，例如「媽媽的眼睛是什麼顏色？爸爸和媽媽誰比較高？媽媽的頭髮是淺色的還是深色的？可能的話，三個問題都必須回答。」、「寫一篇四十個字以上的文章，主題是『我上次的假期是怎麼度過的』或『比較爸爸和媽媽的性格』，任選一題回答。」、「一、描寫媽媽的笑；二、描寫爸爸的笑；三、描寫媽媽的禮服；四、描寫狗窩和裡面的小狗。」

每天問的問題大概是這樣，如果答不出來就打一個叉。約翰的叉叉多得嚇人。當然每道題目都回答的只有史萊特利，沒有人像他那麼希望第一個交卷，然而他的答案都非常地可笑，而且總是倒數第一名，多麼可悲啊。

彼得沒有參加考試。首先，除了溫蒂之外，他瞧不起所有做媽媽的人；其次，他是島上唯一不會讀書寫字的孩子，就連最短的單字都不會。他才不屑做這種事。

順帶一提，所有的問題都是用過去式寫的，例如「過去媽媽的眼睛是什麼顏色？」等等。你看，就連溫蒂也有點忘記了。

冒險的事自然是天天都會發生，下面我們就會提到。但是這幾天，彼得在溫蒂的幫助下，發明了一種令他著迷的新遊戲，但有一天忽然又對它失去了興趣。前面已經提過，他的遊戲一向都是這種結果。這個遊戲是假裝沒有冒險，做約翰和麥可常做的事：坐在小凳子上、向空中丟球、相互推擠、出去散步，回來時一隻灰熊都沒殺死。看彼得無所事事坐在小凳子上的樣子，那才是有意思。在他看來，坐著不動是一件非常可笑的事，而此時他卻擺出一副正經的模樣，他還自誇說，為了自己的身體健康，他出去散了步。一連好幾天，這些對他來說就是所有冒險中最新奇的事，約翰和麥可不得不裝出很高興的樣子，否則彼得會對他們不客氣。

彼得常常獨自外出。他回來時，誰也不能確定他到底有沒有做過什麼冒險的事情。也許是他把事情忘得一乾二淨了，所以就什麼都沒說，可是等你出去時卻赫然發現一具屍體。有時他又會說一大堆，可是你卻始終找不到屍體。有時候他回到家，頭上會綁著繃帶，溫蒂過去安慰他，用溫水替他清洗傷口，此時他會說起一段驚心動魄的故事。不過，你也知道，對於彼得的故事，溫蒂從來都不會完全相信，雖然她知道有許多冒險故事是真的，因為她自己也參與其中；還有更多的故事，她知道至少有部分是真的，因為其他孩子參與了，證明彼得說的都是真的。如果把這些冒險故事全都記錄下來，大概會寫成一本像英文拉丁文雙語字典那麼厚的書。我們最多只能舉一個例子，看看這島上的一小時是怎麼過的。可是難就難在到底要舉哪一個例子。要不我們來說在史萊特利谷和印地安人的衝突吧。那是一場血淋淋的戰爭，特別有趣的是那表現了彼得的一個特質，那就是在戰鬥中他會突然轉變陣營。在山谷裡，當勝利看似時而傾向這一方、時而又傾向那一方時，彼得會大喊：「今天我是印地安人。你是什麼，托托？」

托托說：「印地安人。你是什麼，尼布斯？」尼布斯說：「印地安人。你們是什麼，雙胞胎？」等等。於是他們都成了印地安人。戰爭可能會因此而結束，不過那些真正的印地安人會被彼得的做法所迷惑，也就暫時同意這一次變成遺失的孩子，然後繼續戰鬥，而且比剛才打得更勇猛。

這場冒險有個非比尋常的結局，但是我們還沒決定要不要說這段冒險。也許印地安人夜襲地底的家的故事更有趣。那一次，有好幾個印地安人被卡在樹洞裡，不得不像軟木塞似的被拔出來。或許我們可以說說在美人魚的潟湖上，彼得是如何救了虎蓮，從此雙方結盟的故事。

或許我們還可以說海盜們做的那個蛋糕，孩子們可能會吃了而喪命；說海盜們是如何一次又一次地把它放在巧妙的地方，而溫蒂卻總是把它從孩子們的手中奪走，因此到最後，那顆蛋糕不再鬆軟可口，硬得像塊石頭，可以用來當飛彈。虎克就是在某天夜裡被它打中，摔了一跤。

不然我們可以說彼得的那些飛禽朋友，特別是那隻永無鳥。牠巢築在潟湖上面的一棵樹上。我們來說這個鳥巢是怎麼落入水中，但那隻鳥卻還在孵蛋，而彼得下令不准打擾牠。這是個很美的故事，結局顯示了鳥類有多麼知恩圖報。可是，如果要說這個故事，我們就必須說起潟湖裡發生的整段冒險，這樣一來就得說兩個故事，而不是一個。還有一個比較短的冒險，不過也同樣精彩刺激，那就是叮噹在一些流浪仙子的幫助下，企圖把睡著的溫蒂放在一大片樹葉上，把她送回對岸。幸好樹葉承載不溫蒂的重量，醒來的溫蒂順便洗了澡，游了回來。或者我們還可以說彼得挑戰獅群的故事。他用箭在地上沿著自己畫了一個圈，挑釁獅子們跨進圈子。他等了好幾個鐘頭，其他孩子和溫蒂都屏住呼吸在樹上觀望，可是沒有一隻獅子敢接受他的挑戰。

我們應該選哪一個冒險故事呢？最好的辦法就是擲銅板決定。我擲過了，結果是潟湖的故事獲勝。這樣有人就會希望得勝的是山谷，或是蛋糕，或是叮噹的大樹葉。當然，我可以再擲一次，三次決定勝負，不過，或許直接說潟湖的故事才是最公平的。

第八章

美人魚潟湖

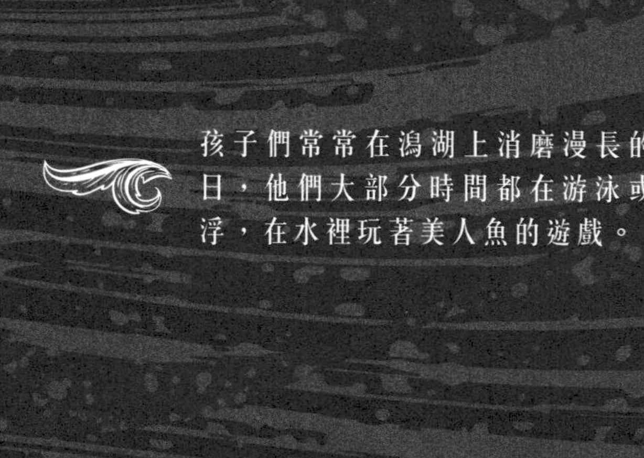

孩子們常常在潟湖上消磨漫長的夏日，他們大部分時間都在游泳或漂浮，在水裡玩著美人魚的遊戲。

有時候如果你閉上雙眼，運氣夠好的話，你會看到一個沒有形狀的湖水懸浮在黑暗之中，湖水的顏色灰白，非常可愛。然後，如果你把眼睛閉緊一點，湖水開始現出形狀，顏色也變得更加鮮明，好像眼睛再閉得更緊一點就會燃燒。但就在燃燒之前，你可以看見那個潟湖。這是在陸地上能看到潟湖最近的景象了，就只有這迷人的一瞬間，如果能有兩瞬間，也許你還能看到海浪，聽到美人魚的歌聲。

孩子們常常在潟湖上消磨漫長的夏日，他們大部分時間都在游泳或漂浮，在水裡玩著美人魚的遊戲。不要因此就以為美人魚和他們很要好，正好相反，溫蒂在島上的這段時間，始終沒聽過美人魚們對她說過一句客氣話，這是溫蒂心中永遠的遺憾。當她躡手躡腳地來到湖邊時，她也許可以看到成群的美人魚，特別是在流放岩上，她們喜歡在那裡曬太陽，用一種溫蒂看不慣的慵懶梳理著她們的長髮。她甚至會躡手躡腳地游到離她們一碼遠的地方。不過這時美人魚發現了她，都紛紛潛入水中，可能還會用尾巴濺得她一身水，這絕對不是不小心，而是故意的。

美人魚們也是如此對待男孩子們。當然彼得例外，他可以和美人魚們坐在流放岩上長談，玩到興起之時，還會騎上她們的尾巴。後來彼得送了溫蒂一把她們的梳子。

想要看美人魚，最令人無法忘懷的時間就是在月亮剛升起時。那時，她們會發出奇特的號泣聲。不過，那時的潟湖對人類來說非常危險，在我們將要提起的那個夜晚之前，溫蒂從沒見過月光下的潟湖。倒不是她害怕，因為彼得肯定會陪著她，而是因為她嚴格規定一到七點，每個人都必須上床睡覺。不過在雨過天晴之後，溫蒂時常會來潟湖。那時候成群的美人魚浮上水面，玩起泡泡。美人魚們把用彩虹中的水氣做成的五顏六色的泡泡當球，開心地用尾巴傳來傳去，試著把它們傳進彩虹，直到破掉為止。球門就在彩虹的兩端，只有守門員才可以用手接球。有時候，潟湖裡會有十幾場比賽同時展開，場面蔚為壯觀。

但是，孩子們剛想加入她們，美人魚們就立刻鑽進水裡消失不見了，孩子們不得不自己玩。然而，我們可以證明她們在暗中注視著這些不速之客，也很樂意向他們學習，因為，約翰發明了新的方法，那就是不要用手，而是用頭頂著泡泡，美人魚們也照著做了。這是約翰留在永無島的一個盛名。

午餐後，看著孩子們躺在岩石上休息半小時，這個場景真的十分賞心悅目。溫蒂堅決要求他們這麼做，即使午飯是假裝的，午休也必須是真的。所以他們全都躺在陽光下，身體被太陽曬得閃閃發亮，溫蒂則坐在他們旁邊，看起來一副很謹慎的樣子。

有一天，他們全都躺在流放岩上。這岩石不比他們的床大，不過他們都知道如何少佔點空間。他們打著瞌睡，至少是閉著眼睛躺在那，趁溫蒂不注意時，偶爾互捏一下。溫蒂則忙著做她的針線活。

正當她縫縫補補的時候，潟湖上起了變化。湖面微微地顫抖了一會，太陽躲了起來，陰影隨即籠罩了整個湖面，湖水也變冷了。溫蒂也沒有辦法看清針線了。她抬頭一看，直到如今一向充滿歡笑的潟湖，此時變得令人生畏、不敢親近。

她知道，並不是黑夜降臨，而是某種像黑夜一樣黑暗，不，比黑夜更黑暗的東西來了。雖然那東西還沒到，卻已經從海上送來了一陣顫抖，預告著它的到來。這是什麼東西呢？

這時溫蒂忽然想起了所有她聽說過關於流放岩的故事。它之所以叫流放岩，是因為邪惡的船長會把水手們丟在這裡，讓他們活活淹死。海水漲潮的時候，岩石被淹沒，水手們就會被淹死。

當然，她應該立刻叫醒孩子們，不僅是因為這股莫名的危險正在逼近，睡在一塊漸漸變冷的岩石上，對他們的身體也不好。然而，她只是一位年輕的母親，根本不懂這個道理。她覺得必須嚴格遵守午飯後休息半個小時的規矩。因此，雖然她非常害怕，渴望聽到男孩子們的聲音，她也不願把他們叫醒。甚至當她聽到一陣壓抑的槳聲的時候，儘管她的心已經跳到了嘴裡，她仍然沒有叫醒他們。溫蒂站在他們身邊，讓他們睡足半個小時。難道她還不勇敢嗎？

幸虧這些男孩當中，有一個人即使睡著了，也能嗅到危險。彼得像狗一樣跳了起來，立刻醒了過來，他發出一聲警告，叫醒了其他孩子。

他一動不動地站著，一隻手放在耳朵上仔細聽著。

「是海盜！」彼得喊。其他孩子都緊緊圍在他身邊。他臉上浮現一絲詭異的笑，溫蒂看了不禁打起寒顫。當他臉上露出那種笑容時，沒人敢跟他說話，他們只能站著，隨時準備好聽從他的指揮。彼得的命令下得又快又乾脆。

「跳下水！」只見一雙雙腿閃過，頃刻間潟湖變得空無一人。

流放岩孤零零地屹立在洶湧的湖水中，彷彿是自願被放逐到那裡。船慢慢靠近，是海盜的小艇，上面有三個人：斯密、斯塔奇、第三個是俘虜，那不是別人，正是虎蓮。她的手腳都被綁著，她知道自己的命運將會如何。她將被扔到流放岩上等死。在她族人看來，這種死法比用火燒或嚴刑拷打還要可怕，因為部落之書上清楚地寫著，透過水路無法通往極樂的狩獵天堂。但是她依舊面無表情，她是酋長的女兒，死也要死得像個酋長的女兒，這樣就夠了。

海盜們是在虎蓮嘴裡銜著一把刀，正要登上海盜船時抓住她的。船上無人看守，因為虎克總是誇口說，他的盛名足以在方圓一英里內保護他的船。如今，虎蓮也只是更加證明虎克的說法。到了夜裡，又將要有另一聲哀號，讓虎克的傳說傳遍四方。

這兩個海盜身處於伴隨他們而來的黑暗中，根本看不清楚，一頭撞上了流放岩。

「快轉舵，你這個笨蛋。」一個愛爾蘭口音喊道，那是斯密的聲音。「石頭就在這裡。現在我們要把這個印地安人放到石頭上，讓她淹死。」

把這樣一位漂亮的女孩丟在岩石上是件相當殘酷的事，可是虎蓮的自尊不允許她作出無謂的反抗。

距離流放岩不遠的地方，有兩顆頭在水裡上上下，那是彼得和溫蒂。溫蒂哭了，這是她看到的第一個悲劇。彼得看過很多悲劇，但是他全都忘了。彼得並不像溫蒂為虎蓮感到遺憾。但令他憤怒的是，他們居然兩個人對付一個。因此，他決定要救虎蓮。最容易的方法就是等海盜走後再去救她，可是彼得從來都不是挑簡單的事去做的人。

彼得幾乎沒有辦不到的事情，於是，他模仿起虎克的聲音。

「喂，那邊的笨蛋。」彼得喊道，這聲音模仿得像極了。

兩個海盜詫異地看著對方說：「是船長。」

兩人四處尋找卻看不到虎克的蹤影，斯塔奇說：「他肯定正往這邊游過來找我們。」

「我們正要把這個印地安人放到石頭上。」斯密大喊。

「放了她。」這回答讓人驚訝。

「放了她？」

「對，割斷繩索，放她走。」

「可是，船長——」

「立刻放了她，聽見沒有？」彼得喊道。「否則我就賞你們一鉤。」

「這真是奇怪。」斯密急促地說。

「還是照船長的命令去做吧。」斯塔奇不安地說。

「沒錯，沒錯。」斯密說著就割斷了的繩子。虎蓮立刻像條泥鰍似的，從斯塔奇的兩腿之間溜進了水裡。

看到彼得如此聰明，溫蒂覺得非常高興，可是她知道，彼得一定也非常高興，很可能會歡呼起來，不小心暴露自己的身份。因此立刻伸手去捂住他的嘴，然而她卻在手快伸到的時候停住了。「喂，那邊的小船！」湖面上傳來虎克的聲音，這次並不是彼得說的。

彼得也許正想要歡呼，可是他卻一臉驚訝的噘著嘴，像是在吹口哨。

「喂，那邊的小船！」又是這個聲音。

此刻溫蒂明白了，真正的虎克也來到了這裡。

虎克正朝著小船游過去，他的手下提著燈籠給他引路，很快地就游到了他們身邊。透過燈籠的光芒，溫蒂看到他的鐵鉤鉤住了船舷，當虎克濕淋淋地從水中爬上去的時候，溫蒂看見了他那張兇狠的黑臉，嚇得渾身發抖，巴不得立刻離開，可是彼得不肯走，他正在興頭上，而且自負過了頭。「我真是個天才，噢，我是個天才！」彼得輕聲地對溫蒂說，雖然溫蒂也這麼認為，但是考慮到他的名譽，她慶幸除了自己之外沒有第二個人聽到。

彼得對她做了個手勢，示意要她仔細聽。

這兩個海盜很想知道是什麼風把船長吹到這裡來了。不過，虎克只是坐在那裡，用鐵鉤托著頭，露出一副非常憂鬱的神情。

「船長，沒事吧？」他們膽怯地問，可是虎克只是深深地嘆了口氣。

「他嘆氣了。」斯密說。

「又嘆氣了。」斯塔奇說。

「第三次嘆氣了。」斯密說。

最後，虎克慷慨激昂地說：「我們的計謀失敗了，那些男孩找到了一個媽媽。」

雖然溫蒂有些害怕，心裡卻充滿了自豪感。

「啊，真糟糕。」斯塔奇喊道。

「什麼是媽媽？」無知的斯密問道。

溫蒂感到很驚訝，大叫：「他居然不知道什麼是媽媽！」從此以後，她一直覺得，如果要養個小海盜當寵物的話，斯密就是最佳人選。

彼得一把將溫蒂拖進水裡，因為虎克忽然站起來驚呼：「什麼聲音？」

「我什麼都沒聽到啊。」斯塔奇邊說邊舉起燈籠照了照湖面。正當海盜們到處東張西望時，他們看到了一個奇怪的場景，就是前面提到過的那個鳥巢飄浮在湖面上，那隻永無鳥臥躺在巢裡。

「看，」虎克回答斯密：「那就是媽媽。這是個很好的例子，鳥巢一定是掉進水裡了，但是鳥媽媽會捨棄她的蛋嗎？不會。」

虎克突然停頓了一下，彷彿想起了那些天真無邪的日子，可是他用鐵鉤揮去了這個軟弱的念頭。

深受感動的斯密凝視著那隻鳥，看著那鳥巢慢慢漂走。可是，多疑的斯塔奇卻說：「如果她是媽媽，那她在這裡漂來漂去，也許是為了幫助彼得。」

虎克畏縮了。「是啊，」他說：「我擔心的正是這個。」

斯密熱切的聲音，把虎克從沮喪中喚醒過來。

「船長，」斯密說：「為什麼我們不把孩子們的媽媽抓來當我們的媽媽呢？」

「這計畫真是太棒了。」虎克喊道，腦海裡立刻就浮現出具體的方案。「我們可以抓住那些孩子，帶他們上船，然後讓他們蒙上眼睛走下木板跳海，這樣溫蒂就變成我們的媽媽了。」

溫蒂再次忘記了自己的處境。

「絕不！」她喊了一聲後又沉到了水中。

「什麼聲音？」

但是海盜們什麼都看不見，他們認為那只是風吹樹葉的聲音。「你們同意這個計畫嗎，夥計們？」虎克問。

「我舉手贊成。」他們倆同時回答說。

「我舉鉤贊成，現在宣誓。」

宣誓後他們都站在岩石上，虎克忽然想起了虎蓮。

「那個印地安人呢？」他突然問道。

虎克時常會開玩笑，耍點幽默，他們以為他在說笑。

「沒事的，船長。」斯密沾沾自喜地回答說：「我們把她給放了。」

「把她給放了！」虎克大叫。

「那是你的命令啊。」水手支支吾吾地說。

「你在水裡的時候，命令我們把她給放了。」斯塔奇說。

「真是氣死我了，」虎克暴跳如雷地喊道：「這是怎麼回事？」他氣得臉色發黑，但是看到手下那麼肯定，他感到很驚訝。

「夥計們，」他微微顫抖地說道：「我從沒下過這種命令啊。」

「這就奇怪了。」斯密說。所有人都坐立不安起來。虎克提高了嗓音，不過這聲音之中夾雜著一絲顫抖。

「今晚在這湖上遊蕩的孤魂野鬼們，」他喊道：「你們都聽見了嗎？」

彼得本該保持沉默的，但這不符合他的個性。他立刻模仿虎克的聲音回答：

「天靈靈地靈靈，鎚子和火鉗，我聽到了。」

在這個節骨眼上，虎克的臉色並沒有嚇得慘白，倒是斯密和斯塔奇早已嚇得抱成一團。

「說！你到底是誰？」虎克問。

「我是詹姆士・虎克。」那聲音回答說：「海盜船的船長。」

「你不是，你不是。」虎克嘶啞地喊著。

「該死的，」那聲音反駁道：「你再說一次，我就把你丟到海裡。」

虎克試著用迎合的方式跟他對話。「如果你是虎克，」他幾乎是低聲下氣地說：「那你告訴我，我又是誰？」

「一條鱈魚，」那聲音回答說：「只不過是一條鱈魚。」

「一條鱈魚！」虎克茫然地重複著，他過去那副驕傲的神情在這一刻破裂了，他看見自己的部下往身後退了退。

「難道至自始至終我們都擁戴一條鱈魚當船長？」他們咕噥著：「真是丟臉啊。」

他們都是虎克的走狗，現在反倒咬了他一口。不過，雖然虎克傷心欲絕，但是他根本沒注意到他們。要反駁一個如此可怕的證詞，他需要的並不是他們對他的信任，而是他自己對自己的信任。他覺得自己的靈魂正慢慢地離他而去。「別拋棄我，惡霸。」他嘶啞地輕聲喚道。

如同所有偉大海盜，虎克兇悍的天性裡，也保留了一些女性的陰柔，有時候也會因此得到一些直覺。忽然間他玩起了猜謎遊戲。

「虎克，」他問：「你還有其他聲音嗎？」

此時，彼得根本無法抵抗遊戲的誘惑。於是他用自己的聲音愉快地回答說：「有啊。」

「有其他名字嗎？」

「有啊，有啊。」

「是蔬菜？」虎克問。

「不是。」

「是礦物？」

「不是。」

「是動物？」

「是。」

「是男人？」

「不是！」這問題回答得頗為輕蔑。

「是男孩？」

「是。」

「普通男孩？」

「不是！」

「奇妙的男孩？」

令溫蒂苦惱的是，彼得這次的回答是「沒錯」。

「你住在英國嗎？」

「不。」

「你住在這裡？」

「對。」

虎克完全被搞鬧糊塗了。「你們兩個也問他幾個問題。」他一邊對另外兩個人說，一邊擦掉他的前額的汗。

斯密思考了一下。「我想不出什麼問題。」他抱歉地說。

「猜不出來啦，猜不出來啦，」彼得愉快地喊道：「你們認輸了吧？」

彼得的驕傲讓惡霸們看到了機會。

「是的，是的。」他們急切地回答。

「那好吧，我來告訴你們，」他喊道：「我是彼得潘！」

是彼得潘！

剎那間，虎克又恢復了兇惡的原形，斯密和斯塔奇又成了他忠實的部下。

「我們終於找到他啦。」虎克大喊：「斯密，下水。斯塔奇，看著船。不管是死是活，都要給我把他抓上來。」

虎克邊說邊跳下了水，與此同時，湖面上也響起彼得那歡樂的聲音。

「準備好了嗎？孩子們？」

「好啦，好啦。」聲音從瀉湖的四面八方傳過來。

「那麼，向海盜進攻吧。」

戰鬥很短，卻很激烈。第一個讓敵人流血的是約翰，他勇敢地爬上小船，抓住了斯塔奇。在激烈的爭鬥中，斯塔奇手中的彎刀落了下來，人也掙扎著掉進了水裡，約翰跟著他跳了下去，小船就漂走了。

湖面上不時地冒出一個個腦袋，刀光一閃，跟著便是一聲慘叫，或是一聲吶喊。在混戰之中，大家都分不清敵我了。斯密的螺旋鑽刺中了托托的第四根肋骨，接著斯密又被捲毛刺傷。離岩石較

遠的地方，斯塔奇正緊緊追趕著史萊特利和雙胞胎兄弟。

這個時候的彼得又在哪呢？他在尋找更大的獵物。

其他孩子都非常勇敢，他們避開海盜船長是無可指責的。虎克的鐵鉤把他的周圍變成了死亡地帶，孩子們就像受到驚嚇的魚一樣急忙逃開。

但是還有一個不怕虎克的人打算闖進這個地帶。

說也奇怪，彼得和虎克從沒有在水裡相遇過。虎克爬上岩石喘了口氣，同一時刻，彼得也從岩石對面爬了上來。這岩石就像球一樣非常光滑，他們沒辦法攀緣，只能慢慢地匍匐著爬上去。兩個人都不知道對方也在往上爬。兩個人都在摸索著一塊能抓緊的地方，不料竟摸到了對方的手。他們驚訝得抬起頭來，兩個人的臉幾乎挨在了一起。他們就這樣相遇了。

一些偉大的英雄都承認，在他們交手之前，心裡也難免會有些不安。如果那時候彼得也是如此，我也不會替他掩飾。畢竟他的對手虎克是唯一能令海上庫克畏懼的人。可是彼得並沒有感到不安，他心裡只有一種感覺：興奮。他愉快地咬緊了他那口漂亮的牙齒。轉念之間，他已經拔出了虎克皮帶上的刀，正準備插入虎克的身體，他突然發現自己所站的岩石比敵人的高，這樣的戰鬥是不公平的。於是，他伸出手把海盜拉了上來。

就在這時，虎克咬了他一口。

彼得感到一陣暈眩，並不是因為疼痛，而是因為不公平。這讓他變得不知所措，只是驚恐地瞪著虎克。每個孩子在他第一次遇到不公平的待遇時，都會受到影響。當他跟你坦誠相見的時候，他心裡所想的只是他有權利受到公平的待遇。如果你對他不公平，他還是會愛你，但是從此之後他就不再是以前的那個孩子了。誰也忘不了第一次受到的不公平待遇，除了彼得。他經常遭遇不公平的事情，不過總是忘記。我想這就是他和別人真正不同之處吧。

所以，此時彼得遇到了不公平，就像他第一次遇到那樣，只能無助地凝視著。虎克的鐵鉤已經抓了他兩次。

沒過多久，其他孩子就看見虎克在水裡瘋狂地掙扎著游向小船。這時，他那討人厭的臉上已經沒有得意洋洋的神情，只剩下慘白的驚恐，原來那隻鱷魚正窮追不捨地跟在他後面。若是在平時，孩子們會一邊游泳，一邊歡呼，但現在他們心裡都非常忐忑不安，因為彼得和溫蒂兩個人都失蹤了。他們紛紛下水四處尋找他們，呼喚他們。孩子們找到了那隻小船，坐了上去，一邊划著船回家，一邊大喊著：「彼得，溫蒂。」但是除了美人魚的嘲笑之外，沒有任何聲音。「他們肯定已經游回去了，要不然就是飛回去了。」孩子們推斷說。他們並沒有非常著急，因為他們對彼得有信心。他們像孩子似的咯咯笑著，因為今晚他們可以晚點睡覺了，這全都是溫蒂媽媽的錯。

當孩子們的笑聲漸漸平息之後，湖面上籠罩著一片冷清的寂靜，之後傳來一聲微弱的叫聲。

「救命啊，救命啊！」

兩個瘦小的身軀朝著岩石游去，女孩已經暈過去，躺在男孩的手臂。彼得使出最後一點力氣，把溫蒂推上岩石，然後倒在她身邊。昏迷之中，他看到湖水正在上漲。他知道他們很快就會被淹死，卻無能為力。

當他們並排躺在岩石上時，一條美人魚抓住溫蒂的腳，輕輕地將她拖入水中。彼得感覺到她正在往下滑，猛地驚醒過來，恰好及時把她拉回來。現在，他不得不把事情告訴溫蒂了。

「我們在岩石上，溫蒂，」他說：「可是這石頭越來越小了，很快湖水就會把它淹沒。」

儘管如此，溫蒂還是聽不懂。

「我們該走了。」她似乎相當清醒地說道。

「是啊。」彼得無精打采地回答。

「彼得，我們是游回去還是飛回去？」

彼得只好告訴她：

「溫蒂，如果沒有我的幫助，你覺得你能游泳或飛到那麼遠的島上去嗎？」

溫蒂不得不承認自己太累了。

彼得呻吟了一聲。

「你怎麼了？」溫蒂問道，立刻擔心起彼得來。

「我沒辦法幫你，溫蒂。虎克把我打傷了，現在我既不會飛，也不會游泳。」

「你是說，我們兩個都會淹死嗎？」

「你看，這湖水漲得多快啊。」

他們用手捂住眼睛，不敢去看眼前的情景，他們心想自己很快就要沒命了。就在他們這樣坐著的時候，有個東西像吻似的輕輕從彼得身上拂過，然後就停在那不動了，彷彿在羞怯地說：「我能派上什麼用場嗎？」

那是一隻風箏的尾巴，這風箏是麥可幾天前剛做出來的。有一天掙脫了麥可的手飛走了。

「是麥可的風箏。」彼得毫無興趣地說，話還沒說完，他突然抓住風箏的尾巴，把它拉到身邊。

「既然這風箏可以把麥可從地上拉起來，」他喊道：「那應該也能把你帶走吧？」

「把我們兩個都帶走！」

「帶不動兩個的，麥可和捲毛試過了。」

「那我們抽籤吧。」溫蒂勇敢地說。

「你是個女孩子，我不能這麼做。」彼得已經把風箏的尾巴繫在她身上。溫蒂緊緊地抱住彼得，彼得不走她就不走。可是，隨著一聲「再見，溫蒂」，彼得就把她推下了岩石。幾分鐘功夫，她就消失在眼前了。彼得則獨自一人留在潟湖上。

此時的岩石已經變得非常小了，很快就會完全被淹沒。一道慘淡的光線躡手躡腳地滑過湖面，不久之後，就會聽到這世上最悅耳動聽也最悲淒的曲調，那是人魚對月亮的呼喚。

雖然彼得和其他孩子很不一樣，但終究也感到害怕了。他渾身一陣顫抖，就像越過海面的波濤。海面上的波濤其實是一個接著一個，直到形成驚濤駭浪，但彼得只感覺到一陣顫抖。轉眼間，他又筆直地站在岩石上，臉上露出他特有的微笑，內心像小鼓敲打似的咚咚吶喊著，彷彿在說：「死亡將是最大的冒險。」

第九章

永無鳥

其實，那不是一張紙，那是帶著巢的永無鳥，她正拚命靠近彼得。

彼得落單前聽到的最後的聲音，是美人魚們一個接著一個回到海底的臥房時發出的聲響。他離得太遠了，聽不到關門的聲音。不過，在她們居住的珊瑚洞穴的每扇門上都有一個小鈴，開門或關門時總會叮噹作響（*就像英國本土最講究的房子那樣*），彼得聽到了這些鈴聲。

海水逐漸上漲，一點一滴地吞噬著彼得的腳。在被海水吞沒之前，他凝視著漂在潟湖上唯一的一樣東西來消磨時間。彼得以為那是一張漂浮的紙，或許是風箏的一部分。他漫不經心地想著那個東西還要多久才能漂到岸邊。

突然間，彼得發現這個東西有點不尋常，它一定是帶著某種目的來到湖面上的，因為它正在逆著海浪而行，有時還戰勝了海浪。每當它勝利時，總是同情弱者的彼得就忍不住為它鼓掌，那是多麼勇敢的一張紙。

其實，那不是一張紙，那是帶著巢的永無鳥，她正拚命靠近彼得。自從鳥巢落水後，她學會了用翅膀划水，現在居然也勉強能操縱她那奇異的小船了。不過，在彼得認出她時，她已經非常疲倦了。她是來救彼得的，儘管巢裡還有蛋，她還是要把巢讓給彼得。我還不能完全理解這隻鳥的舉動，雖然彼得對她好，可是有時候還是會折磨她。我只能猜想，這隻鳥大概也像達林太太一樣，一看到彼得的滿口乳牙就心軟了吧。

那隻鳥向彼得大聲喊著，解釋她來的目的，彼得也大聲詢問大鳥在那裡做什麼。當然他們都聽不懂對方所說的話。在神話裡，人類可以和鳥類自由地交談。我也希望我正在說的故事也是如此，這樣就

可以告訴大家彼得很聰明，能夠和永無鳥自由地交談。但最好還是實話實說，實際上，他們不僅語言不通，而且連禮貌都忘記了。

「我——要——你——到——巢——裡——來，」永無鳥盡可能放慢速度清楚地喊著，「那——樣，你——就——可——以——漂——到——岸——上——去——可——是——我——太——累——了，不——能——離——你——再——近——了 ，你——得——想——辦——法——自——己——游——過——來。」

彼得回答：「你嘰嘰喳喳地在叫什麼呀？為什麼不讓鳥巢隨波漂流呢？」

永無鳥又重複剛才說的話：「我——要——你——」。

接著，彼得也放慢速度清楚地說：

「你——嘰——嘰——喳——喳——地——叫——什——麼——呀？」等等。

永無鳥煩躁起來了，這種鳥的脾氣是很差的。

她尖聲叫道：「你這個呆頭呆腦、囉裡囉嗦的小笨蛋為什麼不照我的話去做？」

彼得覺得她是在罵自己，於是氣沖沖地回敬了一句：

「你才是呢！」

然後他們竟奇怪地對罵起來：

「閉嘴！」

「閉嘴！」

不過，她決心盡力救彼得，最後奮力一推，把鳥巢撞上了岩石就飛了起來，丟下了她的蛋，藉此表明她的用意。

彼得終於明白了，他抓住了鳥巢，向空中飛著的夢幻鳥揮手致謝。永無鳥在空中飛來飛去，並不是為了接受彼得的謝意，也不是要看他怎麼爬進巢裡，而是想看看他會怎樣對待她的蛋。

鳥巢裡有兩隻又大又白的蛋，彼得把它們捧了起來沈思了一會。永無鳥用翅膀捂住臉，不敢看蛋的下場，卻又忍不住從羽毛縫偷看。

我不記得有沒有告訴過你們，岩石上有一塊木板，是很久以前一群西印度海盜釘在那兒，用來標誌寶藏的位置。孩子們發現了這堆閃閃發光的寶藏，有時他們太想惡作劇，就抓起一把一把的金幣、鑽石、珍珠等拋向海鷗，海鷗以為是食物，撲過來啄食，當它們發現這是卑鄙的惡作劇時就生氣得飛走了。那塊木板還在，斯塔奇把他的帽子掛在上面，那是一頂深色寬邊的、高高的防水帽。彼得把蛋放在帽子裡，再把帽子放到水面上，它就平平穩穩地漂起來了。

永無鳥馬上明白了彼得的妙計，高聲歡呼，向他表示欽佩，彼得也應聲歡呼起來。然後他跨進鳥巢，把木板豎起來當桅杆，又掛上他的衣服做船帆。此時，永無鳥也飛到帽子上，安逸地孵起蛋來。永無鳥往那裡漂，彼得往這裡漂，皆大歡喜。

彼得上岸後，當然是把他搭過的「小船」放在一個夢幻鳥容易

發現的地方，可是帽子太好用了，夢幻鳥寧願放棄她的巢。這個巢就漂來漂去，直到最後完全解體。後來，當斯塔奇來到潟湖時，時常看見那隻鳥在他的帽子上孵蛋，這讓他惱怒不已。因為之後我們不會再見到夢幻鳥，所以在這裡值得一提的是，現在所有的夢幻鳥都把巢築成有一道寬邊的樣子，讓小鳥可以在上面散心。

彼得回到地下的家時，溫蒂也剛好被風箏東飄西蕩地帶回家。大家全都興高采烈，每個孩子都有一段冒險故事可以講，不過，他們最大的冒險或許是已經晚睡了好幾個小時。這件事使他們非常得意，於是又磨磨蹭蹭地用包紮傷口之類的理由，拖延上床睡覺的時間。至於溫蒂，雖然她很高興看到他們全都平安地回到家了，但是時間實在太晚了，於是她用那令人不得不服從的語調喊道：「全都給我上床去！」不過到了第二天，溫蒂又變得異常溫柔，她把繃帶還給孩子們，於是他們有的跛著腳，有的吊著手臂，一直玩到上床睡覺。

第十章

快樂家庭

這個景象在地底的家是再熟悉不過的場景，但如今是我們最後一次看到了。

這次潟湖交鋒的一個重大成果，就是和印地安人成為朋友。彼得把虎蓮從可怕的命運中救了出來。現在，她和她的勇士們無不樂於全力以赴地幫助彼得。海盜們的進攻顯然已經迫在眉睫，勇士們整夜坐在地面上，守衛著地下的家，防備著海盜們的大舉進攻。即使在白天，印地安人也在附近一帶巡遊，悠閒地吸著煙斗，看起來倒像是想要點東西吃。

印地安人稱彼得為「偉大的白人父親」，拜倒在他面前。彼得很喜歡這一套，雖然這對他並沒什麼好處。

當印地安人拜倒在他腳下時，彼得會用威嚴的口氣對他們說：「偉大的白人父親很高興看到皮卡尼尼族戰士保衛他的小屋，不受海盜攻擊。」

「我，虎蓮，」這位美女說：「是彼得潘救的，我是他的好朋友，我決不讓海盜傷害他。」

虎蓮實在太漂亮了，如此美麗的女孩不該這樣卑躬屈膝，可是彼得認為他受之無愧：「很好。彼得潘這樣說了。」

每次他說「彼得潘這樣說了」，意思就是叫印地安人閉嘴，他們就會乖乖聽話。但是，他們對其他的孩子可沒這麼恭敬，只把他們看成普通的勇士，只對他們說聲「你好！」之類的話。彼得似乎認為無所謂，這讓孩子們覺得生氣。

私底下，溫蒂有點同情那些孩子，但她是一個非常忠實的家庭主婦，對於抱怨父親的話，一概不聽。無論她個人看法如何，她總是

說「父親的話不會有錯」。但她覺得印地安人不該叫她「婆娘」。

這一天終於到了，他們稱這一天為「夜中之夜」，因為這一夜的冒險及其結局特別重要。白天平靜無事，像是在養精蓄銳。此刻，印地安人在上面裹著毯子站崗，孩子們在地下吃晚飯，只有彼得不在，他出去打聽時間了。在島上，要打聽時間就得去找那條鱷魚，一直在牠旁邊等著聽牠肚裡的鐘報時。

這頓飯是一頓假想的茶點，孩子們圍坐在桌邊，狼吞虎嚥地大嚼，聊天鬥嘴，照溫蒂說的簡直是震耳欲聾。當然，溫蒂並不太在乎吵鬧，但她不能允許他們一邊搶東西吃，一邊說托托撞了自己的手臂。他們有一條吃飯的規矩，就是不能還手打人，而應該禮貌地舉起右手，向溫蒂報告：「我控告某人。」可是實際上，他們不是根本忘了這條規矩，就是做得太過火了。

「不要吵，」溫蒂喊道，她已經第二十次告訴他們不要一起講話了。「你的杯子空了嗎，史萊特利寶貝？」

「還不太空，媽媽。」史萊特利望了一眼假想的杯子後說。

「他連牛奶都還沒喝呢。」尼布斯插嘴說。

他這是告狀，史萊特利抓住了這個機會。

「我控告尼布斯。」他立即喊道。

不過，約翰先舉起了手。

「什麼事，約翰？」

「彼得不在，我可不可以坐他的椅子？」

「坐爸爸的椅子，約翰！」溫蒂認為這簡直不成體統，「當然不可以。」

「他又不是我們真的爸爸，」約翰回答：「他甚至都不知道怎麼當爸爸，還是我教他的呢。」

他這是發牢騷。「我們要抱怨約翰。」雙胞胎喊道。

托托舉起了手。他是孩子們當中最謙遜的一個，說實在的，他也是唯一謙遜的孩子，所以溫蒂對他特別溫和。

托托猶猶豫豫地說：「我不認為我能當父親。」

「你不能，托托。」

托托很少開口，可是他一開口就會傻裡傻氣地說不停。

「既然我當不了父親，」他心情沉重地說：「我猜，麥可，你也不會讓我當寶寶，對吧？」

「我不會。」麥可生氣地叫起來。他早就鑽到搖籃裡了。

「既然我當不了寶寶，」托托說，心情越來越沉重：「你們覺得我能當雙胞胎嗎？」

「當然不能，」雙胞胎回答說：「當雙胞胎真的太難了。」

「既然我不能成為任何重要人，」托托說：「你們有誰想看我表演一個把戲？」

「不要。」大家都回答。

他只能住口。「我真的毫無希望了。」他說。

討人厭的小報告又開始了。

「史萊特利在飯桌上咳嗽。」

「雙胞胎先吃了乳酪蛋糕。」

「捲毛吃了黃油和蜂蜜。」

「尼布斯邊吃邊說話。」

「我要抱怨雙胞胎。」

「我要抱怨捲毛。」

「我要抱怨尼布斯。」

「天啊，天啊，」溫蒂喊道：「我有時覺得沒結婚也是件好事。」

她吩咐孩子們收拾飯桌，之後便坐下做起針線活。針線筐裡堆滿了長襪子，毫不例外地每隻襪子的膝蓋上都有一個洞。

「溫蒂，」麥可提出抗議：「我太大了，睡不下搖籃了。」

「總得有一個人睡搖籃。」溫蒂幾乎用尖酸的語氣回答。「你是最小的，而且搖籃是美滿家庭的居家必備用品。」

溫蒂縫補著襪子的時候，孩子們在她身邊玩耍。在浪漫的爐火之下，這一群歡樂的面孔開心地手足舞蹈。這個景象在地底的家是再熟悉不過的場景，但如今是我們最後一次看到了。

上面有腳步聲，不用說溫蒂是第一個聽出來的。

「孩子們，我聽到你們爸爸的腳步聲了，他喜歡你們到門口迎接他。」

在地面上，印地安人俯伏在彼得面前。

「好好看守，勇士們，我這樣說了。」

然後，歡天喜地的孩子們像從前那樣把彼得從他的樹洞中拉出來。雖說這樣的事以前是常有的，但今後再也不會有了。

彼得給孩子們帶來了堅果，也給溫蒂帶回了正確的時間。

「彼得，你知道嗎？你把他們給寵壞了。」溫蒂傻笑著說。

「是啊，老太婆。」彼得邊說邊把槍掛起來。

「是我告訴他要叫媽媽老太婆的。」麥可悄悄地對捲毛說。

「我要抱怨麥可。」捲毛馬上提出。

雙胞胎中的老大走到彼得跟前說：「爸爸，我們想跳舞。」

彼得說：「那就跳吧，小傢伙。」，他興致很高昂。

「可是我們也想讓你也跳。」

彼得其實是他們當中跳得最好的，但他一臉吃驚的假裝說：

「我？我這把老骨頭會散掉。」

「媽媽也要跳。」

「什麼！」溫蒂喊，「都發福的媽媽了，還跳舞！」

「這可是禮拜六晚上啊！」史萊特利討好地說。

其實那不是禮拜六晚上，不過也許是，因為他們早就把日期給忘了。但是如果他們想做點什麼特別的事，總會說這是禮拜六晚上，然後就開始行動了。

「當然啦，這是禮拜六晚上，彼得。」溫蒂說，她的態度有點軟化。

「像我們這樣……溫蒂。」

「但現在只是跟孩子們一起呀。」

「當然，當然。」

於是孩子們可以跳舞了，不過得先穿上睡衣。

「哎，老太婆。」彼得悄悄地招呼溫蒂。他正在爐前取暖，一邊低頭看著溫蒂坐在那裡補一隻襪子的後跟。「一天的勞累之後，我們坐在火爐前休息，小傢伙在旁邊玩鬧，這樣的晚上真是再愉快不過了。」

「真是甜蜜啊，彼得，你說是不是？」溫蒂心滿意足地說：「彼得，我覺得捲毛的鼻子像你。」

「麥可像你。」

溫蒂走到彼得跟前，兩手搭在他肩上。

溫蒂說，「親愛的彼得，擁有這樣一個大家庭，我也不再年輕了，但你不會變的，對吧？」

「不會的，溫蒂。」

彼得當然不喜歡變來變去，可是他眨著眼睛不安地望著溫蒂，也說不清他究竟是醒著還是睡著了。

「彼得，怎麼了？」

彼得帶著幾分恐慌說：「我在想，這只是假裝的，對吧？假裝我是他們的爸爸。」

「是啊。」溫蒂一本正經地回答。

彼得帶著抱歉意接著說：「你看，如果我是他們真正的爸爸，我會顯得很老。」

「但他們是我們的，彼得，是我們兩個的。」

「但不是真的對吧，溫蒂？」彼得焦慮地問。

「你要是不願意，就不是真的。」溫蒂回答說，她清楚地聽到了彼得放心地嘆了一口氣。「彼得，」她試著不動聲色地問：「你對我究竟是什麼感覺？」

「寶貝兒子的媽媽啊，溫蒂。」

「我想也是。」溫蒂說，走到屋裡最遠的一端，獨自坐下。

「你真怪，」彼得坦白地表示他的困惑：「虎蓮也是這樣。她想要成為我的什麼，可是她又說不是我的媽媽。」

「哼！當然不是。」溫蒂嚴肅地說。現在我們明白她為什麼對印地安人抱持偏見了。

「那是什麼？」

「這可不是一位淑女該說出口的話。」

「那好吧，也許叮噹會告訴我。」彼得有點惱怒地說。

「那當然，叮噹會告訴你。」溫蒂不屑地回頂了他一句：「她是個放蕩的小東西。」

叮噹正在她的臥房裡偷聽，尖聲罵了一些無禮的話。

「她說她以放蕩為榮。」彼得幫忙翻譯。

彼得忽然想到：「也許叮噹願意做我的媽媽吧？」

「你這個笨蛋！」叮噹怒氣衝衝地喊道。

這句話她說了那麼多次，溫蒂不用翻譯也能聽懂了。

「我幾乎要同意她的話了。」溫蒂生氣地說。想想看，溫蒂居然也會這麼說話，可見她已經受夠了。她絕對沒想到這個晚上會發生什麼事。要是她知道的話，就不會這樣說話了。

他們誰也不知道，也許不知道更好。他們的懵懂無知讓他們能多享受一小時的快樂。由於這是他們在島上的最後一小時，大家就盡情享受這六十分鐘吧。他們穿著睡衣又唱又跳，唱著一首美妙的歌，在歌中他們假裝害怕自己的影子，一點都不知道，陰影很快就會籠罩他們，讓他們陷入真正的恐懼。他們的舞跳得那麼愉快熱鬧，還在床上床下互相打鬧，比起跳舞，那更像是一場枕頭戰，打完之後，那些枕頭硬要再打一回合，宛如再也不會見面的夥伴那樣依依不捨。在溫蒂講睡前的故事之前，他們講了多少故事啊！那晚就連史萊特利也想講故事，但故事一開頭就講得沉悶乏味，連他自己也講不下去了。於是他沮喪地說：「對，這個開頭就很無聊。嗯，我們就假裝是故事的結局吧。」

最後，他們都上了床聽溫蒂的故事，這故事是他們最愛聽的，卻是彼得最不喜歡的。平時溫蒂一開始講這個故事，彼得不是離開這屋子，就是用手捂住耳朵。這一次，要是他也這麼做了，他們或許還會留在島上。可是今晚，彼得仍舊坐在他的小凳子上。讓我們看看接著會發生什麼事。

第十一章

溫蒂的故事

「不要吵！」彼得大聲說。他覺得不管這個故事再怎麼無聊，也應該讓溫蒂說完才公平。

「好吧，聽著。」溫蒂說，坐下來準備說她的故事。麥可坐在她腳邊，七個孩子坐在床上。「從前有一位先生……」

「我寧願是位太太。」捲毛說。

「我希望是隻白老鼠。」尼布斯說。

「安靜。」媽媽警告他們。「還有一位太太，而且……」

「啊，媽媽，」雙胞胎中的老大說，「你是說還有一位太太，對不對？她沒有死，對不對？」

「對，沒有。」

「她沒有死，我好高興，」托托說，「你高興嗎，約翰？」

「我當然高興。」

「你高興嗎，尼布斯？」

「很高興。」

「你們高興嗎，雙胞胎？」

「我們也高興。」

「噢，天啊。」溫蒂嘆了口氣。

「不要吵！」彼得大聲說。他覺得不管這個故事再怎麼無聊，也應該讓溫蒂說完才公平。

「這位先生姓達林，」溫蒂接著說，「女士呢，就叫達林太太。」

「我認識他們。」約翰故意激怒其他人。

「我想我認識他們。」麥可有點遲疑地說。

「他們結了婚，你們知道吧？」溫蒂解釋：「你們知道他們有了什麼？」

「白老鼠。」尼布斯靈機一動說。

「不是。」

「真難猜呀。」托托說，儘管這個故事他已經能倒背如流。

「安靜，托托。他們有三個後代。」

「後代是什麼？」

「你就是後代，雙胞胎。」

「聽見了沒有，約翰？我是一個後代。」

「後代就是孩子。」約翰說。

「啊，天啊，天啊，」溫蒂嘆氣說：「好吧，這三個孩子有位忠實的保姆娜娜，可是達林先生生她的氣，把她拴在院子裡，然後三個孩子就都飛走了。」

「這故事真棒！」尼布斯說。

「他們飛到了永無島，」溫蒂接著說：「那裡住著許多遺失的小孩……」

「我就知道他們在那兒，」捲毛興奮地插嘴說，「不知怎麼的，反正我就覺得他們在那兒。」

「溫蒂，」托托喊道：「遺失的孩子裡是不是有一個托托？」

「對。」

「我在故事裡啦，哈哈，我在故事裡啦，尼布斯。」

「別鬧了。現在你們好好想想，孩子們都飛走了，不幸的父母們的心情會怎樣呢？」

「唉！」他們全都嘆起氣來，雖然他們一點也不關心那對不幸的父母的心情。

「想想那些空床！」

「唉。」

「真慘啊。」雙胞胎的老大開心地說。

「我看這故事不會有什麼好結果。」雙胞胎的老二說：「你說呢，尼布斯？」

「我很擔心。」

「要是你們知道母愛有多偉大，」溫蒂得意地告訴他們：「你

們就不會害怕了。」現在講到彼得最討厭的那部分了。

「我喜歡母愛。」托托邊說邊用枕頭砸尼布斯:「你喜歡母愛嗎？尼布斯？」

「我很喜歡。」尼布斯邊反擊邊說道。

「你們看，」溫蒂愉快地說：「我們故事裡的女主角知道，那位母親肯定總是開著窗戶，好讓她的孩子們飛回來。而孩子們卻在外面待許多年，度過了一段愉快的時光。」

「他們回家了嗎？」

「現在，」溫蒂說，鼓起勇氣做最後的努力：「讓我們來瞧瞧後來發生了什麼事吧。」於是大家都扭動了一下，這樣可以更容易看到將來。「很多年以後，一位看不出年紀的優雅小姐在倫敦車站下了火車，她是誰呢？」

「啊，溫蒂，她是誰？」尼布斯喊道，渾身上下都興奮起來，好像他真的不知道似的。

「會不會是——是——不是——正是——美麗的溫蒂！」

「啊！」

「和她在一起的那兩個相貌堂堂的男人又是誰？該不會是約翰和麥可吧？正是他們！」

「啊！」

「『你們看，親愛的弟弟，』溫蒂指著上面說：『那扇窗戶還開著呢。因為我們對母愛的崇高信念，現在我們終於得到回報了。於是他們飛了起來，飛回了媽媽和爸爸的身邊。那重逢的幸福連筆墨都無法形容，故事到此落幕。』」

這個故事就是這樣，聽的人和講的人一樣心滿意足。你看，這是多麼理所當然。我們有時會像那些沒心肝的孩子們那樣，說走就走，但他們又如此討人喜歡。一走了之之後，我們會自私地在外面玩個痛快，當我們需要別人關心時，就又大大方方地回去，而且很有把握地知道自己不但不會受懲罰，還會得到獎賞。

對母愛的深信不疑讓他們覺得再無情一陣子也沒關係。

可是這裡有一個人比他們懂得更多，溫蒂講完後，他發出一聲悶吭。

「怎麼了，彼得？」溫蒂跑到彼得身邊，以為他病了。她關切地摸著他，又彎下腰檢查胸口下方。「你哪裡疼，彼得？」

「不是那種疼。」彼得悶悶不樂地回答。

「那是什麼樣的疼？」

「溫蒂，你對母親的看法不對。」

彼得出乎意料的一番話使得孩子們全都慌亂不安地圍過去。於是彼得一五一十地說出了一直深藏在內心的話。

「很久以前，」彼得說，「我也和你們一樣，相信我的媽媽會永遠開著窗戶等我，所以我在外面玩了一個月又一個月才飛回去，可是窗戶已經鎖上了，因為媽媽已經把我忘了，還有另一個小男孩睡在我的床上。」

我不敢說這是真的，但彼得認為是真的，這把孩子們嚇壞了。

「你確定媽媽們就是這樣嗎？」

「對。」

這就是媽媽們的真面目，冷漠又無情！

不過，還是小心點好，只有小孩子最清楚什麼時候該適可而止。「溫蒂，我們回家吧。」約翰和麥可一同喊道。

「好吧。」溫蒂緊緊抓住他們說。

「該不會是今晚吧？」那些遺失的孩子們迷惑不解地問。這些沒心肝的孩子們其實認為沒有媽媽也可以過得很好，只有媽媽們才以為孩子們沒有她就無法生活。

「馬上就走。」溫蒂果斷地說。因為一個可怕的念頭忽然浮現在她的腦海裡：「說不定媽媽現在已經沒那麼傷心了。」

擔心使她忘了考慮彼得的心情，她不太客氣地對彼得說：「彼得，可以請你安排必要的準備工作嗎？」

「你怎麼說就怎麼做。」彼得冷冷地回答，那冷淡的態度好像溫蒂只是要求他遞堅果過來似的。

他們之間甚至沒有一絲再也見不到面的情緒！要是溫蒂不在乎，那彼得也要讓她知道，他也不在乎。

不過，當然他是非常在乎的，他對那些大人有一肚子的怨氣，那些大人老是把一切都搞砸。所以，每次他鑽進樹洞，他就故意用每秒鐘五次的頻率急促地呼吸。他這麼做是因為在永無島，有個說法是每呼吸一次，就會有一個大人死去。所以彼得就心存報復地想盡全力殺光大人。

彼得向印地安人做了必要交代之後，就回到了地底的家。在他離開的期間，家裡竟發生了不像話的事情。那些遺失的孩子們害怕失去溫蒂，竟步步逼近威脅起她來。

「事情會比她來以前更糟。」他們喊道。

「我們不要讓她走。」

「我們把她關起來吧。」

「對，把她鎖起來。」

在危急的時候溫蒂靈機一動，想到了應該向誰求助。

「托托，」她喊道：「我求求你。」

這不是很奇怪嗎？她竟向最笨的托托求助。

然而，托托的反應卻出乎意料的嚴肅。那一刻，他不再愚笨，充滿尊嚴地回答。

「我不過是托托，」他說：「沒人在意我。但是只要有人對溫蒂的態度不像個英國紳士，我就讓他流血。」

他抽出了短劍。瞬間氣勢如日中天。別的孩子不安地後退。這時彼得回來了，他們立刻就看出來彼得不會支持他們。彼得是不會違背一個女孩的意願，強留她在永無島的。

「溫蒂，」彼得一邊說一邊在房裡走來走去：「我已經叫印地安人護送你們走出樹林了，因為用飛的會讓你們太累。」

「謝謝，彼得。」

「然後，」彼得又用那種令人服從、短促尖銳的聲音說：「叮噹會帶著你們過海。尼布斯，去叫醒她。」

尼布斯敲了兩次門才聽到叮噹來應門。但其實她早已坐在床上偷聽了很久。

「你是誰啊？好大的膽子，走開！」她喊。

「叮噹你該起床啦。」尼布斯喊道：「該帶溫蒂出遠門了。」

叮噹當然很高興聽到溫蒂要離開了，可是她下定決心決不當溫蒂的嚮導，她甚至說了更難聽的話，然後繼續裝睡。

「她說她不要。」尼布斯大聲宣布。叮噹的不服從把他嚇呆了。

於是彼得嚴肅地走向那位小姐的寢室。

「叮噹，」他大喊一聲，「要是你不馬上起床穿衣，我就要拉開門讓所有人都看見你穿睡袍的樣子。」

她一下子跳到了地上，喊道：「誰說我還沒起床的？」

同時，孩子們都傷心地望著溫蒂，覺得自己好像被遺棄了。溫蒂則忙著為約翰和麥可打點旅行裝備，準備上路。這時，孩子們心情沮喪，不僅因為他們就要失去溫蒂，也因為他們感覺溫蒂要去一個好地方，而他們卻沒有收到邀請。他們一向喜歡新奇的事物。

溫蒂相信他們懷著一股高尚的情感，她心軟了。

「親愛的孩子們，」她說：「要是你們和我一起回去，我幾乎可以肯定，我可以說服爸媽收養你們的。」

這個邀請是特別對彼得說的，可是每個孩子都覺得是對自己說的，馬上雀躍不已。

「他們會不會覺得我們人太多？」尼布斯一邊跳一邊問。

「噢，不會的。」溫蒂說，很快地想了想。「只需要在起居室放幾張床就行了。每個月的第一個禮拜四，可以把床藏在屏風後面。」

「彼得，我們可以去嗎？」孩子們一起懇求。他們想當然地認為要是他們都去了，彼得也一定會去，不過他們其實不在乎彼得去不

去。孩子們總是這樣，當新奇的事物來敲門時，隨時準備好遺棄最親愛的人。

「好吧。」彼得苦笑著說，孩子們立刻跑去收拾自己的東西了。

「現在，彼得，」溫蒂想把一切都安排妥當：「在走之前，我要給你吃藥。」她喜歡餵他們吃藥，而且毫無疑問地餵太多了。當然，那只不過是水，但那是從一個葫蘆裡倒出來的水。溫蒂總是搖晃著葫蘆算好有幾滴藥水，因此賦予了這些藥水某種程度的藥效。但是，這一次她沒有餵彼得吃，因為當她在準備藥水的時候，忽然看到彼得臉上的神情，讓她心頭一沉。

「去收拾你的東西，彼得。」溫蒂顫抖著喊道。

「不要。」彼得回答，裝作若無其事的樣子。「我不跟你們去。」

「你應該跟我們一起走，彼得！」

「不要。」

為了表示對溫蒂離去的無動於衷，彼得在房裡走來走去，興高采烈地吹著他那把聽起來格外冷漠的笛子。溫蒂只能追著他跑，就算那樣很沒面子。

「去找你的媽媽吧。」溫蒂慫恿他說。

就算彼得曾經有個媽媽，他也已經不記得了。沒有媽媽他照樣過得很好，他已經徹底想過了，想起的只有她們的缺點。

「不要！不要！」彼得果斷地告訴溫蒂：「也許她會說我已經長大了，可是我只想永遠當個小男孩，永遠玩下去。」

「可是，彼得……」

「不要。」

這件事必須告訴其他人。

「彼得不打算走。」

彼得不走！孩子們茫然地望著他。他們每個人的肩上扛著一根木棍、挑著一個包袱。他們的第一個念頭是，要是彼得不去，他或許會改變主意也不讓他們去。

但是彼得太驕傲了，不會這麼做。「要是你們找到了媽媽，」他陰沉地說：「但願你們會喜歡她們。」

這句帶有很重的譏諷意味的話，讓孩子們感到很不自在，多數人都露出疑惑的神色，臉上寫著：「不管怎麼說，想離開永無島是不是很傻？」

「好啦，」彼得喊道：「不要哭哭啼啼，不要大驚小怪。再見，溫蒂。」他痛快地伸出手，好像真的要他們快走，因為他還有重要的事要做。

溫蒂不得不和他握手，因為沒有任何跡象顯示彼得比較想要一個「頂針」。

「別忘了換內衣，彼得！」溫蒂說，她總是很在意他們的內衣。

「好。」

「還有，要記得吃藥，知道嗎？」

「知道。」

該說的似乎都說了，接著是一陣尷尬的沉默。但彼得不是會在人前失控的人。「叮噹，你準備好了嗎？」他大喊。

「好了！好了！」

「那就趕快帶路吧。」

叮噹飛上了最近的一棵樹，可是沒人跟上去。就在此時，海盜們對印地安人發動了一場可怕的進攻，地面上原本平靜的空氣被吶喊聲和刀劍撞擊聲給劃破。地底下卻是一片死寂，一張張嘴張得大大的，只見溫蒂跪了下來，向彼得伸出雙臂。所有的手臂都伸向彼得，像花一樣朝他綻放。孩子們無聲地懇求彼得不要拋下他們。彼得則一把抓住他的劍，就是那把殺死了巴比克的劍，眼睛裡閃耀著渴望作戰的光芒。

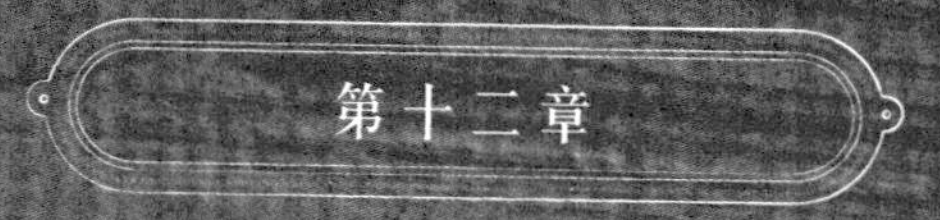

第十二章

孩子們被抓走了

不過，這一晚的工作還沒結束。虎克要摧毀的目標並不是印地安人，他們不過是必須用煙燻走的蜜蜂，好讓他奪取到蜂蜜。

海盜的襲擊完全出乎意料，這就足以證明不擇手段的虎克指揮不當。因為要想出其不意地襲擊印地安人，完全超過白人的智慧。

在部落戰爭的不成文法規中，總是由印地安人首先發動攻擊。印地安人是很狡黠的，他們總是在天亮前發動攻勢，因為他們知道這是白人士氣最低落的時候。另一方面，白人總是在遠處地勢起伏的最高處搭建簡陋的營地，山腳下還有一條小河流過，因為離水太遠是自取滅亡。白人就在那等待印地安人襲擊。缺乏經驗的新手緊握著手槍，踏在枯枝上；老手則安穩地睡到天快亮。漫長的黑夜裡，印地安人的偵察兵在草叢裡像蛇一樣匍匐，不驚動一絲刀光劍影，那片矮樹叢在他們身後悄然合起，就像鼴鼠寂靜無聲地鑽進沙地一樣。大地萬籟俱寂，除了偶爾傳來逼真的土狼孤寂號叫聲。這呼聲又得到其他勇士的呼應，有的勇士甚至叫得比那不擅長號叫的土狼更好。令人戰慄的時間就這樣緩慢流逝，長時間的懸疑對於那些初次上陣的白人來說真的特別難熬，可是對有經驗的老手來說，那些陰森可怕的號叫聲，以及更加陰森可怕的寂靜無聲，只不過是在宣告黑夜將如何進行。

這種情況虎克是一清二楚的，如果他忽略了，我們就不能把這想成是因為他無知而原諒他。

至於皮卡尼尼族，他們對虎克的榮譽感是深信不疑的，他們在這一夜的行動，和虎克的行動形成強烈對比。他們做了所有符合部落名譽的事。他們的敏銳使文明人既驚訝又害怕，只要一個海盜踩了一根乾樹枝，他們立刻就知道海盜來了。接著在短到不可思議的時間內，土狼的號叫聲就開始傳響。從虎克的隊伍登陸的海岸，到大樹下

的地底的家，每一寸土地都被一群倒穿鹿皮鞋的勇士暗地裡勘察過了。他們只發現一座土丘底下有一條小河流過，所以虎克別無選擇，只能在這裡暫駐，等待天亮。印地安人根據這樣的情勢，規劃有如惡魔般狡猾的作戰計畫。主力部隊裹著毯子，以他們最引以為傲的鎮定，守候在孩子們地底的家上方，等待著與白臉死神決一死戰的嚴峻時刻。

這些容易相信別人的印地安人就這樣睜大眼睛，幻想黎明時要怎麼折磨虎克。不料卻被奸詐的虎克先馳得點。據逃過這場大屠殺的印地安偵察兵描述，儘管在灰暗的光線中他一定看到了那座土丘，虎克似乎不曾在小土丘停留。在他那詭計多端的腦海中始終沒有等著被印地安人攻擊的想法，他甚至沒有等待黑夜將盡。他的策略不是別的，而是毫無原則、不分青紅皂白的猛然發動攻勢。那些困惑的印地安偵察兵能怎麼辦呢？儘管他們精通多種戰術（*除了這種*）也無法堤防，只能無助地在虎克後面追著跑，一邊發出可悲土狼的哀號聲，冒著生命危險地暴露了自己。

勇敢的老虎莉莉身邊聚集了十二名最勇猛強悍的戰士，他們突然發現詭計多端的海盜正向他們襲來。此刻，蒙蔽著他們的雙眼，讓他們以為勝利在望的那層薄霧散去，他們要想以酷刑對付虎克是辦不到了。他們很明白現在正是痛快狩獵的時刻，但為了表現出自己是印地安人的後代，必須極力自持。假如他們很快地聚攏，列成密集的陣式，那仍是很難攻破的。但是印地安族的傳統禁止他們這麼做。部落有一條規定：凡是尊貴的印地安人，在白人面前決不可以表現得驚慌失措。所以儘管海盜的突然出現使他們驚訝，他們仍巍然屹立，沒有一絲動搖，就好像敵人是應邀來做客似的。這樣英勇地遵從了傳統之後，他們才拿起武器，發出了震天的喊殺聲，可惜為時已晚。

這不是什麼戰鬥，而是一場大屠殺，我們就不細說了。印地安部落許多優秀的戰士就這樣被殺了。不過他們也沒有白白死去，瘦狼和阿爾夫・梅森一起送了命，後者再也不能侵擾西班牙海岸了；還有喬治・斯庫利、查理・托利和阿爾塞人福格蒂等也一命嗚呼。托利死在可怕的小黑豹的斧頭下，小黑豹、虎蓮以及少數殘餘部隊，最後終於殺出一條血路，逃了出去。

這場戰役中虎克的戰略應該受到什麼樣的譴責，就等歷史學家去判斷吧。倘若他待在土丘上等待正當的時刻再交手，他和他的部下說不定會全軍覆沒。在論斷功過的時候，必須把這一點列入考慮才公平。也許他應該預先讓對手知道他打算採取一套新的策略。不過如果那樣，就不能做到出其不意、攻其不備，他的戰略計畫也會落空。所以這個問題真讓人為難。不過，儘管不情願，也不得不佩服他能想出這麼大膽的計畫，以及實現這項計畫的邪惡才能。

這個勝利的時刻，虎克對自己又有什麼感覺呢？我想他的爪牙會很高興知道，但他們只能聚在一起，在沈重的呼吸中擦拭短彎刀，和虎克的鐵鉤保持安全距離，眯著雙眼窺探著這個奇特的人。虎克心裡當然是既得意又興奮，不過他完全沒展露出來。他的心靈和身體都與手下保持距離，他永遠是個陰暗孤獨，謎一般的人。

不過，這一晚的工作還沒結束。虎克要摧毀的目標並不是印地安人，他們不過是必須用煙燻走的蜜蜂，好讓他奪取蜂蜜。他的目標是彼得潘、溫蒂以及那些孩子，但主要目標是彼得潘。

彼得只不過是個小男孩，為什麼虎克那麼恨他實在讓人想不透。沒錯，他曾把虎克的手臂丟去餵鱷魚，而因為鱷魚的窮追不捨使虎克越來越難安穩過日子。不過，這也無法完全解釋如此長久而惡毒的懷恨。事實是，彼得身上的某種特質刺激到這位海盜船長，使他為之發狂。不是因為彼得的勇敢，不是因為他迷人的外表，不是因為……我們就不拐彎抹角了，我們都很清楚那是什麼，就老實說吧，就是因為彼得的自大。

這一點觸怒了虎克，使得他的鐵爪陣陣抽痛，在夜裡像一隻惱人的蟲子害他輾轉難眠。只要彼得活著，這個飽受折磨的人就覺得自己像是一頭被關在籠子裡的獅子，不斷地被一隻闖進籠中的麻雀騷擾。

現在虎克要面對的是，該怎樣從那些樹通到地底下，或者說，該怎樣把他的手下弄下去。虎克尖銳的目光掃視著，想找一個最瘦小的人。海盜們侷促不安地扭動身體，因為他們知道虎克會不惜用棍子把他們擠下去。

這時，孩子們的情況又如何呢？在聽到了第一聲武器撞擊時，我們看到他們一動也不動像石像一樣，張著嘴，伸出手臂向彼得懇求。現在回頭來看，只見他們閉上了嘴，垂下了手臂。上方的動亂停止得幾乎和開始一樣突然，宛如一陣狂風掃過。但他們知道，這陣狂風決定了他們的命運。

哪一方得勝了呢？

海盜們爬在樹洞口屏息傾聽，聽到了每個孩子提出的問題，不幸的是，也聽到了彼得的回答。

彼得說：「要是印地安人贏了，他們一定會打手鼓，那是他們的信號。」

斯密已經找到手鼓了，此刻他正坐在鼓上。「你們再也別想聽到手鼓聲了。」斯密低聲嘲笑著說，不過斯密當然沒有發出聲音，因為虎克嚴令不許出聲。使他驚訝萬分的是，虎克竟示意他擊手鼓。斯密這才慢慢地了解，這個命令是多麼陰險毒辣。這個單純的人從來沒有像現在這麼崇拜虎克。

斯密敲了兩次鼓，然後幸災樂禍的停下來傾聽。

「手鼓！」海盜們聽見彼得喊道：「印地安人勝利了！」

地底下前途黑暗的孩子們發出歡呼聲，在上面的人聽來簡直是美妙的音樂。接著，他們重新向彼得告別。這使得海盜們困惑不已。不過，他們所有的情緒都被卑鄙的歡喜蓋過了，因為敵人就要從樹洞裡爬上來了。他們奸笑著，摩拳擦掌。虎克迅速、悄悄地下令一個人守著一顆樹，其他人排成一行，彼此間隔兩公尺。

第十三章

你們相信有仙子嗎？

彼得對著孩子們大喊：「要是你們相信就拍拍手，不要讓叮噹死掉。」

這段恐怖的經歷越快解決越好。第一個鑽出樹洞的是捲毛，他一出來，立刻就落到了伽可的手裡，伽可把他扔給了斯密，斯密把他扔給了斯塔奇，斯塔奇把他扔給了比爾・裘克斯，比爾・裘克斯又把他扔給了努德勒。就這樣，他被他們一個接一個扔過去，最後被扔到了虎克腳邊。所有孩子都被殘忍地從樹洞裡拖了出來，有幾個孩子像傳遞貨物似的被拋到半空中。

最後一個出來的是溫蒂，她受到的待遇稍微不一樣。虎克嘲弄地裝作彬彬有禮的樣子，向她脫帽致意，還用手臂挽著她，把她送到孩子們被囚禁的地方。虎克如此風度翩翩，讓溫蒂著迷到忘了要喊出聲來。畢竟她只是個小女孩。

洩露虎克一下子就迷倒溫蒂這件事，或許像在打小報告，但我們提到這一點，是因為溫蒂的失誤引起了意想不到的後果。假如她驕傲地推開虎克的手臂（*我們當然會很開心地寫下這件事*），她就會像別的孩子一樣被拋在空中，那麼虎克也許就不會盯著手下捆綁孩子；假如他當時不在場，也就不會發現史萊特利的秘密；假如沒有發現這個秘密，他就不會用卑鄙的手段想要奪取彼得的性命。

為了防止孩子們飛走，海盜們把他們綁了起來，膝蓋貼著耳朵綁成一團。黑海盜把一條繩子割成相等的九段，一切都很順利，直到輪到史萊特利時，發現他像一個惱人的包裹一樣，繞完一圈剛好用掉整段繩子，沒有可以打結的繩頭。海盜們惱怒之下就像在踢包裹一樣（*雖然其實該踢的是繩子才對*）踢他。沒想到虎克叫他們住手。虎克撇著嘴，露出邪惡的勝利神情，看著手下忙得滿頭大汗，試著從一端綁緊這個不幸的孩子，另一端總是會凸出來。精明的虎克看透了史萊特利的把戲，他發現的不是結果，而是原因。他那副洋洋得意的樣子說明他已經發現了秘密。史萊特利臉色慘白，他知道虎克已經發現了，一個這麼胖的孩子不可能鑽得進中等身材的男人用棍子戳才進得去的樹洞。可憐的史萊特利，他現在是所有孩子們中最不幸的一個。他為彼得擔心，深深地懊悔他所做的事。他因為天氣熱而不可自拔的拼命喝水，把肚子脹得像現在這麼大，他沒有想辦法讓自己縮回符合樹洞的尺寸，而是瞞著其他人，把樹洞削成符合他身材的大小。

這就夠了，虎克相信彼得現在終於落進了他的手掌心。不過他陰暗的腦子裡成形的這個計謀，也沒有一個字爬上他的雙唇，他只打了個手勢，命令把俘虜押上船去，他要獨自留下來。

要怎麼運送呢？他們被繩子捆成一團，原本可以像木桶一樣滾下山坡，但是遇到沼澤就沒辦法了。虎克的天才再次克服了困難。他指示手下利用那間小屋子作為運輸工具。孩子們被扔進了小屋子，四個強壯的海盜把它扛在肩上，其餘的海盜跟在後面，唱著那首討人厭的海盜歌。這支奇怪的隊伍出發了，穿過了樹林。我不知道孩子們是否有人在哭，即使有，那哭聲也被歌聲淹沒了。可是，當小屋消失在樹林裡時，小屋的煙囪升起了一縷細小但勇敢的青煙，彷佛在向虎克抗議。

沒想到這縷青煙幫了彼得一個倒忙。原本虎克怒火焚燒的心還有一絲對彼得的惻隱之心，此時卻隨之煙消雲散。

夜幕低垂中落單的虎克做的第一件事，就是悄悄地走到史萊特利的那棵樹前，確認他能不能從那裡鑽進去。他沉思許久，他把那頂代表著不祥惡兆的帽子放在草地上，清風輕撫他的頭髮，使他的精神為之一振。雖然他的心思黑暗，他藍色的眼睛卻像長春花一樣溫柔。他屏息聽著地下的動靜，可是下面也和上面一樣寂靜無聲。地底的家像是一座空無一人的荒宅。那孩子睡著了嗎？還是正站在史萊特利的樹底下，手裡拿著刀在等著他？

除非親自去探個究竟，否則沒有人會知道。虎克讓外套輕輕滑落在地，緊緊地咬著嘴唇，直到滲了一滴血。然後他踏進了樹洞。他是個英勇的海盜，可是這一刻竟不得不停下來擦額頭上的汗，他的汗像蠟燭的蠟油一樣一直低落。接著，他悄悄地落入未知的世界。

他平安無恙地來到了樹洞底下，站穩後重新找回剛才幾乎遺忘了的呼吸。等到他的眼睛逐漸習慣昏暗的光線之後，才慢慢看清楚地底的家裡的各樣東西。但是他目光貪婪地緊盯著某樣東西，那是他找了好久終於找到的：那張大床，床上躺著熟睡的彼得。

彼得完全不知道上面發生的悲劇。孩子們離開後，他還愉快地吹了一會兒笛子。毫無疑問，他只是無謂的想證明他一點都不在乎。為了讓溫蒂傷心，他決定不吃藥。接著他直接躺在床罩上，好讓溫蒂更生氣，因為溫蒂總是用床罩牢牢的裹住孩子們，以免半夜著涼。彼得幾乎要哭出來了，但他忽然又想到，如果他不是哭而是笑的話，溫蒂會有多生氣呢！於是他傲慢地大笑，笑著笑著就睡著了。

有時，雖然不太常，彼得會做比別的孩子的夢更痛苦的夢，而且一連好幾個小時都擺脫不了糾纏，任憑彼得淒慘的哭喊也無法醒來。他的夢，我想大概是和他那來歷不明的身世有關，每到這種時候，溫蒂總會把他抱下床，讓他坐在自己的膝上，用她發明的各種親暱的方法安撫他，等他稍微平靜下來，沒等他醒來又把他放回床上，為的是不讓他知道溫蒂做了讓他沒面子的那些事。可是這一次，彼得睡得很熟，完全沒有做夢，手臂從床沿垂下，一條腿拱了起來，嘴角還留著一抹笑意，張著嘴，露出兩排珍珠般的小牙齒。

彼得就在這樣毫無防備的狀態下被虎克發現了。虎克一聲不響地站在樹洞底下，隔著房間遠遠望著他的敵人。虎克那陰暗的心，難道沒有半點惻隱之心嗎？這個男人並不是只有邪惡的一面，他愛花（*我是這樣聽說的*），也愛美妙的音樂（*他很會彈大鍵琴*）。我們得坦白承認，眼前這幅動人的景象深深地感動了他。在良心的驅使之下，他差點就不情願地從樹洞回到地面上，但有件事把他留了下來。

讓虎克留下的是彼得睡覺時那倨傲不恭的樣子：張開的嘴、下垂的手臂、彎曲的膝蓋。那些姿態看起來十分盛氣淩人，加在一起從虎克敏感的眼裡看來，再也沒有比這更氣人的了。這使虎克鐵了心。如果說他的怒火已經把他燒成了千百片，那麼每一片都會不顧一切地撲向沉睡的彼得。

一盞微弱的燈照在床上，虎克站在黑暗中。他才偷偷地前進一步，就遇到了障礙，那是史萊特利樹洞的門。這扇門沒有完全遮住出入口，所以虎克是從門上面往裡面看。他伸手去摸門閂，卻火冒三丈的發現門閂很低，他搆不著。在他那狂怒的頭腦裡，彼得的睡姿展現的惱人特質似乎更可惡了。他使勁搖晃著門，還用身體去撞門。他的敵人究竟能不能逃出他的手掌心呢？

那是什麼？虎克血紅的眼睛看見了彼得的藥，放在他伸手就能拿到的架子上。他一下子就明白了那是什麼，立刻知道這個熟睡的孩子已經落入了他的手掌心。

虎克怕自己被人活捉，總是隨身帶著一瓶可怕的毒藥，那是他把到手的各種致命物質混在一起調配而成的。他把這些物質熬煮濃縮成一種黃色液體，連科學家都沒見過，這可能是世界上最毒的一種毒藥了。

虎克在彼得的藥杯裡滴了五滴這種毒藥。他的手不停顫抖，不是因為羞愧，而是因為狂喜。虎克滴藥時，儘量不去看睡著的彼得，不是因為怕心軟下不了手，只是避免把藥灑出來。然後，他幸災樂禍地向他的受害者投以深長的一瞥後，轉身艱難地往上爬。當虎克回到地面時，看起來就像邪惡的靈魂破洞而出。他瀟灑地戴上帽子，圍上披風，拉起披風的一角擋在身前，像是要把整個人藏起來，不被黑夜看見。其實他才是黑夜中最黑暗的部分。接著虎克悄悄穿過樹林，一邊古怪地自言自語。

彼得還在睡。燈火搖曳閃爍一陣之後熄滅了，屋裡一片黑暗，他依然繼續沈睡。後來彼得不知道被什麼驚醒了，這時一定已經超過鱷魚報時的十點了。彼得突然從床上坐起來，吵醒他的是那棵樹洞門上傳來的一陣有禮貌的敲門聲。

雖然聲音輕柔而謹慎，但在寂靜的深夜裡，仍顯得格外不祥。彼得伸手去摸短劍。他手握短劍問道：「是誰？」

等了一段時間沒有回答，接著再次傳來敲門聲。

「是誰？」

沒有回答。

彼得感到興奮，這正是他最喜歡的刺激。他三步併兩步跨到門前。這門不像史萊特利的門，它和樹洞密合，所以他看不到外面，敲門的人也看不到他。

「你不說話，我就不開門。」彼得喊道。

敲門的人終於開口了，發出了小鈴鐺似可愛的聲音。

「讓我進去，彼得。」

是叮噹，彼得馬上打開門讓她進來。她飛了進來，神情激動，臉色通紅，衣服上沾滿了泥巴。

「怎麼回事？」

「噢，你絕對猜不到！」她喊。她讓彼得猜三次。彼得大聲喊：「快說！」於是，叮噹用語無倫次的長句子，長得像從魔術師嘴裡抽出來的絲帶一樣，說出了溫蒂和孩子們被抓上船的經過。

彼得一邊聽，心臟一邊撲通撲通的跳。溫蒂被抓到海盜船上，喜歡每件事都有條有理的溫蒂。

彼得喊：「我要去救她。」他跳起來去拿武器。跳起來的時候，突然想起有件事可以讓溫蒂高興，就是把他的藥喝掉。

他的手伸向那杯致命的藥水。

「別喝！」叮噹尖叫，因為她聽到了虎克匆匆穿過樹林時，喃喃嘟噥著他做的好事。

「為什麼？」

「藥裡有毒。」

「有毒？誰會下毒？」

「虎克。」

「別說傻話。虎克怎麼能到這裡來？」

唉！這一點叮噹也無法解釋，因為就連她也不知道史萊特利的樹的秘密。不過，虎克的話是無庸置疑的，的確下了毒。

「而且，」彼得信心十足地說：「我根本沒睡著。」

彼得舉起了杯子。沒時間解釋了，叮噹只能立即行動。叮噹像閃電一般，以迅雷不及掩耳的速度鑽到彼得的嘴唇和杯子之間，一口喝完藥水。

「哎呀，叮噹？你竟敢喝我的藥？」

叮噹沒有回答。她已經搖搖晃晃地在空中旋轉了。

「你怎麼了？」彼得突然害怕了起來。

「藥裡有毒，彼得，」叮噹輕聲對他說：「現在我快死了。」

「噢，叮噹，你是為了救我才喝的嗎？」

「對。」

「為什麼，叮噹？」

叮噹的翅膀已經托不住她了，她落到了彼得的肩上，在他的鼻子上愛憐地咬了一口，然後在他耳邊悄悄地說：「你這個笨蛋。」然後她搖搖晃晃地回到她的寢室，倒在床上。

彼得傷心地跪在她身邊，他的頭幾乎填滿了整個寢室。叮噹的亮光越來越暗了。彼得知道，一旦這亮光熄滅了，叮噹就不存在了。叮噹喜歡彼得的眼淚，她伸出美麗的手指，讓眼淚滾過她的手指。

叮噹的聲音很微弱。一開始彼得幾乎聽不清楚她在說什麼。後來他聽懂了。她說要是孩子們相信有仙子，她就會好起來。

彼得伸出了雙臂。可是眼前沒有孩子，而且現在是深夜。不過，他跟所有夢到了永無島的孩子們說話：穿著睡衣的小男孩和小女孩，還有光著身子、睡在在樹上的吊籃裡的印地安小嬰兒。他們其實離彼得都很近，不像你所想的那麼遠。

「你們相信不相信有仙子？」他大喊。

叮噹一下子從床上坐了起來，屏住氣，聆聽她的命運。

她感覺她彷彿聽到了肯定的回答，但又不是很確定。

「你覺得呢？」叮噹問彼得。

彼得對著孩子們大喊：「要是你們相信就拍拍手，不要讓叮噹死掉。」

很多孩子拍了手。

有些孩子沒拍。

少數幾個沒心肝的搗蛋鬼還發出了噓聲。

拍手聲突然停止了。好像有數不清的母親們奔進了育兒室，看看到底發生了什麼事，不過叮噹已經得救了。她的聲音變大了，然後她一陣風似的跳下床。接著她滿屋子亂飛，比以往然來得愉快和放肆。她絕對沒想到要感謝那些拍手的孩子，一心只想著對付那些發出噓聲的小東西。

「現在該去救溫蒂了。」

彼得鑽出樹洞時，月亮正在雲裡行走。他全副武裝，幾乎沒穿戴其他東西，就這樣踏上了冒險。他並不想選在這樣的夜晚去冒險。他原本想靠近地面低飛，這樣所有不尋常的事都逃不過他的眼睛。但是，在忽隱忽現的月光下低飛，就會把他的身影投射在樹上驚動鳥兒，警覺的敵人就會發現他的行蹤。

彼得現在後悔替島上的鳥兒取了些奇怪的名字，那讓牠們變得很野，很難接近。

沒有別的辦法了，只能學印地安人的樣子，貼著地面爬，幸好他已經習慣了。可是該朝什麼方向爬呢？他還不確定孩子們是不是被帶上了船。一場小雪覆蓋了所有的腳印，島上籠罩著一片死寂，彷彿剛才發生的大屠殺連大自然也被嚇呆了。彼得曾經把從虎蓮和叮噹那裡學過的一些森林求生知識傳給孩子們，他相信到了緊要關頭他們是不會忘記的。例如，如果有機會，史萊特利會在樹上刻上標記，捲毛會沿路撒樹種子，溫蒂會在重要的地點扔下她的手帕。可是要找到這些目標需要等到天亮，彼得不能再等了，上面的世界在召喚他，卻不給他一點幫助。

除了從彼得身邊爬過的鱷魚以外，再也沒有別的生物了。沒有一點聲音，沒有一絲動靜。彼得很清楚，死神也許就等在前面的下一棵樹，或者正在身後悄悄地跟著他。

彼得發下毒誓：「虎克，這次不是你死就是我死！」

現在，彼得像蛇一樣向前爬著，時而起身飛快地跑過一片被月光照亮的空地，一根手指頭按著嘴唇，一手握刀做好準備，興奮得不得了。

第十四章

海盜船

「好啦，惡霸們，」虎克興奮地說：「今晚你們六個人要走木板跳海，不過我可以留下兩個人。會是誰呢？」

靠近河流出海口之處，一盞燈斜射在基德灣上，標示出歡樂羅傑號的位置。這艘外型輕巧的雙桅帆船吃水很深，整艘船髒亂不堪，每根樑都很噁心，跟地板一樣黏滿了羽毛。歡樂羅傑號是海上食人魔，幾乎不需要看守，因為光是邪惡的名聲就足以使人卻步。

這整艘船被夜幕籠罩著，一點聲音都沒傳到岸上。其實船上也沒有多少聲音，就算有，也是讓人不快的聲音。唯一的例外是縫紉機發出的噠噠轉動聲，坐在縫紉機前的斯密，永遠是那麼殷勤與樂於助人，既平凡又可憐的斯密。我不知道他為什麼這麼可憐，也許正是因為他自己沒有察覺自己很可憐吧。即使是那些堅強的男人，也不忍心多看他一眼。在夏天的夜晚，他竟不只一次觸動了虎克的淚腺。然而對於這件事和其他事一樣，斯密絲毫沒有察覺。

幾個海盜靠在船舷邊，在夜間的瘴氣中喝酒，其餘的海盜都懶洋洋的趴在木桶旁擲骰子、玩紙牌，而那四個抬小屋的海盜則精疲力竭地趴在甲板上睡著了。即使在睡夢中，他們也靈活地滾來滾去，避開虎克伸手可及的範圍，以免虎克經過時習慣性的攻擊他們。

虎克在甲板上踱步沉思。這個高深莫測的男人，他大獲全勝的時刻來了。彼得已經被除掉了，再也不能擋他的路了，其他的孩子全都被捉到了船上，等著走木板跳海。自從他制伏了巴比克以來，這算是他最輝煌的戰績了。我們都知道，人是多麼虛榮，如果他現在因為勝利而趾高氣揚，在甲板上大搖大擺地晃來晃去，那也不足為奇。

但是，他的步伐絲毫沒有得意的樣子，反而和他陰鬱的心情相呼應。虎克的情緒相當低落。

每當夜深人靜時，虎克經常在船上和自己對話，因為他感到非常孤獨。這個神秘莫測的男人，越被走狗圍繞著就越孤獨。因為他們無法和他平起平坐。

虎克不是他的真名。要是把他的真實身份透露出來，就算在今天也會轟動全國。但是，那些聽出言外之意的人一定早就猜到了，虎克曾就讀一所有名的公立學校，這所學校的傳統至今還像衣服一樣緊緊跟著他，例如對於服裝的講究，所以直到今日，虎克仍然堅持從對一艘船發動攻擊到登船時，不能穿同一套衣服。他走起路來依然堅持那所校鬆散慵懶的招牌姿態。不過最重要的是，他仍保有對「風度」的熱切追求。

風度！不管他怎麼墮落，他也知道這是真正重要的事。

從他內心深處，他隱約聽到了嘎吱聲，彷彿打開了一扇生鏽的鐵門，門外傳來頑固的敲門聲，在睡不著的夜晚就像鎚子的敲擊聲，那聲音永遠問著他一成不變的問題：「你今天有風度嗎？」

虎克喊道：「名聲，名聲，那華而不實的玩意是屬於我的。」

他的學校的敲門聲回答：「在某方面出名就是有風度嗎？」

虎克極力辯駁：「巴比克就只怕我一人，至於弗林特，他甚至害怕巴比克。」

「巴比克和弗林特是哪個學派的？」傳來尖厲地反駁。

最令虎克焦慮不安的想法是一心想要保持良好的風度，這不就是一種沒風度的表現嗎？

這個問題使虎克的身心飽受折磨，就像一個比他的鐵爪還要鋒利的爪子撕裂著他的心，汗水從他灰黃的臉上滴了下來，在他那具有文藝復興風格的緊身上衣留下汗漬。他不時用袖子擦臉，但依舊止不住不斷落下的汗珠。

啊，虎克實在沒什麼好羨慕的。

虎克忽然有種死期將近的不祥預感，好像彼得的毒誓隨風登上了船。虎克突然沮喪地想到得說幾句遺言，以免來不及說。

虎克大聲喊道：「要是虎克的野心沒那麼大就好了。」只有在他心情最陰鬱的時候，他才會用第三人稱稱呼自己。

「沒有一個孩子愛我。」

說也奇怪，他居然想到了這一點，這是以前從來沒有困擾過他的事，也許是那台縫紉機讓他想到的。他一邊喃喃自語，一邊凝視著斯密許久，斯密正靜靜地在車邊，深信所有的孩子都怕他。

怕他！怕斯密！那一晚，被抓上船的孩子們沒有一個不愛他的。斯密對他們口出惡言，還用手掌打他們，因為他無法向他們揮拳，這卻使孩子們越是纏著他不放，麥可還試著戴他的眼鏡。

如果告訴可憐的斯密，孩子們覺得他很討人喜歡，他會有什麼反應呢？虎克有股衝動想告訴他，但是這似乎太殘忍了。於是，虎克決定在心中反覆思索這個謎：「為什麼孩子們會喜歡斯密呢？」虎克

像警犬一樣，對這個問題窮追不捨。「如果斯密討人喜愛，那原因又是什麼呢？」一個可怕的回答突然冒了出來：「是因為他有風度？」

難道他的水手長是個有風度的人，卻渾然不覺？這豈不是達到了風度的最高境界嗎？

虎克想起了以前學校的菁英社團波普社，你必須證明你不知道自己有風度，才有資格獲選加入社團。

虎克怒吼一聲舉起鐵爪，卻停在斯密頭上沒有揮下。一個念頭阻止了他：

「因為一個人有風度而殺他，那算什麼呢？」

「沒風度！」

痛苦的虎克既沮喪又無力，像被剪下的花一樣向前撲倒。

手下們以為虎克昏了過去，不管他們了，紀律立刻鬆懈下來，開始狂歡作樂，喝酒跳舞。這使得虎克頓時振作起來，他再站起來時，所有的軟弱一掃而空，好像被一桶冷水當頭澆灌而清醒過來。

虎克喊道：「安靜，你們這些人渣，否則我就把你們丟進海底。」喧鬧聲立刻停止。「那些孩子們都上好了鎖鏈，不能飛了嗎？」

「對，船長。」

「把他們帶上來。」

除了溫蒂，這些不幸的囚犯被拖了出來，在虎克面前排成一排。有一會兒，虎克好像沒看見他們。他懶洋洋地坐在那，哼著一首粗俗的歌曲，手裡撥弄著紙牌，雪茄的火光替他的臉增添一絲顏色。

「好啦，惡霸們，」虎克興奮地說，「今晚你們六個人要走木板跳海，不過我可以留下兩個人。會是誰呢？」

溫蒂曾在貨艙裡告訴孩子們：「沒必要的話別激怒他。」所以托托很有禮貌地走上前去。他不願意當這個人手下，但直覺告訴他，可以把責任推給一個不在場的人。雖然他有點笨，還是知道只有媽媽總是樂意扮演緩衝的角色。所有的孩子們都知道這一點，也因此輕視她們，卻常常加以利用。

於是，托托謹慎地解釋：「是這樣的，閣下，我想我媽媽是不願意讓我當海盜的。你媽媽願意讓你當海盜嗎，史萊特利？」

他對史萊特利眨眼示意，史萊特利裝出一副遺憾的樣子悲傷地說：「我想她不願意。你媽媽願意讓你們當海盜嗎，雙胞胎？」

「我想她不願意。」老大說，他和其他人一樣聰明。「尼布斯，你呢？」

「廢話少說。」虎克吼道，擔任發言人的托托被拖回隊伍。「小子，你，」虎克對約翰說：「你看起來倒有點骨氣，你想過要當海盜嗎，我的小朋友？」

的確，約翰在做數學習題的時候曾有過這樣的渴望，虎克只選中他，讓他有些感動。

約翰猶豫地說：「我曾想過把自己叫作紅手傑克。」。

「好名字！要是你加入，我們就這樣叫你。」

「麥可，你怎麼想？」約翰問。

「要是我加入的話，你們叫我什麼？」麥可問。

「黑鬍子喬。」

麥可深受感動。「你怎麼想，約翰？」他要約翰決定，約翰則是要他決定。

「我們還是效忠國王陛下的百姓嗎？」約翰問。

虎克咬牙切齒地回答：「你們必須發誓打倒國王。」

約翰或許到目前一直表現得不太理想，但這次他大放異彩。

「那我拒絕。」他敲了虎克前面的木桶大喊。

「我也拒絕。」麥可喊。

「英王萬歲！」捲毛高喊。

氣急敗壞的海盜們打他們的嘴巴。虎克大吼：「這是你們自找的。把他們的媽媽帶上來，準備好跳板。」

他們只是孩子，看到裘克斯和伽可準備著通往死亡的跳板，不禁臉色蒼白。可是，當溫蒂被帶來時，他們卻裝出一副勇敢的樣子。

溫蒂對這些海盜的鄙視，已超過我的言語所能形容。男孩們覺得當海盜多少還有點吸引人，但溫蒂只看到這艘船好幾年沒有打掃了，每扇舷窗的玻璃都髒到可以用手指在上面寫字，當然她已經在好幾扇舷窗上寫了「髒鬼」。可是，當男孩們圍上來時，她一心只想著他們。

「我的小美人，」虎克說，嘴巴像是抹了蜜糖：「你就要看你的孩子們踏上跳板了。」

儘管虎克是一位體面的紳士，但是先前內心的劇烈掙扎弄亂了他輪狀皺摺的衣領。他發現溫蒂正注視著他的衣領，便急忙想遮蓋，可是已經太遲了。

溫蒂問:「他們要死了？」她的神情十分不屑，虎克差點昏倒。

虎克狠狠地說：「對。」接著他又幸災樂禍地宣布：「所有人安靜，讓媽媽和她的孩子們說最後一段話。」

這時的溫蒂非常了不起。她堅定地說：「親愛的孩子們，這是我最後要對你們說的話。我想代替你們真正的媽媽轉達給你們:『我們希望我們的兒子死得像個英國紳士。』」

聽了這話，就連海盜們也深感敬畏。托托發狂似的大叫：「我要照我媽媽希望的去做。你呢，尼布斯？」

「照我媽媽希望的去做。你們呢，雙胞胎？」

「照我媽媽希望的去做。約翰，你呢？」

此時虎克重新找回了他的聲音。

「把她綁起來。」虎克大喊。

斯密趁著把溫蒂綁到船桅時，悄悄地對她說：「親愛的，要是你答應當我的媽媽，我就救你。」

就算是斯密，溫蒂也不肯答應，她不屑地回答：「我寧願沒有孩子。」

說來悲哀，在斯密把溫蒂綁在船桅上的時，沒有一個孩子看著她。所有人的目光全都集中在跳板上，這是他們將要走的最後幾步路。他們已經不敢指望自己能走得雄赳赳氣昂昂，他們已經失去了思考能力，能做的只有乾瞪著眼和發抖。

虎克對著他們咬牙切齒地微笑，他朝溫蒂走近了一步，想要讓溫蒂轉過臉來，看著孩子們一個個走跳板。但是他沒碰到她，也沒能聽見他期待從溫蒂口中發出痛苦呼喊的聲音，他反而聽到了另一個聲音：鱷魚可怕的滴答聲。

所有人都聽到了，海盜們、孩子們和溫蒂。刹那間，所有人的頭都被吹向同一個方向。不是朝向聲音傳來的水面，而是朝向虎克。大家都知道，將要發生的事只和他一個人有關。大家一下子從參與者變成了旁觀者。

虎克身上發生的變化令人不忍直視，彷彿他全身的每個關節都被剪斷，他癱軟地縮成一小團。

滴答聲越來越近了，隨著聲音持續接近，一個恐怖的念頭馬上浮現：鱷魚就要爬上船了。

虎克的鐵爪一動也不動地垂下，彷彿以為自己不是正在進攻的敵人真正想要得到的一部分。在這樣孤立無援的情況下，換作是其他人，早就閉上眼睛倒地等死了，可是虎克碩大的腦袋依然在運轉，在大腦指揮下，他雙膝著地，跪在甲板上往前爬，儘量爬到離滴答聲最遠的地方。海盜們恭敬地讓出一條路，他一直爬到了船舷那邊，才開口說話。

「把我藏起來。」他沙啞地喊。

海盜團團圍住他，所有的目光都避開不去看那個就要爬上船來的東西，他們沒有一點抵抗的念頭，因為這是宿命。

等虎克藏起來以後，好奇心鬆綁了孩子們的手腳，他們衝到船邊去看鱷魚爬上船。這時，他們看到了這一晚最令人驚訝的畫面。來救他們的不是鱷魚，是彼得。

彼得向他們打手勢，示意他們不要發出任何會引起懷疑的讚美，一面繼續發出滴答聲。

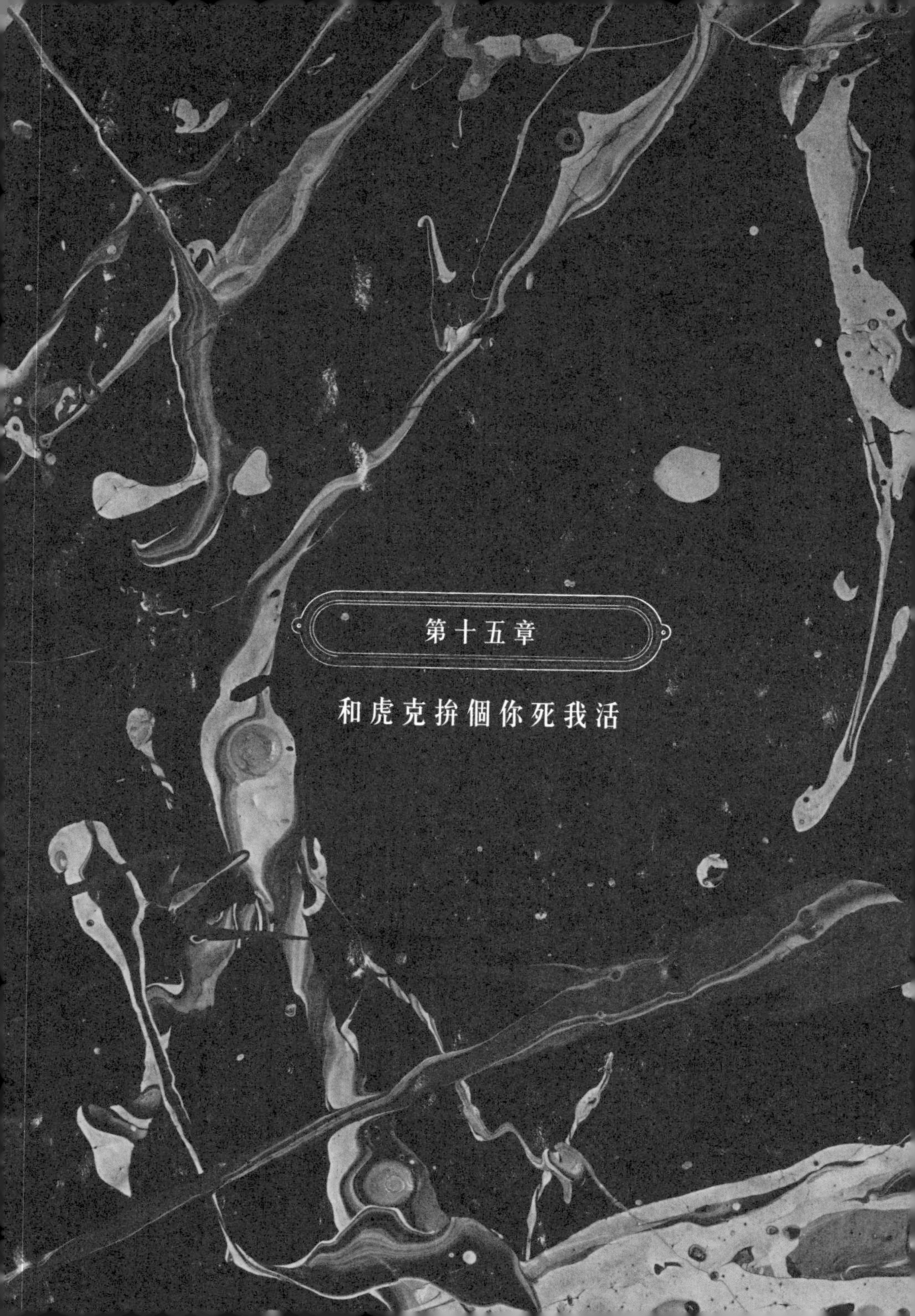

第十五章

和虎克拚個你死我活

他游泳的時候心裡只有一個念頭：
「這次不是虎克死，就是我死。」

我們一生中都曾遇到過奇怪的事，卻有好一段時間絲毫沒察覺這些事。舉例來說，我們突然發現一邊耳朵聽不見了，卻不知道這情況持續了多久，只好說半個小時。那天晚上，彼得就遇到了這種情況。上次我們說他正悄悄地穿越永無島，一根手指頭放在嘴巴上，一手握刀做好準備。他看見鱷魚從他身邊爬過，不覺得有什麼不對勁，可是過了一會兒他突然想起來，那隻鱷魚不再滴答作響了。起初，他覺得這件事有點奇怪，不過很快地他就得到了正確的結論，鱷魚肚子裡的鐘停了。

鱷魚突然間失去了最親密的夥伴會有什麼感受，彼得並不在乎，而是立刻想到可以怎麼利用這個悲劇。他決定學著發出滴答聲，野獸聽到時會以為是鱷魚，就不會打擾他通過。他的滴答聲模仿得唯妙唯肖，卻引來了一個意想不到的結果。鱷魚跟別的動物一樣聽到了滴答聲，就跟在他後面。那隻鱷魚究竟是想找回失去的東西，還是以為牠的時鐘好友又滴答作響了，我們永遠不會知道，因為鱷魚是個很蠢的動物，固守成規而且非常死腦筋。

彼得平安無事地抵達了海岸。當他的雙腳碰到水時，好像絲毫渾然不覺那是另一種物質。許多動物從陸地到水裡都是這樣的自然，可是我知道的人類當中，只有彼得有這樣的能耐。他游泳的時候心裡只有一個念頭：「這次不是虎克死，就是我死。」他發出滴答聲已經很久了，以致於沒發現自己還繼續發出滴答聲。要是他曾注意到，他早就停止了。他是藉著滴答聲登上海盜船的，雖然這是個絕妙的點子，但他從沒想過這個方法。

彼得的想法恰巧相反，他自以為自己像隻老鼠安靜無聲地爬到了船邊。他驚訝的看見海盜們十分害怕地避著他，而虎克躲在中間，失魂落魄的樣子像是聽到了鱷魚的聲音。

鱷魚！彼得剛想起鱷魚，就聽到了滴答聲。起初，他還以為是鱷魚發出的聲音，於是迅速地回頭看，這才發現發出滴答聲的原來是自己，這一瞬間他才明白了事情的來龍去脈。他的第一個想法是：「我真是太聰明了！」於是他向孩子們做手勢，示意他們不要拍手歡呼。

就在此時，舵手愛德華．坦特從水手艙走上甲板。各位讀者，現在請用你的錶開始計時。彼得一刀砍下去，又狠又準，約翰用手蒙住不幸的海盜的嘴，不讓他發出臨死的呻吟。海盜往前倒，四個孩子上前接住他，以免落地時發出聲音。彼得用手打信號，屍體被拋下海，水花四濺，然後就是一陣寂靜。整個過程花了多少時間？

「一！」（*史萊特利開始計數。*）

不只一名海盜鼓起勇氣東張西望。說時遲，那時快，彼得一溜煙鑽進了船艙，現在海盜們只聽到彼此驚慌的喘息聲，那個更可怕的聲音已經消失了。

「消失了，船長。」斯密擦著眼鏡說：「一切又恢復平靜了。」

虎克的頭慢慢地從皺褶衣領中探出，用力聆聽，用力到可以聽到滴答聲的回音。確認沒有半點聲音之後，他又重新站穩，恢復到原本的身高。

「現在該走跳板啦。」虎克厚著臉皮喊道。他現在更加恨那些男孩了，因為他們看到了他的糗態。虎克突然開始唱起難聽的歌：

唷呵，唷呵，晃動的木板，
踩著木板走到底；
連人帶板掉下去，
去到海底見閻王！

為了讓這些犯人更害怕，虎克不顧尊嚴，沿著想像中的跳板跳舞，邊唱邊對孩子們扮鬼臉。唱完後他喊道：「走跳板以前，要不要嚐嚐九尾鞭的味道？」

聽到這話，孩子們都跪了下來。「不，不。」他們可憐兮兮地喊著。海盜們都忍不住笑了。

「裘克斯，去把鞭子拿來，」虎克說：「鞭子在船艙裡。」

船艙！彼得就在船艙裡！孩子們互相看著彼此。

「是，是。」裘克斯愉快地回答，大步走進船艙。孩子們的目光追隨著裘克斯，以至於沒注意到虎克又唱起歌來，而他的手下們應聲唱道：

唷呵，唷呵，犀利的鞭子，
長長尾巴有九條，
要是鞭子落在你背上……

最後一行歌詞是什麼，我們永遠都不會知道了。因為，船艙裡冷不防的傳來一聲可怕的尖叫，響徹全船，使歌聲戛然停止。接著又聽到響亮的叫喊聲，那是孩子們所熟悉的，可是聽在海盜耳裡，卻比那聲尖叫更令人毛骨悚然。

「那是什麼？」虎克喊道。

「二。」史萊特利鄭重地數。

義大利人伽可猶豫了一下，然後搖搖晃晃地走下船艙去。他倉皇的逃了出來，一臉驚恐。

「比爾．裘克斯，到底發生了什麼事，你這個廢物？」虎克宛如一座高塔聳立在他面前，低聲責問。

「發生在他身上的事就是他死了，被刺死了。」伽可用空洞的聲音回答。

「比爾．裘克斯死了！」海盜們驚慌失色，齊聲喊道。

「船艙黑得像地獄一樣，」伽可幾乎連話都說不清楚了：「可是裡面有個嚇人的東西，你們剛也聽見那東西在叫。」

孩子們的興高采烈和海盜們的垂頭喪氣，虎克全都看在眼裡。

「伽可，」虎克用最強硬的聲音說：「去船艙裡把那個鬼吼鬼叫的搗蛋鬼給抓出來。」

伽可，這個最勇敢的海盜，在船長面前恐懼地喊道：「不，不。」但是虎克自顧自地對著鐵爪低聲呢喃。

「你是說你要去，是吧，伽可？」虎克故作深思道。

伽可絕望地高舉雙手走下去。再也沒有人唱歌了，所有的人都在傾聽著。又是臨死前的哀號，又是歡呼聲。

沒有人說話，只有史萊特利數：「三。」

虎克示意招聚他的手下。「混蛋，豈有此理，」他暴跳如雷地吼道：「誰去把那個搗蛋的傢伙給我抓來？」

「等伽可出來再說吧。」斯塔奇喊道，其他的人也紛紛附和。

「我好像聽到你說，你要自告奮勇下去。」虎克又開始對著鐵爪喃喃自語。

「不，天打雷劈！」斯塔奇喊道。

「我的鐵鉤認為你想去，」虎克向他逼近：「我看，你還是遷就一下這鐵鉤為妙，斯塔奇。」

「我寧可吊死也不去。」斯塔奇頑強抵抗，他得到了所有水手的支持。

「要造反嗎？」虎克的語氣從未如此和善：「斯塔奇是叛徒頭目。」

「船長，放過我吧。」斯塔奇渾身發抖嗚咽著說。

「握握手吧，斯塔奇。」虎克伸出了鐵爪。

斯塔奇環顧四周求援，但是所有的人都棄他而去。他步步後退，虎克則步步逼近。這時，虎克的眼睛裡發出了紅光。隨著一聲絕望的哀嚎，斯塔奇跳上了長湯姆大炮，縱身躍入大海。

「四。」史萊特利叫著。

「現在，」虎克彬彬有禮地問：「還有哪位先生要造反？」他抓來一盞燈，威嚇地舉起鐵鉤：「我要親自下去把那個搗蛋鬼抓上來。」他說著並快步走進了船艙。

「五。」史萊特利多麼渴望這樣說，他潤了潤嘴唇準備，可是虎克搖搖擺擺地退了出來，手裡沒有了燈。

「有個東西吹熄了我的燈。」虎克有點不安地說。

「有個東西！」馬林斯應聲說。

「伽可怎麼樣了？」努德勒問。

「死了，像裘克斯一樣。」虎克簡短回答。

虎克遲疑不願再進船艙，這讓海盜們感覺不妙，反抗的聲浪再次爆發。海盜們都很迷信，庫克森喊道：「人們都說，一艘船遭咒詛的跡象是船上莫名其妙多了一個人。」

「我還聽說，」馬林斯喃喃的說：「那個人總是最後一個登上海盜船。船長上船的時候後面還有人嗎？」

另一個海盜不懷好意地看著虎克說：「他們說，那個人出現的時候，長得就像船上那個最邪惡的人。」

「他有鐵鉤嗎，船長？」庫克森傲慢地問，於是，海盜們一個接一個鼓譟起來：「這艘船完蛋了。」聽到這話，孩子們忍不住歡呼起來。虎克幾乎忘了這批犯人，這時他迅速轉身面對他們，臉上再次露出喜色。

虎克對他的水手喊道，「弟兄們，我有個主意。打開艙門，把他們推下去，讓他們跟那個搗蛋鬼拚個你死我活吧。要是他們殺了那個搗蛋鬼，那再好不過；要是那搗蛋鬼把他們給殺了，對我們也沒差。」

這是虎克的走狗最後一次對他表示欽佩，並且熱忱地照著他的指示執行。男孩們假裝掙扎，被推進船艙，艙門在他們身後關上。

「現在，聽著！」虎克喊道，大家都安靜地聽著，沒有一個敢直視艙門。不，有一個人，那是溫蒂，她一直被綁在船桅上。她盯著門看不是為了等待哀嚎聲，而是靜候彼得再次現身。

溫蒂沒等太久。彼得在船艙裡到了他要找的東西：解開男孩們鐐銬的鑰匙。現在他們一起偷偷地溜到各處，身上佩戴著搜刮到的武器。彼得先做手勢叫男孩們藏起來，然後他溜出來割斷了綁著溫蒂的繩子。現在，最簡單的方法就是全部人一起飛走，但是有一件事阻止了他們，就是那句誓言「不是虎克死，就是我死」。所以，彼得替溫蒂鬆綁後，悄悄地讓她和別的孩子一起躲好，他自己則取代溫蒂的位置，披上溫蒂的斗篷，假裝她仍被綁在船桅上。然後彼得深深地吸進一口氣，發出啼叫聲。

海盜們聽了這叫聲，以為艙裡所有的孩子都被殺死了，他們嚇得魂不守舍。虎克想替他們打氣，可是被他當作走狗的手下現在對他齜牙咧嘴。虎克心裡明白，要是一個不留神，他們就會撲上來反咬他一口。

虎克準備好視情況動武或用甜言蜜語哄騙，但是此刻不能在他們面前表現出畏懼。他說：「兄弟們，我想起來了，這船上有一個約拿。」

水手們凶狠地說：「對，一個帶鐵鉤的人。」

「不，兄弟們，是那個女孩。海盜船上來了個女的準沒好事。如果她走了，船上就會太平了。」

有些海盜想起來了，弗林特船長的確說過這樣的話。水手們半信半疑地說：「不妨試試。」

虎克高聲喊道：「把那個女孩扔到海裡去。」海盜們衝向那個披著斗篷的身影。

「現在沒人能救你了，小姐。」馬林斯壓低嗓子嘲笑的說。

「有一個人。」那人回答。

「誰？」

「復仇者彼得潘！」隨著這駭人的回答，彼得揭開了斗篷。這下海盜們知道了是誰在船艙裡作怪。虎克兩次試圖想說話，都沒說出來。在這難堪的時刻，我想虎克的心都碎了。

最後他喊了出來：「將他碎屍萬段！」可是他已經沒有什麼信心了。

彼得大喊：「上啊，孩子們，打倒他們。」轉眼間，船上刀劍的撞擊聲響徹雲霄。如果海盜們團結起來一定會贏的，可是在遭到突襲時，他們如同一盤散沙，毫無準備，東奔西竄，瘋狂砍殺。人人都以為自己是最後的倖存者。要是一對一的話，當然是海盜們比較厲害，可是他們是被動挨打的一方，這使得孩子們能夠兩個對付一個，追捕選定的獵物。有些海盜跳進海裡，有些則躲在陰暗的角落，最後全都被史萊特利找出來了。史萊特利沒有參加戰鬥，只是提著一盞燈跑來跑去，用燈光照在海盜的臉上，使他們什麼也看不清楚，這樣其他男孩子就可以輕而易舉地揮動利劍殺他們。船上除了聽到兵器鏗鏘，偶爾也傳來慘叫聲或落水聲，還有史萊特利那單調的數數聲：五個、六個、七個、八個、九個、十個、十一個。

我想所有的海盜都被解決了。野蠻的孩子們團團圍住虎克，虎克像有魔法一樣，孩子們竟無法靠近他，彷彿他周圍有個火圈。孩子們已經解決了他所有的手下，可是，他一個人似乎就能對付他們所有人。男孩們一次又一次逼近，卻一次又一次被他逼退了。虎克還用鉤子舉起一個男孩當成盾牌，這時，另一個剛剛用劍刺穿馬林斯的男孩跳過來加入戰鬥。

新來的男孩喊：「收起你們的刀，這個人讓我來對付。」

忽然間，虎克發現他和彼得面對面，其他人都退了下去，圍著他們站成一圈。

這兩個死對頭對看了許久，虎克微微顫抖，彼得的臉上則綻放怪異的笑容。

最後虎克說：「那麼說，彼得，這全是你做的。」

「對，詹姆士・虎克，這全都是我做的。」彼得堅定地回答。

「驕傲無禮的小子，準備迎接你的末日吧。」虎克說。

「陰險毒辣的男人，前來受死吧。」彼得回答。

兩人不再多說，開始對打，一時分不出勝負。彼得劍法高超，躲閃迅速，使人眼花繚亂。他不時虛晃一招，趁敵人不備猛刺一劍，可惜他的攻擊範圍較短，這對他不利，無法命中要害。虎克的劍法也毫不遜色，不過，他手腕上的功夫不如彼得靈活，靠著猛烈的攻勢逼退了彼得。他滿心期待用巴比克先前在里約教他的致命招數，一下就能結束敵人的性命，卻錯愕的發現他屢刺不中，偏離目標。他的鐵鉤一直在空中胡亂飛舞，他想用鐵鉤給予致命的一擊。不料彼得彎身躲開鐵鉤，向前猛刺，刺進了虎克的肋骨。他看到了自己的血——各位應該還記得，那血的顏色最讓他受不了——虎克手中的劍墜落在地上，他現在完全任憑彼得擺佈。

「快！」孩子們齊聲喊到。可是，彼得做了個優雅的手勢，示意敵人撿起他的劍。虎克立刻照做，不過心裡感到一陣悲哀，因為彼得展現了絕佳的風度。

在這之前，虎克一直認為和他作戰的對手是個惡魔，現在卻有更糟的念頭湧上心頭。

「彼得，你到底是何方神聖？」虎克聲音沙啞的喊道。

彼得隨口回答：「我是青春，我是快樂，我是剛破殼的小鳥。」

這當然是一派胡言。但是，在不幸的虎克看來，這就足以證明彼得根本不知道他自己是誰，而這正是有風度的最高境界。

「又來了。」虎克絕望地吶喊。

現在的虎克像個人形風車頻頻揮舞著他的劍。這凌厲的刀法足以把每個大人或小孩切成兩段。可是彼得在他身邊飄來飄去，好像那把劍帶來的風把他吹出了危險地帶，使他可以靈巧地反擊和進攻。

虎克現在對勝負已不抱希望。他也不再期望活命了，只求在死前得到個痛快，那就是看到彼得失態的表現。

虎克終於放棄廝殺，衝到彈藥庫放火。

虎克喊道：「兩分鐘內，這整艘船就會被炸得粉碎。」

這下好了，虎克想，看看每個人的真面目吧。

可是彼得從彈藥庫捧著彈藥走出來，不慌不忙地把彈藥扔進了海裡。

虎克自己展現出什麼樣的風度呢？儘管他誤入歧途，並不能博得別人的同情，但我們還是很高興看到在最後他依然遵守了海盜的傳統。這時，其他的男孩圍著他，冷嘲熱諷的嘲笑他。他蹣跚地走過甲板，有氣無力地還擊。他的心思已經不在他們身上，而是回到了兒時的遊戲場，在那裡懶洋洋地遊蕩，或是觀看一場精彩的壁球遊戲。他穿著端正整潔的鞋子，背心，領結，和襪子。

詹姆士・虎克，不能說你不是一條好漢，永別了。

因為他的最後時刻已經來了。

看到彼得舉著劍慢慢地淩空朝著他飛來，他跳上了船舷，準備縱身跳下海。他不知道鱷魚正在水裡等著他。因為，我們故意讓鐘停擺，免得讓他察覺這件事，算是最後對他表示的一點敬意吧。

我們也不妨提一提，虎克獲得了最後一次的勝利，他站在船舷上回頭看著彼得向他飛來時，他要彼得用腳踢。於是彼得果然用腳踢，沒有用劍刺。

虎克總算得到了他渴望的痛快。「沒風度。」虎克嘲諷地喊道，然後心滿意足地落入鱷魚的口中。

詹姆士・虎克就此殞沒。

「十七個。」史萊特利唱了出來。不過他的算數不太正確。當天晚上十五個海盜因為他們犯的錯而付出代價，但有兩個逃回了岸上。斯塔奇被印地安人捕獲，被迫給印地安嬰孩當保姆，對於一個海盜，不得不說是個悲慘的下場。斯密從此戴著眼鏡到處流浪，有一餐沒一餐過著朝夕不保的生活，四處吹噓自己是詹姆士・虎克唯一害怕的人。

溫蒂當然沒有參與打鬥，只是旁觀，她又大又明亮的眼睛一直目不轉睛地注視著彼得。現在都結束了，她再次成了重要的人物。她一視同仁地表揚了每一個人。麥可指給她看他殺了一個海盜的地點時，她嚇得直發抖。然後，她把孩子們都帶到虎克的船艙裡，指著掛在釘子上虎克的錶，上面顯示的時間是「一點半」。

時間這麼晚了，現在睡覺是最重要的事。於是溫蒂很快地把孩子們安頓在海盜的臥鋪。只有彼得沒睡，他在甲板上來回踱步，最後，他倒在長炮旁睡著了。那夜，他做了很多夢，在夢中哭喊了很久，溫蒂則緊緊地抱著他。

第十六章

回家

「噢，娜娜，我夢見我的寶貝們回來了。」

第二天清晨鐘敲過三響後，孩子們就都東奔西跑地忙碌起來，海上的大風大浪正滾滾而來。托托這位水手長，手裡握著繩子的一端，嘴裡嚼著煙草。他們全都穿上了剪短及膝的海盜服，鬍子刮得乾乾淨淨的，像真正的水手那樣，提著褲子，兩步作一步，匆匆忙忙地走到甲板。

船長是誰就不用說了，尼布斯和約翰是大副和二副。船上還有一個女人，其餘都是普通船員，住在前艙。彼得已經將自己牢牢地綁在船舵，接著又吹笛把全體船員召集到甲板上來，做了一個簡短的演講，希望他們都像英勇的海上男兒一樣恪盡職守。不過他知道，他們都是來自里約和黃金海岸的敗類，誰敢違抗命令就把他給撕碎。他那幾句嚇唬人的粗話，擺足了水手的架勢，孩子們為彼得喝彩歡呼。接著，彼得下了幾道嚴厲的命令，然後他們掉轉船頭，朝本土駛去。

船長彼得查過航海圖之後推算，依照目前的天氣，他們將於六月二十一日抵達亞速爾群島。到那裡後再飛回去就省時多了。

有些孩子希望將這艘船改造成一艘普通的船，有些則希望仍是海盜船。可是船長把他們當成狗一樣對待，所以他們不敢表達意見，連遞交一份陳情書也不敢。絕對服從是唯一的辦法。史萊特利有一次奉命探測水深時臉上露出了迷惑的表情，就被打了十二下。大家都覺得彼得暫時假裝正派，為的是消除溫蒂的疑心，等到新衣服做好之後或許還會有變化。這件衣服是溫蒂原本不願意使用的虎克最邪惡的一件海盜服為彼得修改剪裁的。彼得穿上這件衣服的第一個晚上大家都在竊竊私語。他在艙裡坐了很久，嘴裡叼著虎克的煙斗，一手握拳，只伸出了食指，這根食指彎曲著，像個鉤子，高高舉起，做出恐嚇威脅的姿態。

現在我們暫時將目光從船上轉過來看看那個寂寞的家。我們的三個主角已經無情地離家出走很久了。說也慚愧，我們這麼久都沒提起十四號的情形。不過我們可以確定，達林太太一定不會責怪我們的。假如我們早一點回到這裡，帶著懊悔和同情來探望她，她多半會喊：「別做傻事，我有什麼關係？快回去照顧孩子們吧。」母親們總是這樣，難怪孩子們都會利用她們的這個弱點，遲遲不肯回家。

即使我們現在冒險地走進那間熟悉的育嬰室，也只是因為它的合法主人已經在回家的路上了，我們只不過比他們早了一步，提前看看他們的床是不是都鋪好了，並確認達林先生和達林太太那晚沒出門，我們不過是跑腿的罷了。不過，既然他們離開時走得匆忙，連句感謝的話都沒說，又何必替他們鋪床呢？要是他們回到家裡發現父母正好都到鄉下去度週末，那也是他們活該應得的對吧？這是從我們和他們相識以來，他們應得的教訓。不過，如果事情果真這樣發展，達林太太永遠也不會原諒我們的。

此刻我很想做一件事，就是利用作者的特權告訴達林太太，孩子們就要回來了，下週四他們就會到家。這樣一來，溫蒂、約翰和麥可預先設想要給家裡一個意外驚喜的計畫，就會完全落空了。他們在船上一直想像著——母親將欣喜若狂，父親會開心的歡呼，娜娜則是搶先撲上前擁抱他們，儘管其實他們應得的是頓痛打。如果我預先把消息洩露出來，破壞他們的計畫，那該多麼有趣啊。這樣一來，當他們大搖大擺地走進家門時，達林太太甚至不會去親吻溫蒂，達林先生還可能會煩躁地嚷道：「真討厭，這兩個臭小子又回來了。」不過這樣做我們也得不到感謝。我們現在已經越來越了解達林太太了，可以確定的是，她會責怪我們剝奪了孩子們的樂趣。

「可是，太太，到下週四還有十天，我們把實情告訴您，可以幫您減少十天的不快樂。」

「是沒錯，但是得為此付上多大的代價呀！剝奪了孩子們整整十分鐘的快樂。」

「噢，如果您是這樣看的話……」

「不然還能有什麼別的看法？」

你看，這個女人就是這樣不可理喻。我本想讚美她幾句，但我現在瞧不起她，不想再提孩子們的事了。其實也用不著提醒達林太太安排好一切，因為一切都已準備好了。三張床上都鋪著洗曬過的床單，她足不出戶的在家等待著——請看，窗戶是開著的。若說我們對她能夠有點用處，大概就是回到船上去。不過，我們既然來了，不妨留下來看看吧。我們本來就是旁觀者，沒有人真正需要我們。所以就讓我們在一旁觀望著，說幾句不好聽的話，希望能讓某些人聽了不開心。

育嬰室裡唯一的變化是從九點到六點狗屋不在裡面。自從孩子們飛走以後，達林先生就打心裡覺得千錯萬錯都錯在自己把娜娜拴了起來，而且娜娜自始至終都比他聰明。當然，我們已經見識到，達林先生是個很單純的人。倘若他的頭沒禿，他甚至會被誤認為是一個男孩。但是，他也有一種高尚的正義感，凡是他認為正確的事，他都有極大的勇氣去做。孩子們飛走後，他在焦慮中把這件事徹底地想了一遍，然後他趴著鑽進了狗屋。達林太太再三懇求勸他出來，他悲哀但是堅定地回答：

「不，親愛的，這才是我應該待的地方。」

達林先生悔恨至極，發誓只要孩子們一天不回來，他就一天不出狗屋。這當然是件遺憾的事，不過，達林先生要做什麼都喜歡極端，要不很快就停止不做。過去那個驕傲的喬治・達林，如今變得再謙遜不過了。有一天晚上，他坐在狗屋裡，和妻子談著孩子們和他們可愛的舉動。

他對娜娜的尊敬真讓人感動。除了不讓娜娜進狗屋之外，其他事情他也都對娜娜言聽計從。

每天早上，達林先生坐在狗屋裡被搬到出租馬車上前往辦公室，下午六點再以同樣的方式回家。要是我們還記得這個人把鄰居的觀感看得多麼重要，就更可以看出他的性格有多麼堅強。現在這個人的一舉一動都引人側目。他內心一定忍受著極大的痛苦，甚至當年輕人們指著他的小屋子說三道四時，他外表還能保持鎮靜。要是有哪位太太探頭向狗屋裡張望時，他總是彬彬有禮的脫帽致意。

這也許有點唐吉訶德式的理想主義，卻也挺偉大的。不久，這件事情的來龍去脈迅速地傳開了，大家深受感動。成群的人跟在他的車後面歡呼，漂亮的女孩爬上車去要求他親筆簽名，各大報紙都刊載了他的專訪，社會名流也紛紛邀請他出席晚宴，並且總是加上一句：「請務必攜帶狗屋蒞臨。」

在那個重要的星期四，達林太太坐在育嬰室等著達林先生回家，眼神充滿憂鬱。現在，我們來仔細看看她，想想她昔日的活潑愉快，現在那些風采都蕩然無存了，因為她失去了她最疼愛的孩子們。我發現我實在不忍心說她的壞話了。要說她太愛她的那幾個壞孩子，那也難怪。她坐在椅子上睡著了。看看她吧。首先看到的是她的嘴角，現在幾乎變得憔悴了；她的手不停地撫摸著胸口，就好像那裡在隱隱作痛。有的人最喜歡彼得，有的人最喜歡溫蒂，可是我最喜歡達林太太。為了讓她高興起來，我們要不要趁她睡著的時候在她耳邊悄悄告訴她，那三個小壞蛋要回來了？其實孩子們現在離窗口不到三公里，而且正在加速飛行，我們只需悄悄地對她說，他們已在回家的路上了。我們就這樣說吧。

很糟糕的是，我們真的這樣說了，達林太太忽然驚醒過來，呼喚著孩子們的名字。可是屋裡一個人也沒有，只有娜娜。

「娜娜，我夢見我的寶貝們回來了。」

娜娜睡眼惺忪，她能做的只有輕輕地把爪子放在女主人的膝蓋上，就這樣坐著這時，狗屋被運回來了。達林先生探出頭來吻他的妻子時，我們看到他的臉比以前憔悴多了，但表情變得更柔和。

達林先生把帽子交給莉莎，她鄙夷地接了過去，莉莎缺乏想像力，沒辦法理解這個人的所作所為。屋外隨車而來的一群人還在歡呼。達林先生當然不會無動於衷。

「聽聽他們，」他說：「真讓人欣慰。」

「一群小孩子。」莉莎嘲笑地說。

「今天人群裡有好幾個大人呢。」達林先生紅著臉告訴莉莎，可是她卻不屑地搖搖頭，達林先生也沒有責備她。大出風頭並沒有

使他得意忘形，反倒使他變得更謙虛了。有一陣子，他半個身體坐在狗屋裡，和達林太太談著他的出名。達林太太說。希望這不會讓他沖昏頭，他緊緊握著達林太太的手，要她放心。

「幸虧我不是一個軟弱的人。」達林先生說：「天哪，要是我是一個軟弱的人就糟了。」

「喬治，」達林太太怯生生地說：「你還是滿心的悔恨，是不是？」

「還是滿心的悔恨，親愛的！你看我怎麼懲罰自己？住在狗屋裡。」

「你是在懲罰自己，是不是，喬治？你能肯定你不是把它當作一種樂趣嗎？」

「什麼話，親愛的。」

當然，達林太太請求原諒。然後達林先生覺得睏了，他蜷著身子在狗屋裡躺下。

「你可以為我彈鋼琴催眠嗎？」他請求道。達林太太向臥房走去時，他漫不經心地說：「關上窗戶，我感覺有風。」

「啊，喬治，千萬別叫我關窗戶。窗戶是永遠要為孩子們開著的，永遠，永遠。」

現在，輪到達林先生請求她原諒了。達林太太走到孩子們白天遊戲的房間，彈起鋼琴來，達林先生很快就睡著了。就在他睡著的時候，溫蒂、約翰、麥可飛進了房間。

不對，不是這樣的。我們這樣寫是因為在我們離開船以前，這就是他們安排的迷人計劃。可是在我們離開船後，一定發生了什麼事，因為飛進來的不是他們三個，而是彼得和叮噹。

彼得說的第一句話就說明了一切。

「快，叮噹，」彼得低聲說：「關上窗子，上閂。對了。現在我們得從門口飛出去了，等溫蒂回來時，她會以為她母親把她關在外面了，然後她就得跟我一起回去。」

我腦子裡一直有一個疑問：「殺了海盜以後，彼得為什麼不回島上去，讓叮噹護送孩子們回家？」現在，這個讓我不解的謎團解開了，原來彼得腦子裡一直藏著這個詭計。

彼得並不覺得這樣做有什麼不對，反而開心地跳起舞來。然後他向遊戲室裡偷看，看是誰在彈鋼琴。他輕輕地對叮噹說：「那是溫蒂的媽媽。她是一位漂亮的太太，不過沒有我的媽媽漂亮。她嘴上滿是頂針，不過還是沒有我媽媽嘴上的多。」

當然，關於他的母親，他知道得不多，可是他有時就喜歡吹噓她有多好。

彼得不知道鋼琴上彈的是什麼曲子，那其實是「甜蜜的家」，可是他知道，那曲子在不斷地唱著「回來吧，溫蒂，溫蒂，溫蒂。」彼得洋洋得意地說：「太太，你再也別想見到溫蒂啦，因為窗戶已

經門上啦。」

彼得又向房間裡偷看了一眼，想看看琴聲為什麼停了，他看見達林太太把頭靠在琴箱上，眼裡含著兩顆淚珠。

「她要我把窗戶打開，」彼得心想：「可是我才不要呢，絕不。」

彼得又偷看了一下，只見兩顆淚珠還在眼裡待著，不過已經換了兩顆。

「她真的很愛溫蒂。」彼得對自己說。他現在很恨達林太太，因為她不明白為什麼她不能留下溫蒂。

這道理再簡單也不過：「因為我也愛溫蒂，太太，我們兩個人不能都擁有溫蒂呀。」

可是這位太太偏偏不肯善罷甘休，彼得覺得不高興，就不再看她。但就算是這樣，她也不放過彼得。彼得在房裡蹦蹦跳跳，做著鬼臉，但當他一停下來，達林太太彷彿在他心裡不停地敲打。

「啊，那好吧。」最後，彼得忍著怒氣說。然後他打開了窗戶。「來，叮噹，我們不需要什麼笨媽媽！」他喊，語氣中充滿對自然法則的不屑，然後就飛走了。

所以，當溫蒂、約翰和麥可飛回來的時候，窗戶還是開著的，這當然是他們不配得到的。他們落到了地板上，一點也不感到慚愧，最小的一個甚至已經忘了他的家。

「約翰，」他疑惑地四處張望說：「這裡，我好像來過。」

「你當然來過，笨蛋。那不是你的舊床嗎？」

「對。」麥可說，可是還不太確定。

「看，狗屋！」約翰喊，他跑去裡面看。

「或許娜娜在裡面。」溫蒂說。

於是約翰吹了一聲口哨。「裡面有個男人。」他說。

「是爸爸！」溫蒂驚叫。

「讓我看看爸爸。」麥可迫切地請求，他仔細地看了一眼。「他還沒有我殺死的那個海盜那麼壯呢。」他坦率地帶著失望的口氣說。幸好達林先生睡著了，要是他聽見他的小麥可一見面就說出這樣的一句話，會多傷心啊。

看見父親睡在狗屋裡，溫蒂和約翰嚇了一跳。

「真的，」約翰像一個對自己的記憶力失去信心的人說道：「他不是一直都睡在狗屋裡吧？」

「約翰，」溫蒂猶豫地說：「也許我們對過去生活的記憶，不像我們想的那樣準確吧。」

他們覺得身上一陣寒意。活該。

「我們回來的時候，」約翰這個小壞蛋說，「媽媽也沒在這裡

等著，真是太粗心了。」

這時候，達林太太又彈起琴來了。

「是媽媽！」溫蒂喊道，向那邊偷看。

「可不是嗎！」約翰說。

「那麼，溫蒂，你並不是我們真正的媽媽囉？」麥可問。他一定是睏了。

「噢，我的天！」溫蒂驚叫道，她第一次真正感到了後悔：「我們該回來的時候到了。」

「我們偷偷地溜進去，」約翰提議：「用手蒙住她的眼睛。」

可是溫蒂認為應該用一種更溫和的辦法宣布好消息，她想到了一個更好的辦法。

「我們都上床去，等媽媽進來的時候我們都在床上躺著，就好像從來沒有離開過一樣。」

於是，當達林太太回到孩子們的育嬰室，看看達林先生是不是睡著了的時候，她看到了每張床上都睡了一個孩子。孩子們正急切地等著聽到她的歡呼，可是她沒有。她看到了他們，但她不相信他們在那兒。原來，她時常在夢裡看到孩子們躺在床上，所以達林太太以為她現在還在做夢。

達林太太在火爐邊的椅子上坐了下來，從前，她總是坐在這兒給孩子們餵奶。

孩子們不明白這是怎麼回事，三個孩子都覺得渾身發冷。

「媽媽！」溫蒂喊道。

「這是溫蒂。」達林太太說，可是她還以為這是夢。

「媽媽！」

「這是約翰！」達林太太說。

「媽媽！」麥可喊。他現在認出媽媽來了。

「這是麥可。」達林太太說。她伸出雙臂擁抱那三個自私的孩子，她還以為自己再也抱不到他們了。沒錯，她確實抱著了，她摟住了溫蒂、約翰和麥可。他們三個早已溜下床，跑到了她身邊。

「喬治，喬治。」達林太太好不容易才叫出聲來。達林先生醒來，分享了她的歡樂，娜娜也衝了進來。再也沒有比這更美妙動人的景象了。不過，沒人觀賞，只有一個陌生的小男孩從窗外向裡張望。他快樂的事數也數不清，那是別的孩子永遠得不到的。但是，只有這一種快樂，他隔著窗戶看到的那種快樂，是他永遠也得不到的。

第十七章

溫蒂長大了

我希望你想知道別的孩子後來怎麼了。他們都在樓下等著，好讓溫蒂有時間解釋。

我希望你想知道別的孩子後來怎麼了。他們都在樓下等著，好讓溫蒂有時間解釋。當他們數到五百的時候就會上樓。他們是沿樓梯走上來的，因為他們覺得這樣會給人好印象。他們在達林太太面前站成一排，脫掉了帽子，心裡恨不得沒有穿海盜服。他們沒有說話，眼睛卻在懇求達林太太收留他們。他們原本也應該也看達林先生，可是他們忘了。

當然，達林太太立刻就說她願意收留他們，可是達林先生很不高興，孩子們猜想他是嫌六個人太多了。

「我告訴你，」達林先生對溫蒂說：「做事從來不能只做一半。」雙胞胎覺得這句埋怨顯然是針對他們的。

老大自尊心比較強，他紅著臉對達林先生說：「先生，你覺得我們人太多了嗎？如果是的話，我們可以走。」

「爸爸！」溫蒂驚訝地叫了一聲，但是，達林先生的臉上還是滿臉陰霾。他知道不值得這樣做，卻又無法控制。

「我們可以擠在一起睡。」尼布斯說。

「我可以經常幫他們剪頭髮。」溫蒂說。

「喬治！」達林太太驚嘆了一聲，看到她親愛的丈夫表現得這麼丟臉，心裡很難過。

達林先生突然哭了起來，於是真相大白。他說，他也和達林太太一樣願意收留他們，只不過他們在徵求她的意見時，也應徵求他

的意見，不該在他自己的家裡把他看成一個可有可無的人。

「我並不覺得他是一個可有可無的人。」托托立刻大聲說，「你呢，捲毛？」

「我不覺得，你呢，史萊特利？」

「我也不覺得，雙胞胎，你們呢？」

到頭來，沒有一個孩子認為達林先生是個可有可無的人。他高興極了，並說要是合適的話，他可以把他們統統安置在客廳裡。

「非常合適，先生。」孩子們向他擔保。

「那麼，跟我來。」他興沖沖地喊：「請注意，我不確定我有沒有一間客廳，不過我們可以假裝有一間客廳，反正一樣。啊哈！」

他手舞足蹈地滿屋子轉著，孩子們也全都高喊：「啊哈！」，手舞足蹈地跟著他尋找那間客廳。我也不記得他們究竟找到了沒有，不管怎麼樣，他們總算找到一些角落，所有的人都擠進去了。

至於彼得，他飛走前又來看了溫蒂。但他並沒有特地來到窗前，只是在飛過時擦了一下窗子，如果溫蒂想的話，可以打開窗子呼喚他。溫蒂果然這麼做了。

「哈囉，溫蒂，再見。」他說。

「你要走了嗎？」

「對。」

「彼得，你不想跟我爸媽談那個甜蜜的話題嗎？」溫蒂有點遲疑地說。

「不想。」

「關於我的事，彼得？」

「不想。」

這時達林太太走到窗前，她現在一直在密切地注視著溫蒂。她告訴彼得，她已經收養了所有的孩子，也願意收養他。

「你會送我去上學？」彼得機警地問。

「對。」

「然後再送我上班？」

「我想是這樣。」

「我很快就會變成大人？」

「很快。」

「我不要去學校學那些正經的東西。」彼得激動地對達林太太說：「我不要變成大人。溫蒂的媽媽，要是我一覺醒來，摸到自己有鬍子怎麼辦！」

「彼得！」溫蒂安慰他：「你有鬍子我也會愛你的。」達林太太向他伸出雙臂，但是彼得拒絕了她。

「女士，別靠近我，誰也不能把我變成大人。」

「可是你要住在哪呢？」

「和叮噹一起住在我們替溫蒂蓋的小房子裡。仙子們會把它高高地抬上樹梢的，她們晚上就住在樹上。」

「好棒。」溫蒂羨慕地喊道。達林太太不由得把她抓得更緊。

「我以為所有的仙子都死了。」達林太太說。

「總會有許多年輕的仙子出生。」溫蒂解釋。關於仙子的事，她現在可以說是個專家了。「每個嬰兒第一次笑出聲的時候，就有一個新的仙子誕生。既然總是有新的嬰兒，就總會有新的仙子，他們住在樹梢上的巢裡。淡紫色的是男生，白色的是女生，藍色的是不確定自己是誰的小笨蛋。」

「我會很快樂的。」彼得邊說邊用一隻眼睛看著溫蒂說。

「晚上一個人坐在火爐邊很寂寞的。」溫蒂說。

「我有叮噹。」

「叮噹可做不了什麼事。」她有點刻薄地提醒他。

「背後說人壞話的人！」叮噹不知從哪兒鑽出來，罵了一句。

「沒關係。」彼得說。

「彼得，有關係，你知道的。」溫蒂說。

「那你跟我一起去小房子吧。」

「媽媽，我可以去嗎？」

「當然不可以，你好不容易回家了，我絕不讓你再離開。」

「可是他真的需要一個母親啊。」

「你也需要一個母親啊，寶貝。」

「沒關係。」彼得說，好像他邀請溫蒂只是出於禮貌。但是，達林太太看到彼得的嘴抽動了，於是她提出一個慷慨的建議：每年讓溫蒂去他那兒住一個禮拜，幫他春季大掃除。溫蒂寧願有更長遠的安排，而且她覺得，春天還要等很久。但是，這個承諾卻讓彼得高興地走了。他沒有時間觀念，又有那麼多冒險，我告訴你們的只不過是其中微乎其微的一點。我想，大概溫蒂非常明白這一點，所以她最後向他說了一句悲傷的話：

「彼得，你不會忘記我吧？在春季大掃除以前，你會忘記我嗎？」

「當然不會。」彼得向她保證，然後就飛走了。他帶走了達林太太的吻，這個吻是誰也得不到的，彼得卻毫不費力地得到了。真有趣。可是溫蒂好像也心滿意足了。

所有的孩子都進了學校，多數人上第三班。不過，史萊特利一開始被安排到第四班，後來又改上第五班。第一班是最好的。他們上學還不到一個禮拜就後悔了，覺得不該離開永無島，可是現在已經太遲了。他們也很快安心下來，像你、我或小詹金斯一樣過著普通的生活。說來怪可憐的，他們漸漸失去了飛行的能力。起初，娜娜把他們的腳綁在床柱上，防止他們夜裡飛走。白天，他們的遊戲是假裝從公車上掉下來。過了一陣子，他們不再拉扯床柱的繩子，而且他們從公車掉下時會痛。後來，帽子被風吹刮走，他們不能飛過去抓住了。他們說這是因為缺少練習，其實，真正的原因是他們不再相信這一切了。

麥可比別的孩子相信的時間長了點，他們老是嘲笑他。所以，第一年彼得來找溫蒂時，他還和溫蒂在一起。溫蒂和彼得一起飛走時，身上穿著她在永無島時用樹葉和漿果編織成的罩衫。她害怕彼得看出罩衫已經變得那麼短了，可是彼得根本沒注意，他自己的事就多到不完。

溫蒂期盼著和他談起那些令人激動的往事，可是新的冒險趣事已經從他腦中擠走了那些舊事。

溫蒂提起那個死對頭時，彼得很感興趣地問：「虎克是誰？」

「你不記得了嗎？」溫蒂驚訝地問，「你是怎麼殺了他，救了我們大家的？」

「我殺了他們以後就把他們忘了。」彼得漫不經心地回答。

當溫蒂猶豫地表示希望叮噹會高興見到她時，彼得卻問：「叮噹是誰？」

「啊，彼得。」溫蒂非常驚訝。可是就算她再怎麼解釋，彼得仍然想不起來。

「這種小東西多的是，」他說：「我想她已經不在了。」

我想彼得大概是對的，因為仙子是活不長的。不過，因為她們很小，所以很短的時間在她們看來很長。

還有一點也讓溫蒂感到難過，過去的一年，對於彼得來說彷彿只是昨天，可是對她來說，這一年的等待真是漫長啊。不過彼得還像以前一樣令人喜歡，他們在樹梢上的小屋裡度過了愉快的春季大掃除。

第二年，彼得沒有來接她。她穿上一件新衣服等著他，因為那件舊的已經穿不下了。可是彼得沒有來。

「彼得也許是病了吧。」麥可說。

「你知道彼得從來不生病的。」

麥可湊到溫蒂跟前，打了個冷顫，悄悄地說：「也許根本就沒有這個人，溫蒂！」那時就算麥可沒哭，溫蒂也會哭的。

再下一年，彼得又來接她去進行春季大掃除了。奇怪的是他竟然不知道自己漏掉了一年。

這是小女孩溫蒂最後一次見到彼得。有一段時間，因為彼得的關係，她努力不讓自己越來越痛苦。當她在常識課上得了獎時，她覺得自己是對彼得不忠實。但是一年一年過去了，這位粗心大意的孩子再也沒來。等到他們再見面時，溫蒂已經是一位結了婚的婦人，彼得對於她，只不過變成了玩具盒裡的一點灰塵。溫蒂長大了。你不必為她感到遺憾，她是喜歡長大的那種人，她是心甘情願長大的，而且心甘情願比別的女孩子長得更快一點。

男孩子們這時全都長大了，所以沒什麼好說的。你隨便哪天都可以看到雙胞胎、尼布斯和捲毛提著公事包和雨傘走去辦公室。麥可是位火車司機。史萊特利娶了一位貴族女子，所以他成了一位勳爵。你看見一位戴假髮的法官從鐵門裡走出來嗎？那就是過去的托托。那個從來不會給他的孩子講故事的有鬍子的男人，他就是原來的約翰。

溫蒂結婚時穿著白色的婚紗，繫著一條粉紅色的飾帶。說來也奇怪，彼得竟然沒有飛進教堂反對這樁婚事。

時光飛逝，溫蒂有了一個女兒。這件事不該用墨水寫下，該用金粉寫下來。

她的女兒名叫珍，小女孩總是一臉好發問的古怪神情，彷彿她一來到世上就有許多問題要問。等她長到可以發問的時候，她的問題多半是關於彼得潘的。她愛聽彼得的事，溫蒂把她自己還記得的事情全講給女兒聽。她講這些故事的地點，正是那間發生過那次有名的飛行的育嬰室。現在，這裡成了珍的育嬰室，因為，她父親以百分之三的廉價從溫蒂的父親手裡買下了這房子。溫蒂的父親已經不喜歡爬樓梯了。達林太太已經去世，人們已經忘記她了。

現在育嬰室裡只有兩張床，珍一張，她的保姆一張。已經沒有狗屋了，因為娜娜也死了。她是老死的，最後幾年她的脾氣變得很難相處，因為她非常固執己見，認為除了她誰也不懂照顧孩子。

珍的保姆每個禮拜有一天晚上休息，這時就由溫蒂照顧珍上床睡覺。這是講故事的時間。珍別出心裁地用床單罩在自己和媽媽的頭上，當作一頂帳篷。在黑暗裡，兩人說著悄悄話：

「現在我們看到什麼了？」

「今晚我什麼也沒看見到。」溫蒂說，她感覺要是娜娜在的話，一定不會讓她們再說下去。

「你看得到，」珍說：「你是一個小姑娘的時候就看得到。」

「那是很久很久以前的事了，我的寶貝，」溫蒂說：「唉，時間飛得多快呀！」

「時間也會飛嗎？」這個機靈的孩子問：「就像你小時候那樣嗎？」

「像我那樣飛！你知道，珍，我有時候真的不知道我是不是真的飛過。」

「你飛過。」

「我會飛的那個大好時光，已經回不來了。」

「為什麼現在你不能飛了，媽媽？」

「因為我長大了，親愛的。人一長大就忘了怎麼飛。」

「為什麼他們會忘了怎麼飛呢？」

「因為他們不再是無憂無慮、天真無邪、毫無心機的人了。只有無憂無慮、天真無邪、毫無心機的人才會飛。」

「什麼叫無憂無慮、天真無邪、毫無心機的人呢？我真希望我也是這種人呀。」

或許這時候溫蒂真的領悟到了什麼。「我想都是因為這間育嬰室。」她說。

「我想也是，」珍說：「繼續說吧。」

於是她們開始談到了大冒險的那一夜，彼得飛進來找他的影子。

「那個傻孩子，」溫蒂說：「他想用肥皂把影子黏上，黏不上他就哭，哭聲把我驚醒了，我就用針線替他縫上。」

「你漏掉了一點。」珍插嘴說，她現在比母親知道的還清楚了。「你看見他坐在地板上哭的時候，你說了什麼？」

「我從床上坐起來說：『孩子，你為什麼在哭？』」

「對了，就是這樣。」珍說，深呼吸了一下。

「後來，他帶我飛到了永無島，那裡有仙子，有海盜，有印地安人，有美人魚的潟湖，有地下的家，還有那間小房子。」

「對！你最喜歡的是什麼？」

「我想是地下的家。」

「我也最喜歡。彼得最後對你說了什麼？」

「他最後對我說了：『你只要永遠等著我，總有一天晚上你會聽到我的叫聲。』」

「對。」

「可是，唉！他已經完全把我給忘了。」溫蒂微笑著。她已經長得那麼大了。

「彼得的叫聲是什麼樣子的？」珍有一晚問。

「是這樣的。」溫蒂說，她試著學彼得叫。

「不對，不是這樣，」珍鄭重地說：「是這樣。」她學得比母親像多了。

溫蒂有點吃驚：「寶貝，你怎麼知道？」

「我睡覺的時候常常聽到。」珍說。

「啊，是啊，許多女孩睡覺的時候都曾聽到，可是只有我是醒著的時候聽到了。」

「你好幸運。」珍說。

有一夜悲劇發生了。那是在春天，晚上剛講完了故事，珍躺在床上睡著了。溫蒂坐在地板上，靠近壁爐，藉著火光補襪子，因為育兒室裡沒有別的亮光。補著補著，她聽到一聲叫聲。窗戶像過去一樣吹開了，彼得跳了進來，落在地板上。

彼得和從前一樣一點也沒變，溫蒂馬上就看到了他還長著滿口的乳牙。

彼得還是一個小男孩，但溫蒂已經是一個大人了。她在火邊縮成一團，一動也不敢動，既尷尬又難堪，一個大人。

「你好，溫蒂。」彼得向她打招呼，他並沒注意到有什麼不一樣，因為他只想到自己。在昏暗的光下，溫蒂穿的那件白衣服，很像他第一次見到她時穿的那件睡衣。

「你好，彼得。」溫蒂有氣無力地回答。她緊縮著身子，儘量把自己變得小些。她內心有個聲音在說：「女人，女人，放開我。」

「約翰在哪？」彼得問，突然發現少了第三張床。

「約翰現在不在這。」溫蒂喘息著說。

「麥可睡著了嗎？」他隨便瞄了珍一眼問道。

「對。」溫蒂回答，可她立刻感到自己對珍和彼得都不誠實。

「那不是麥可。」她連忙改口說。

彼得走過去看：「這是個新孩子嗎？」

「對。」

「男孩還是女孩？」

「女孩。」

現在彼得該懂了吧，可是他一點都不懂。

「彼得，」溫蒂結結巴巴地說：「你希望我跟你一起飛走嗎？」

「當然啦，我正是為這個來的。」彼得有點嚴厲地說，「你忘了是春季大掃除的時候了嗎？」

溫蒂知道，不用告訴他有好多次春季大掃除都被他漏掉了。

「我不能去，」她抱歉地說：「我忘了怎麼飛了。」

「我可以重新教你。」

「啊，彼得，別浪費仙粉在我身上了。」

溫蒂站了起來，這時，彼得突然感到一陣恐懼。「怎麼回事？」他喊，往後退縮著。

「我去開燈，」溫蒂說：「你自己看就知道了。」

就我所知，這是彼得有生以來第一次感到害怕。「不要開燈。」他喊道。

溫蒂用手撫弄著這可憐的孩子的頭髮。她已經不是一個為他傷心的小女孩，她是一個成年婦人，微笑地看待這一切，那是帶著淚的微笑。

然後溫蒂開了燈。彼得看見了，他痛苦地叫了一聲。這位高大、美麗的婦人正要彎下身去把他抱起來，他猛然後退。

「怎麼回事？」他又喊了一聲。

溫蒂不得不告訴他。

「我老了，彼得。我已經二十幾歲了，早就長大成人了。」

「你答應過我你不長大的！」

「我沒有辦法不長大⋯⋯我是一個結了婚的女人，彼得。」

「不，你不是。」

「是，床上那個小女孩就是我的女兒。」

「不，她不是。」

可是，彼得想這個小女孩大概真的是溫蒂的小孩，他高高舉起了手中的短劍，朝熟睡的孩子走了幾步。當然他沒有砍她。他坐在地板上抽泣起來。溫蒂不知道怎麼安慰他才好，雖然她曾經輕而易舉就能做到這一點。她現在只是一個女人，於是她走出房間去好好思考。

彼得還在哭，哭聲很快就驚醒了珍。珍從床上坐起來，覺得眼前這一切非常有趣。

「孩子，」她說：「你為什麼在哭？」

彼得站起來，向她鞠了躬，她也在床上向彼得鞠了躬。

「你好。」彼得說。

「你好。」珍說。

「我叫彼得潘。」他告訴她。

「我知道。」

「我回來找媽媽，」彼得解釋：「我要帶她去永無島。」

「我知道，」珍說，「我正在等你。」

溫蒂忐忑不安地走回房間時，看到彼得正坐在床上洋洋得意地叫喊著，珍正穿著睡衣開心地繞著房間飛。

「她是我的媽媽了。」彼得對溫蒂解釋，珍落下來，站在彼得身旁，臉上露出了女孩們注視他時的神情，那是彼得最喜歡看到的。

「他太需要一個媽媽了。」珍說。

「是呀，我知道，」溫蒂多少有點淒涼地承認：「沒有人比我更清楚了。」

「再見。」彼得對溫蒂說，他飛到了空中，毫無顧忌的珍也隨他飛起，飛行已經是她最容易的活動方式了。

溫蒂衝到了窗前。

「不，不。」她大喊。

「只是去進行春季大掃除罷了，」珍說，「他要我總去幫他進行春季大掃除。」

「要是我能跟你們一起去就好了。」溫蒂嘆了一口氣。

「可是你不能飛呀。」珍說。

當然，溫蒂最後還是讓他們一起飛走了。我們最後看到溫蒂時，她正站在窗前，望著他們向天空裡遠去，直到他們小得像星星。

你再見到溫蒂時，會看到她頭髮變白了，身體又縮小了。這些事是很久以前發生的。珍現在是普通的成年女子了，她的女兒叫瑪格麗特，每到春季大掃除的時後，除非他自己忘記了，否則彼得總是會來帶瑪格麗特去永無島。她在那兒給彼得講她自己的故事，彼得總是聚精會神地聽著。瑪格麗特長大後，又會有一個女兒，這個女孩又成了彼得的母親。事情就這樣周而復始，只要孩子們一直無憂無慮、天真無邪，就會一代又一代一直傳下去。

Chapter 1

Peter Breaks Through

There never was a simpler happier family until the coming of Peter Pan.

All children, except one, grow up. They soon know that they will grow up, and the way Wendy knew was this. One day when she was two years old she was playing in a garden, and she plucked another flower and ran with it to her mother. I suppose she must have looked rather delightful, for Mrs. Darling put her hand to her heart and cried, "Oh, why can't you remain like this for ever!" This was all that passed between them on the subject, but henceforth Wendy knew that she must grow up. You always know after you are two. Two is the beginning of the end.

Of course they lived at 14 (*their house number on their street*), and until Wendy came her mother was the chief one. She was a lovely lady, with a romantic mind and such a sweet mocking mouth. Her romantic mind was like the tiny boxes, one within the other, that come from the puzzling East, however many you discover there is always one more; and her sweet mocking mouth had one kiss on it that Wendy could never get, though there it was, perfectly conspicuous in the right-hand corner.

The way Mr. Darling won her was this: the many gentlemen who had been boys when she was a girl discovered simultaneously that they loved her, and they all ran to her house to propose to her except Mr. Darling, who took a cab and nipped in first, and so he got her. He got all of her, except the innermost box and the kiss. He never knew about the box, and in time he gave up trying for the kiss. Wendy thought Napoleon could have got it, but I can picture him trying, and then going off in a passion, slamming the door.

Mr. Darling used to boast to Wendy that her mother not only loved him but respected him. He was one of those deep ones who know about stocks and shares. Of course no one really knows, but he quite seemed to know, and he often said stocks were up and shares were down in a way that would have made any woman respect him.

Mrs. Darling was married in white, and at first she kept the books perfectly, almost gleefully, as if it were a game, not so much as a Brussels sprout was missing; but by and by whole cauliflowers dropped out, and instead of them there were pictures of babies without faces. She drew them when she should have been totting up. They were Mrs. Darling's guesses.

Wendy came first, then John, then Michael.

For a week or two after Wendy came it was doubtful whether they would be able to keep her, as she was another mouth to feed. Mr. Darling was frightfully proud of her, but he was very honourable, and he sat on the edge of Mrs. Darling's bed, holding her hand and calculating expenses, while she looked at him imploringly. She wanted to risk it, come what might, but that was not his way; his way was with a pencil and a piece of paper, and if she confused him with suggestions he had to begin at the beginning again.

"Now don't interrupt," he would beg of her.

"I have one pound seventeen here, and two and six at the office; I can cut off my coffee at the office, say ten shillings, making two nine and six, with your eighteen and three makes three nine seven, with five naught naught in my cheque-book makes eight nine seven, – who is that moving? – eight nine seven, dot and carry seven – don't speak, my own – and the pound you lent to that man who came to the door – quiet, child – dot and carry child – there, you've done it! – did I say nine nine seven? yes, I said nine nine seven; the question is, can we try it for a year on nine nine seven?"

"Of course we can, George," she cried. But she was prejudiced in Wendy's favour, and he was really the grander character of the two.

"Remember mumps," he warned her almost threateningly, and off he went again. "Mumps one pound, that is what I have put down, but I daresay it will be more like thirty shillings – don't speak – measles one five, German measles half a guinea, makes two fifteen six – don't waggle your finger – whooping-cough, say fifteen shillings" – and so on it went, and it added up differently each time; but at last Wendy just got through, with mumps reduced to twelve six, and the two kinds of measles treated as one.

There was the same excitement over John, and Michael had even a narrower squeak; but both were kept, and soon, you might have seen the three of them going in a row to Miss Fulsom's Kindergarten school, accompanied by their nurse.

Mrs. Darling loved to have everything just so, and Mr. Darling had a passion for being exactly like his neighbours; so, of course, they had a nurse. As they were poor, owing to the amount of milk the children drank, this nurse was a prim Newfoundland dog, called Nana, who had belonged to no one in particular until the Darlings engaged her. She had always thought children important, however, and the Darlings had become acquainted with her in Kensington Gardens, where she spent most of her spare time peeping into perambulators, and was much hated by careless nursemaids, whom she followed to their homes and complained of to their mistresses. She proved to be quite a treasure of a nurse. How thorough she was at bath-time, and up at any moment of the night if one of her charges made the slightest cry. Of course her kennel was in the nursery. She had a genius for knowing when a cough is a thing to have no patience with and when it needs stocking around your throat. She believed to her last day in old-fashioned remedies like rhubarb leaf, and made sounds of contempt over all this new-fangled talk about germs, and so on. It was a lesson in propriety to see her escorting the children to school, walking sedately by their side when they were well behaved, and butting them back into line if they strayed. On John's footer (*in England soccer was called football, "footer" for short*) days she never once forgot his sweater, and she usually carried an umbrella in her mouth in case of rain. There is a room in the basement of Miss Fulsom's school where the nurses wait. They sat on forms, while Nana lay on the floor, but that was the only difference. They affected to ignore her as of an inferior social status to themselves, and she despised their light talk. She resented visits to the nursery from Mrs. Darling's friends, but if they did come she first whipped off Michael's pinafore and put him into the one with blue braiding, and smoothed out Wendy and made a dash at John's hair.

No nursery could possibly have been conducted more correctly, and

Mr. Darling knew it, yet he sometimes wondered uneasily whether the neighbours talked.

He had his position in the city to consider.

Nana also troubled him in another way. He had sometimes a feeling that she did not admire him. "I know she admires you tremendously, George," Mrs. Darling would assure him, and then she would sign to the children to be specially nice to father. Lovely dances followed, in which the only other servant, Liza, was sometimes allowed to join. Such a midget she looked in her long skirt and maid's cap, though she had sworn, when engaged, that she would never see ten again. The gaiety of those romps! And gayest of all was Mrs. Darling, who would pirouette so wildly that all you could see of her was the kiss, and then if you had dashed at her you might have got it. There never was a simpler happier family until the coming of Peter Pan.

Mrs. Darling first heard of Peter when she was tidying up her children's minds. It is the nightly custom of every good mother after her children are asleep to rummage in their minds and put things straight for next morning, repacking into their proper places the many articles that have wandered during the day. If you could keep awake (*but of course you can't*) you would see your own mother doing this, and you would find it very interesting to watch her. It is quite like tidying up drawers. You would see her on her knees, I expect, lingering humorously over some of your contents, wondering where on earth you had picked this thing up, making discoveries sweet and not so sweet, pressing this to her cheek as if it were as nice as a kitten, and hurriedly stowing that out of sight. When you wake in the morning, the naughtiness and evil passions with which you went to bed have been folded up small and placed at the bottom of your mind and on the top, beautifully aired, are spread out your prettier thoughts, ready for you to put on.

I don't know whether you have ever seen a map of a person's mind. Doctors sometimes draw maps of other parts of you, and your own map can become intensely interesting, but catch them trying to draw a map of a child's mind, which is not only confused, but keeps going round all the time. There are zigzag lines on it, just like your temperature on a card, and these are probably roads in the island, for the Neverland is always more or less an island, with astonishing splashes of colour here and there, and coral reefs and rakish-looking craft in the offing, and savages and lonely lairs, and gnomes who are mostly tailors, and caves through which a river runs, and princes with six elder brothers, and a hut fast going to decay, and one very small old lady with a hooked nose. It would be an easy map if that were all, but there is also first day at school, religion, fathers, the round pond, needle-work, murders, hangings, verbs that take the dative, chocolate pudding day, getting into braces, say ninety-nine, three-pence for pulling out your tooth yourself, and so on, and either these are part of the island or they are another map showing through, and it is all rather confusing, especially as nothing will stand still.

Of course the Neverlands vary a good deal. John's, for instance, had a lagoon with flamingoes flying over it at which John was shooting, while Michael, who was very small, had a flamingo with lagoons flying over it. John lived in a boat turned upside down on the sands, Michael in a wigwam, Wendy in a house of leaves deftly sewn together. John had no friends, Michael had friends at night, Wendy had a pet wolf forsaken by its parents, but on the whole the Neverlands have a family resemblance, and if they stood still in a row you could say of them that they have each other's nose, and so forth. On these magic shores children at play are for ever beaching their coracles (*simple boat*). We too have been there; we can still hear the sound of the surf, though we shall land no more.

Of all delectable islands the Neverland is the snuggest and most compact, not large and sprawly, you know, with tedious distances between one adventure and another, but nicely crammed. When you play at it by day with the chairs and table-cloth, it is not in the least alarming, but in the two minutes before you go to sleep it becomes very real. That is why there are night-lights.

Occasionally in her travels through her children's minds Mrs. Darling found things she could not understand, and of these quite the most perplexing was the word Peter. She knew of no Peter, and yet he was here and there in John and Michael's minds, while Wendy's began to be scrawled all over with him. The name stood out in bolder letters than any of the other words, and as Mrs. Darling gazed she felt that it had an oddly cocky appearance.

"Yes, he is rather cocky," Wendy admitted with regret. Her mother

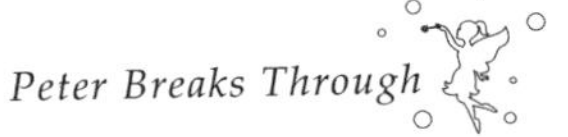

had been questioning her.

"But who is he, my pet?"

"He is Peter Pan, you know, mother."

At first Mrs. Darling did not know, but after thinking back into her childhood she just remembered a Peter Pan who was said to live with the fairies. There were odd stories about him, as that when children died he went part of the way with them, so that they should not be frightened. She had believed in him at the time, but now that she was married and full of sense she quite doubted whether there was any such person.

"Besides," she said to Wendy, "he would be grown up by this time."

"Oh no, he isn't grown up," Wendy assured her confidently, "and he is just my size." She meant that he was her size in both mind and body; she didn't know how she knew, she just knew it.

Mrs. Darling consulted Mr. Darling, but he smiled pooh-pooh. "Mark my words," he said, "it is some nonsense Nana has been putting into their heads; just the sort of idea a dog would have. Leave it alone, and it will blow over."

But it would not blow over and soon the troublesome boy gave Mrs. Darling quite a shock.

Children have the strangest adventures without being troubled by them. For instance, they may remember to mention, a week after the event happened, that when they were in the wood they had met their dead father and had a game with him. It was in this casual way that Wendy one morning made a disquieting revelation. Some leaves of a tree had been found on the nursery floor, which certainly were not there when the children went to bed, and Mrs. Darling was puzzling over them when Wendy said with a tolerant smile:

"I do believe it is that Peter again!"

"Whatever do you mean, Wendy?"

"It is so naughty of him not to wipe," Wendy said, sighing. She was a tidy child.

She explained in quite a matter-of-fact way that she thought Peter sometimes came to the nursery in the night and sat on the foot of her bed and played on his pipes to her. Unfortunately she never woke, so she didn't know how she knew, she just knew.

"What nonsense you talk, precious! No one can get into the house without knocking."

"I think he comes in by the window," she said.

"My love, it is three floors up."

"Weren't the leaves at the foot of the window, mother?"

It was quite true; the leaves had been found very near the window.

Mrs. Darling did not know what to think, for it all seemed so natural to Wendy that you could not dismiss it by saying she had been dreaming.

"My child," the mother cried, "why did you not tell me of this before?"

"I forgot," said Wendy lightly. She was in a hurry to get her breakfast.

Oh, surely she must have been dreaming.

But, on the other hand, there were the leaves. Mrs. Darling examined them very carefully; they were skeleton leaves, but she was sure they did not come from any tree that grew in England. She crawled about the floor, peering at it with a candle for marks of a strange foot. She rattled the poker up the chimney and tapped the walls. She let down a tape from the window to the pavement, and it was a sheer drop of thirty feet, without so much as a spout to climb up by.

Certainly Wendy had been dreaming.

But Wendy had not been dreaming, as the very next night showed, the night on which the extraordinary adventures of these children may be said to have begun.

On the night we speak of all the children were once more in bed. It happened to be Nana's evening off, and Mrs. Darling had bathed them and sung to them till one by one they had let go her hand and slid away into the land of sleep.

All were looking so safe and cosy that she smiled at her fears now and sat down tranquilly by the fire to sew.

It was something for Michael, who on his birthday was getting into shirts. The fire was warm, however, and the nursery dimly lit by three night-lights, and presently the sewing lay on Mrs. Darling's lap. Then her head nodded, oh, so gracefully. She was asleep. Look at the four of them, Wendy and Michael over there, John here, and Mrs. Darling by the fire. There should have been a fourth night-light.

While she slept she had a dream. She dreamt that the Neverland had come too near and that a strange boy had broken through from it. He did not alarm her, for she thought she had seen him before in the faces of many women who have no children. Perhaps he is to be found in the faces of some mothers also. But in her dream he had rent the film that obscures the Neverland, and she saw Wendy and John and Michael peeping through the gap.

The dream by itself would have been a trifle, but while she was dreaming the window of the nursery blew open, and a boy did drop on the floor. He was accompanied by a strange light, no bigger than your fist, which darted about the room like a living thing and I think it must have been this light that wakened Mrs. Darling.

She started up with a cry, and saw the boy, and somehow she knew at once that he was Peter Pan. If you or I or Wendy had been there

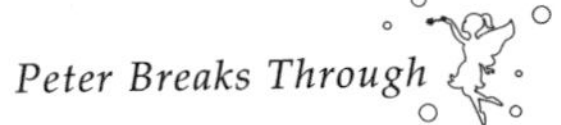

we should have seen that he was very like Mrs. Darling's kiss. He was a lovely boy, clad in skeleton leaves and the juices that ooze out of trees, but the most entrancing thing about him was that he had all his first teeth. When he saw she was a grown-up, he gnashed the little pearls at her.

Chapter 2

The Shadow

She returned to the nursery, and found Nana with something in her mouth, which proved to be the boy's shadow.

Mrs. Darling screamed, and, as if in answer to a bell, the door opened, and Nana entered, returned from her evening out. She growled and sprang at the boy, who leapt lightly through the window. Again Mrs. Darling screamed, this time in distress for him, for she thought he was killed, and she ran down into the street to look for his little body, but it was not there; and she looked up, and in the black night she could see nothing but what she thought was a shooting star.

She returned to the nursery, and found Nana with something in her mouth, which proved to be the boy's shadow. As he leapt at the window Nana had closed it quickly, too late to catch him, but his shadow had not had time to get out; slam went the window and snapped it off.

You may be sure Mrs. Darling examined the shadow carefully, but it was quite the ordinary kind.

Nana had no doubt of what was the best thing to do with this shadow. She hung it out at the window, meaning "He is sure to come back for it; let us put it where he can get it easily without disturbing the children."

But unfortunately Mrs. Darling could not leave it hanging out at the window, it looked so like the washing and lowered the whole tone of the house. She thought of showing it to Mr. Darling, but he was totting up winter great-coats for John and Michael, with a wet towel around his head to keep his brain clear, and it seemed a shame to trouble him; besides, she knew exactly what he would say: "It all comes of having a dog for a nurse."

She decided to roll the shadow up and put it away carefully in a drawer, until a fitting opportunity came for telling her husband. Ah me!

The opportunity came a week later, on that never-to-be-forgotten Friday. Of course it was a Friday.

"I ought to have been specially careful on a Friday," she used to say afterwards to her husband, while perhaps Nana was on the other side of her, holding her hand.

"No, no," Mr. Darling always said, "I am responsible for it all. I, George Darling, did it. Mea culpa, mea culpa." He had had a classical education.

They sat thus night after night recalling that fatal Friday, till every detail of it was stamped on their brains and came through on the other side like the faces on a bad coinage.

"If only I had not accepted that invitation to dine at 27," Mrs. Darling said.

"If only I had not poured my medicine into Nana's bowl," said Mr. Darling.

"If only I had pretended to like the medicine," was what Nana's wet eyes said.

"My liking for parties, George."

"My fatal gift of humour, dearest."

"My touchiness about trifles, dear master and mistress."

Then one or more of them would break down altogether; Nana at the thought, "It's true, it's true, they ought not to have had a dog for a nurse." Many a time it was Mr. Darling who put the handkerchief to Nana's eyes.

"That fiend!" Mr. Darling would cry, and Nana's bark was the echo of it, but Mrs. Darling never upbraided Peter; there was something in the right-hand corner of her mouth that wanted her not to call Peter names.

They would sit there in the empty nursery, recalling fondly every smallest detail of that dreadful evening. It had begun so uneventfully, so precisely like a hundred other evenings, with Nana putting on the water for Michael's bath and carrying him to it on her back.

"I won't go to bed," he had shouted, like one who still believed that he had the last word on the subject, "I won't, I won't. Nana, it isn't six o'clock yet. Oh dear, oh dear, I shan't love you any more, Nana. I tell you I won't be bathed, I won't, I won't!"

Then Mrs. Darling had come in, wearing her white evening-gown. She had dressed early because Wendy so loved to see her in her evening-gown, with the necklace George had given her. She was wearing Wendy's bracelet on her arm; she had asked for the loan of it. Wendy so loved to lend her bracelet to her mother.

She had found her two older children playing at being herself and

father on the occasion of Wendy's birth, and John was saying:

"I am happy to inform you, Mrs. Darling, that you are now a mother," in just such a tone as Mr. Darling himself may have used on the real occasion.

Wendy had danced with joy, just as the real Mrs. Darling must have done.

Then John was born, with the extra pomp that he conceived due to the birth of a male, and Michael came from his bath to ask to be born also, but John said brutally that they did not want any more.

Michael had nearly cried. "Nobody wants me," he said, and of course the lady in the evening-dress could not stand that.

"I do," she said, "I so want a third child."

"Boy or girl?" asked Michael, not too hopefully.

"Boy."

Then he had leapt into her arms. Such a little thing for Mr. and Mrs. Darling and Nana to recall now, but not so little if that was to be Michael's last night in the nursery.

They go on with their recollections.

"It was then that I rushed in like a tornado, wasn't it?" Mr. Darling would say, scorning himself; and indeed he had been like a tornado.

Perhaps there was some excuse for him. He, too, had been dressing for the party, and all had gone well with him until he came to his tie. It is an astounding thing to have to tell, but this man, though he knew about stocks and shares, had no real mastery of his tie. Sometimes the thing yielded to him without a contest, but there were occasions when it would have been better for the house if he had swallowed his pride and used a made-up tie.

This was such an occasion. He came rushing into the nursery with the crumpled little brute of a tie in his hand.

"Why, what is the matter, father dear?"

"Matter!" he yelled; he really yelled. "This tie, it will not tie." He became dangerously sarcastic. "Not round my neck! Round the bed-post! Oh yes, twenty times have I made it up round the bed-post, but round my neck, no! Oh dear no! begs to be excused!"

He thought Mrs. Darling was not sufficiently impressed, and he went on sternly, "I warn you of this, mother, that unless this tie is round my neck we don't go out to dinner to-night, and if I don't go out to dinner to-night, I never go to the office again, and if I don't go to the office again, you and I starve, and our children will be flung into the streets."

Even then Mrs. Darling was placid. "Let me try, dear," she said, and indeed that was what he had come to ask her to do, and with her nice cool hands she tied his tie for him, while the children stood around to see their fate decided. Some men would have resented her being able to do it so easily, but Mr. Darling had far too fine a nature for that; he

thanked her carelessly, at once forgot his rage, and in another moment was dancing round the room with Michael on his back.

"How wildly we romped!" says Mrs. Darling now, recalling it.

"Our last romp!" Mr. Darling groaned.

"O George, do you remember Michael suddenly said to me, `How did you get to know me, mother?'"

"I remember!"

"They were rather sweet, don't you think, George?"

"And they were ours, ours! and now they are gone."

The romp had ended with the appearance of Nana, and most unluckily Mr. Darling collided against her, covering his trousers with hairs. They were not only new trousers, but they were the first he had ever had with braid on them, and he had had to bite his lip to prevent the tears coming. Of course Mrs. Darling brushed him, but he began to talk again about its being a mistake to have a dog for a nurse.

"George, Nana is a treasure."

"No doubt, but I have an uneasy feeling at times that she looks upon the children as puppies."

"Oh no, dear one, I feel sure she knows they have souls."

"I wonder," Mr. Darling said thoughtfully, "I wonder." It was an opportunity, his wife felt, for telling him about the boy. At first he pooh-poohed the story, but he became thoughtful when she showed him the shadow.

"It is nobody I know," he said, examining it carefully, "but it does look a scoundrel."

"We were still discussing it, you remember," says Mr. Darling, "when Nana came in with Michael's medicine. You will never carry the bottle in your mouth again, Nana, and it is all my fault."

Strong man though he was, there is no doubt that he had behaved rather foolishly over the medicine. If he had a weakness, it was for thinking that all his life he had taken medicine boldly, and so now, when Michael dodged the spoon in Nana's mouth, he had said reprovingly, "Be a man, Michael."

"Won't; won't!" Michael cried naughtily. Mrs. Darling left the room to get a chocolate for him, and Mr. Darling thought this showed want of firmness.

"Mother, don't pamper him," he called after her. "Michael, when I was your age I took medicine without a murmur. I said, 'Thank you, kind parents, for giving me bottles to make we well.'"

He really thought this was true, and Wendy, who was now in her night-gown, believed it also, and she said, to encourage Michael, "That medicine you sometimes take, father, is much nastier, isn't it?"

"Ever so much nastier," Mr. Darling said bravely, "and I would take it now as an example to you, Michael, if I hadn't lost the bottle."

He had not exactly lost it; he had climbed in the dead of night to the top of the wardrobe and hidden it there. What he did not know was that the faithful Liza had found it, and put it back on his wash-stand.

"I know where it is, father," Wendy cried, always glad to be of service. "I'll bring it," and she was off before he could stop her. Immediately his spirits sank in the strangest way.

"John," he said, shuddering, "it's most beastly stuff. It's that nasty, sticky, sweet kind."

"It will soon be over, father," John said cheerily, and then in rushed Wendy with the medicine in a glass.

"I have been as quick as I could," she panted.

"You have been wonderfully quick," her father retorted, with a vindictive politeness that was quite thrown away upon her. "Michael first," he said doggedly.

"Father first," said Michael, who was of a suspicious nature.

"I shall be sick, you know," Mr. Darling said threateningly.

"Come on, father," said John.

"Hold your tongue, John," his father rapped out.

Wendy was quite puzzled. "I thought you took it quite easily, father."

"That is not the point," he retorted. "The point is, that there is more in my glass than in Michael's spoon." His proud heart was nearly bursting. "And it isn't fair; I would say it though it were with my last breath; it isn't fair."

"Father, I am waiting," said Michael coldly.

"It's all very well to say you are waiting; so am I waiting."

"Father's a cowardly custard."

"So are you a cowardly custard."

"I'm not frightened."

"Neither am I frightened."

"Well, then, take it."

"Well, then, you take it."

Wendy had a splendid idea. "Why not both take it at the same time?"

"Certainly," said Mr. Darling. "Are you ready, Michael?"

Wendy gave the words, one, two, three, and Michael took his medicine, but Mr. Darling slipped his behind his back.

There was a yell of rage from Michael, and "O father!" Wendy exclaimed.

"What do you mean by 'O father'?" Mr. Darling demanded. "Stop that row, Michael. I meant to take mine, but I – I missed it."

It was dreadful the way all the three were looking at him, just as if they did not admire him. "Look here, all of you," he said entreatingly, as soon as Nana had gone into the bathroom, "I have just thought of a splendid joke. I shall pour my medicine into Nana's bowl, and she will drink it, thinking it is milk!"

It was the colour of milk; but the children did not have their father's sense of humour, and they looked at him reproachfully as he poured the medicine into Nana's bowl. "What fun!" he said doubtfully, and they did not dare expose him when Mrs. Darling and Nana returned.

"Nana, good dog," he said, patting her, "I have put a little milk into your bowl, Nana."

Nana wagged her tail, ran to the medicine, and began lapping it. Then she gave Mr. Darling such a look, not an angry look: she showed him the great red tear that makes us so sorry for noble dogs, and crept into her kennel.

Mr. Darling was frightfully ashamed of himself, but he would not give in. In a horrid silence Mrs. Darling smelt the bowl. "O George," she said, "it's your medicine!"

"It was only a joke," he roared, while she comforted her boys, and Wendy hugged Nana. "Much good," he said bitterly, "my wearing myself to the bone trying to be funny in this house."

And still Wendy hugged Nana. "That's right," he shouted. "Coddle her! Nobody coddles me. Oh dear no! I am only the breadwinner, why should I be coddled – why, why, why!"

"George," Mrs. Darling entreated him, "not so loud; the servants will hear you." Somehow they had got into the way of calling Liza the servants.

"Let them!" he answered recklessly. "Bring in the whole world. But I refuse to allow that dog to lord it in my nursery for an hour longer."

The children wept, and Nana ran to him beseechingly, but he waved her back. He felt he was a strong man again. "In vain, in vain," he cried; "the proper place for you is the yard, and there you go to be tied up this instant."

"George, George," Mrs. Darling whispered, "remember what I told you about that boy."

Alas, he would not listen. He was determined to show who was master in that house, and when commands would not draw Nana from the kennel, he lured her out of it with honeyed words, and seizing her roughly, dragged her from the nursery. He was ashamed of himself, and yet he did it. It was all owing to his too affectionate

nature, which craved for admiration. When he had tied her up in the back-yard, the wretched father went and sat in the passage, with his knuckles to his eyes.

In the meantime Mrs. Darling had put the children to bed in unwonted silence and lit their night-lights. They could hear Nana barking, and John whimpered, "It is because he is chaining her up in the yard," but Wendy was wiser.

"That is not Nana's unhappy bark," she said, little guessing what was about to happen; "that is her bark when she smells danger."

Danger!

"Are you sure, Wendy?"

"Oh, yes."

Mrs. Darling quivered and went to the window. It was securely fastened. She looked out, and the night was peppered with stars. They were crowding round the house, as if curious to see what was to take place there, but she did not notice this, nor that one or two of the smaller ones winked at her. Yet a nameless fear clutched at her heart and made her cry, "Oh, how I wish that I wasn't going to a party to-night!"

Even Michael, already half asleep, knew that she was perturbed, and he asked, "Can anything harm us, mother, after the night- lights are lit?"

"Nothing, precious," she said; "they are the eyes a mother leaves behind her to guard her children."

She went from bed to bed singing enchantments over them, and little Michael flung his arms round her. "Mother," he cried, "I'm glad of you." They were the last words she was to hear from him for a long time.

No. 27 was only a few yards distant, but there had been a slight fall of snow, and Father and Mother Darling picked their way over it deftly not to soil their shoes. They were already the only persons in the street, and all the stars were watching them. Stars are beautiful, but they may not take an active part in anything, they must just look on for ever. It is a punishment put on them for something they did so long ago that no star now knows what it was. So the older ones have become glassy-eyed and seldom speak (*winking is the star language*), but the little ones still wonder. They are not really friendly to Peter, who had a mischievous way of stealing up behind them and trying to blow them out; but they are so fond of fun that they were on his side to-night, and anxious to get the grown-ups out of the way. So as soon as the door of 27 closed on Mr. and Mrs. Darling there was a commotion in the firmament, and the smallest of all the stars in the Milky Way screamed out:"Now, Peter!"

Chapter 3

Come Away, Come Away!

They were not nearly so elegant as Peter, they could not help kicking a little, but their heads were bobbing against the ceiling, and there is almost nothing so delicious as that.

For a moment after Mr. and Mrs. Darling left the house the night-lights by the beds of the three children continued to burn clearly. They were awfully nice little night-lights, and one cannot help wishing that they could have kept awake to see Peter; but Wendy's light blinked and gave such a yawn that the other two yawned also, and before they could close their mouths all the three went out.

There was another light in the room now, a thousand times brighter than the night-lights, and in the time we have taken to say this, it had been in all the drawers in the nursery, looking for Peter's shadow, rummaged the wardrobe and turned every pocket inside out. It was not really a light; it made this light by flashing about so quickly, but when it came to rest for a second you saw it was a fairy, no longer than your hand, but still growing. It was a girl called Tinker Bell exquisitely gowned in a skeleton leaf, cut low and square, through which her figure could be seen to the best advantage. She was slightly inclined to embonpoint. (*plump hourglass figure*)

A moment after the fairy's entrance the window was blown open by the breathing of the little stars, and Peter dropped in. He had carried Tinker Bell part of the way, and his hand was still messy with the fairy dust.

"Tinker Bell," he called softly, after making sure that the children were asleep, "Tink, where are you?" She was in a jug for the moment, and liking it extremely; she had never been in a jug before.

"Oh, do come out of that jug, and tell me, do you know where they put my shadow?"

The loveliest tinkle as of golden bells answered him. It is the fairy language. You ordinary children can never hear it, but if you were to hear it you would know that you had heard it once before.

Tink said that the shadow was in the big box. She meant the chest of drawers, and Peter jumped at the drawers, scattering their contents to the floor with both hands, as kings toss ha'pence to the crowd. In a moment he had recovered his shadow, and in his delight he forgot that he had shut Tinker Bell up in the drawer.

If he thought at all, but I don't believe he ever thought, it was that he and his shadow, when brought near each other, would join like drops of water, and when they did not he was appalled. He tried to stick it on with soap from the bathroom, but that also failed. A shudder passed through Peter, and he sat on the floor and cried.

His sobs woke Wendy, and she sat up in bed. She was not alarmed to see a stranger crying on the nursery floor; she was only pleasantly interested.

"Boy," she said courteously, "why are you crying?"

Peter could be exceeding polite also, having learned the grand manner at fairy ceremonies, and he rose and bowed to her beautifully. She was much pleased, and bowed beautifully to him from the bed.

"What's your name?" he asked.

"Wendy Moira Angela Darling," she replied with some satisfaction. "What is your name?"

"Peter Pan."

She was already sure that he must be Peter, but it did seem a comparatively short name.

"Is that all?"

"Yes," he said rather sharply. He felt for the first time that it was a shortish name.

"I'm so sorry," said Wendy Moira Angela.

"It doesn't matter," Peter gulped.

She asked where he lived.

"Second to the right," said Peter, "and then straight on till morning."

"What a funny address!"

Peter had a sinking. For the first time he felt that perhaps it was a funny address.

"No, it isn't," he said.

"I mean," Wendy said nicely, remembering that she was hostess, "is that what they put on the letters?"

He wished she had not mentioned letters.

"Don't get any letters," he said contemptuously.

"But your mother gets letters?"

"Don't have a mother," he said. Not only had he no mother, but he had not the slightest desire to have one. He thought them very over-rated persons. Wendy, however, felt at once that she was in the presence of a tragedy.

"O Peter, no wonder you were crying," she said, and got out of bed and ran to him.

"I wasn't crying about mothers," he said rather indignantly. "I was crying because I can't get my shadow to stick on. Besides, I wasn't crying."

"It has come off?"

"Yes."

Then Wendy saw the shadow on the floor, looking so draggled, and she was frightfully sorry for Peter. "How awful!" she said, but she could not help smiling when she saw that he had been trying to stick it on with soap. How exactly like a boy!

Fortunately she knew at once what to do. "It must be sewn on," she said, just a little patronisingly.

"What's sewn?" he asked.

"You're dreadfully ignorant."

"No, I'm not."

But she was exulting in his ignorance. "I shall sew it on for you, my little man," she said, though he was tall as herself, and she got out her housewife (*sewing bag*), and sewed the shadow on to Peter's foot.

"I daresay it will hurt a little," she warned him.

"Oh, I shan't cry," said Peter, who was already of the opinion that he had never cried in his life. And he clenched his teeth and did not cry, and soon his shadow was behaving properly, though still a little creased.

"Perhaps I should have ironed it," Wendy said thoughtfully, but Peter, boylike, was indifferent to appearances, and he was now jumping about in the wildest glee. Alas, he had already forgotten that he owed his bliss to Wendy. He thought he had attached the shadow himself. "How clever I am!" he crowed rapturously, "oh, the cleverness of me!"

It is humiliating to have to confess that this conceit of Peter was one of his most fascinating qualities. To put it with brutal frankness, there never was a cockier boy.

But for the moment Wendy was shocked. "You conceit (*braggart*)," she exclaimed, with frightful sarcasm; "of course I did nothing!"

"You did a little," Peter said carelessly, and continued to dance.

"A little!" she replied with hauteur (*pride*). "if I am no use I can at least withdraw," and she sprang in the most dignified way into bed and covered her face with the blankets.

To induce her to look up he pretended to be going away, and when this failed he sat on the end of the bed and tapped her gently with his foot. "Wendy," he said, "don't withdraw. I can't help crowing, Wendy, when I'm pleased with myself." Still she would not look up, though she was listening eagerly. "Wendy," he continued, in a voice that no woman has ever yet been able to resist, "Wendy, one girl is more use than twenty boys."

Now Wendy was every inch a woman, though there were not very many inches, and she peeped out of the bed-clothes.

"Do you really think so, Peter?"

"Yes, I do."

"I think it's perfectly sweet of you," she declared, "and I'll get up again," and she sat with him on the side of the bed. She also said she would give him a kiss if he liked, but Peter did not know what she meant, and he held out his hand expectantly.

"Surely you know what a kiss is?" she asked, aghast.

"I shall know when you give it to me," he replied stiffly, and not to hurt his feeling she gave him a thimble.

"Now," said he, "shall I give you a kiss?" and she replied with a slight primness, "If you please." She made herself rather cheap by inclining her face toward him, but he merely dropped an acorn button into her hand, so she slowly returned her face to where it had been before, and said nicely that she would wear his kiss on the chain around her neck. It was lucky that she did put it on that chain, for it was afterwards to save her life.

When people in our set are introduced, it is customary for them to ask each other's age, and so Wendy, who always liked to do the correct thing, asked Peter how old he was. It was not really a happy question to ask him; it was like an examination paper that asks grammar, when what you want to be asked is Kings of England.

"I don't know," he replied uneasily, "but I am quite young." He really knew nothing about it, he had merely suspicions, but he said at a venture, "Wendy, I ran away the day I was born."

Wendy was quite surprised, but interested; and she indicated in the charming drawing-room manner, by a touch on her night-gown, that he could sit nearer her.

"It was because I heard father and mother," he explained in a low voice, "talking about what I was to be when I became a man." He was extraordinarily agitated now. "I don't want ever to be a man," he said with passion. "I want always to be a little boy and to have fun. So I ran away to Kensington Gardens and lived a long long time among the fairies."

She gave him a look of the most intense admiration, and he thought it was because he had run away, but it was really because he knew fairies. Wendy had lived such a home life that to know fairies struck her as quite delightful. She poured out questions about them, to his surprise, for they were rather a nuisance to him, getting in his way and so on, and indeed he sometimes had to give them a hiding (*spanking*). Still, he liked them on the whole, and he told her about the beginning of fairies.

"You see, Wendy, when the first baby laughed for the first time, its laugh broke into a thousand pieces, and they all went skipping about, and that was the beginning of fairies."

Tedious talk this, but being a stay-at-home she liked it.

"And so," he went on good-naturedly, "there ought to be one fairy for every boy and girl."

"Ought to be? Isn't there?"

"No. You see children know such a lot now, they soon don't believe in fairies, and every time a child says, 'I don't believe in fairies,' there is a fairy somewhere that falls down dead."

Really, he thought they had now talked enough about fairies, and it struck him that Tinker Bell was keeping very quiet. "I can't think where she has gone to," he said, rising, and he called Tink by name. Wendy's heart went flutter with a sudden thrill.

"Peter," she cried, clutching him, "you don't mean to tell me that there is a fairy in this room!"

"She was here just now," he said a little impatiently. "You don't hear her, do you?" and they both listened.

"The only sound I hear," said Wendy, "is like a tinkle of bells."

"Well, that's Tink, that's the fairy language. I think I hear her too."

The sound come from the chest of drawers, and Peter made a merry face. No one could ever look quite so merry as Peter, and the loveliest of gurgles was his laugh. He had his first laugh still.

"Wendy," he whispered gleefully, "I do believe I shut her up in the drawer!"

He let poor Tink out of the drawer, and she flew about the nursery screaming with fury. "You shouldn't say such things," Peter retorted. "Of course I'm very sorry, but how could I know you were in the drawer?"

Wendy was not listening to him. "O Peter," she cried, "if she would only stand still and let me see her!"

"They hardly ever stand still," he said, but for one moment Wendy saw the romantic figure come to rest on the cuckoo clock. "O the lovely!" she cried, though Tink's face was still distorted with passion.

"Tink," said Peter amiably, "this lady says she wishes you were her fairy."

Tinker Bell answered insolently.

"What does she say, Peter?"

He had to translate. "She is not very polite. She says you are a great ugly girl, and that she is my fairy."

He tried to argue with Tink. "You know you can't be my fairy, Tink, because I am an gentleman and you are a lady."

To this Tink replied in these words, "You silly ass," and disappeared into the bathroom. "She is quite a common fairy," Peter explained apologetically, "she is called Tinker Bell because she mends the pots and kettles

They were together in the armchair by this time, and Wendy plied him with more questions.

"If you don't live in Kensington Gardens now – "

"Sometimes I do still."

"But where do you live mostly now?"

"With the lost boys."

"Who are they?"

"They are the children who fall out of their perambulators when the nurse is looking the other way. If they are not claimed in seven days they are sent far away to the Neverland to defray expenses. I'm captain."

"What fun it must be!"

"Yes," said cunning Peter, "but we are rather lonely. You see we have no female companionship."

"Are none of the others girls?"

"Oh, no; girls, you know, are much too clever to fall out of their prams."

This flattered Wendy immensely. "I think," she said, "it is perfectly lovely the way you talk about girls; John there just despises us."

For reply Peter rose and kicked John out of bed, blankets and all; one kick. This seemed to Wendy rather forward for a first meeting, and she told him with spirit that he was not captain in her house. However, John continued to sleep so placidly on the floor that she allowed him to remain there. "And I know you meant to be kind," she said, relenting, "so you may give me a kiss."

For the moment she had forgotten his ignorance about kisses. "I thought you would want it back," he said a little bitterly, and offered to return her the thimble.

"Oh dear," said the nice Wendy, "I don't mean a kiss, I mean a thimble."

"What's that?"

"It's like this." She kissed him.

"Funny!" said Peter gravely. "Now shall I give you a thimble?"

"If you wish to," said Wendy, keeping her head erect this time.

Peter thimbled her, and almost immediately she screeched. "What is it, Wendy?"

"It was exactly as if someone were pulling my hair."

"That must have been Tink. I never knew her so naughty before."

And indeed Tink was darting about again, using offensive language.

"She says she will do that to you, Wendy, every time I give you a thimble."

"But why?"

"Why, Tink?"

Again Tink replied, "You silly ass." Peter could not understand why, but Wendy understood, and she was just slightly disappointed when he admitted that he came to the nursery window not to see her but to listen to stories.

"You see, I don't know any stories. None of the lost boys knows any stories."

"How perfectly awful," Wendy said.

"Do you know," Peter asked "why swallows build in the eaves of houses? It is to listen to the stories. O Wendy, your mother was telling you such a lovely story."

"Which story was it?"

"About the prince who couldn't find the lady who wore the glass slipper."

"Peter," said Wendy excitedly, "that was Cinderella, and he found her, and they lived happily ever after."

Peter was so glad that he rose from the floor, where they had been sitting, and hurried to the window.

"Where are you going?" she cried with misgiving.

"To tell the other boys."

"Don't go, Peter," she entreated, "I know such lots of stories."

Those were her precise words, so there can be no denying that it was she who first tempted him.

He came back, and there was a greedy look in his eyes now which ought to have alarmed her, but did not.

"Oh, the stories I could tell to the boys!" she cried, and then Peter gripped her and began to draw her toward the window.

"Let me go!" she ordered him.

"Wendy, do come with me and tell the other boys."

Of course she was very pleased to be asked, but she said, "Oh dear, I can't. Think of mummy! Besides, I can't fly."

"I'll teach you."

"Oh, how lovely to fly."

"I'll teach you how to jump on the wind's back, and then away we go."

"Oo!" she exclaimed rapturously.

"Wendy, Wendy, when you are sleeping in your silly bed you might be flying about with me saying funny things to the stars."

"Oo!"

"And, Wendy, there are mermaids."

"Mermaids! With tails?"

"Such long tails."

"Oh," cried Wendy, "to see a mermaid!"

He had become frightfully cunning. "Wendy," he said, "how we should all respect you."

She was wriggling her body in distress. It was quite as if she were trying to remain on the nursery floor.

But he had no pity for her.

"Wendy," he said, the sly one, "you could tuck us in at night."

"Oo!"

"None of us has ever been tucked in at night."

"Oo," and her arms went out to him.

"And you could darn our clothes, and make pockets for us. None of us has any pockets."

How could she resist. "Of course it's awfully fascinating!" she cried. "Peter, would you teach John and Michael to fly too?"

"If you like," he said indifferently, and she ran to John and Michael and shook them. "Wake up," she cried, "Peter Pan has come and he is to teach us to fly."

John rubbed his eyes. "Then I shall get up," he said. Of course he was on the floor already. "Hallo," he said, "I am up!"

Michael was up by this time also, looking as sharp as a knife with six blades and a saw, but Peter suddenly signed silence. Their faces assumed the awful craftiness of children listening for sounds from the grown-up world. All was as still as salt. Then everything was right. No, stop! Everything was wrong. Nana, who had been barking distressfully all the evening, was quiet now. It was her silence they had heard!

"Out with the light! Hide! Quick!" cried John, taking command for the only time throughout the whole adventure. And thus when Liza entered, holding Nana, the nursery seemed quite its old self, very dark, and you would have sworn you heard its three wicked inmates breathing angelically as they slept. They were really doing it artfully from behind the window curtains.

Liza was in a bad temper, for she was mixing the Christmas puddings in the kitchen, and had been drawn from them, with a raisin still on her cheek, by Nana's absurd suspicions. She thought the best way of getting a little quiet was to take Nana to the nursery for a moment, but in custody of course.

"There, you suspicious brute," she said, not sorry that Nana was in disgrace. "They are perfectly safe, aren't they? Every one of the little angels sound asleep in bed. Listen to their gentle breathing."

Here Michael, encouraged by his success, breathed so loudly that they were nearly detected. Nana knew that kind of breathing, and she tried to drag herself out of Liza's clutches.

But Liza was dense. "No more of it, Nana," she said sternly, pulling her out of the room. "I warn you if bark again I shall go straight for master and missus and bring them home from the party, and then, oh, won't master whip you, just."

She tied the unhappy dog up again, but do you think Nana ceased to bark? Bring master and missus home from the party? Why, that was just what she wanted. Do you think she cared whether she was whipped so long as her charges were safe? Unfortunately Liza returned to her puddings, and Nana, seeing that no help would come from her, strained and strained at the chain until at last she broke it. In another moment she had burst into the dining-room of 27 and flung up her paws to heaven, her most expressive way of making a communication. Mr. and Mrs. Darling knew at once that something terrible was happening in their nursery, and without a good-bye to their hostess they rushed into the street.

But it was now ten minutes since three scoundrels had been breathing behind the curtains, and Peter Pan can do a great deal in ten minutes.

We now return to the nursery.

"It's all right," John announced, emerging from his hiding-place. "I say, Peter, can you really fly?"

Instead of troubling to answer him Peter flew around the room, taking the mantelpiece on the way.

"How topping!" said John and Michael.

"How sweet!" cried Wendy.

"Yes, I'm sweet, oh, I am sweet!" said Peter, forgetting his manners again.

It looked delightfully easy, and they tried it first from the floor and then from the beds, but they always went down instead of up.

"I say, how do you do it?" asked John, rubbing his knee. He was quite a practical boy.

"You just think lovely wonderful thoughts," Peter explained, "and they lift you up in the air."

He showed them again.

"You're so nippy at it," John said, "couldn't you do it very slowly once?"

Peter did it both slowly and quickly. "I've got it now, Wendy!" cried John, but soon he found he had not. Not one of them could fly an inch, though even Michael was in words of two syllables, and Peter did not know A from Z.

Of course Peter had been trifling with them, for no one can fly unless the fairy dust has been blown on him. Fortunately, as we have mentioned, one of his hands was messy with it, and he blew some on each of them, with the most superb results.

"Now just wiggle your shoulders this way," he said, "and let go."

They were all on their beds, and gallant Michael let go first. He did not quite mean to let go, but he did it, and immediately he was borne across the room.

"I flewed!" he screamed while still in mid-air.

John let go and met Wendy near the bathroom.

"Oh, lovely!"

"Oh, ripping!"

"Look at me!"

"Look at me!"

"Look at me!"

They were not nearly so elegant as Peter, they could not help kicking a little, but their heads were bobbing against the ceiling, and there is almost nothing so delicious as that. Peter gave Wendy a hand at first, but had to desist, Tink was so indignant.

Up and down they went, and round and round. Heavenly was Wendy's word.

"I say," cried John, "why shouldn't we all go out!"

Of course it was to this that Peter had been luring them.

Michael was ready: he wanted to see how long it took him to do a billion miles. But Wendy hesitated.

"Mermaids!" said Peter again.

"Oo!"

"And there are pirates."

"Pirates," cried John, seizing his Sunday hat, "let us go at once!"

It was just at this moment that Mr. and Mrs. Darling hurried with Nana out of 27. They ran into the middle of the street to look up at the nursery window; and, yes, it was still shut, but the room was ablaze with light, and most heart-gripping sight of all, they could see in shadow on the curtain three little figures in night attire circling round and round, not on the floor but in the air.

Not three figures, four!

In a tremble they opened the street door. Mr. Darling would have rushed upstairs, but Mrs. Darling signed him to go softly. She even tried to make her heart go softly.

Will they reach the nursery in time? If so, how delightful for them, and we shall all breathe a sigh of relief, but there will be no story. On the other hand, if they are not in time, I solemnly promise that it will all come right in the end.

They would have reached the nursery in time had it not been that the little stars were watching them. Once again the stars blew the window open, and that smallest star of all called out:

"Cave, Peter!"

Then Peter knew that there was not a moment to lose. "Come," he cried imperiously, and soared out at once into the night, followed by John and Michael and Wendy.

Mr. and Mrs. Darling and Nana rushed into the nursery too late. The birds were flown.

Chapter 4

The Flight

So with occasional tiffs, but on the whole rollicking, they drew near the Neverland.

"Second to the right, and straight on till morning."

That, Peter had told Wendy, was the way to the Neverland; but even birds, carrying maps and consulting them at windy corners, could not have sighted it with these instructions. Peter, you see, just said anything that came into his head.

At first his companions trusted him implicitly, and so great were the delights of flying that they wasted time circling round church spires or any other tall objects on the way that took their fancy.

John and Michael raced, Michael getting a start.

They recalled with contempt that not so long ago they had thought themselves fine fellows for being able to fly round a room.

Not long ago. But how long ago? They were flying over the sea before this thought began to disturb Wendy seriously. John thought it was their second sea and their third night.

Sometimes it was dark and sometimes light, and now they were very cold and again too warm. Did they really feel hungry at times, or were they merely pretending, because Peter had such a jolly new way of feeding them? His way was to pursue birds who had food in their mouths suitable for humans and snatch it from them; then the birds would follow and snatch it back; and they would all go chasing each other gaily for miles, parting at last with mutual expressions of good-will. But Wendy noticed with gentle concern that Peter did not seem to

know that this was rather an odd way of getting your bread and butter, nor even that there are other ways.

Certainly they did not pretend to be sleepy, they were sleepy; and that was a danger, for the moment they popped off, down they fell. The awful thing was that Peter thought this funny.

"There he goes again!" he would cry gleefully, as Michael suddenly dropped like a stone.

"Save him, save him!" cried Wendy, looking with horror at the cruel sea far below. Eventually Peter would dive through the air, and catch Michael just before he could strike the sea, and it was lovely the way he did it; but he always waited till the last moment, and you felt it was his cleverness that interested him and not the saving of human life. Also he was fond of variety, and the sport that engrossed him one moment would suddenly cease to engage him, so there was always the possibility that the next time you fell he would let you go.

He could sleep in the air without falling, by merely lying on his back and floating, but this was, partly at least, because he was so light that if you got behind him and blew he went faster.

"Do be more polite to him," Wendy whispered to John, when they were playing "Follow my Leader."

"Then tell him to stop showing off," said John.

When playing Follow my Leader, Peter would fly close to the water and touch each shark's tail in passing, just as in the street you may run your finger along an iron railing. They could not follow him in this with much success, so perhaps it was rather like showing off, especially as he kept looking behind to see how many tails they missed.

"You must be nice to him," Wendy impressed on her brothers. "What could we do if he were to leave us!"

"We could go back," Michael said.

"How could we ever find our way back without him?"

"Well, then, we could go on," said John.

"That is the awful thing, John. We should have to go on, for we don't know how to stop."

This was true, Peter had forgotten to show them how to stop.

John said that if the worst came to the worst, all they had to do was to go straight on, for the world was round, and so in time they must come back to their own window.

"And who is to get food for us, John?"

"I nipped a bit out of that eagle's mouth pretty neatly, Wendy."

"After the twentieth try," Wendy reminded him. "And even though we became good a picking up food, see how we bump against clouds and things if he is not near to give us a hand."

Indeed they were constantly bumping. They could now fly strongly, though they still kicked far too much; but if they saw a cloud in front of them, the more they tried to avoid it, the more certainly did they bump into it. If Nana had been with them, she would have had a bandage round Michael's forehead by this time.

Peter was not with them for the moment, and they felt rather lonely up there by themselves. He could go so much faster than they that he would suddenly shoot out of sight, to have some adventure in which they had no share. He would come down laughing over something fearfully funny he had been saying to a star, but he had already forgotten what it was, or he would come up with mermaid scales still sticking to him, and yet not be able to say for certain what had been happening. It was really rather irritating to children who had never seen a mermaid.

"And if he forgets them so quickly," Wendy argued, "how can we expect that he will go on remembering us?"

Indeed, sometimes when he returned he did not remember them, at least not well. Wendy was sure of it. She saw recognition come into his eyes as he was about to pass them the time of day and go on; once even she had to call him by name.

"I'm Wendy," she said agitatedly.

He was very sorry. "I say, Wendy," he whispered to her, "always if you see me forgetting you, just keep on saying 'I'm Wendy,' and then I'll remember."

Of course this was rather unsatisfactory. However, to make amends he showed them how to lie out flat on a strong wind that was going their way, and this was such a pleasant change that they tried it several times and found that they could sleep thus with security. Indeed they would have slept longer, but Peter tired quickly of sleeping, and soon he would cry in his captain voice, "We get off here." So with occasional tiffs, but on the whole rollicking, they drew near the Neverland; for after many moons they did reach it, and, what is more, they had been going pretty straight all the time, not perhaps so much owing to the guidance of Peter or Tink as because the island was looking for them. It is only thus that any one may sight those magic shores.

"There it is," said Peter calmly.

"Where, where?"

"Where all the arrows are pointing."

Indeed a million golden arrows were pointing it out to the children, all directed by their friend the sun, who wanted them to be sure of their way before leaving them for the night.

Wendy and John and Michael stood on tip-toe in the air to get their first sight of the island. Strange to say, they all recognized it at once, and until fear fell upon them they hailed it, not as something long dreamt of and seen at last, but as a familiar friend to whom they were returning home for the holidays.

"John, there's the lagoon!"

"Wendy, look at the turtles burying their eggs in the sand."

"I say, John, I see your flamingo with the broken leg!"

"Look, Michael, there's your cave!"

"John, what's that in the brushwood?"

"It's a wolf with her whelps. Wendy, I do believe that's your little whelp!"

"There's my boat, John, with her sides stove in!"

"No, it isn't. Why, we burned your boat."

"That's her, at any rate. I say, John, I see the smoke of the redskin camp!"

"Where? Show me, and I'll tell you by the way smoke curls whether they are on the war-path."

"There, just across the Mysterious River."

"I see now. Yes, they are on the war-path right enough."

Peter was a little annoyed with them for knowing so much, but if he wanted to lord it over them his triumph was at hand, for have I not told you that anon fear fell upon them?

It came as the arrows went, leaving the island in gloom.

In the old days at home the Neverland had always begun to look a little dark and threatening by bedtime. Then unexplored patches arose in it and spread, black shadows moved about in them, the roar of the beasts of prey was quite different now, and above all, you lost the certainty that you would win. You were quite glad that the night-lights were on. You even liked Nana to say that this was just the mantelpiece over here, and that the Neverland was all make-believe.

Of course the Neverland had been make-believe in those days, but it was real now, and there were no night-lights, and it was getting darker every moment, and where was Nana?

They had been flying apart, but they huddled close to Peter now. His careless manner had gone at last, his eyes were sparkling, and a tingle went through them every time they touched his body. They were now over the fearsome island, flying so low that sometimes a tree grazed their feet. Nothing horrid was visible in the air, yet their progress had become slow and laboured, exactly as if they were pushing their way through hostile forces. Sometimes they hung in the air until Peter had beaten on it with his fists.

"They don't want us to land," he explained.

"Who are they?" Wendy whispered, shuddering.

But he could not or would not say. Tinker Bell had been asleep on his shoulder, but now he wakened her and sent her on in front.

Sometimes he poised himself in the air, listening intently, with his

hand to his ear, and again he would stare down with eyes so bright that they seemed to bore two holes to earth. Having done these things, he went on again.

His courage was almost appalling. "Would you like an adventure now," he said casually to John, "or would you like to have your tea first?"

Wendy said "tea first" quickly, and Michael pressed her hand in gratitude, but the braver John hesitated.

"What kind of adventure?" he asked cautiously.

"There's a pirate asleep in the pampas just beneath us," Peter told him. "If you like, we'll go down and kill him."

"I don't see him," John said after a long pause.

"I do."

"Suppose," John said, a little huskily, "he were to wake up."

Peter spoke indignantly. "You don't think I would kill him while he was sleeping! I would wake him first, and then kill him. That's the way I always do."

"I say! Do you kill many?"

"Tons."

John said "How ripping," but decided to have tea first. He asked if there were many pirates on the island just now, and Peter said he had never known so many.

"Who is captain now?"

"Hook," answered Peter, and his face became very stern as he said that hated word.

"Jas. Hook?"

"Ay."

Then indeed Michael began to cry, and even John could speak in gulps only, for they knew Hook's reputation.

"He was Blackbeard's bo'sun," John whispered huskily. "He is the worst of them all. He is the only man of whom Barbecue was afraid."

"That's him," said Peter.

"What is he like? Is he big?"

"He is not so big as he was."

"How do you mean?"

"I cut off a bit of him."

"You!"

"Yes, me," said Peter sharply.

"I wasn't meaning to be disrespectful."

"Oh, all right."

"But, I say, what bit?"

"His right hand."

"Then he can't fight now?"

"Oh, can't he just!"

"Left-hander?"

"He has an iron hook instead of a right hand, and he claws with it."

"Claws!"

"I say, John," said Peter.

"Yes."

"Say, 'Ay, ay, sir.'"

"Ay, ay, sir."

"There is one thing," Peter continued, "that every boy who serves under me has to promise, and so must you."

John paled.

"It is this, if we meet Hook in open fight, you must leave him to me."

"I promise," John said loyally.

For the moment they were feeling less eerie, because Tink was flying with them, and in her light they could distinguish each other. Unfortunately she could not fly so slowly as they, and so she had to go round and round them in a circle in which they moved as in a halo. Wendy quite liked it, until Peter pointed out the drawbacks.

"She tells me," he said, "that the pirates sighted us before the darkness came, and got Long Tom out."

"The big gun?"

"Yes. And of course they must see her light, and if they guess we are near it they are sure to let fly."

"Wendy!"

"John!"

"Michael!"

"Tell her to go away at once, Peter," the three cried simultaneously, but he refused.

"She thinks we have lost the way," he replied stiffly, "and she is rather frightened. You don't think I would send her away all by herself when she is frightened!"

For a moment the circle of light was broken, and something gave Peter a loving little pinch.

"Then tell her," Wendy begged, "to put out her light."

"She can't put it out. That is about the only thing fairies can't do. It just goes out of itself when she falls asleep, same as the stars."

"Then tell her to sleep at once," John almost ordered.

"She can't sleep except when she's sleepy. It is the only other thing fairies can't do."

"Seems to me," growled John, "these are the only two things worth doing."

Here he got a pinch, but not a loving one.

"If only one of us had a pocket," Peter said, "we could carry her in it." However, they had set off in such a hurry that there was not a pocket between the four of them.

He had a happy idea. John's hat!

Tink agreed to travel by hat if it was carried in the hand. John carried it, though she had hoped to be carried by Peter. Presently Wendy took the hat, because John said it struck against his knee as he flew; and this, as we shall see, led to mischief, for Tinker Bell hated to be under an obligation to Wendy.

In the black topper the light was completely hidden, and they flew on in silence. It was the stillest silence they had ever known, broken once by a distant lapping, which Peter explained was the wild beasts drinking at the ford, and again by a rasping sound that might have been the branches of trees rubbing together, but he said it was the redskins sharpening their knives.

Even these noises ceased. To Michael the loneliness was dreadful. "If only something would make a sound!" he cried.

As if in answer to his request, the air was rent by the most tremendous crash he had ever heard. The pirates had fired Long Tom at them.

The roar of it echoed through the mountains, and the echoes seemed to cry savagely, "Where are they, where are they, where are they?"

Thus sharply did the terrified three learn the difference between an island of make-believe and the same island come true.

When at last the heavens were steady again, John and Michael found themselves alone in the darkness. John was treading the air mechanically, and Michael without knowing how to float was floating.

"Are you shot?" John whispered tremulously.

"I haven't tried (*myself out*) yet," Michael whispered back.

We know now that no one had been hit. Peter, however, had been

carried by the wind of the shot far out to sea, while Wendy was blown upwards with no companion but Tinker Bell.

It would have been well for Wendy if at that moment she had dropped the hat.

I don't know whether the idea came suddenly to Tink, or whether she had planned it on the way, but she at once popped out of the hat and began to lure Wendy to her destruction.

Tink was not all bad; or, rather, she was all bad just now, but, on the other hand, sometimes she was all good. Fairies have to be one thing or the other, because being so small they unfortunately have room for one feeling only at a time. They are, however, allowed to change, only it must be a complete change. At present she was full of jealousy of Wendy. What she said in her lovely tinkle Wendy could not of course understand, and I believe some of it was bad words, but it sounded kind, and she flew back and forward, plainly meaning "Follow me, and all will be well."

What else could poor Wendy do? She called to Peter and John and Michael, and got only mocking echoes in reply. She did not yet know that Tink hated her with the fierce hatred of a very woman. And so, bewildered, and now staggering in her flight, she followed Tink to her doo.

Chapter 5

The Island Come True

All are keeping a sharp look-out in front, but none suspects that the danger may be creeping up from behind. This shows how real the island was.

Feeling that Peter was on his way back, the Neverland had again woke into life. We ought to use the pluperfect and say wakened, but woke is better and was always used by Peter.

In his absence things are usually quiet on the island. The fairies take an hour longer in the morning, the beasts attend to their young, the redskins feed heavily for six days and nights, and when pirates and lost boys meet they merely bite their thumbs at each other. But with the coming of Peter, who hates lethargy, they are under way again: if you put your ear to the ground now, you would hear the whole island seething with life.

On this evening the chief forces of the island were disposed as follows. The lost boys were out looking for Peter, the pirates were out looking for the lost boys, the redskins were out looking for the pirates, and the beasts were out looking for the redskins. They were going round and round the island, but they did not meet because all were going at the same rate.

All wanted blood except the boys, who liked it as a rule, but to-night were out to greet their captain. The boys on the island vary, of course, in numbers, according as they get killed and so on; and when they seem to be growing up, which is against the rules, Peter thins them out; but at this time there were six of them, counting the twins as two. Let us pretend to lie here among the sugar-cane and watch them as they steal by in single file, each with his hand on his dagger.

They are forbidden by Peter to look in the least like him, and they wear the skins of the bears slain by themselves, in which they are so round and furry that when they fall they roll. They have therefore become very sure-footed.

The first to pass is Tootles, not the least brave but the most unfortunate of all that gallant band. He had been in fewer adventures than any of them, because the big things constantly happened just when he had stepped round the corner; all would be quiet, he would take the opportunity of going off to gather a few sticks for firewood, and then when he returned the others would be sweeping up the blood. This ill-luck had given a gentle melancholy to his countenance, but instead of souring his nature had sweetened it, so that he was quite the humblest of the boys. Poor kind Tootles, there is danger in the air for you to-night. Take care lest an adventure is now offered you, which, if accepted, will plunge you in deepest woe. Tootles, the fairy Tink, who is bent on mischief this night is looking for a tool (*for doing her mischief*), and she thinks you are the most easily tricked of the boys. 'Ware Tinker Bell'

Would that he could hear us, but we are not really on the island, and he passes by, biting his knuckles.

Next comes Nibs, the gay and debonair, followed by Slightly, who cuts whistles out of the trees and dances ecstatically to his own tunes. Slightly is the most conceited of the boys. He thinks he remembers the days before he was lost, with their manners and customs, and this has given his nose an offensive tilt. Curly is fourth; he is a pickle, (*a person who gets in pickles-predicaments*) and so often has he had to deliver up his person when Peter said sternly, "Stand forth the one who did this thing," that now at the command he stands forth automatically whether he has done it or not. Last come the Twins, who cannot be described because we should be sure to be describing the wrong one. Peter never quite knew what twins were, and his band were not allowed to know anything he did not know, so these two were always vague about themselves, and did their best to give satisfaction by keeping close together in an apologetic sort of way.

The boys vanish in the gloom, and after a pause, but not a long pause, for things go briskly on the island, come the pirates on their track. We hear them before they are seen, and it is always the same dreadful song:

"Avast belay, yo ho, heave to,
A-pirating we go,
And if we're parted by a shot
We're sure to meet below!"

A more villainous-looking lot never hung in a row on Execution dock. Here, a little in advance, ever and again with his head to the ground listening, his great arms bare, pieces of eight in his ears as ornaments, is the handsome Italian Cecco, who cut his name in letters of blood on the back of the governor of the prison at Gao. That gigantic black behind him has had many names since he dropped the one with which dusky mothers still terrify their children on the banks of the Guadjo-mo. Here is Bill Jukes, every inch of him tattooed, the same Bill Jukes who got six dozen on the walrus from Flint before he would drop the bag of moidores (*Portuguese gold pieces*); and Cookson, said to be Black Murphy's brother (*but this was never proved*), and Gentleman Starkey, once an usher in a public school and still dainty in his ways of killing; and Skylights (*Morgan's Skylights*); and the Irish bo'sun Smee, an oddly genial man who stabbed, so to speak, without offence, and was the only Non-conformist in Hook's crew; and Noodler, whose hands were fixed on backwards; and Robt. Mullins and Alf Mason and many another ruffian long known and feared on the Spanish Main.

In the midst of them, the blackest and largest in that dark setting, reclined James Hook, or as he wrote himself, Jas. Hook, of whom it is said he was the only man that the Sea-Cook feared. He lay at his ease in a rough chariot drawn and propelled by his men, and instead of a right hand he had the iron hook with which ever and anon he encouraged them to increase their pace. As dogs this terrible man treated and addressed them, and as dogs they obeyed him. In person he was cadaverous (*dead looking*) and blackavized (*dark faced*), and his hair was dressed in long curls, which at a little distance looked like black candles, and gave a singularly threatening expression to his handsome countenance. His eyes were of the blue of the forget-me-not, and of a profound melancholy, save when he was plunging his hook into you, at which time two red spots appeared in them and lit them up horribly. In manner, something of the grand seigneur still clung to him, so that he even ripped you up with an air, and I have been told that he was a raconteur (*storyteller*) of repute. He was never more sinister than when he was most polite, which is probably the truest test of breeding;

and the elegance of his diction, even when he was swearing, no less than the distinction of his demeanour, showed him one of a different cast from his crew. A man of indomitable courage, it was said that the only thing he shied at was the sight of his own blood, which was thick and of an unusual colour. In dress he somewhat aped the attire associated with the name of Charles II, having heard it said in some earlier period of his career that he bore a strange resemblance to the ill-fated Stuarts; and in his mouth he had a holder of his own contrivance which enabled him to smoke two cigars at once. But undoubtedly the grimmest part of him was his iron claw.

Let us now kill a pirate, to show Hook's method. Skylights will do. As they pass, Skylights lurches clumsily against him, ruffling his lace collar; the hook shoots forth, there is a tearing sound and one screech, then the body is kicked aside, and the pirates pass on. He has not even taken the cigars from his mouth.

Such is the terrible man against whom Peter Pan is pitted. Which will win?

On the trail of the pirates, stealing noiselessly down the war-path, which is not visible to inexperienced eyes, come the redskins, every one of them with his eyes peeled. They carry tomahawks and knives, and their naked bodies gleam with paint and oil. Strung around them are scalps, of boys as well as of pirates, for these are the Piccaninny tribe, and not to be confused with the softer-hearted Delawares or the Hurons. In the van, on all fours, is Great Big Little Panther, a brave of so many scalps that in his present position they somewhat impede his progress. Bringing up the rear, the place of greatest danger, comes Tiger Lily, proudly erect, a princess in her own right. She is the most beautiful of dusky Dianas (*Diana = goddess of the woods*) and the belle of the Piccaninnies, coquettish (*flirting*), cold and amorous (*loving*) by turns; there is not a brave who would not have the wayward thing to wife, but she staves off the altar with a hatchet. Observe how they pass over fallen twigs without making the slightest noise. The only sound to be heard is their somewhat heavy breathing. The fact is that they are all a little fat just now after the heavy gorging, but in time they will work this off. For the moment, however, it constitutes their chief danger.

The redskins disappear as they have come like shadows, and soon their place is taken by the beasts, a great and motley procession: lions, tigers, bears, and the innumerable smaller savage things that flee from them, for every kind of beast, and, more particularly, all the man-eaters, live cheek by jowl on the favoured island. Their tongues are hanging out, they are hungry to-night.

When they have passed, comes the last figure of all, a gigantic crocodile. We shall see for whom she is looking presently.

The crocodile passes, but soon the boys appear again, for the procession must continue indefinitely until one of the parties stops or changes its pace. Then quickly they will be on top of each other.

All are keeping a sharp look-out in front, but none suspects that the danger may be creeping up from behind. This shows how real the island was.

The first to fall out of the moving circle was the boys. They flung themselves down on the sward (*turf*), close to their underground home.

"I do wish Peter would come back," every one of them said nervously, though in height and still more in breadth they were all larger than their captain.

"I am the only one who is not afraid of the pirates," Slightly said, in the tone that prevented his being a general favourite; but perhaps some distant sound disturbed him, for he added hastily, "but I wish he would come back, and tell us whether he has heard anything more about Cinderella."

They talked of Cinderella, and Tootles was confident that his mother must have been very like her.

It was only in Peter's absence that they could speak of mothers, the subject being forbidden by him as silly.

"All I remember about my mother," Nibs told them, "is that she often said to my father, 'Oh, how I wish I had a cheque-book of my own!' I don't know what a cheque-book is, but I should just love to give my mother one."

While they talked they heard a distant sound. You or I, not being wild things of the woods, would have heard nothing, but they heard it, and it was the grim song:

"Yo ho, yo ho, the pirate life,
The flag o' skull and bones,
A merry hour, a hempen rope,
And hey for Davy Jones."

At once the lost boys – but where are they? They are no longer there. Rabbits could not have disappeared more quickly.

I will tell you where they are. With the exception of Nibs, who has darted away to reconnoitre (*look around*), they are already in their home under the ground, a very delightful residence of which we shall see a good deal presently. But how have they reached it? for there is no entrance to be seen, not so much as a large stone, which if rolled away, would disclose the mouth of a cave. Look closely, however, and you may note that there are here seven large trees, each with a hole in its hollow trunk as large as a boy. These are the seven entrances to the home under the ground, for which Hook has been searching in vain these many moons. Will he find it tonight?

As the pirates advanced, the quick eye of Starkey sighted Nibs disappearing through the wood, and at once his pistol flashed out. But an iron claw gripped his shoulder.

"Captain, let go!" he cried, writhing.

Now for the first time we hear the voice of Hook. It was a black voice. "Put back that pistol first," it said threateningly.

"It was one of those boys you hate. I could have shot him dead."

"Ay, and the sound would have brought Tiger Lily's redskins upon us. Do you want to lose your scalp?"

"Shall I after him, Captain," asked pathetic Smee, "and tickle him with Johnny Corkscrew?" Smee had pleasant names for everything, and his cutlass was Johnny Corkscrew, because he wiggled it in the wound. One could mention many lovable traits in Smee. For instance, after killing, it was his spectacles he wiped instead of his weapon.

"Johnny's a silent fellow," he reminded Hook.

"Not now, Smee," Hook said darkly. "He is only one, and I want to mischief all the seven. Scatter and look for them."

The pirates disappeared among the trees, and in a moment their Captain and Smee were alone. Hook heaved a heavy sigh, and I know not why it was, perhaps it was because of the soft beauty of the evening, but there came over him a desire to confide to his faithful bo'sun the story of his life. He spoke long and earnestly, but what it was all about Smee, who was rather stupid, did not know in the least.

Anon (*later*) he caught the word Peter.

"Most of all," Hook was saying passionately, "I want their captain, Peter Pan. 'Twas he cut off my arm." He brandished the hook threateningly. "I've waited long to shake his hand with this. Oh, I'll tear him!"

"And yet," said Smee, "I have often heard you say that hook was worth a score of hands, for combing the hair and other homely uses."

"Ay," the captain answered, "if I was a mother I would pray to have my children born with this instead of that," and he cast a look of pride upon his iron hand and one of scorn upon the other. Then again he frowned.

"Peter flung my arm," he said, wincing, "to a crocodile that happened to be passing by."

"I have often," said Smee, "noticed your strange dread of crocodiles."

"Not of crocodiles," Hook corrected him, "but of that one crocodile." He lowered his voice. "It liked my arm so much, Smee, that it has followed me ever since, from sea to sea and from land to land, licking its lips for the rest of me."

"In a way," said Smee, "it's sort of a compliment."

"I want no such compliments," Hook barked petulantly. "I want Peter Pan, who first gave the brute its taste for me."

He sat down on a large mushroom, and now there was a quiver in his voice. "Smee," he said huskily, "that crocodile would have had me before this, but by a lucky chance it swallowed a clock which goes tick tick inside it, and so before it can reach me I hear the tick and bolt." He laughed, but in a hollow way.

"Some day," said Smee, "the clock will run down, and then he'll get you."

Hook wetted his dry lips. "Ay," he said, "that's the fear that haunts me."

Since sitting down he had felt curiously warm. "Smee," he said, "this seat is hot." He jumped up. "Odds bobs, hammer and tongs I'm burning."

They examined the mushroom, which was of a size and solidity unknown on the mainland; they tried to pull it up, and it came away at once in their hands, for it had no root. Stranger still, smoke began at once to ascend. The pirates looked at each other. "A chimney!" they both exclaimed.

They had indeed discovered the chimney of the home under the ground. It was the custom of the boys to stop it with a mushroom when enemies were in the neighbourhood.

Not only smoke came out of it. There came also children's voices, for so safe did the boys feel in their hiding-place that they were gaily chattering. The pirates listened grimly, and then replaced the mushroom. They looked around them and noted the holes in the seven trees.

"Did you hear them say Peter Pan's from home?" Smee whispered, fidgeting with Johnny Corkscrew.

Hook nodded. He stood for a long time lost in thought, and at last a curdling smile lit up his swarthy face. Smee had been waiting for it. "Unrip your plan, captain," he cried eagerly.

"To return to the ship," Hook replied slowly through his teeth, "and cook a large rich cake of a jolly thickness with green sugar on it. There can be but one room below, for there is but one chimney. The silly moles had not the sense to see that they did not need a door apiece. That shows they have no mother. We will leave the cake on the shore of the Mermaids' Lagoon. These boys are always swimming about there, playing with the mermaids. They will find the cake and they will gobble it up, because, having no mother, they don't know how dangerous 'tis to eat rich damp cake." He burst into laughter, not hollow laughter now, but honest laughter. "Aha, they will die!"

Smee had listened with growing admiration.

"It's the wickedest, prettiest policy ever I heard of!" he cried, and in their exultation they danced and sang:

"Avast, belay, when I appear,
By fear they're overtook,
Nought's left upon your bones when you
Have shaken claws with Hook."

They began the verse, but they never finished it, for another sound broke in and stilled them. There was at first such a tiny sound that a leaf might have fallen on it and smothered it, but as it came nearer it was more distinct.

Tick tick tick tick!

Hook stood shuddering, one foot in the air.

"The crocodile!" he gasped, and bounded away, followed by his bo'sun.

It was indeed the crocodile. It had passed the redskins, who were now on the trail of the other pirates. It oozed on after Hook.

Once more the boys emerged into the open; but the dangers of the night were not yet over, for presently Nibs rushed breathless into their midst, pursued by a pack of wolves. The tongues of the pursuers were hanging out; the baying of them was horrible.

"Save me, save me!" cried Nibs, falling on the ground.

"But what can we do, what can we do?"

It was a high compliment to Peter that at that dire moment their thoughts turned to him.

"What would Peter do?" they cried simultaneously.

Almost in the same breath they cried, "Peter would look at them through his legs."

And then, "Let us do what Peter would do."

It is quite the most successful way of defying wolves, and as one boy they bent and looked through their legs. The next moment is the long one, but victory came quickly, for as the boys advanced upon them in the terrible attitude, the wolves dropped their tails and fled.

Now Nibs rose from the ground, and the others thought that his staring eyes still saw the wolves. But it was not wolves he saw.

"I have seen a wonderfuller thing," he cried, as they gathered round him eagerly. "A great white bird. It is flying this way."

"What kind of a bird, do you think?"

"I don't know," Nibs said, awestruck, "but it looks so weary, and as it flies it moans, 'Poor Wendy,'"

"Poor Wendy?"

"I remember," said Slightly instantly, "there are birds called Wendies."

"See, it comes!" cried Curly, pointing to Wendy in the heavens.

Wendy was now almost overhead, and they could hear her plaintive cry. But more distinct came the shrill voice of Tinker Bell. The jealous fairy had now cast off all disguise of friendship, and was darting at her victim from every direction, pinching savagely each time she touched.

"Hullo, Tink," cried the wondering boys.

Tink's reply rang out: "Peter wants you to shoot the Wendy."

It was not in their nature to question when Peter ordered. "Let us do what Peter wishes!" cried the simple boys. "Quick, bows and arrows!"

All but Tootles popped down their trees. He had a bow and arrow with him, and Tink noted it, and rubbed her little hands.

"Quick, Tootles, quick," she screamed. "Peter will be so pleased."

Tootles excitedly fitted the arrow to his bow. "Out of the way, Tink," he shouted, and then he fired, and Wendy fluttered to the ground with an arrow in her breast.

Chapter 6

The Little House

"See," he said, "the arrow struck against this. It is the kiss I gave her. It has saved her life."

Foolish Tootles was standing like a conqueror over Wendy's body when the other boys sprang, armed, from their trees.

"You are too late," he cried proudly, "I have shot the Wendy. Peter will be so pleased with me."

Overhead Tinker Bell shouted "Silly ass!" and darted into hiding. The others did not hear her.

They had crowded round Wendy, and as they looked a terrible silence fell upon the wood. If Wendy's heart had been beating they would all have heard it.

Slightly was the first to speak. "This is no bird," he said in a scared voice. "I think this must be a lady."

"A lady?" said Tootles, and fell a-trembling.

"And we have killed her," Nibs said hoarsely.

They all whipped off their caps.

"Now I see," Curly said: "Peter was bringing her to us." He threw himself sorrowfully on the ground.

"A lady to take care of us at last," said one of the twins, "and you have killed her!"

They were sorry for him, but sorrier for themselves, and when he took a step nearer them they turned from him.

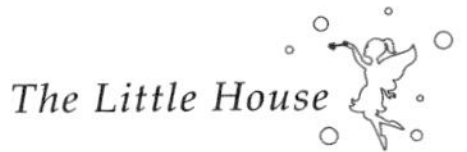

Tootles' face was very white, but there was a dignity about him now that had never been there before.

"I did it," he said, reflecting. "When ladies used to come to me in dreams, I said, 'Pretty mother, pretty mother.' But when at last she really came, I shot her."

He moved slowly away.

"Don't go," they called in pity.

"I must," he answered, shaking; "I am so afraid of Peter."

It was at this tragic moment that they heard a sound which made the heart of every one of them rise to his mouth. They heard Peter crow.

"Peter!" they cried, for it was always thus that he signalled his return.

"Hide her," they whispered, and gathered hastily around Wendy. But Tootles stood aloof.

Again came that ringing crow, and Peter dropped in front of them. "Greetings, boys," he cried, and mechanically they saluted, and then again was silence.

He frowned.

"I am back," he said hotly, "why do you not cheer?"

They opened their mouths, but the cheers would not come. He

overlooked it in his haste to tell the glorious tidings.

"Great news, boys," he cried, "I have brought at last a mother for you all."

Still no sound, except a little thud from Tootles as he dropped on his knees.

"Have you not seen her?" asked Peter, becoming troubled. "She flew this way."

"Ah me!" once voice said, and another said, "Oh, mournful day."

Tootles rose. "Peter," he said quietly, "I will show her to you," and when the others would still have hidden her he said, "Back, twins, let Peter see."

So they all stood back, and let him see, and after he had looked for a little time he did not know what to do next.

"She is dead," he said uncomfortably. "Perhaps she is frightened at being dead."

He thought of hopping off in a comic sort of way till he was out of sight of her, and then never going near the spot any more. They would all have been glad to follow if he had done this.

But there was the arrow. He took it from her heart and faced his band.

"Whose arrow?" he demanded sternly.

"Mine, Peter," said Tootles on his knees.

"Oh, dastard hand," Peter said, and he raised the arrow to use it as a dagger.

Tootles did not flinch. He bared his breast. "Strike, Peter," he said firmly, "strike true."

Twice did Peter raise the arrow, and twice did his hand fall. "I cannot strike," he said with awe, "there is something stays my hand."

All looked at him in wonder, save Nibs, who fortunately looked at Wendy.

"It is she," he cried, "the Wendy lady, see, her arm!"

Wonderful to relate, Wendy had raised her arm. Nibs bent over her and listened reverently. "I think she said, 'Poor Tootles,'" he whispered.

"She lives," Peter said briefly.

Slightly cried instantly, "The Wendy lady lives."

Then Peter knelt beside her and found his button. You remember she had put it on a chain that she wore round her neck.

"See," he said, "the arrow struck against this. It is the kiss I gave her. It has saved her life."

"I remember kisses," Slightly interposed quickly, "let me see it. Ay, that's a kiss."

Peter did not hear him. He was begging Wendy to get better quickly, so that he could show her the mermaids. Of course she could not answer yet, being still in a frightful faint; but from overhead came a wailing note.

"Listen to Tink," said Curly, "she is crying because the Wendy lives."

Then they had to tell Peter of Tink's crime, and almost never had they seen him look so stern.

"Listen, Tinker Bell," he cried, "I am your friend no more. Begone from me for ever."

She flew on to his shoulder and pleaded, but he brushed her off. Not until Wendy again raised her arm did he relent sufficiently to say, "Well, not for ever, but for a whole week."

Do you think Tinker Bell was grateful to Wendy for raising her arm? Oh dear no, never wanted to pinch her so much. Fairies indeed are strange, and Peter, who understood them best, often cuffed (*slapped*) them.

But what to do with Wendy in her present delicate state of health?

"Let us carry her down into the house," Curly suggested.

"Ay," said Slightly, "that is what one does with ladies."

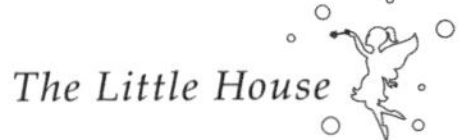

“No, no,” Peter said, “you must not touch her. It would not be sufficiently respectful.”

“That,” said Slightly, “is what I was thinking.”

“But if she lies there,” Tootles said, “she will die.”

“Ay, she will die,” Slightly admitted, “but there is no way out.”

“Yes, there is,” cried Peter. “Let us build a little house round her.”

They were all delighted. “Quick,” he ordered them, “bring me each of you the best of what we have. Gut our house. Be sharp.”

In a moment they were as busy as tailors the night before a wedding. They skurried this way and that, down for bedding, up for firewood, and while they were at it, who should appear but John and Michael. As they dragged along the ground they fell asleep standing, stopped, woke up, moved another step and slept again.

“John, John,” Michael would cry, “wake up! Where is Nana, John, and mother?”

And then John would rub his eyes and mutter, “It is true, we did fly.”

You may be sure they were very relieved to find Peter.

“Hullo, Peter,” they said.

“Hullo,” replied Peter amicably, though he had quite forgotten them. He was very busy at the moment measuring Wendy with his feet to see how large a house she would need. Of course he meant to leave room for chairs and a table. John and Michael watched him.

"Is Wendy asleep?" they asked.

"Yes."

"John," Michael proposed, "let us wake her and get her to make supper for us," but as he said it some of the other boys rushed on carrying branches for the building of the house. "Look at them!" he cried.

"Curly," said Peter in his most captainy voice, "see that these boys help in the building of the house."

"Ay, ay, sir."

"Build a house?" exclaimed John.

"For the Wendy," said Curly.

"For Wendy?" John said, aghast. "Why, she is only a girl!"

"That," explained Curly, "is why we are her servants."

"You? Wendy's servants!"

"Yes," said Peter, "and you also. Away with them."

The astounded brothers were dragged away to hack and hew and carry. "Chairs and a fender (*fireplace*) first," Peter ordered. "Then we

shall build a house round them."

"Ay," said Slightly, "that is how a house is built; it all comes back to me."

Peter thought of everything. "Slightly," he cried, "fetch a doctor."

"Ay, ay," said Slightly at once, and disappeared, scratching his head. But he knew Peter must be obeyed, and he returned in a moment, wearing John's hat and looking solemn.

"Please, sir," said Peter, going to him, "are you a doctor?"

The difference between him and the other boys at such a time was that they knew it was make-believe, while to him make-believe and true were exactly the same thing. This sometimes troubled them, as when they had to make-believe that they had had their dinners.

If they broke down in their make-believe he rapped them on the knuckles.

"Yes, my little man," Slightly anxiously replied, who had chapped knuckles.

"Please, sir," Peter explained, "a lady lies very ill."

She was lying at their feet, but Slightly had the sense not to see her.

"Tut, tut, tut," he said, "where does she lie?"

"In yonder glade."

"I will put a glass thing in her mouth," said Slightly, and he made-believe to do it, while Peter waited. It was an anxious moment when the glass thing was withdrawn.

"How is she?" inquired Peter.

"Tut, tut, tut," said Slightly, "this has cured her."

"I am glad!" Peter cried.

"I will call again in the evening," Slightly said; "give her beef tea out of a cup with a spout to it"; but after he had returned the hat to John he blew big breaths, which was his habit on escaping from a difficulty.

In the meantime the wood had been alive with the sound of axes; almost everything needed for a cosy dwelling already lay at Wendy's feet.

"If only we knew," said one, "the kind of house she likes best."

"Peter," shouted another, "she is moving in her sleep."

"Her mouth opens," cried a third, looking respectfully into it. "Oh, lovely!"

"Perhaps she is going to sing in her sleep," said Peter. "Wendy, sing the kind of house you would like to have."

Immediately, without opening her eyes, Wendy began to sing:

"I wish I had a pretty house,
The littlest ever seen,
With funny little red walls
And roof of mossy green."

They gurgled with joy at this, for by the greatest good luck the branches they had brought were sticky with red sap, and all the ground was carpeted with moss. As they rattled up the little house they broke into song themselves:

"We've built the little walls and roof
And made a lovely door,
So tell us, mother Wendy,
What are you wanting more?"

To this she answered greedily:

"Oh, really next I think I'll have
Gay windows all about,
With roses peeping in, you know,
And babies peeping out."

With a blow of their fists they made windows, and large yellow leaves were the blinds. But roses – ?

"Roses!" cried Peter sternly.

Quickly they made-believe to grow the loveliest roses up the walls.

Babies?

To prevent Peter ordering babies they hurried into song again:

“We’ve made the roses peeping out,
The babes are at the door,
We cannot make ourselves, you know,
‘cos we’ve been made before.”

Peter, seeing this to be a good idea, at once pretended that it was his own. The house was quite beautiful, and no doubt Wendy was very cosy within, though, of course, they could no longer see her. Peter strode up and down, ordering finishing touches. Nothing escaped his eagle eyes. Just when it seemed absolutely finished:

“There’s no knocker on the door,” he said.

They were very ashamed, but Tootles gave the sole of his shoe, and it made an excellent knocker.

Absolutely finished now, they thought.

Not of bit of it. “There’s no chimney,” Peter said; “we must have a chimney.”

“It certainly does need a chimney,” said John importantly. This gave Peter an idea. He snatched the hat off John’s head, knocked out the bottom (*top*), and put the hat on the roof. The little house was so

pleased to have such a capital chimney that, as if to say thank you, smoke immediately began to come out of the hat.

Now really and truly it was finished. Nothing remained to do but to knock.

"All look your best," Peter warned them; "first impressions are awfully important."

He was glad no one asked him what first impressions are; they were all too busy looking their best.

He knocked politely, and now the wood was as still as the children, not a sound to be heard except from Tinker Bell, who was watching from a branch and openly sneering.

What the boys were wondering was, would any one answer the knock? If a lady, what would she be like?

The door opened and a lady came out. It was Wendy. They all whipped off their hats.

She looked properly surprised, and this was just how they had hoped she would look.

"Where am I?" she said.

Of course Slightly was the first to get his word in. "Wendy lady," he said rapidly, "for you we built this house."

"Oh, say you're pleased," cried Nibs.

"Lovely, darling house," Wendy said, and they were the very words they had hoped she would say.

"And we are your children," cried the twins.

Then all went on their knees, and holding out their arms cried, "O Wendy lady, be our mother."

"Ought I?" Wendy said, all shining. "Of course it's frightfully fascinating, but you see I am only a little girl. I have no real experience."

"That doesn't matter," said Peter, as if he were the only person present who knew all about it, though he was really the one who knew least. "What we need is just a nice motherly person."

"Oh dear!" Wendy said, "you see, I feel that is exactly what I am."

"It is, it is," they all cried; "we saw it at once."

"Very well," she said, "I will do my best. Come inside at once, you naughty children; I am sure your feet are damp. And before I put you to bed I have just time to finish the story of Cinderella."

In they went; I don't know how there was room for them, but you can squeeze very tight in the Neverland. And that was the first of the many joyous evenings they had with Wendy. By and by she tucked them up in the great bed in the home under the trees, but she herself slept that night in the little house, and Peter kept watch outside with drawn sword, for the pirates could be heard carousing far away and

the wolves were on the prowl. The little house looked so cosy and safe in the darkness, with a bright light showing through its blinds, and the chimney smoking beautifully, and Peter standing on guard. After a time he fell asleep, and some unsteady fairies had to climb over him on their way home from an orgy. Any of the other boys obstructing the fairy path at night they would have mischiefed, but they just tweaked Peter's nose and passed on.

Chapter 7

The Home Under the Ground

This is a difficult question, because it is quite impossible to say how time does wear on in the Neverland, where it is calculated by moons and suns, and there are ever so many more of them than on the mainland.

One of the first things Peter did next day was to measure Wendy and John and Michael for hollow trees. Hook, you remember, had sneered at the boys for thinking they needed a tree apiece, but this was ignorance, for unless your tree fitted you it was difficult to go up and down, and no two of the boys were quite the same size. Once you fitted, you drew in (*let out*) your breath at the top, and down you went at exactly the right speed, while to ascend you drew in and let out alternately, and so wriggled up. Of course, when you have mastered the action you are able to do these things without thinking of them, and nothing can be more graceful.

But you simply must fit, and Peter measures you for your tree as carefully as for a suit of clothes: the only difference being that the clothes are made to fit you, while you have to be made to fit the tree. Usually it is done quite easily, as by your wearing too many garments or too few, but if you are bumpy in awkward places or the only available tree is an odd shape, Peter does some things to you, and after that you fit. Once you fit, great care must be taken to go on fitting, and this, as Wendy was to discover to her delight, keeps a whole family in perfect condition.

Wendy and Michael fitted their trees at the first try, but John had to be altered a little.

After a few days' practice they could go up and down as gaily as buckets in a well. And how ardently they grew to love their home under the ground; especially Wendy! It consisted of one large room, as all houses should do, with a floor in which you could dig (*for worms*) if you wanted to go fishing, and in this floor grew stout mushrooms of a charming colour, which were used as stools. A Never tree tried hard to grow in the centre of the room, but every morning they sawed the trunk through, level with the floor. By tea-time it was always about two feet high, and then they put a door on top of it, the whole thus becoming a table; as soon as they cleared away, they sawed off the trunk again, and thus there was more room to play. There was an enormous fireplace which was in almost any part of the room where you cared to light it, and across this Wendy stretched strings, made of fibre, from which she suspended her washing. The bed was tilted against the wall by day, and let down at 6:30, when it filled nearly half the room; and all the boys slept in it, except Michael, lying like sardines in a tin. There was a strict rule against turning round until one gave the signal, when all turned at once. Michael should have used it also, but Wendy would have (*desired*) a baby, and he was the littlest, and you know what women are, and the short and long of it is that he was hung up in a basket.

It was rough and simple, and not unlike what baby bears would have made of an underground house in the same circumstances. But there was one recess in the wall, no larger than a bird-cage, which was the private apartment of Tinker Bell. It could be shut off from the rest of the house by a tiny curtain, which Tink, who was most fastidious (*particular*), always kept drawn when dressing or undressing. No woman, however large, could have had a more exquisite boudoir (*dressing room*) and bed-chamber combined. The couch, as she always called it, was a genuine Queen Mab, with club legs; and she varied the bedspreads according to what fruit- blossom was in season. Her mirror was a Puss-in-Boots, of which there are now only three, unchipped, known to fairy dealers; the washstand was Pie-crust and reversible, the chest of drawers an authentic Charming the Sixth, and the carpet and rugs the best (*the early*) period of Margery and Robin. There was a chandelier from Tiddlywinks for the look of the thing, but of course she lit the residence herself. Tink was very contemptuous of the rest of the house, as indeed was perhaps inevitable, and her chamber, though beautiful, looked rather conceited, having the appearance of a nose permanently turned up.

I suppose it was all especially entrancing to Wendy, because those rampageous boys of hers gave her so much to do. Really there were whole weeks when, except perhaps with a stocking in the evening, she was never above ground. The cooking, I can tell you, kept her nose to the pot, and even if there was nothing in it, even if there was no pot, she had to keep watching that it came aboil just the same. You never exactly knew whether there would be a real meal or just a make-believe, it all depended upon Peter's whim: he could eat, really eat, if it was part of a game, but he could not stodge (*cram down the food*) just to feel stodgy (*stuffed with food*), which is what most children like better than anything else; the next best thing being to talk about it. Make-believe was so real to him that during a meal of it you could see him getting rounder. Of course it was trying, but you simply had to follow his lead, and if you could prove to him that you were getting loose for your tree he let you stodge.

Wendy's favourite time for sewing and darning was after they had all gone to bed. Then, as she expressed it, she had a breathing time for herself; and she occupied it in making new things for them, and putting double pieces on the knees, for they were all most frightfully hard on their knees.

When she sat down to a basketful of their stockings, every heel with a hole in it, she would fling up her arms and exclaim, "Oh dear, I am sure I sometimes think spinsters are to be envied!"

Her face beamed when she exclaimed this.

You remember about her pet wolf. Well, it very soon discovered that she had come to the island and it found her out, and they just ran into each other's arms. After that it followed her about everywhere.

As time wore on did she think much about the beloved parents she had left behind her? This is a difficult question, because it is quite impossible to say how time does wear on in the Neverland, where it is calculated by moons and suns, and there are ever so many more of them than on the mainland. But I am afraid that Wendy did not really worry about her father and mother; she was absolutely confident that they would always keep the window open for her to fly back by, and this gave her complete ease of mind. What did disturb her at times was that John remembered his parents vaguely only, as people he had once known, while Michael was quite willing to believe that she was really his mother. These things scared her a little, and nobly anxious to do her duty, she tried to fix the old life in their minds by setting them examination papers on it, as like as possible to the ones she used to do at school. The other boys thought this awfully interesting, and insisted on joining, and they made slates for themselves, and sat round the table, writing and thinking hard about the questions she had written on another slate and passed round. They were the most ordinary questions: "What was the colour of Mother's eyes? Which was taller, Father or Mother? Was Mother blonde or brunette? Answer all three questions if possible." "(A) Write an essay of not less than 40 words on How I spent my last Holidays, or The Characters of Father and Mother compared. Only one of these to be attempted." or "(1) Describe Mother's laugh; (2) Describe Father's laugh; (3) Describe Mother's Party Dress; (4) Describe the Kennel and its Inmate."

They were just everyday questions like these, and when you could not answer them you were told to make a cross; and it was really dreadful what a number of crosses even John made. Of course the only boy who replied to every question was Slightly, and no one could have been more hopeful of coming out first, but his answers were perfectly ridiculous, and he really came out last: a melancholy thing.

Peter did not compete. For one thing he despised all mothers except Wendy, and for another he was the only boy on the island who could neither write nor spell; not the smallest word. He was above all that sort of thing.

By the way, the questions were all written in the past tense. What was the colour of Mother's eyes, and so on. Wendy, you see, had been forgetting, too.

Adventures, of course, as we shall see, were of daily occurrence; but about this time Peter invented, with Wendy's help, a new game that fascinated him enormously, until he suddenly had no more interest in it, which, as you have been told, was what always happened with his games. It consisted in pretending not to have adventures, in doing the sort of thing John and Michael had been doing all their lives, sitting on stools flinging balls in the air, pushing each other, going out for walks and coming back without having killed so much as a grizzly. To see Peter doing nothing on a stool was a great sight; he could not help looking solemn at such times, to sit still seemed to him such a comic thing to do. He boasted that he had gone walking for the good of his health. For several suns these were the most novel of all adventures to him; and John and Michael had to pretend to be delighted also; otherwise he would have treated them severely.

He often went out alone, and when he came back you were never absolutely certain whether he had had an adventure or not. He might have forgotten it so completely that he said nothing about it; and then when you went out you found the body; and, on the other hand, he might say a great deal about it, and yet you could not find the body. Sometimes he came home with his head bandaged, and then Wendy cooed over him and bathed it in lukewarm water, while he told a dazzling tale. But she was never quite sure, you know. There were, however, many adventures which she knew to be true because she was in them herself, and there were still more that were at least partly true, for the other boys were in them and said they were wholly true. To describe them all would require a book as large as an English-

Latin, Latin-English Dictionary, and the most we can do is to give one as a specimen of an average hour on the island. The difficulty is which one to choose. Should we take the brush with the redskins at Slightly Gulch? It was a sanguinary (*cheerful*) affair, and especially interesting as showing one of Peter's peculiarities, which was that in the middle of a fight he would suddenly change sides. At the Gulch, when victory was still in the balance, sometimes leaning this way and sometimes that, he called out, "I'm redskin to-day; what are you, Tootles?" And Tootles answered, "Redskin; what are you, Nibs?" and Nibs said, "Redskin; what are you Twin?" and so on; and they were all redskins; and of course this would have ended the fight had not the real redskins fascinated by Peter's methods, agreed to be lost boys for that once, and so at it they all went again, more fiercely than ever.

The extraordinary upshot of this adventure was – but we have not decided yet that this is the adventure we are to narrate. Perhaps a better one would be the night attack by the redskins on the house under the ground, when several of them stuck in the hollow trees and had to be pulled out like corks. Or we might tell how Peter saved Tiger Lily's life in the Mermaids' Lagoon, and so made her his ally.

Or we could tell of that cake the pirates cooked so that the boys might eat it and perish; and how they placed it in one cunning spot after another; but always Wendy snatched it from the hands of her children, so that in time it lost its succulence, and became as hard as a stone, and was used as a missile, and Hook fell over it in the dark.

Or suppose we tell of the birds that were Peter's friends, particularly of the Never bird that built in a tree overhanging the lagoon, and how the nest fell into the water, and still the bird sat on her eggs, and Peter gave orders that she was not to be disturbed. That is a pretty story, and the end shows how grateful a bird can be; but if we tell it we must also tell the whole adventure of the lagoon, which would of course be telling two adventures rather than just one. A shorter adventure, and quite as exciting, was Tinker Bell's attempt, with the help of some street fairies, to have the sleeping Wendy conveyed on a great floating leaf to the mainland. Fortunately the leaf gave way and Wendy woke, thinking it was bath-time, and swam back. Or again, we might choose Peter's defiance of the lions, when he drew a circle round him on the ground with an arrow and dared them to cross it; and though he waited for hours, with the other boys and Wendy looking on breathlessly from trees, not one of them dared to accept his challenge.

Which of these adventures shall we choose? The best way will be to toss for it.

I have tossed, and the lagoon has won. This almost makes one wish that the gulch or the cake or Tink's leaf had won. Of course I could do it again, and make it best out of three; however, perhaps fairest to stick to the lagoon.

Chapter 8

The Mermaids' Lagoon

The children often spent long summer days on this lagoon, swimming or floating most of the time, playing the mermaid games in the water, and so forth.

If you shut your eyes and are a lucky one, you may see at times a shapeless pool of lovely pale colours suspended in the darkness; then if you squeeze your eyes tighter, the pool begins to take shape, and the colours become so vivid that with another squeeze they must go on fire. But just before they go on fire you see the lagoon. This is the nearest you ever get to it on the mainland, just one heavenly moment; if there could be two moments you might see the surf and hear the mermaids singing.

The children often spent long summer days on this lagoon, swimming or floating most of the time, playing the mermaid games in the water, and so forth. You must not think from this that the mermaids were on friendly terms with them: on the contrary, it was among Wendy's lasting regrets that all the time she was on the island she never had a civil word from one of them. When she stole softly to the edge of the lagoon she might see them by the score, especially on Marooners' Rock, where they loved to bask, combing out their hair in a lazy way that quite irritated her; or she might even swim, on tiptoe as it were, to within a yard of them, but then they saw her and dived, probably splashing her with their tails, not by accident, but intentionally.

They treated all the boys in the same way, except of course Peter, who chatted with them on Marooners' Rock by the hour, and sat on their tails when they got cheeky. He gave Wendy one of their combs.

The most haunting time at which to see them is at the turn of the moon, when they utter strange wailing cries; but the lagoon is dangerous for mortals then, and until the evening of which we have now to tell, Wendy had never seen the lagoon by moonlight, less from fear, for of course Peter would have accompanied her, than because she had strict rules about every one being in bed by seven. She was often at the lagoon, however, on sunny days after rain, when the mermaids come up in extraordinary numbers to play with their bubbles. The bubbles of many colours made in rainbow water they treat as balls, hitting them gaily from one to another with their tails, and trying to keep them in the rainbow till they burst. The goals are at each end of the rainbow, and the keepers only are allowed to use their hands. Sometimes a dozen of these games will be going on in the lagoon at a time, and it is quite a pretty sight.

But the moment the children tried to join in they had to play by themselves, for the mermaids immediately disappeared. Nevertheless we have proof that they secretly watched the interlopers, and were not above taking an idea from them; for John introduced a new way of hitting the bubble, with the head instead of the hand, and the mermaids adopted it. This is the one mark that John has left on the Neverland.

It must also have been rather pretty to see the children resting on a rock for half an hour after their mid-day meal. Wendy insisted on their doing this, and it had to be a real rest even though the meal was make-believe. So they lay there in the sun, and their bodies glistened in it, while she sat beside them and looked important.

It was one such day, and they were all on Marooners' Rock. The rock was not much larger than their great bed, but of course they all knew how not to take up much room, and they were dozing, or at least lying with their eyes shut, and pinching occasionally when they thought Wendy was not looking. She was very busy, stitching.

While she stitched a change came to the lagoon. Little shivers ran over it, and the sun went away and shadows stole across the water, turning it cold. Wendy could no longer see to thread her needle, and when she looked up, the lagoon that had always hitherto been such a laughing place seemed formidable and unfriendly.

It was not, she knew, that night had come, but something as dark as night had come. No, worse than that. It had not come, but it had sent that shiver through the sea to say that it was coming. What was it?

There crowded upon her all the stories she had been told of Marooners' Rock, so called because evil captains put sailors on it and leave them there to drown. They drown when the tide rises, for then it is submerged.

Of course she should have roused the children at once; not merely because of the unknown that was stalking toward them, but because it was no longer good for them to sleep on a rock grown chilly. But she was a young mother and she did not know this; she thought you simply must stick to your rule about half an hour after the mid-day meal. So, though fear was upon her, and she longed to hear male voices, she would not waken them. Even when she heard the sound of muffled oars, though her heart was in her mouth, she did not waken them. She stood over them to let them have their sleep out. Was it not brave of Wendy?

It was well for those boys then that there was one among them who could sniff danger even in his sleep. Peter sprang erect, as wide awake at once as a dog, and with one warning cry he roused the others.

He stood motionless, one hand to his ear.

"Pirates!" he cried. The others came closer to him. A strange smile was playing about his face, and Wendy saw it and shuddered. While that smile was on his face no one dared address him; all they could do was to stand ready to obey. The order came sharp and incisive.

"Dive!"

There was a gleam of legs, and instantly the lagoon seemed deserted. Marooners' Rock stood alone in the forbidding waters as if it were itself marooned.

The boat drew nearer. It was the pirate dinghy, with three figures in her, Smee and Starkey, and the third a captive, no other than Tiger Lily. Her hands and ankles were tied, and she knew what was to be her fate. She was to be left on the rock to perish, an end to one of her race more terrible than death by fire or torture, for is it not written in the book of the tribe that there is no path through water to the happy hunting-ground? Yet her face was impassive; she was the daughter of a chief, she must die as a chief's daughter, it is enough.

They had caught her boarding the pirate ship with a knife in her mouth. No watch was kept on the ship, it being Hook's boast that the wind of his name guarded the ship for a mile around. Now her fate would help to guard it also. One more wail would go the round in that wind by night.

In the gloom that they brought with them the two pirates did not see the rock till they crashed into it.

"Luff, you lubber," cried an Irish voice that was Smee's; "here's the rock. Now, then, what we have to do is to hoist the redskin on to it and leave her here to drown."

It was the work of one brutal moment to land the beautiful girl on the rock; she was too proud to offer a vain resistance.

Quite near the rock, but out of sight, two heads were bobbing up and down, Peter's and Wendy's. Wendy was crying, for it was the first tragedy she had seen. Peter had seen many tragedies, but he had forgotten them all. He was less sorry than Wendy for Tiger Lily: it was two against one that angered him, and he meant to save her. An easy way would have been to wait until the pirates had gone, but he was never one to choose the easy way.

There was almost nothing he could not do, and he now imitated the voice of Hook.

"Ahoy there, you lubbers!" he called. It was a marvellous imitation.

"The captain!" said the pirates, staring at each other in surprise.

"He must be swimming out to us," Starkey said, when they had looked for him in vain.

"We are putting the redskin on the rock," Smee called out.

"Set her free," came the astonishing answer.

"Free!"

"Yes, cut her bonds and let her go."

"But, captain – "

"At once, d'ye hear," cried Peter, "or I'll plunge my hook in you."

"This is queer!" Smee gasped.

"Better do what the captain orders," said Starkey nervously.

"Ay, ay." Smee said, and he cut Tiger Lily's cords. At once like an eel she slid between Starkey's legs into the water.

Of course Wendy was very elated over Peter's cleverness; but she knew that he would be elated also and very likely crow and thus betray himself, so at once her hand went out to cover his mouth. But it was stayed even in the act, for "Boat ahoy!" rang over the lagoon in Hook's voice, and this time it was not Peter who had spoken.

Peter may have been about to crow, but his face puckered in a whistle of surprise instead.

"Boat ahoy!" again came the voice.

Now Wendy understood. The real Hook was also in the water.

He was swimming to the boat, and as his men showed a light to guide him he had soon reached them. In the light of the lantern Wendy saw his hook grip the boat's side; she saw his evil swarthy face as he rose dripping from the water, and, quaking, she would have liked to swim away, but Peter would not budge. He was tingling with life and also top-heavy with conceit. "Am I not a wonder, oh, I am a wonder!" he whispered to her, and though she thought so also, she was really glad for the sake of his reputation that no one heard him except herself.

He signed to her to listen.

The two pirates were very curious to know what had brought their captain to them, but he sat with his head on his hook in a position of profound melancholy.

"Captain, is all well?" they asked timidly, but he answered with a hollow moan.

"He sighs," said Smee.

"He sighs again," said Starkey.

"And yet a third time he sighs," said Smee.

Then at last he spoke passionately.

"The game's up," he cried, "those boys have found a mother."

Affrighted though she was, Wendy swelled with pride.

"O evil day!" cried Starkey.

"What's a mother?" asked the ignorant Smee.

Wendy was so shocked that she exclaimed. "He doesn't know!" and always after this she felt that if you could have a pet pirate Smee would be her one.

Peter pulled her beneath the water, for Hook had started up, crying, "What was that?"

"I heard nothing," said Starkey, raising the lantern over the waters, and as the pirates looked they saw a strange sight. It was the nest I have told you of, floating on the lagoon, and the Never bird was sitting on it.

"See," said Hook in answer to Smee's question, "that is a mother. What a lesson! The nest must have fallen into the water, but would the mother desert her eggs? No."

There was a break in his voice, as if for a moment he recalled innocent days when – but he brushed away this weakness with his hook.

Smee, much impressed, gazed at the bird as the nest was borne past, but the more suspicious Starkey said, "If she is a mother, perhaps she is hanging about here to help Peter."

Hook winced. "Ay," he said, "that is the fear that haunts me."

He was roused from this dejection by Smee's eager voice.

"Captain," said Smee, "could we not kidnap these boys' mother and make her our mother?"

"It is a princely scheme," cried Hook, and at once it took practical shape in his great brain. "We will seize the children and carry them to the boat: the boys we will make walk the plank, and Wendy shall be our mother."

Again Wendy forgot herself.

"Never!" she cried, and bobbed.

"What was that?"

But they could see nothing. They thought it must have been a leaf in the wind. "Do you agree, my bullies?" asked Hook.

"There is my hand on it," they both said.

"And there is my hook. Swear."

They all swore. By this time they were on the rock, and suddenly Hook remembered Tiger Lily.

"Where is the redskin?" he demanded abruptly.

He had a playful humour at moments, and they thought this was one of the moments.

"That is all right, captain," Smee answered complacently; "we let her go."

"Let her go!" cried Hook.

"'Twas your own orders," the bo'sun faltered.

"You called over the water to us to let her go," said Starkey.

"Brimstone and gall," thundered Hook, "what cozening (*cheating*) is going on here!" His face had gone black with rage, but he saw that they believed their words, and he was startled. "Lads," he said, shaking a little, "I gave no such order."

"It is passing queer," Smee said, and they all fidgeted uncomfortably. Hook raised his voice, but there was a quiver in it.

"Spirit that haunts this dark lagoon to-night," he cried, "dost hear me?"

Of course Peter should have kept quiet, but of course he did not. He immediately answered in Hook's voice:

"Odds, bobs, hammer and tongs, I hear you."

In that supreme moment Hook did not blanch, even at the gills, but Smee and Starkey clung to each other in terror.

"Who are you, stranger? Speak!" Hook demanded.

"I am James Hook," replied the voice, "captain of the Jolly Roger."

"You are not; you are not," Hook cried hoarsely.

"Brimstone and gall," the voice retorted, "say that again, and I'll cast anchor in you."

Hook tried a more ingratiating manner. "If you are Hook," he said almost humbly, "come tell me, who am I?"

"A codfish," replied the voice, "only a codfish."

"A codfish!" Hook echoed blankly, and it was then, but not till then, that his proud spirit broke. He saw his men draw back from him.

"Have we been captained all this time by a codfish!" they muttered. "It is lowering to our pride."

They were his dogs snapping at him, but, tragic figure though he had become, he scarcely heeded them. Against such fearful evidence it was not their belief in him that he needed, it was his own. He felt his ego slipping from him. "Don't desert me, bully," he whispered hoarsely to it.

In his dark nature there was a touch of the feminine, as in all the great pirates, and it sometimes gave him intuitions. Suddenly he tried the guessing game.

"Hook," he called, "have you another voice?"

Now Peter could never resist a game, and he answered blithely in his own voice, "I have."

"And another name?"

"Ay, ay."

"Vegetable?" asked Hook.

"No."

"Mineral?"

"No."

"Animal?"

"Yes."

"Man?"

"No!" This answer rang out scornfully.

"Boy?"

"Yes."

"Ordinary boy?"

"No!"

"Wonderful boy?"

To Wendy's pain the answer that rang out this time was "Yes."

"Are you in England?"

"No."

"Are you here?"

"Yes."

Hook was completely puzzled. "You ask him some questions," he said to the others, wiping his damp brow.

Smee reflected. "I can't think of a thing," he said regretfully.

"Can't guess, can't guess!" crowed Peter. "Do you give it up?"

Of course in his pride he was carrying the game too far, and the miscreants (*villains*) saw their chance.

"Yes, yes," they answered eagerly.

"Well, then," he cried, "I am Peter Pan."

Pan!

In a moment Hook was himself again, and Smee and Starkey were his faithful henchmen.

"Now we have him," Hook shouted. "Into the water, Smee. Starkey, mind the boat. Take him dead or alive!"

He leaped as he spoke, and simultaneously came the gay voice of Peter.

"Are you ready, boys?"

"Ay, ay," from various parts of the lagoon.

"Then lam into the pirates."

The fight was short and sharp. First to draw blood was John, who gallantly climbed into the boat and held Starkey. There was fierce struggle, in which the cutlass was torn from the pirate's grasp. He wriggled overboard and John leapt after him. The dinghy drifted away.

Here and there a head bobbed up in the water, and there was a flash of steel followed by a cry or a whoop. In the confusion some struck at their own side. The corkscrew of Smee got Tootles in the fourth rib, but he was himself pinked (*nicked*) in turn by Curly. Farther from the rock Starkey was pressing Slightly and the twins hard.

Where all this time was Peter? He was seeking bigger game.

The others were all brave boys, and they must not be blamed for backing from the pirate captain. His iron claw made a circle of dead water round him, from which they fled like affrighted fishes.

But there was one who did not fear him: there was one prepared to enter that circle.

Strangely, it was not in the water that they met. Hook rose to the rock to breathe, and at the same moment Peter scaled it on the opposite side. The rock was slippery as a ball, and they had to crawl rather than climb. Neither knew that the other was coming. Each feeling for a grip met the other's arm: in surprise they raised their heads; their faces were almost touching; so they met.

Some of the greatest heroes have confessed that just before they fell to (*began combat*) they had a sinking (*feeling in the stomach*). Had it been so with Peter at that moment I would admit it. After all, he was the only man that the Sea-Cook had feared. But Peter had no sinking, he had one feeling only, gladness; and he gnashed his pretty teeth with joy. Quick as thought he snatched a knife from Hook's belt and was about to drive it home, when he saw that he was higher up the rock that his foe. It would not have been fighting fair. He gave the pirate a hand to help him up.

It was then that Hook bit him.

Not the pain of this but its unfairness was what dazed Peter. It made him quite helpless. He could only stare, horrified. Every child is affected thus the first time he is treated unfairly. All he thinks he has a right to when he comes to you to be yours is fairness. After you have been unfair to him he will love you again, but will never afterwards be quite the same boy. No one ever gets over the first unfairness; no one except Peter. He often met it, but he always forgot it. I suppose that was the real difference between him and all the rest.

So when he met it now it was like the first time; and he could just stare, helpless. Twice the iron hand clawed him.

A few moments afterwards the other boys saw Hook in the water striking wildly for the ship; no elation on the pestilent face now, only white fear, for the crocodile was in dogged pursuit of him. On ordinary occasions the boys would have swum alongside cheering; but now they were uneasy, for they had lost both Peter and Wendy, and were scouring the lagoon for them, calling them by name. They found the dinghy and went home in it, shouting "Peter, Wendy" as they went, but no answer came save mocking laughter from the mermaids. "They must be swimming back or flying," the boys concluded. They were not very anxious, because they had such faith in Peter. They chuckled, boylike, because they would be late for bed; and it was all mother Wendy's fault!

When their voices died away there came cold silence over the lagoon, and then a feeble cry.

"Help, help!"

Two small figures were beating against the rock; the girl had fainted and lay on the boy's arm. With a last effort Peter pulled her up the rock and then lay down beside her. Even as he also fainted he saw that the water was rising. He knew that they would soon be drowned, but he could do no more.

As they lay side by side a mermaid caught Wendy by the feet, and began pulling her softly into the water. Peter, feeling her slip from him, woke with a start, and was just in time to draw her back. But he had to tell her the truth.

"We are on the rock, Wendy," he said, "but it is growing smaller. Soon the water will be over it."

She did not understand even now.

"We must go," she said, almost brightly.

"Yes," he answered faintly.

"Shall we swim or fly, Peter?"

He had to tell her.

"Do you think you could swim or fly as far as the island, Wendy, without my help?"

She had to admit that she was too tired.

He moaned.

"What is it?" she asked, anxious about him at once.

"I can't help you, Wendy. Hook wounded me. I can neither fly nor swim."

"Do you mean we shall both be drowned?"

"Look how the water is rising."

They put their hands over their eyes to shut out the sight. They thought they would soon be no more. As they sat thus something brushed against Peter as light as a kiss, and stayed there, as if saying timidly, "Can I be of any use?"

It was the tail of a kite, which Michael had made some days

before. It had torn itself out of his hand and floated away.

"Michael's kite," Peter said without interest, but next moment he had seized the tail, and was pulling the kite toward him.

"It lifted Michael off the ground," he cried; "why should it not carry you?"

"Both of us!"

"It can't lift two; Michael and Curly tried."

"Let us draw lots," Wendy said bravely.

"And you a lady; never." Already he had tied the tail round her. She clung to him; she refused to go without him; but with a "Good-bye, Wendy," he pushed her from the rock; and in a few minutes she was borne out of his sight. Peter was alone on the lagoon.

The rock was very small now; soon it would be submerged. Pale rays of light tiptoed across the waters; and by and by there was to be heard a sound at once the most musical and the most melancholy in the world: the mermaids calling to the moon.

Peter was not quite like other boys; but he was afraid at last. A tremor ran through him, like a shudder passing over the sea; but on the sea one shudder follows another till there are hundreds of them, and Peter felt just the one. Next moment he was standing erect on the rock again, with that smile on his face and a drum beating within him. It was saying, "To die will be an awfully big adventure."

Chapter 9

The Never Bird

It was not really a piece of paper; it was the Never bird, making desperate efforts to reach Peter on the nest.

The last sounds Peter heard before he was quite alone were the mermaids retiring one by one to their bedchambers under the sea. He was too far away to hear their doors shut; but every door in the coral caves where they live rings a tiny bell when it opens or closes (*as in all the nicest houses on the mainland*), and he heard the bells.

Steadily the waters rose till they were nibbling at his feet; and to pass the time until they made their final gulp, he watched the only thing on the lagoon. He thought it was a piece of floating paper, perhaps part of the kite, and wondered idly how long it would take to drift ashore.

Presently he noticed as an odd thing that it was undoubtedly out upon the lagoon with some definite purpose, for it was fighting the tide, and sometimes winning; and when it won, Peter, always sympathetic to the weaker side, could not help clapping; it was such a gallant piece of paper.

It was not really a piece of paper; it was the Never bird, making desperate efforts to reach Peter on the nest. By working her wings, in a way she had learned since the nest fell into the water, she was able to some extent to guide her strange craft, but by the time Peter recognised her she was very exhausted. She had come to save him, to give him her nest, though there were eggs in it. I rather wonder at the bird, for though he had been nice to her, he had also sometimes tormented her. I can suppose only that, like Mrs. Darling and the rest of them, she was melted because he had all his first teeth.

She called out to him what she had come for, and he called out to

her what she was doing there; but of course neither of them understood the other's language. In fanciful stories people can talk to the birds freely, and I wish for the moment I could pretend that this were such a story, and say that Peter replied intelligently to the Never bird; but truth is best, and I want to tell you only what really happened. Well, not only could they not understand each other, but they forgot their manners.

"I – want – you – to – get – into – the – nest," the bird called, speaking as slowly and distinctly as possible, "and – then – you – can – drift – ashore, but – I – am – too – - tired – to – bring – it – any – nearer – so – you – must – try – to – swim – to – it."

"What are you quacking about?" Peter answered. "Why don't you let the nest drift as usual?"

"I – want – you – " the bird said, and repeated it all over.

Then Peter tried slow and distinct.

"What – are – you – quacking – about?" and so on.

The Never bird became irritated; they have very short tempers.

"You dunderheaded little jay," she screamed, "Why don't you do as I tell you?"

Peter felt that she was calling him names, and at a venture he retorted hotly:

"So are you!"

Then rather curiously they both snapped out the same remark:

"Shut up!"

"Shut up!"

Nevertheless the bird was determined to save him if she could, and by one last mighty effort she propelled the nest against the rock. Then up she flew; deserting her eggs, so as to make her meaning clear.

Then at last he understood, and clutched the nest and waved his thanks to the bird as she fluttered overhead. It was not to receive his thanks, however, that she hung there in the sky; it was not even to watch him get into the nest; it was to see what he did with her eggs.

There were two large white eggs, and Peter lifted them up and reflected. The bird covered her face with her wings, so as not to see the last of them; but she could not help peeping between the feathers.

I forget whether I have told you that there was a stave on the rock, driven into it by some buccaneers of long ago to mark the site of buried treasure. The children had discovered the glittering hoard, and when in a mischievous mood used to fling showers of moidores, diamonds, pearls and pieces of eight to the gulls, who pounced upon them for food, and then flew away, raging at the scurvy trick that had been played upon them. The stave was still there, and on it Starkey had hung his hat, a deep tarpaulin, watertight, with a broad brim. Peter put the eggs into this hat and set it on the lagoon. It floated beautifully.

 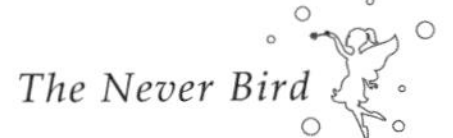

The Never bird saw at once what he was up to, and screamed her admiration of him; and, alas, Peter crowed his agreement with her. Then he got into the nest, reared the stave in it as a mast, and hung up his shirt for a sail. At the same moment the bird fluttered down upon the hat and once more sat snugly on her eggs. She drifted in one direction, and he was borne off in another, both cheering.

Of course when Peter landed he beached his barque (*small ship, actually the Never Bird's nest in this particular case in point*) in a place where the bird would easily find it; but the hat was such a great success that she abandoned the nest. It drifted about till it went to pieces, and often Starkey came to the shore of the lagoon, and with many bitter feelings watched the bird sitting on his hat. As we shall not see her again, it may be worth mentioning here that all Never birds now build in that shape of nest, with a broad brim on which the youngsters take an airing.

Great were the rejoicings when Peter reached the home under the ground almost as soon as Wendy, who had been carried hither and thither by the kite. Every boy had adventures to tell; but perhaps the biggest adventure of all was that they were several hours late for bed. This so inflated them that they did various dodgy things to get staying up still longer, such as demanding bandages; but Wendy, though glorying in having them all home again safe and sound, was scandalised by the lateness of the hour, and cried, "To bed, to bed," in a voice that had to be obeyed. Next day, however, she was awfully tender, and gave out bandages to every one, and they played till bed-time at limping about and carrying their arms in slings.

Chapter 10

The Happy Home

It had become a very familiar scene, this, in the home under the ground, but we are looking on it for the last time.

One important result of the brush *(with the pirates)* on the lagoon was that it made the redskins their friends. Peter had saved Tiger Lily from a dreadful fate, and now there was nothing she and her braves would not do for him. All night they sat above, keeping watch over the home under the ground and awaiting the big attack by the pirates which obviously could not be much longer delayed. Even by day they hung about, smoking the pipe of peace, and looking almost as if they wanted tit-bits to eat.

They called Peter the Great White Father, prostrating themselves (*lying down*) before him; and he liked this tremendously, so that it was not really good for him.

"The great white father," he would say to them in a very lordly manner, as they grovelled at his feet, "is glad to see the Piccaninny warriors protecting his wigwam from the pirates."

"Me Tiger Lily," that lovely creature would reply. "Peter Pan save me, me his velly nice friend. Me no let pirates hurt him."

She was far too pretty to cringe in this way, but Peter thought it his due, and he would answer condescendingly, "It is good. Peter Pan has spoken."

Always when he said, "Peter Pan has spoken," it meant that they must now shut up, and they accepted it humbly in that spirit; but they were by no means so respectful to the other boys, whom they looked upon as just ordinary braves. They said "How-do?" to them, and things like that; and what annoyed the boys was that Peter seemed to think

this all right.

Secretly Wendy sympathised with them a little, but she was far too loyal a housewife to listen to any complaints against father. "Father knows best," she always said, whatever her private opinion must be. Her private opinion was that the redskins should not call her a squaw.

We have now reached the evening that was to be known among them as the Night of Nights, because of its adventures and their upshot. The day, as if quietly gathering its forces, had been almost uneventful, and now the redskins in their blankets were at their posts above, while, below, the children were having their evening meal; all except Peter, who had gone out to get the time. The way you got the time on the island was to find the crocodile, and then stay near him till the clock struck.

The meal happened to be a make-believe tea, and they sat around the board, guzzling in their greed; and really, what with their chatter and recriminations, the noise, as Wendy said, was positively deafening. To be sure, she did not mind noise, but she simply would not have them grabbing things, and then excusing themselves by saying that Tootles had pushed their elbow. There was a fixed rule that they must never hit back at meals, but should refer the matter of dispute to Wendy by raising the right arm politely and saying, "I complain of so-and-so;" but what usually happened was that they forgot to do this or did it too much.

"Silence," cried Wendy when for the twentieth time she had told them that they were not all to speak at once. "Is your mug empty, Slightly darling?"

"Not quite empty, mummy," Slightly said, after looking into an imaginary mug.

"He hasn't even begun to drink his milk," Nibs interposed.

This was telling, and Slightly seized his chance.

"I complain of Nibs," he cried promptly.

John, however, had held up his hand first.

"Well, John?"

"May I sit in Peter's chair, as he is not here?"

"Sit in father's chair, John!" Wendy was scandalised. "Certainly not."

"He is not really our father," John answered. "He didn't even know how a father does till I showed him."

This was grumbling. "We complain of John," cried the twins.

Tootles held up his hand. He was so much the humblest of them, indeed he was the only humble one, that Wendy was specially gentle with him.

"I don't suppose," Tootles said diffidently (*bashfully or timidly*), "that

I could be father."

"No, Tootles."

Once Tootles began, which was not very often, he had a silly way of going on.

"As I can't be father," he said heavily, "I don't suppose, Michael, you would let me be baby?"

"No, I won't," Michael rapped out. He was already in his basket.

"As I can't be baby," Tootles said, getting heavier and heavier and heavier, "do you think I could be a twin?"

"No, indeed," replied the twins; "it's awfully difficult to be a twin."

"As I can't be anything important," said Tootles, "would any of you like to see me do a trick?"

"No," they all replied.

Then at last he stopped. "I hadn't really any hope," he said.

The hateful telling broke out again.

"Slightly is coughing on the table."

"The twins began with cheese-cakes."

"Curly is taking both butter and honey."

"Nibs is speaking with his mouth full."

"I complain of the twins."

"I complain of Curly."

"I complain of Nibs."

"Oh dear, oh dear," cried Wendy, "I'm sure I sometimes think that spinsters are to be envied."

She told them to clear away, and sat down to her work-basket, a heavy load of stockings and every knee with a hole in it as usual.

"Wendy," remonstrated Michael, "I'm too big for a cradle."

"I must have somebody in a cradle," she said almost tartly, "and you are the littlest. A cradle is such a nice homely thing to have about a house."

While she sewed they played around her; such a group of happy faces and dancing limbs lit up by that romantic fire. It had become a very familiar scene, this, in the home under the ground, but we are looking on it for the last time.

There was a step above, and Wendy, you may be sure, was the first to recognize it.

"Children, I hear your father's step. He likes you to meet him at the door."

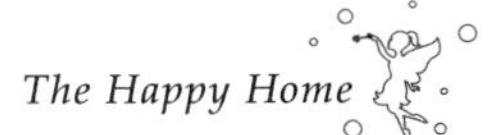

Above, the redskins crouched before Peter.

"Watch well, braves. I have spoken."

And then, as so often before, the gay children dragged him from his tree. As so often before, but never again.

He had brought nuts for the boys as well as the correct time for Wendy.

"Peter, you just spoil them, you know," Wendy simpered (*exaggerated a smile*).

"Ah, old lady," said Peter, hanging up his gun.

"It was me told him mothers are called old lady," Michael whispered to Curly.

"I complain of Michael," said Curly instantly.

The first twin came to Peter. "Father, we want to dance."

"Dance away, my little man," said Peter, who was in high good humour.

"But we want you to dance."

Peter was really the best dancer among them, but he pretended to be scandalised.

"Me! My old bones would rattle!"

"And mummy too."

"What," cried Wendy, "the mother of such an armful, dance!"

"But on a Saturday night," Slightly insinuated.

It was not really Saturday night, at least it may have been, for they had long lost count of the days; but always if they wanted to do anything special they said this was Saturday night, and then they did it.

"Of course it is Saturday night, Peter," Wendy said, relenting.

"People of our figure, Wendy!"

"But it is only among our own progeny (*children*)."

"True, true."

So they were told they could dance, but they must put on their nighties first.

"Ah, old lady," Peter said aside to Wendy, warming himself by the fire and looking down at her as she sat turning a heel, "there is nothing more pleasant of an evening for you and me when the day's toil is over than to rest by the fire with the little ones near by."

"It is sweet, Peter, isn't it?" Wendy said, frightfully gratified. "Peter, I think Curly has your nose."

"Michael takes after you."

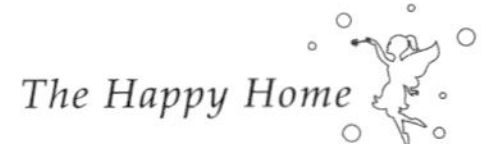

She went to him and put her hand on his shoulder.

"Dear Peter," she said, "with such a large family, of course, I have now passed my best, but you don't want to (*ex*) change me, do you?"

"No, Wendy."

Certainly he did not want a change, but he looked at her uncomfortably, blinking, you know, like one not sure whether he was awake or asleep.

"Peter, what is it?"

"I was just thinking," he said, a little scared. "It is only make-believe, isn't it, that I am their father?"

"Oh yes," Wendy said primly (*formally and properly*).

"You see," he continued apologetically, "it would make me seem so old to be their real father."

"But they are ours, Peter, yours and mine."

"But not really, Wendy?" he asked anxiously.

"Not if you don't wish it," she replied; and she distinctly heard his sigh of relief. "Peter," she asked, trying to speak firmly, "what are your exact feelings to me?"

"Those of a devoted son, Wendy."

"I thought so," she said, and went and sat by herself at the extreme end of the room.

"You are so queer," he said, frankly puzzled, "and Tiger Lily is just the same. There is something she wants to be to me, but she says it is not my mother."

"No, indeed, it is not," Wendy replied with frightful emphasis. Now we know why she was prejudiced against the redskins.

"Then what is it?"

"It isn't for a lady to tell."

"Oh, very well," Peter said, a little nettled. "Perhaps Tinker Bell will tell me."

"Oh yes, Tinker Bell will tell you," Wendy retorted scornfully. "She is an abandoned little creature."

Here Tink, who was in her bedroom, eavesdropping, squeaked out something impudent.

"She says she glories in being abandoned," Peter interpreted.

He had a sudden idea. "Perhaps Tink wants to be my mother?"

"You silly ass!" cried Tinker Bell in a passion.

She had said it so often that Wendy needed no translation.

"I almost agree with her," Wendy snapped. Fancy Wendy snapping! But she had been much tried, and she little knew what was to happen before the night was out. If she had known she would not have snapped.

None of them knew. Perhaps it was best not to know. Their ignorance gave them one more glad hour; and as it was to be their last hour on the island, let us rejoice that there were sixty glad minutes in it. They sang and danced in their night-gowns. Such a deliciously creepy song it was, in which they pretended to be frightened at their own shadows, little witting that so soon shadows would close in upon them, from whom they would shrink in real fear. So uproariously gay was the dance, and how they buffeted each other on the bed and out of it! It was a pillow fight rather than a dance, and when it was finished, the pillows insisted on one bout more, like partners who know that they may never meet again. The stories they told, before it was time for Wendy's good-night story! Even Slightly tried to tell a story that night, but the beginning was so fearfully dull that it appalled not only the others but himself, and he said happily:

"Yes, it is a dull beginning. I say, let us pretend that it is the end."

And then at last they all got into bed for Wendy's story, the story they loved best, the story Peter hated. Usually when she began to tell this story he left the room or put his hands over his ears; and possibly if he had done either of those things this time they might all still be on the island. But to-night he remained on his stool; and we shall see what happened.

Chapter 11

Wendy's Story

"Little less noise there," Peter called out, determined that she should have fair play, however beastly a story it might be in his opinion.

"Listen, then," said Wendy, settling down to her story, with Michael at her feet and seven boys in the bed. "There was once a gentleman – "

"I had rather he had been a lady," Curly said.

"I wish he had been a white rat," said Nibs.

"Quiet," their mother admonished (*cautioned*) them. "There was a lady also, and – "

"Oh, mummy," cried the first twin, "you mean that there is a lady also, don't you? She is not dead, is she?"

"Oh, no."

"I am awfully glad she isn't dead," said Tootles. "Are you glad, John?"

"Of course I am."

"Are you glad, Nibs?"

"Rather."

"Are you glad, Twins?"

"We are glad."

"Oh dear," sighed Wendy.

"Little less noise there," Peter called out, determined that she should

have fair play, however beastly a story it might be in his opinion.

"The gentleman's name," Wendy continued, "was Mr. Darling, and her name was Mrs. Darling."

"I knew them," John said, to annoy the others.

"I think I knew them," said Michael rather doubtfully.

"They were married, you know," explained Wendy, "and what do you think they had?"

"White rats," cried Nibs, inspired.

"No."

"It's awfully puzzling," said Tootles, who knew the story by heart.

"Quiet, Tootles. They had three descendants."

"What is descendants?"

"Well, you are one, Twin."

"Did you hear that, John? I am a descendant."

"Descendants are only children," said John.

"Oh dear, oh dear," sighed Wendy. "Now these three children had a faithful nurse called Nana; but Mr. Darling was angry with her and chained her up in the yard, and so all the children flew away."

"It's an awfully good story," said Nibs.

"They flew away," Wendy continued, "to the Neverland, where the lost children are."

"I just thought they did," Curly broke in excitedly. "I don't know how it is, but I just thought they did!"

"O Wendy," cried Tootles, "was one of the lost children called Tootles?"

"Yes, he was."

"I am in a story. Hurrah, I am in a story, Nibs."

"Hush. Now I want you to consider the feelings of the unhappy parents with all their children flown away."

"Oo!" they all moaned, though they were not really considering the feelings of the unhappy parents one jot.

"Think of the empty beds!"

"Oo!"

"It's awfully sad," the first twin said cheerfully.

"I don't see how it can have a happy ending," said the second twin. "Do you, Nibs?"

"I'm frightfully anxious."

"If you knew how great is a mother's love," Wendy told them triumphantly, "you would have no fear." She had now come to the part that Peter hated.

"I do like a mother's love," said Tootles, hitting Nibs with a pillow. "Do you like a mother's love, Nibs?"

"I do just," said Nibs, hitting back.

"You see," Wendy said complacently, "our heroine knew that the mother would always leave the window open for her children to fly back by; so they stayed away for years and had a lovely time."

"Did they ever go back?"

"Let us now," said Wendy, bracing herself up for her finest effort, "take a peep into the future"; and they all gave themselves the twist that makes peeps into the future easier. "Years have rolled by, and who is this elegant lady of uncertain age alighting at London Station?"

"O Wendy, who is she?" cried Nibs, every bit as excited as if he didn't know.

"Can it be – yes – no – it is – the fair Wendy!"

"Oh!"

"And who are the two noble portly figures accompanying her, now grown to man's estate? Can they be John and Michael? They are!"

"Oh!"

"'See, dear brothers,'"says Wendy pointing upwards, "'there is the window still standing open. Ah, now we are rewarded for our sublime faith in a mother's love.' So up they flew to their mummy and daddy, and pen cannot describe the happy scene, over which we draw a veil."

That was the story, and they were as pleased with it as the fair narrator herself. Everything just as it should be, you see. Off we skip like the most heartless things in the world, which is what children are, but so attractive; and we have an entirely selfish time, and then when we have need of special attention we nobly return for it, confident that we shall be rewarded instead of smacked.

So great indeed was their faith in a mother's love that they felt they could afford to be callous for a bit longer.

But there was one there who knew better, and when Wendy finished he uttered a hollow groan.

"What is it, Peter?" she cried, running to him, thinking he was ill. She felt him solicitously, lower down than his chest. "Where is it, Peter?"

"It isn't that kind of pain," Peter replied darkly.

"Then what kind is it?"

"Wendy, you are wrong about mothers."

They all gathered round him in affright, so alarming was his agitation; and with a fine candour he told them what he had hitherto

concealed.

"Long ago," he said, "I thought like you that my mother would always keep the window open for me, so I stayed away for moons and moons and moons, and then flew back; but the window was barred, for mother had forgotten all about me, and there was another little boy sleeping in my bed."

I am not sure that this was true, but Peter thought it was true; and it scared them.

"Are you sure mothers are like that?"

"Yes."

So this was the truth about mothers. The toads!

Still it is best to be careful; and no one knows so quickly as a child when he should give in. "Wendy, let us go home," cried John and Michael together.

"Yes," she said, clutching them.

"Not to-night?" asked the lost boys bewildered. They knew in what they called their hearts that one can get on quite well without a mother, and that it is only the mothers who think you can't.

"At once," Wendy replied resolutely, for the horrible thought had come to her: "Perhaps mother is in half mourning by this time."

This dread made her forgetful of what must be Peter's feelings, and she said to him rather sharply, "Peter, will you make the necessary arrangements?"

"If you wish it," he replied, as coolly as if she had asked him to pass the nuts.

Not so much as a sorry-to-lose-you between them! If she did not mind the parting, he was going to show her, was Peter, that neither did he.

But of course he cared very much; and he was so full of wrath against grown-ups, who, as usual, were spoiling everything, that as soon as he got inside his tree he breathed intentionally quick short breaths at the rate of about five to a second. He did this because there is a saying in the Neverland that, every time you breathe, a grown-up dies; and Peter was killing them off vindictively as fast as possible.

Then having given the necessary instructions to the redskins he returned to the home, where an unworthy scene had been enacted in his absence. Panic-stricken at the thought of losing Wendy the lost boys had advanced upon her threateningly.

"It will be worse than before she came," they cried.

"We shan't let her go."

"Let's keep her prisoner."

"Ay, chain her up."

In her extremity an instinct told her to which of them to turn.

"Tootles," she cried, "I appeal to you."

Was it not strange? She appealed to Tootles, quite the silliest one.

Grandly, however, did Tootles respond. For that one moment he dropped his silliness and spoke with dignity.

"I am just Tootles," he said, "and nobody minds me. But the first who does not behave to Wendy like an English gentleman I will blood him severely."

He drew back his hanger; and for that instant his sun was at noon. The others held back uneasily. Then Peter returned, and they saw at once that they would get no support from him. He would keep no girl in the Neverland against her will.

"Wendy," he said, striding up and down, "I have asked the redskins to guide you through the wood, as flying tires you so."

"Thank you, Peter."

"Then," he continued, in the short sharp voice of one accustomed to be obeyed, "Tinker Bell will take you across the sea. Wake her, Nibs."

Nibs had to knock twice before he got an answer, though Tink had really been sitting up in bed listening for some time.

"Who are you? How dare you? Go away," she cried.

"You are to get up, Tink," Nibs called, "and take Wendy on a journey."

Of course Tink had been delighted to hear that Wendy was going; but she was jolly well determined not to be her courier, and she said so in still more offensive language. Then she pretended to be asleep again.

"She says she won't!" Nibs exclaimed, aghast at such insubordination, whereupon Peter went sternly toward the young lady's chamber.

"Tink," he rapped out, "if you don't get up and dress at once I will open the curtains, and then we shall all see you in your negligée (*nightgown*)."

This made her leap to the floor. "Who said I wasn't getting up?" she cried.

In the meantime the boys were gazing very forlornly at Wendy, now equipped with John and Michael for the journey. By this time they were dejected, not merely because they were about to lose her, but also because they felt that she was going off to something nice to which they had not been invited. Novelty was beckoning to them as usual.

Crediting them with a nobler feeling Wendy melted.

"Dear ones," she said, "if you will all come with me I feel almost sure I can get my father and mother to adopt you."

The invitation was meant specially for Peter, but each of the boys

was thinking exclusively of himself, and at once they jumped with joy.

"But won't they think us rather a handful?" Nibs asked in the middle of his jump.

"Oh no," said Wendy, rapidly thinking it out, "it will only mean having a few beds in the drawing-room; they can be hidden behind the screens on first Thursdays."

"Peter, can we go?" they all cried imploringly. They took it for granted that if they went he would go also, but really they scarcely cared. Thus children are ever ready, when novelty knocks, to desert their dearest ones.

"All right," Peter replied with a bitter smile, and immediately they rushed to get their things.

"And now, Peter," Wendy said, thinking she had put everything right, "I am going to give you your medicine before you go." She loved to give them medicine, and undoubtedly gave them too much. Of course it was only water, but it was out of a bottle, and she always shook the bottle and counted the drops, which gave it a certain medicinal quality. On this occasion, however, she did not give Peter his draught (*portion*), for just as she had prepared it, she saw a look on his face that made her heart sink.

"Get your things, Peter," she cried, shaking.

"No," he answered, pretending indifference, "I am not going with you, Wendy."

"Yes, Peter."

"No."

To show that her departure would leave him unmoved, he skipped up and down the room, playing gaily on his heartless pipes. She had to run about after him, though it was rather undignified.

"To find your mother," she coaxed.

Now, if Peter had ever quite had a mother, he no longer missed her. He could do very well without one. He had thought them out, and remembered only their bad points.

"No, no," he told Wendy decisively; "perhaps she would say I was old, and I just want always to be a little boy and to have fun."

"But, Peter – "

"No."

And so the others had to be told.

"Peter isn't coming."

Peter not coming! They gazed blankly at him, their sticks over their backs, and on each stick a bundle. Their first thought was that if Peter was not going he had probably changed his mind about letting them go.

But he was far too proud for that. "If you find your mothers," he said darkly, "I hope you will like them."

The awful cynicism of this made an uncomfortable impression, and most of them began to look rather doubtful. After all, their faces said, were they not noodles to want to go?

"Now then," cried Peter, "no fuss, no blubbering; good-bye, Wendy"; and he held out his hand cheerily, quite as if they must really go now, for he had something important to do.

She had to take his hand, and there was no indication that he would prefer a thimble.

"You will remember about changing your flannels, Peter?" she said, lingering over him. She was always so particular about their flannels.

"Yes."

"And you will take your medicine?"

"Yes."

That seemed to be everything, and an awkward pause followed. Peter, however, was not the kind that breaks down before other people. "Are you ready, Tinker Bell?" he called out.

"Ay! Ay!"

"Then lead the way."

Tink darted up the nearest tree; but no one followed her, for it was at this moment that the pirates made their dreadful attack upon the redskins. Above, where all had been so still, the air was rent with shrieks and the clash of steel. Below, there was dead silence. Mouths opened and remained open. Wendy fell on her knees, but her arms were extended toward Peter. All arms were extended to him, as if suddenly blown in his direction; they were beseeching him mutely not to desert them. As for Peter, he seized his sword, the same he thought he had slain Barbecue with, and the lust of battle was in his eye.

Chapter 12

The Children Are Carried Off

The night's work was not yet over, for it was not the redskins he had come out to destroy; they were but the bees to be smoked, so that he should get at the honey.

The pirate attack had been a complete surprise: a sure proof that the unscrupulous Hook had conducted it improperly, for to surprise redskins fairly is beyond the wit of the white man.

By all the unwritten laws of savage warfare it is always the redskin who attacks, and with the wiliness of his race he does it just before the dawn, at which time he knows the courage of the whites to be at its lowest ebb. The white men have in the meantime made a rude stockade on the summit of yonder undulating ground, at the foot of which a stream runs, for it is destruction to be too far from water. There they await the onslaught, the inexperienced ones clutching their revolvers and treading on twigs, but the old hands sleeping tranquilly until just before the dawn. Through the long black night the savage scouts wriggle, snake-like, among the grass without stirring a blade. The brushwood closes behind them, as silently as sand into which a mole has dived. Not a sound is to be heard, save when they give vent to a wonderful imitation of the lonely call of the coyote. The cry is answered by other braves; and some of them do it even better than the coyotes, who are not very good at it. So the chill hours wear on, and the long suspense is horribly trying to the paleface who has to live through it for the first time; but to the trained hand those ghastly calls and still ghastlier silences are but an intimation of how the night is marching.

That this was the usual procedure was so well known to Hook that in disregarding it he cannot be excused on the plea of ignorance.

The Piccaninnies, on their part, trusted implicitly to his honour, and their whole action of the night stands out in marked contrast to his. They left nothing undone that was consistent with the reputation of their tribe. With that alertness of the senses which is at once the marvel and despair of civilised peoples, they knew that the pirates were on the island from the moment one of them trod on a dry stick; and in an incredibly short space of time the coyote cries began. Every foot of ground between the spot where Hook had landed his forces and the home under the trees was stealthily examined by braves wearing their mocassins with the heels in front. They found only one hillock with a stream at its base, so that Hook had no choice; here he must establish himself and wait for just before the dawn. Everything being thus mapped out with almost diabolical cunning, the main body of the redskins folded their blankets around them, and in the phlegmatic manner that is to them, the pearl of manhood squatted above the children's home, awaiting the cold moment when they should deal pale death.

Here dreaming, though wide-awake, of the exquisite tortures to which they were to put him at break of day, those confiding savages were found by the treacherous Hook. From the accounts afterwards supplied by such of the scouts as escaped the carnage, he does not seem even to have paused at the rising ground, though it is certain that in that grey light he must have seen it: no thought of waiting to be attacked appears from first to last to have visited his subtle mind; he would not even hold off till the night was nearly spent; on he pounded with no policy but to fall to (*get into combat*). What could the bewildered scouts do, masters as they were of every war-like artifice save this one, but trot helplessly after him, exposing themselves fatally to view, while they gave pathetic utterance to the coyote cry.

Around the brave Tiger Lily were a dozen of her stoutest warriors, and they suddenly saw the perfidious pirates bearing down upon them. Fell from their eyes then the film through which they had looked at victory. No more would they torture at the stake. For them the happy hunting-grounds was now. They knew it; but as their father's sons they acquitted themselves. Even then they had time to gather in a phalanx (*dense formation*) that would have been hard to break had they risen quickly, but this they were forbidden to do by the traditions of their race. It is written that the noble savage must never express surprise in the presence of the white. Thus terrible as the sudden appearance of the pirates must have been to them, they remained stationary for a moment, not a muscle moving; as if the foe had come by invitation. Then, indeed, the tradition gallantly upheld, they seized their weapons, and the air was torn with the war-cry; but it was now too late.

It is no part of ours to describe what was a massacre rather than a fight. Thus perished many of the flower of the Piccaninny tribe. Not all unavenged did they die, for with Lean Wolf fell Alf Mason, to disturb the Spanish Main no more, and among others who bit the dust were Geo. Scourie, Chas. Turley, and the Alsatian Foggerty. Turley fell to the tomahawk of the terrible Panther, who ultimately cut a way through the pirates with Tiger Lily and a small remnant of the tribe.

To what extent Hook is to blame for his tactics on this occasion is for the historian to decide. Had he waited on the rising ground till the proper hour he and his men would probably have been butchered; and in judging him it is only fair to take this into account. What he should perhaps have done was to acquaint his opponents that he proposed to follow a new method. On the other hand, this, as destroying the element of surprise, would have made his strategy of no avail, so that the whole question is beset with difficulties. One cannot at least withhold a reluctant admiration for the wit that had conceived so bold a scheme, and the fell genius with which it was carried out.

What were his own feelings about himself at that triumphant moment? Fain would his dogs have known, as breathing heavily and wiping their cutlasses, they gathered at a discreet distance from his hook, and squinted through their ferret eyes at this extraordinary man. Elation must have been in his heart, but his face did not reflect it: ever a dark and solitary enigma, he stood aloof from his followers in spirit as in substance.

The night's work was not yet over, for it was not the redskins he had come out to destroy; they were but the bees to be smoked, so that he should get at the honey. It was Pan he wanted, Pan and Wendy and their band, but chiefly Pan.

Peter was such a small boy that one tends to wonder at the man's hatred of him. True he had flung Hook's arm to the crocodile, but even this and the increased insecurity of life to which it led, owing to the crocodile's pertinacity, hardly account for a vindictiveness so relentless and malignant. The truth is that there was a something about Peter which goaded the pirate captain to frenzy. It was not his courage, it was not his engaging appearance, it was not – . There is no beating about the bush, for we know quite well what it was, and have got to tell. It was Peter's cockiness.

This had got on Hook's nerves; it made his iron claw twitch, and at night it disturbed him like an insect. While Peter lived, the tortured man felt that he was a lion in a cage into which a sparrow had come.

The question now was how to get down the trees, or how to get his dogs down? He ran his greedy eyes over them, searching for the thinnest ones. They wriggled uncomfortably, for they knew he would not scruple to ram them down with poles.

In the meantime, what of the boys? We have seen them at the first clang of the weapons, turned as it were into stone figures, open-mouthed, all appealing with outstretched arms to Peter; and we return to them as their mouths close, and their arms fall to their sides. The pandemonium above has ceased almost as suddenly as it arose, passed like a fierce gust of wind; but they know that in the passing it has determined their fate.

Which side had won?

The pirates, listening avidly at the mouths of the trees, heard the question put by every boy, and alas, they also heard Peter's answer.

"If the redskins have won," he said, "they will beat the tom- tom; it is always their sign of victory."

Now Smee had found the tom-tom, and was at that moment sitting on it. "You will never hear the tom-tom again," he muttered, but inaudibly of course, for strict silence had been enjoined . To his amazement Hook signed him to beat the tom-tom, and slowly there came to Smee an understanding of the dreadful wickedness of the order. Never, probably, had this simple man admired Hook so much.

Twice Smee beat upon the instrument, and then stopped to listen gleefully.

"The tom-tom," the miscreants heard Peter cry; "an Indian victory!"

The doomed children answered with a cheer that was music to the black hearts above, and almost immediately they repeated their good-byes to Peter. This puzzled the pirates, but all their other feelings were swallowed by a base delight that the enemy were about to come up the trees. They smirked at each other and rubbed their hands. Rapidly and silently Hook gave his orders: one man to each tree, and the others to arrange themselves in a line two yards apart.

Chapter 13

Do You Believe in Fairies?

"If you believe," he shouted to them, "clap your hands; don't let Tink die."

The more quickly this horror is disposed of the better. The first to emerge from his tree was Curly. He rose out of it into the arms of Cecco, who flung him to Smee, who flung him to Starkey, who flung him to Bill Jukes, who flung him to Noodler, and so he was tossed from one to another till he fell at the feet of the black pirate. All the boys were plucked from their trees in this ruthless manner; and several of them were in the air at a time, like bales of goods flung from hand to hand.

A different treatment was accorded to Wendy, who came last. With ironical politeness Hook raised his hat to her, and, offering her his arm, escorted her to the spot where the others were being gagged. He did it with such an air, he was so frightfully DISTINGUE , that she was too fascinated to cry out. She was only a little girl.

Perhaps it is tell-tale to divulge that for a moment Hook entranced her, and we tell on her only because her slip led to strange results. Had she haughtily unhanded him (*and we should have loved to write it of her*), she would have been hurled through the air like the others, and then Hook would probably not have been present at the tying of the children; and had he not been at the tying he would not have discovered Slightly's secret, and without the secret he could not presently have made his foul attempt on Peter's life.

They were tied to prevent their flying away, doubled up with their knees close to their ears; and for this job the black pirate had cut a rope into nine equal pieces. All went well until Slightly's turn came, when he was found to be like those irritating parcels that use up all the string in going round and leave no tags with which to tie a knot. The pirates kicked him in their rage, just as you kick the parcel (*though in fairness you should kick the string*); and strange to say it was Hook who told them to belay their violence. His lip was curled with malicious triumph. While his dogs were merely sweating because every time they tried to pack the unhappy lad tight in one part he bulged out in another, Hook's master mind had gone far beneath Slightly's surface, probing not for effects but for causes; and his exultation showed that he had found them. Slightly, white to the gills, knew that Hook had surprised his secret, which was this, that no boy so blown out could use a tree wherein an average man need stick. Poor Slightly, most wretched of all the children now, for he was in a panic about Peter, bitterly regretted what he had done. Madly addicted to the drinking of water when he was hot, he had swelled in consequence to his present girth, and instead of reducing himself to fit his tree he had, unknown to the others, whittled his tree to make it fit him.

Sufficient of this Hook guessed to persuade him that Peter at last lay at his mercy, but no word of the dark design that now formed in the subterranean caverns of his mind crossed his lips; he merely signed that the captives were to be conveyed to the ship, and that he would be alone.

How to convey them? Hunched up in their ropes they might indeed be rolled down hill like barrels, but most of the way lay through a morass. Again Hook's genius surmounted difficulties. He indicated that the little house must be used as a conveyance. The children were flung into it, four stout pirates raised it on their shoulders, the others fell in behind, and singing the hateful pirate chorus the strange procession set off through the wood. I don't know whether any of the children were crying; if so, the singing drowned the sound; but as the little house disappeared in the forest, a brave though tiny jet of smoke issued from its chimney as if defying Hook.

Hook saw it, and it did Peter a bad service. It dried up any trickle of pity for him that may have remained in the pirate's infuriated breast.

The first thing he did on finding himself alone in the fast falling night was to tiptoe to Slightly's tree, and make sure that it provided him with a passage. Then for long he remained brooding; his hat of ill omen on the sward, so that any gentle breeze which had arisen might play refreshingly through his hair. Dark as were his thoughts his blue eyes were as soft as the periwinkle. Intently he listened for any sound from the nether world, but all was as silent below as above; the house under the ground seemed to be but one more empty tenement in the void. Was that boy asleep, or did he stand waiting at the foot of Slightly's tree, with his dagger in his hand?

There was no way of knowing, save by going down. Hook let his cloak slip softly to the ground, and then biting his lips till a lewd blood stood on them, he stepped into the tree. He was a brave man, but for a moment he had to stop there and wipe his brow, which was dripping like a candle. Then silently he let himself go into the unknown.

He arrived unmolested at the foot of the shaft, and stood still again, biting at his breath, which had almost left him. As his eyes became accustomed to the dim light various objects in the home under the trees took shape; but the only one on which his greedy gaze rested, long sought for and found at last, was the great bed. On the bed lay Peter fast asleep.

Unaware of the tragedy being enacted above, Peter had continued, for a little time after the children left, to play gaily on his pipes: no doubt rather a forlorn attempt to prove to himself that he did not care. Then he decided not to take his medicine, so as to grieve Wendy. Then he lay down on the bed outside the coverlet, to vex her still more; for she had always tucked them inside it, because you never know that you may not grow chilly at the turn of the night. Then he nearly cried; but it struck him how indignant she would be if he laughed instead; so he laughed a haughty laugh and fell asleep in the middle of it.

Sometimes, though not often, he had dreams, and they were more painful than the dreams of other boys. For hours he could not be separated from these dreams, though he wailed piteously in them. They had to do, I think, with the riddle of his existence. At such times it had been Wendy's custom to take him out of bed and sit with him on her lap, soothing him in dear ways of her own invention, and when he grew calmer to put him back to bed before he quite woke up, so that he should not know of the indignity to which she had subjected him. But on this occasion he had fallen at once into a dreamless sleep. One arm dropped over the edge of the bed, one leg was arched, and the unfinished part of his laugh was stranded on his mouth, which was open, showing the little pearls.

Thus defenceless Hook found him. He stood silent at the foot of the tree looking across the chamber at his enemy. Did no feeling of compassion disturb his sombre breast? The man was not wholly evil; he loved flowers (*I have been told*) and sweet music (*he was himself no mean performer on the harpsichord*); and, let it be frankly admitted, the idyllic nature of the scene stirred him profoundly. Mastered by his better self he would have returned reluctantly up the tree, but for one thing.

What stayed him was Peter's impertinent appearance as he slept. The open mouth, the drooping arm, the arched knee: they were such a personification of cockiness as, taken together, will never again, one may hope, be presented to eyes so sensitive to their offensiveness. They steeled Hook's heart. If his rage had broken him into a hundred pieces every one of them would have disregarded the incident, and leapt at the sleeper.

Though a light from the one lamp shone dimly on the bed, Hook stood in darkness himself, and at the first stealthy step forward he discovered an obstacle, the door of Slightly's tree. It did not entirely fill the aperture, and he had been looking over it. Feeling for the catch, he found to his fury that it was low down, beyond his reach. To his disordered brain it seemed then that the irritating quality in Peter's face and figure visibly increased, and he rattled the door and flung himself against it. Was his enemy to escape him after all?

But what was that? The red in his eye had caught sight of Peter's medicine standing on a ledge within easy reach. He fathomed what it was straightaway, and immediately knew that the sleeper was in his power.

Lest he should be taken alive, Hook always carried about his person a dreadful drug, blended by himself of all the death- dealing rings that had come into his possession. These he had boiled down into a yellow liquid quite unknown to science, which was probably the most virulent poison in existence.

Five drops of this he now added to Peter's cup. His hand shook, but it was in exultation rather than in shame. As he did it he avoided glancing at the sleeper, but not lest pity should unnerve him; merely to avoid spilling. Then one long gloating look he cast upon his victim, and turning, wormed his way with difficulty up the tree. As he emerged at the top he looked the very spirit of evil breaking from its hole. Donning his hat at its most rakish angle, he wound his cloak around him, holding one end in front as if to conceal his person from the night, of which it was the blackest part, and muttering strangely to himself, stole away through the trees.

Peter slept on. The light guttered and went out, leaving the tenement in darkness; but still he slept. It must have been not less than ten o'clock by the crocodile, when he suddenly sat up in his bed, wakened by he knew not what. It was a soft cautious tapping on the door of his tree.

Soft and cautious, but in that stillness it was sinister. Peter felt for his dagger till his hand gripped it. Then he spoke.

"Who is that?"

For long there was no answer: then again the knock.

"Who are you?"

No answer.

He was thrilled, and he loved being thrilled. In two strides he reached the door. Unlike Slightly's door, it filled the aperture, so that he could not see beyond it, nor could the one knocking see him.

"I won't open unless you speak," Peter cried.

Then at last the visitor spoke, in a lovely bell-like voice.

"Let me in, Peter."

It was Tink, and quickly he unbarred to her. She flew in excitedly, her face flushed and her dress stained with mud.

"What is it?"

"Oh, you could never guess!" she cried, and offered him three guesses. "Out with it!" he shouted, and in one ungrammatical sentence, as long as the ribbons that conjurers pull from their mouths, she told of the capture of Wendy and the boys.

Peter's heart bobbed up and down as he listened. Wendy bound, and on the pirate ship; she who loved everything to be just so!

"I'll rescue her!" he cried, leaping at his weapons. As he leapt he thought of something he could do to please her. He could take his medicine.

His hand closed on the fatal draught.

"No!" shrieked Tinker Bell, who had heard Hook mutter about his deed as he sped through the forest.

"Why not?"

"It is poisoned."

"Poisoned? Who could have poisoned it?"

"Hook."

"Don't be silly. How could Hook have got down here?"

Alas, Tinker Bell could not explain this, for even she did not know the dark secret of Slightly's tree. Nevertheless Hook's words had left no room for doubt. The cup was poisoned.

"Besides," said Peter, quite believing himself "I never fell asleep."

He raised the cup. No time for words now; time for deeds; and with one of her lightning movements Tink got between his lips and the draught, and drained it to the dregs.

"Why, Tink, how dare you drink my medicine?"

But she did not answer. Already she was reeling in the air.

"What is the matter with you?" cried Peter, suddenly afraid.

"It was poisoned, Peter," she told him softly; "and now I am going to be dead."

"O Tink, did you drink it to save me?"

"Yes."

"But why, Tink?"

Her wings would scarcely carry her now, but in reply she alighted on his shoulder and gave his nose a loving bite. She whispered in his ear "You silly ass," and then, tottering to her chamber, lay down on the bed.

His head almost filled the fourth wall of her little room as he knelt near her in distress. Every moment her light was growing fainter; and he knew that if it went out she would be no more. She liked his tears so much that she put out her beautiful finger and let them run over it.

Her voice was so low that at first he could not make out what she said. Then he made it out. She was saying that she thought she could get well again if children believed in fairies.

Peter flung out his arms. There were no children there, and it was night time; but he addressed all who might be dreaming of the

Neverland, and who were therefore nearer to him than you think: boys and girls in their nighties, and naked papooses in their baskets hung from trees.

"Do you believe?" he cried.

Tink sat up in bed almost briskly to listen to her fate.

She fancied she heard answers in the affirmative, and then again she wasn't sure.

"What do you think?" she asked Peter.

"If you believe," he shouted to them, "clap your hands; don't let Tink die."

Many clapped.

Some didn't.

A few beasts hissed.

The clapping stopped suddenly; as if countless mothers had rushed to their nurseries to see what on earth was happening; but already Tink was saved. First her voice grew strong, then she popped out of bed, then she was flashing through the room more merry and impudent than ever. She never thought of thanking those who believed, but she would have like to get at the ones who had hissed.

"And now to rescue Wendy!"

The moon was riding in a cloudy heaven when Peter rose from his tree, begirt with weapons and wearing little else, to set out upon his perilous quest. It was not such a night as he would have chosen. He had hoped to fly, keeping not far from the ground so that nothing unwonted should escape his eyes; but in that fitful light to have flown low would have meant trailing his shadow through the trees, thus disturbing birds and acquainting a watchful foe that he was astir.

He regretted now that he had given the birds of the island such strange names that they are very wild and difficult of approach.

There was no other course but to press forward in redskin fashion, at which happily he was an adept But in what direction, for he could not be sure that the children had been taken to the ship? A light fall of snow had obliterated all footmarks; and a deathly silence pervaded the island, as if for a space Nature stood still in horror of the recent carnage. He had taught the children something of the forest lore that he had himself learned from Tiger Lily and Tinker Bell, and knew that in their dire hour they were not likely to forget it. Slightly, if he had an opportunity, would blaze the trees, for instance, Curly would drop seeds, and Wendy would leave her handkerchief at some important place. The morning was needed to search for such guidance, and he could not wait. The upper world had called him, but would give no help.

The crocodile passed him, but not another living thing, not a sound, not a movement; and yet he knew well that sudden death might be at the next tree, or stalking him from behind.

He swore this terrible oath: “Hook or me this time.”

Now he crawled forward like a snake; and again, erect, he darted across a space on which the moonlight played, one finger on his lip and his dagger at the ready. He was frightfully happy.

Chapter 14

The Pirate Ship

"Now then, bullies," he said briskly, "six of you walk the plank tonight, but I have room for two cabin boys. Which of you is it to be?"

One green light squinting over Kidd's Creek, which is near the mouth of the pirate river, marked where the brig, the JOLLY ROGER, lay, low in the water; a rakish-looking craft foul to the hull, every beam in her detestable, like ground strewn with mangled feathers. She was the cannibal of the seas, and scarce needed that watchful eye, for she floated immune in the horror of her name.

She was wrapped in the blanket of night, through which no sound from her could have reached the shore. There was little sound, and none agreeable save the whir of the ship's sewing machine at which Smee sat, ever industrious and obliging, the essence of the commonplace, pathetic Smee. I know not why he was so infinitely pathetic, unless it were because he was so pathetically unaware of it; but even strong men had to turn hastily from looking at him, and more than once on summer evenings he had touched the fount of Hook's tears and made it flow. Of this, as of almost everything else, Smee was quite unconscious.

A few of the pirates leant over the bulwarks, drinking in the miasma of the night; others sprawled by barrels over games of dice and cards; and the exhausted four who had carried the little house lay prone on the deck, where even in their sleep they rolled skillfully to this side or that out of Hook's reach, lest he should claw them mechanically in passing.

Hook trod the deck in thought. O man unfathomable. It was his hour of triumph. Peter had been removed for ever from his path, and all the other boys were in the brig, about to walk the plank. It was his grimmest deed since the days when he had brought Barbecue to

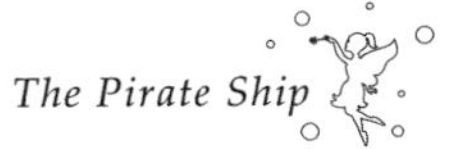

heel; and knowing as we do how vain a tabernacle is man, could we be surprised had he now paced the deck unsteadily, bellied out by the winds of his success?

But there was no elation in his gait, which kept pace with the action of his sombre mind. Hook was profoundly dejected.

He was often thus when communing with himself on board ship in the quietude of the night. It was because he was so terribly alone. This inscrutable man never felt more alone than when surrounded by his dogs. They were socially inferior to him.

Hook was not his true name. To reveal who he really was would even at this date set the country in a blaze; but as those who read between the lines must already have guessed, he had been at a famous public school; and its traditions still clung to him like garments, with which indeed they are largely concerned. Thus it was offensive to him even now to board a ship in the same dress in which he grappled her, and he still adhered in his walk to the school's distinguished slouch. But above all he retained the passion for good form.

Good form! However much he may have degenerated, he still knew that this is all that really matters.

From far within him he heard a creaking as of rusty portals, and through them came a stern tap-tap-tap, like hammering in the night when one cannot sleep. "Have you been good form to-day?" was their eternal question.

"Fame, fame, that glittering bauble, it is mine!" he cried.

"Is it quite good form to be distinguished at anything?" the tap-tap from his school replied.

"I am the only man whom Barbecue feared," he urged, "and Flint feared Barbecue."

"Barbecue, Flint – what house?" came the cutting retort.

Most disquieting reflection of all, was it not bad form to think about good form?

His vitals were tortured by this problem. It was a claw within him sharper than the iron one; and as it tore him, the perspiration dripped down his tallow countenance and streaked his doublet. Ofttimes he drew his sleeve across his face, but there was no damming that trickle.

Ah, envy not Hook.

There came to him a presentiment of his early dissolution. It was as if Peter's terrible oath had boarded the ship. Hook felt a gloomy desire to make his dying speech, lest presently there should be no time for it.

"Better for Hook," he cried, "if he had had less ambition!" It was in his darkest hours only that he referred to himself in the third person.

"No little children to love me!"

Strange that he should think of this, which had never troubled him before; perhaps the sewing machine brought it to his mind. For long

he muttered to himself, staring at Smee, who was hemming placidly, under the conviction that all children feared him.

Feared him! Feared Smee! There was not a child on board the brig that night who did not already love him. He had said horrid things to them and hit them with the palm of his hand, because he could not hit with his fist, but they had only clung to him the more. Michael had tried on his spectacles.

To tell poor Smee that they thought him lovable! Hook itched to do it, but it seemed too brutal. Instead, he revolved this mystery in his mind: why do they find Smee lovable? He pursued the problem like the sleuth-hound that he was. If Smee was lovable, what was it that made him so? A terrible answer suddenly presented itself – "Good form?"

Had the bo'sun good form without knowing it, which is the best form of all?

He remembered that you have to prove you don't know you have it before you are eligible for Pop.

With a cry of rage he raised his iron hand over Smee's head; but he did not tear. What arrested him was this reflection:

"To claw a man because he is good form, what would that be?"

"Bad form!"

The unhappy Hook was as impotent as he was damp, and he fell forward like a cut flower.

His dogs thinking him out of the way for a time, discipline instantly relaxed; and they broke into a bacchanalian dance, which brought him to his feet at once, all traces of human weakness gone, as if a bucket of water had passed over him.

"Quiet, you scugs," he cried, "or I'll cast anchor in you"; and at once the din was hushed. "Are all the children chained, so that they cannot fly away?"

"Ay, ay."

"Then hoist them up."

The wretched prisoners were dragged from the hold, all except Wendy, and ranged in line in front of him. For a time he seemed unconscious of their presence. He lolled at his ease, humming, not unmelodiously, snatches of a rude song, and fingering a pack of cards. Ever and anon the light from his cigar gave a touch of colour to his face.

"Now then, bullies," he said briskly, "six of you walk the plank tonight, but I have room for two cabin boys. Which of you is it to be?"

"Don't irritate him unnecessarily," had been Wendy's instructions in the hold; so Tootles stepped forward politely. Tootles hated the idea of signing under such a man, but an instinct told him that it would be prudent to lay the responsibility on an absent person; and though a somewhat silly boy, he knew that mothers alone are always willing to be the buffer. All children know this about mothers, and despise them for it, but make constant use of it.

So Tootles explained prudently, "You see, sir, I don't think my mother would like me to be a pirate. Would your mother like you to be a pirate, Slightly?"

He winked at Slightly, who said mournfully, "I don't think so," as if he wished things had been otherwise. "Would your mother like you to be a pirate, Twin?"

"I don't think so," said the first twin, as clever as the others. "Nibs, would – "

"Stow this gab," roared Hook, and the spokesmen were dragged back. "You, boy," he said, addressing John, "you look as if you had a little pluck in you. Didst never want to be a pirate, my hearty?"

Now John had sometimes experienced this hankering at maths. prep; and he was struck by Hook's picking him out.

"I once thought of calling myself Red-handed Jack," he said diffidently.

"And a good name too. We'll call you that here, bully, if you join."

"What do you think, Michael?" asked John.

"What would you call me if I join?" Michael demanded.

"Blackbeard Joe."

Michael was naturally impressed. “What do you think, John?” He wanted John to decide, and John wanted him to decide.

“Shall we still be respectful subjects of the King?” John inquired.

Through Hook’s teeth came the answer: “You would have to swear, ‘Down with the King.’”

Perhaps John had not behaved very well so far, but he shone out now.

“Then I refuse,” he cried, banging the barrel in front of Hook.

“And I refuse,” cried Michael.

“Rule Britannia!” squeaked Curly.

The infuriated pirates buffeted them in the mouth; and Hook roared out, “That seals your doom. Bring up their mother. Get the plank ready.”

They were only boys, and they went white as they saw Jukes and Cecco preparing the fatal plank. But they tried to look brave when Wendy was brought up.

No words of mine can tell you how Wendy despised those pirates. To the boys there was at least some glamour in the pirate calling; but all that she saw was that the ship had not been tidied for years. There was not a porthole on the grimy glass of which you might not have written with your finger “Dirty pig”; and she had already written it

on several. But as the boys gathered round her she had no thought, of course, save for them.

"So, my beauty," said Hook, as if he spoke in syrup, "you are to see your children walk the plank."

Fine gentlemen though he was, the intensity of his communings had soiled his ruff, and suddenly he knew that she was gazing at it. With a hasty gesture he tried to hide it, but he was too late.

"Are they to die?" asked Wendy, with a look of such frightful contempt that he nearly fainted.

"They are," he snarled. "Silence all," he called gloatingly, "for a mother's last words to her children."

At this moment Wendy was grand. "These are my last words, dear boys," she said firmly. "I feel that I have a message to you from your real mothers, and it is this: 'We hope our sons will die like English gentlemen.'"

Even the pirates were awed, and Tootles cried out hysterically, "I am going to do what my mother hopes. What are you to do, Nibs?"

"What my mother hopes. What are you to do, Twin?"

"What my mother hopes. John, what are – "

But Hook had found his voice again.

"Tie her up!" he shouted.

It was Smee who tied her to the mast. “See here, honey,” he whispered, “I’ll save you if you promise to be my mother.”

But not even for Smee would she make such a promise. “I would almost rather have no children at all,” she said disdainfully .

It is sad to know that not a boy was looking at her as Smee tied her to the mast; the eyes of all were on the plank: that last little walk they were about to take. They were no longer able to hope that they would walk it manfully, for the capacity to think had gone from them; they could stare and shiver only.

Hook smiled on them with his teeth closed, and took a step toward Wendy. His intention was to turn her face so that she should see they boys walking the plank one by one. But he never reached her, he never heard the cry of anguish he hoped to wring from her. He heard something else instead.

It was the terrible tick-tick of the crocodile.

They all heard it – pirates, boys, Wendy; and immediately every head was blown in one direction; not to the water whence the sound proceeded, but toward Hook. All knew that what was about to happen concerned him alone, and that from being actors they were suddenly become spectators.

Very frightful was it to see the change that came over him. It was as if he had been clipped at every joint. He fell in a little heap.

The sound came steadily nearer; and in advance of it came this ghastly thought, "The crocodile is about to board the ship!"

Even the iron claw hung inactive; as if knowing that it was no intrinsic part of what the attacking force wanted. Left so fearfully alone, any other man would have lain with his eyes shut where he fell: but the gigantic brain of Hook was still working, and under its guidance he crawled on the knees along the deck as far from the sound as he could go. The pirates respectfully cleared a passage for him, and it was only when he brought up against the bulwarks that he spoke.

"Hide me!" he cried hoarsely.

They gathered round him, all eyes averted from the thing that was coming aboard. They had no thought of fighting it. It was Fate.

Only when Hook was hidden from them did curiosity loosen the limbs of the boys so that they could rush to the ship's side to see the crocodile climbing it. Then they got the strangest surprise of the Night of Nights; for it was no crocodile that was coming to their aid. It was Peter.

He signed to them not to give vent to any cry of admiration that might rouse suspicion. Then he went on ticking.

Chapter 15

Hook or Me This Time

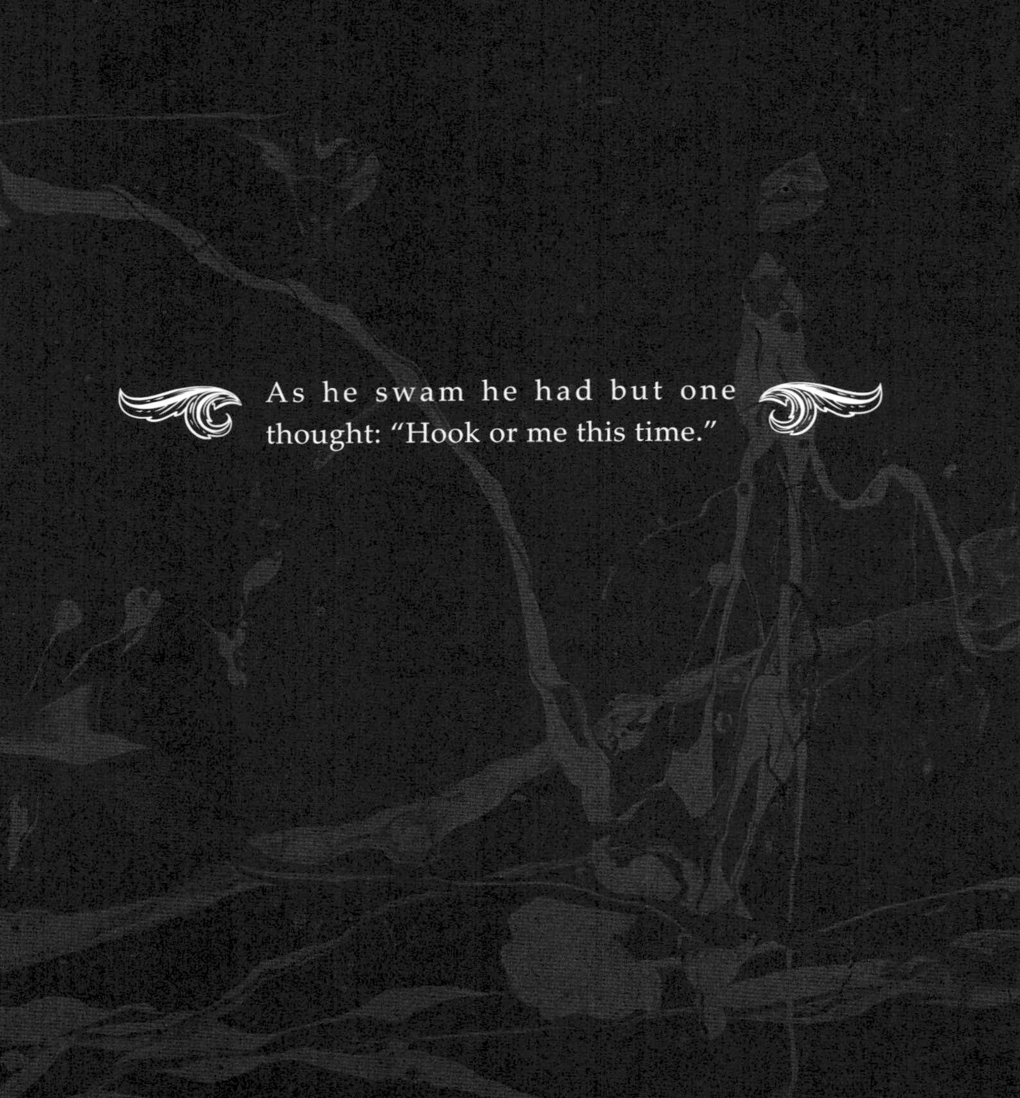

As he swam he had but one thought: "Hook or me this time."

Odd things happen to all of us on our way through life without our noticing for a time that they have happened. Thus, to take an instance, we suddenly discover that we have been deaf in one ear for we don't know how long, but, say, half an hour. Now such an experience had come that night to Peter. When last we saw him he was stealing across the island with one finger to his lips and his dagger at the ready. He had seen the crocodile pass by without noticing anything peculiar about it, but by and by he remembered that it had not been ticking. At first he thought this eerie, but soon concluded rightly that the clock had run down.

Without giving a thought to what might be the feelings of a fellow-creature thus abruptly deprived of its closest companion, Peter began to consider how he could turn the catastrophe to his own use; and he decided to tick, so that wild beasts should believe he was the crocodile and let him pass unmolested. He ticked superbly, but with one unforeseen result. The crocodile was among those who heard the sound, and it followed him, though whether with the purpose of regaining what it had lost, or merely as a friend under the belief that it was again ticking itself, will never be certainly known, for, like slaves to a fixed idea, it was a stupid beast.

Peter reached the shore without mishap, and went straight on, his legs encountering the water as if quite unaware that they had entered a new element. Thus many animals pass from land to water, but no other human of whom I know. As he swam he had but one thought: "Hook or me this time." He had ticked so long that he now went on ticking without knowing that he was doing it. Had he known he would have stopped, for to board the brig by help of the tick, though an ingenious idea, had not occurred to him.

On the contrary, he thought he had scaled her side as noiseless as a mouse; and he was amazed to see the pirates cowering from him, with Hook in their midst as abject as if he had heard the crocodile.

The crocodile! No sooner did Peter remember it than he heard the ticking. At first he thought the sound did come from the crocodile, and he looked behind him swiftly. They he realised that he was doing it himself, and in a flash he understood the situation. "How clever of me!" he thought at once, and signed to the boys not to burst into applause.

It was at this moment that Ed Teynte the quartermaster emerged from the forecastle and came along the deck. Now, reader, time what happened by your watch. Peter struck true and deep. John clapped his hands on the ill-fated pirate's mouth to stifle the dying groan. He fell forward. Four boys caught him to prevent the thud. Peter gave the signal, and the carrion was cast overboard. There was a splash, and then silence. How long has it taken?

"One!" (*Slightly had begun to count.*)

None too soon, Peter, every inch of him on tiptoe, vanished into the cabin; for more than one pirate was screwing up his courage to look round. They could hear each other's distressed breathing now, which showed them that the more terrible sound had passed.

"It's gone, captain," Smee said, wiping off his spectacles. "All's still again."

Slowly Hook let his head emerge from his ruff, and listened so intently that he could have caught the echo of the tick. There was not a sound, and he drew himself up firmly to his full height.

"Then here's to Johnny Plank!" he cried brazenly, hating the boys more than ever because they had seen him unbend. He broke into the villainous ditty:

"Yo ho, yo ho, the frisky plank,
You walk along it so,
Till it goes down and you goes down
To Davy Jones below!"

To terrorize the prisoners the more, though with a certain loss of dignity, he danced along an imaginary plank, grimacing at them as he sang; and when he finished he cried, "Do you want a touch of the cat before you walk the plank?"

At that they fell on their knees. "No, no!" they cried so piteously that every pirate smiled.

"Fetch the cat, Jukes," said Hook; "it's in the cabin."

The cabin! Peter was in the cabin! The children gazed at each other.

"Ay, ay," said Jukes blithely, and he strode into the cabin. They followed him with their eyes; they scarce knew that Hook had resumed his song, his dogs joining in with him:

"Yo ho, yo ho, the scratching cat,
Its tails are nine, you know,
And when they're writ upon your back – "

What was the last line will never be known, for of a sudden the song was stayed by a dreadful screech from the cabin. It wailed through the ship, and died away. Then was heard a crowing sound which was well understood by the boys, but to the pirates was almost more eerie than the screech.

"What was that?" cried Hook.

"Two," said Slightly solemnly.

The Italian Cecco hesitated for a moment and then swung into the cabin. He tottered out, haggard.

"What's the matter with Bill Jukes, you dog?" hissed Hook, towering over him.

"The matter wi' him is he's dead, stabbed," replied Cecco in a hollow voice.

"Bill Jukes dead!" cried the startled pirates.

"The cabin's as black as a pit," Cecco said, almost gibbering, "but there is something terrible in there: the thing you heard crowing."

The exultation of the boys, the lowering looks of the pirates, both were seen by Hook.

"Cecco," he said in his most steely voice, "go back and fetch me out that doodle-doo."

Cecco, bravest of the brave, cowered before his captain, crying "No, no"; but Hook was purring to his claw.

"Did you say you would go, Cecco?" he said musingly.

Cecco went, first flinging his arms despairingly. There was no more singing, all listened now; and again came a death-screech and again a crow.

No one spoke except Slightly. "Three," he said.

Hook rallied his dogs with a gesture. "'S'death and odds fish," he thundered, "who is to bring me that doodle-doo?"

"Wait till Cecco comes out," growled Starkey, and the others took up the cry.

"I think I heard you volunteer, Starkey," said Hook, purring again.

"No, by thunder!" Starkey cried.

"My hook thinks you did," said Hook, crossing to him. "I wonder if it would not be advisable, Starkey, to humour the hook?"

"I'll swing before I go in there," replied Starkey doggedly, and again he had the support of the crew.

"Is this mutiny?" asked Hook more pleasantly than ever. "Starkey's ringleader!"

"Captain, mercy!" Starkey whimpered, all of a tremble now.

"Shake hands, Starkey," said Hook, proffering his claw.

Starkey looked round for help, but all deserted him. As he backed up Hook advanced, and now the red spark was in his eye. With a despairing scream the pirate leapt upon Long Tom and precipitated himself into the sea.

"Four," said Slightly.

"And now," Hook said courteously, "did any other gentlemen say mutiny?" Seizing a lantern and raising his claw with a menacing gesture, "I'll bring out that doodle-doo myself," he said, and sped into the cabin.

"Five." How Slightly longed to say it. He wetted his lips to be ready, but Hook came staggering out, without his lantern.

"Something blew out the light," he said a little unsteadily.

"Something!" echoed Mullins.

"What of Cecco?" demanded Noodler.

"He's as dead as Jukes," said Hook shortly.

His reluctance to return to the cabin impressed them all

unfavourably, and the mutinous sounds again broke forth. All pirates are superstitious, and Cookson cried, "They do say the surest sign a ship's accurst is when there's one on board more than can be accounted for."

"I've heard," muttered Mullins, "he always boards the pirate craft last. Had he a tail, captain?"

"They say," said another, looking viciously at Hook, "that when he comes it's in the likeness of the wickedest man aboard."

"Had he a hook, captain?" asked Cookson insolently; and one after another took up the cry, "The ship's doomed!" At this the children could not resist raising a cheer. Hook had well-nigh forgotten his prisoners, but as he swung round on them now his face lit up again.

"Lads," he cried to his crew, "now here's a notion. Open the cabin door and drive them in. Let them fight the doodle-doo for their lives. If they kill him, we're so much the better; if he kills them, we're none the worse."

For the last time his dogs admired Hook, and devotedly they did his bidding. The boys, pretending to struggle, were pushed into the cabin and the door was closed on them.

"Now, listen!" cried Hook, and all listened. But not one dared to face the door. Yes, one, Wendy, who all this time had been bound to the mast. It was for neither a scream nor a crow that she was watching, it was for the reappearance of Peter.

She had not long to wait. In the cabin he had found the thing for which he had gone in search: the key that would free the children of their manacles, and now they all stole forth, armed with such weapons as they could find. First signing them to hide, Peter cut Wendy's bonds, and then nothing could have been easier than for them all to fly off together; but one thing barred the way, an oath, "Hook or me this time." So when he had freed Wendy, he whispered for her to conceal herself with the others, and himself took her place by the mast, her cloak around him so that he should pass for her. Then he took a great breath and crowed.

To the pirates it was a voice crying that all the boys lay slain in the cabin; and they were panic-stricken. Hook tried to hearten them; but like the dogs he had made them they showed him their fangs, and he knew that if he took his eyes off them now they would leap at him.

"Lads," he said, ready to cajole or strike as need be, but never quailing for an instant, "I've thought it out. There's a Jonah aboard."

"Ay," they snarled, "a man wi' a hook."

"No, lads, no, it's the girl. Never was luck on a pirate ship wi' a woman on board. We'll right the ship when she's gone."

Some of them remembered that this had been a saying of Flint's. "It's worth trying," they said doubtfully.

"Fling the girl overboard," cried Hook; and they made a rush at the figure in the cloak.

“There’s none can save you now, missy,” Mullins hissed jeeringly.

“There’s one,” replied the figure.

“Who’s that?”

“Peter Pan the avenger!” came the terrible answer; and as he spoke Peter flung off his cloak. Then they all knew who ’twas that had been undoing them in the cabin, and twice Hook essayed to speak and twice he failed. In that frightful moment I think his fierce heart broke.

At last he cried, “Cleave him to the brisket!” but without conviction.

“Down, boys, and at them!” Peter’s voice rang out; and in another moment the clash of arms was resounding through the ship. Had the pirates kept together it is certain that they would have won; but the onset came when they were still unstrung, and they ran hither and thither, striking wildly, each thinking himself the last survivor of the crew. Man to man they were the stronger; but they fought on the defensive only, which enabled the boys to hunt in pairs and choose their quarry. Some of the miscreants leapt into the sea; others hid in dark recesses, where they were found by Slightly, who did not fight, but ran about with a lantern which he flashed in their faces, so that they were half blinded and fell as an easy prey to the reeking swords of the other boys. There was little sound to be heard but the clang of weapons, an occasional screech or splash, and Slightly monotonously counting – five – six – seven – eight – nine – ten – eleven.

I think all were gone when a group of savage boys surrounded Hook, who seemed to have a charmed life, as he kept them at bay in that circle of fire. They had done for his dogs, but this man alone seemed to be a match for them all. Again and again they closed upon him, and again and again he hewed a clear space. He had lifted up one boy with his hook, and was using him as a buckler (*shield*), when another, who had just passed his sword through Mullins, sprang into the fray.

"Put up your swords, boys," cried the newcomer, "this man is mine."

Thus suddenly Hook found himself face to face with Peter. The others drew back and formed a ring around them.

For long the two enemies looked at one another, Hook shuddering slightly, and Peter with the strange smile upon his face.

"So, Pan," said Hook at last, "this is all your doing."

"Ay, James Hook," came the stern answer, "it is all my doing."

"Proud and insolent youth," said Hook, "prepare to meet thy doom."

"Dark and sinister man," Peter answered, "have at thee."

Without more words they fell to, and for a space there was no advantage to either blade. Peter was a superb swordsman, and parried with dazzling rapidity; ever and anon he followed up a feint with a lunge that got past his foe's defence, but his shorter reach stood him in ill stead, and he could not drive the steel home. Hook, scarcely his inferior in brilliancy, but not quite so nimble in wrist play, forced him back by the weight of his onset, hoping suddenly to end all with a favourite thrust, taught him long ago by Barbecue at Rio; but to his astonishment he found this thrust turned aside again and again. Then he sought to close and give the quietus with his iron hook, which all this time had been pawing the air; but Peter doubled under it and, lunging fiercely, pierced him in the ribs. At the sight of his own blood, whose peculiar colour, you remember, was offensive to him, the sword fell from Hook's hand, and he was at Peter's mercy.

"Now!" cried all the boys, but with a magnificent gesture Peter invited his opponent to pick up his sword. Hook did so instantly, but with a tragic feeling that Peter was showing good form.

Hitherto he had thought it was some fiend fighting him, but darker suspicions assailed him now.

"Pan, who and what art thou?" he cried huskily.

"I'm youth, I'm joy," Peter answered at a venture, "I'm a little bird that has broken out of the egg."

This, of course, was nonsense; but it was proof to the unhappy Hook that Peter did not know in the least who or what he was, which is the very pinnacle of good form.

"To't again," he cried despairingly.

He fought now like a human flail, and every sweep of that terrible sword would have severed in twain any man or boy who obstructed it; but Peter fluttered round him as if the very wind it made blew him out of the danger zone. And again and again he darted in and pricked.

Hook was fighting now without hope. That passionate breast no longer asked for life; but for one boon it craved: to see Peter show bad form before it was cold forever.

Abandoning the fight he rushed into the powder magazine and fired it.

"In two minutes," he cried, "the ship will be blown to pieces."

Now, now, he thought, true form will show.

But Peter issued from the powder magazine with the shell in his hands, and calmly flung it overboard.

What sort of form was Hook himself showing? Misguided man though he was, we may be glad, without sympathising with him, that in the end he was true to the traditions of his race. The other boys were flying around him now, flouting, scornful; and he staggered about the deck striking up at them impotently, his mind was no longer with them; it was slouching in the playing fields of long ago, or being sent up for good, or watching the wall-game from a famous wall. And his shoes were right, and his waistcoat was right, and his tie was right, and his socks were right.

James Hook, thou not wholly unheroic figure, farewell.

For we have come to his last moment.

Seeing Peter slowly advancing upon him through the air with dagger poised, he sprang upon the bulwarks to cast himself into the sea. He did not know that the crocodile was waiting for him; for we purposely stopped the clock that this knowledge might be spared him: a little mark of respect from us at the end.

He had one last triumph, which I think we need not grudge him. As he stood on the bulwark looking over his shoulder at Peter gliding through the air, he invited him with a gesture to use his foot. It made Peter kick instead of stab.

At last Hook had got the boon for which he craved.

"Bad form," he cried jeeringly, and went content to the crocodile.

Thus perished James Hook.

"Seventeen," Slightly sang out; but he was not quite correct in his figures. Fifteen paid the penalty for their crimes that night; but two reached the shore: Starkey to be captured by the redskins, who made him nurse for all their papooses, a melancholy come-down for a pirate; and Smee, who henceforth wandered about the world in his spectacles, making a precarious living by saying he was the only man that Jas. Hook had feared.

Wendy, of course, had stood by taking no part in the fight, though watching Peter with glistening eyes; but now that all was over she became prominent again. She praised them equally, and shuddered delightfully when Michael showed her the place where he had killed one; and then she took them into Hook's cabin and pointed to his watch which was hanging on a nail. It said "half- past one!"

The lateness of the hour was almost the biggest thing of all. She got them to bed in the pirates' bunks pretty quickly, you may be sure; all but Peter, who strutted up and down on the deck, until at last he fell asleep by the side of Long Tom. He had one of his dreams that night, and cried in his sleep for a long time, and Wendy held him tightly.

Chapter 16

The Return Home

 "O Nana, I dreamt my dear ones had come back." 

By three bells that morning they were all stirring their stumps; for there was a big sea running; and Tootles, the bo'sun, was among them, with a rope's end in his hand and chewing tobacco. They all donned pirate clothes cut off at the knee, shaved smartly, and tumbled up, with the true nautical roll and hitching their trousers.

It need not be said who was the captain. Nibs and John were first and second mate. There was a woman aboard. The rest were tars before the mast, and lived in the fo'c'sle. Peter had already lashed himself to the wheel; but he piped all hands and delivered a short address to them; said he hoped they would do their duty like gallant hearties, but that he knew they were the scum of Rio and the Gold Coast, and if they snapped at him he would tear them. The bluff strident words struck the note sailors understood, and they cheered him lustily. Then a few sharp orders were given, and they turned the ship round, and nosed her for the mainland.

Captain Pan calculated, after consulting the ship's chart, that if this weather lasted they should strike the Azores about the 21st of June, after which it would save time to fly.

Some of them wanted it to be an honest ship and others were in favour of keeping it a pirate; but the captain treated them as dogs, and they dared not express their wishes to him even in a round robin. Instant obedience was the only safe thing. Slightly got a dozen for looking perplexed when told to take soundings. The general feeling was that Peter was honest just now to lull Wendy's suspicions, but that there might be a change when the new suit was ready, which, against

her will, she was making for him out of some of Hook's wickedest garments. It was afterwards whispered among them that on the first night he wore this suit he sat long in the cabin with Hook's cigar-holder in his mouth and one hand clenched, all but for the forefinger, which he bent and held threateningly aloft like a hook.

Instead of watching the ship, however, we must now return to that desolate home from which three of our characters had taken heartless flight so long ago. It seems a shame to have neglected No. 14 all this time; and yet we may be sure that Mrs. Darling does not blame us. If we had returned sooner to look with sorrowful sympathy at her, she would probably have cried, "Don't be silly; what do I matter? Do go back and keep an eye on the children." So long as mothers are like this their children will take advantage of them; and they may lay to that.

Even now we venture into that familiar nursery only because its lawful occupants are on their way home; we are merely hurrying on in advance of them to see that their beds are properly aired and that Mr. and Mrs. Darling do not go out for the evening. We are no more than servants. Why on earth should their beds be properly aired, seeing that they left them in such a thankless hurry? Would it not serve them jolly well right if they came back and found that their parents were spending the week-end in the country? It would be the moral lesson they have been in need of ever since we met them; but if we contrived things in this way Mrs. Darling would never forgive us.

One thing I should like to do immensely, and that is to tell her, in the way authors have, that the children are coming back, that indeed they will be here on Thursday week. This would spoil so completely the surprise to which Wendy and John and Michael are looking forward. They have been planning it out on the ship: mother's rapture, father's shout of joy, Nana's leap through the air to embrace them first, when what they ought to be prepared for is a good hiding. How delicious to spoil it all by breaking the news in advance; so that when they enter grandly Mrs. Darling may not even offer Wendy her mouth, and Mr. Darling may exclaim pettishly, "Dash it all, here are those boys again." However, we should get no thanks even for this. We are beginning to know Mrs. Darling by this time, and may be sure that she would upbraid us for depriving the children of their little pleasure.

"But, my dear madam, it is ten days till Thursday week; so that by telling you what's what, we can save you ten days of unhappiness."

"Yes, but at what a cost! By depriving the children of ten minutes of delight."

"Oh, if you look at it in that way!"

"What other way is there in which to look at it?"

You see, the woman had no proper spirit. I had meant to say extraordinarily nice things about her; but I despise her, and not one of them will I say now. She does not really need to be told to have things ready, for they are ready. All the beds are aired, and she never leaves the house, and observe, the window is open. For all the use we are to her, we might well go back to the ship. However, as we are here we may as well stay and look on. That is all we are, lookers-on. Nobody

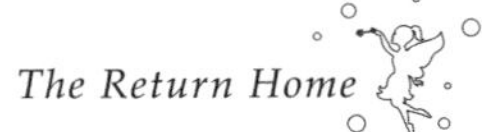

really wants us. So let us watch and say jaggy things, in the hope that some of them will hurt.

The only change to be seen in the night-nursery is that between nine and six the kennel is no longer there. When the children flew away, Mr. Darling felt in his bones that all the blame was his for having chained Nana up, and that from first to last she had been wiser than he. Of course, as we have seen, he was quite a simple man; indeed he might have passed for a boy again if he had been able to take his baldness off; but he had also a noble sense of justice and a lion's courage to do what seemed right to him; and having thought the matter out with anxious care after the flight of the children, he went down on all fours and crawled into the kennel. To all Mrs. Darling's dear invitations to him to come out he replied sadly but firmly:

"No, my own one, this is the place for me."

In the bitterness of his remorse he swore that he would never leave the kennel until his children came back. Of course this was a pity; but whatever Mr. Darling did he had to do in excess, otherwise he soon gave up doing it. And there never was a more humble man than the once proud George Darling, as he sat in the kennel of an evening talking with his wife of their children and all their pretty ways.

Very touching was his deference to Nana. He would not let her come into the kennel, but on all other matters he followed her wishes implicitly.

Every morning the kennel was carried with Mr. Darling in it to a cab, which conveyed him to his office, and he returned home in the same way at six. Something of the strength of character of the man will be seen if we remember how sensitive he was to the opinion of neighbours: this man whose every movement now attracted surprised attention. Inwardly he must have suffered torture; but he preserved a calm exterior even when the young criticised his little home, and he always lifted his hat courteously to any lady who looked inside.

It may have been quixotic, but it was magnificent. Soon the inward meaning of it leaked out, and the great heart of the public was touched. Crowds followed the cab, cheering it lustily; charming girls scaled it to get his autograph; interviews appeared in the better class of papers, and society invited him to dinner and added, "Do come in the kennel."

On that eventful Thursday week, Mrs. Darling was in the night-nursery awaiting George's return home; a very sad-eyed woman. Now that we look at her closely and remember the gaiety of her in the old days, all gone now just because she has lost her babes, I find I won't be able to say nasty things about her after all. If she was too fond of her rubbishy children, she couldn't help it. Look at her in her chair, where she has fallen asleep. The corner of her mouth, where one looks first, is almost withered up. Her hand moves restlessly on her breast as if she had a pain there. Some like Peter best, and some like Wendy best, but I like her best. Suppose, to make her happy, we whisper to her in her sleep that the brats are coming back. They are really within two miles of the window now, and flying strong, but all

we need whisper is that they are on the way. Let's.

It is a pity we did it, for she has started up, calling their names; and there is no one in the room but Nana.

"O Nana, I dreamt my dear ones had come back."

Nana had filmy eyes, but all she could do was put her paw gently on her mistress's lap; and they were sitting together thus when the kennel was brought back. As Mr. Darling puts his head out to kiss his wife, we see that his face is more worn than of yore, but has a softer expression.

He gave his hat to Liza, who took it scornfully; for she had no imagination, and was quite incapable of understanding the motives of such a man. Outside, the crowd who had accompanied the cab home were still cheering, and he was naturally not unmoved.

"Listen to them," he said; "it is very gratifying."

"Lots of little boys," sneered Liza.

"There were several adults to-day," he assured her with a faint flush; but when she tossed her head he had not a word of reproof for her. Social success had not spoilt him; it had made him sweeter. For some time he sat with his head out of the kennel, talking with Mrs. Darling of this success, and pressing her hand reassuringly when she said she hoped his head would not be turned by it.

"But if I had been a weak man," he said. "Good heavens, if I had been a weak man!"

"And, George," she said timidly, "you are as full of remorse as ever, aren't you?"

"Full of remorse as ever, dearest! See my punishment: living in a kennel."

"But it is punishment, isn't it, George? You are sure you are not enjoying it?"

"My love!"

You may be sure she begged his pardon; and then, feeling drowsy, he curled round in the kennel.

"Won't you play me to sleep," he asked, "on the nursery piano?" and as she was crossing to the day-nursery he added thoughtlessly, "And shut that window. I feel a draught."

"O George, never ask me to do that. The window must always be left open for them, always, always."

Now it was his turn to beg her pardon; and she went into the day-nursery and played, and soon he was asleep; and while he slept, Wendy and John and Michael flew into the room.

Oh no. We have written it so, because that was the charming arrangement planned by them before we left the ship; but something must have happened since then, for it is not they who have flown in,

it is Peter and Tinker Bell.

Peter's first words tell all.

"Quick Tink," he whispered, "close the window; bar it! That's right. Now you and I must get away by the door; and when Wendy comes she will think her mother has barred her out; and she will have to go back with me."

Now I understand what had hitherto puzzled me, why when Peter had exterminated the pirates he did not return to the island and leave Tink to escort the children to the mainland. This trick had been in his head all the time.

Instead of feeling that he was behaving badly he danced with glee; then he peeped into the day-nursery to see who was playing. He whispered to Tink, "It's Wendy's mother! She is a pretty lady, but not so pretty as my mother. Her mouth is full of thimbles, but not so full as my mother's was."

Of course he knew nothing whatever about his mother; but he sometimes bragged about her.

He did not know the tune, which was "Home, Sweet Home," but he knew it was saying, "Come back, Wendy, Wendy, Wendy"; and he cried exultantly, "You will never see Wendy again, lady, for the window is barred!"

He peeped in again to see why the music had stopped, and now he saw that Mrs. Darling had laid her head on the box, and that two tears were sitting on her eyes.

"She wants me to unbar the window," thought Peter, "but I won't, not I!"

He peeped again, and the tears were still there, or another two had taken their place.

"She's awfully fond of Wendy," he said to himself. He was angry with her now for not seeing why she could not have Wendy.

The reason was so simple: "I'm fond of her too. We can't both have her, lady."

But the lady would not make the best of it, and he was unhappy. He ceased to look at her, but even then she would not let go of him. He skipped about and made funny faces, but when he stopped it was just as if she were inside him, knocking.

"Oh, all right," he said at last, and gulped. Then he unbarred the window. "Come on, Tink," he cried, with a frightful sneer at the laws of nature; "we don't want any silly mothers"; and he flew away.

Thus Wendy and John and Michael found the window open for them after all, which of course was more than they deserved. They alighted on the floor, quite unashamed of themselves, and the youngest one had already forgotten his home.

"John," he said, looking around him doubtfully, "I think I have

 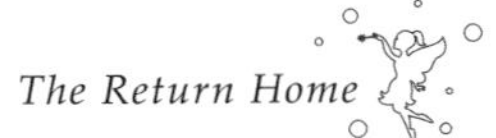

been here before."

"Of course you have, you silly. There is your old bed."

"So it is," Michael said, but not with much conviction.

"I say," cried John, "the kennel!" and he dashed across to look into it.

"Perhaps Nana is inside it," Wendy said.

But John whistled. "Hullo," he said, "there's a man inside it."

"It's father!" exclaimed Wendy.

"Let me see father," Michael begged eagerly, and he took a good look. "He is not so big as the pirate I killed," he said with such frank disappointment that I am glad Mr. Darling was asleep; it would have been sad if those had been the first words he heard his little Michael say.

Wendy and John had been taken aback somewhat at finding their father in the kennel.

"Surely," said John, like one who had lost faith in his memory, "he used not to sleep in the kennel?"

"John," Wendy said falteringly, "perhaps we don't remember the old life as well as we thought we did."

A chill fell upon them; and serve them right.

"It is very careless of mother," said that young scoundrel John, "not to be here when we come back."

It was then that Mrs. Darling began playing again.

"It's mother!" cried Wendy, peeping.

"So it is!" said John.

"Then are you not really our mother, Wendy?" asked Michael, who was surely sleepy.

"Oh dear!" exclaimed Wendy, with her first real twinge of remorse, "it was quite time we came back."

"Let us creep in," John suggested, "and put our hands over her eyes."

But Wendy, who saw that they must break the joyous news more gently, had a better plan.

"Let us all slip into our beds, and be there when she comes in, just as if we had never been away."

And so when Mrs. Darling went back to the night-nursery to see if her husband was asleep, all the beds were occupied. The children waited for her cry of joy, but it did not come. She saw them, but she did not believe they were there. You see, she saw them in their beds so often in her dreams that she thought this was just the dream hanging around her still.

She sat down in the chair by the fire, where in the old days she had nursed them.

They could not understand this, and a cold fear fell upon all the three of them.

"Mother!" Wendy cried.

"That's Wendy," she said, but still she was sure it was the dream.

"Mother!"

"That's John," she said.

"Mother!" cried Michael. He knew her now.

"That's Michael," she said, and she stretched out her arms for the three little selfish children they would never envelop again. Yes, they did, they went round Wendy and John and Michael, who had slipped out of bed and run to her.

"George, George!" she cried when she could speak; and Mr. Darling woke to share her bliss, and Nana came rushing in. There could not have been a lovelier sight; but there was none to see it except a little boy who was staring in at the window. He had had ecstasies innumerable that other children can never know; but he was looking through the window at the one joy from which he must be for ever barred.

Chapter 17

When Wendy Grew Up

I hope you want to know what became of the other boys. They were waiting below to give Wendy time to explain about them.

I hope you want to know what became of the other boys. They were waiting below to give Wendy time to explain about them; and when they had counted five hundred they went up. They went up by the stair, because they thought this would make a better impression. They stood in a row in front of Mrs. Darling, with their hats off, and wishing they were not wearing their pirate clothes. They said nothing, but their eyes asked her to have them. They ought to have looked at Mr. Darling also, but they forgot about him.

Of course Mrs. Darling said at once that she would have them; but Mr. Darling was curiously depressed, and they saw that he considered six a rather large number.

"I must say," he said to Wendy, "that you don't do things by halves," a grudging remark which the twins thought was pointed at them.

The first twin was the proud one, and he asked, flushing, "Do you think we should be too much of a handful, sir? Because, if so, we can go away."

"Father!" Wendy cried, shocked; but still the cloud was on him. He knew he was behaving unworthily, but he could not help it.

"We could lie doubled up," said Nibs.

"I always cut their hair myself," said Wendy.

"George!" Mrs. Darling exclaimed, pained to see her dear one showing himself in such an unfavourable light.

Then he burst into tears, and the truth came out. He was as glad to have them as she was, he said, but he thought they should have asked his consent as well as hers, instead of treating him as a cypher in his own house.

"I don't think he is a cypher," Tootles cried instantly. "Do you think he is a cypher, Curly?"

"No, I don't. Do you think he is a cypher, Slightly?"

"Rather not. Twin, what do you think?"

It turned out that not one of them thought him a cypher; and he was absurdly gratified, and said he would find space for them all in the drawing-room if they fitted in.

"We'll fit in, sir," they assured him.

"Then follow the leader," he cried gaily. "Mind you, I am not sure that we have a drawing-room, but we pretend we have, and it's all the same. Hoop la!"

He went off dancing through the house, and they all cried "Hoop la!" and danced after him, searching for the drawing-room; and I forget whether they found it, but at any rate they found corners, and they all fitted in.

As for Peter, he saw Wendy once again before he flew away. He did not exactly come to the window, but he brushed against it in passing so that she could open it if she liked and call to him. That is what she did.

"Hullo, Wendy, good-bye," he said.

"Oh dear, are you going away?"

"Yes."

"You don't feel, Peter," she said falteringly, "that you would like to say anything to my parents about a very sweet subject?"

"No."

"About me, Peter?"

"No."

Mrs. Darling came to the window, for at present she was keeping a sharp eye on Wendy. She told Peter that she had adopted all the other boys, and would like to adopt him also.

"Would you send me to school?" he inquired craftily.

"Yes."

"And then to an office?"

"I suppose so."

"Soon I would be a man?"

"Very soon."

"I don't want to go to school and learn solemn things," he told her passionately. “I don’t want to be a man. O Wendy’s mother, if I was to wake up and feel there was a beard!”

“Peter,” said Wendy the comforter, “I should love you in a beard;” and Mrs. Darling stretched out her arms to him, but he repulsed her.

“Keep back, lady, no one is going to catch me and make me a man.”

“But where are you going to live?”

“With Tink in the house we built for Wendy. The fairies are to put it high up among the tree tops where they sleep at nights.”

“How lovely,” cried Wendy so longingly that Mrs. Darling tightened her grip.

“I thought all the fairies were dead,” Mrs. Darling said.

“There are always a lot of young ones,” explained Wendy, who was now quite an authority, “because you see when a new baby laughs for the first time a new fairy is born, and as there are always new babies there are always new fairies. They live in nests on the tops of trees; and the mauve ones are boys and the white ones are girls, and the blue ones are just little sillies who are not sure what they are.”

“I shall have such fun,” said Peter, with eye on Wendy.

“It will be rather lonely in the evening,” she said, “sitting by the fire.”

“I shall have Tink.”

"Tink can't go a twentieth part of the way round," she reminded him a little tartly.

"Sneaky tell-tale!" Tink called out from somewhere round the corner.

"It doesn't matter," Peter said.

"O Peter, you know it matters."

"Well, then, come with me to the little house."

"May I, mummy?"

"Certainly not. I have got you home again, and I mean to keep you."

"But he does so need a mother."

"So do you, my love."

"Oh, all right," Peter said, as if he had asked her from politeness merely; but Mrs. Darling saw his mouth twitch, and she made this handsome offer: to let Wendy go to him for a week every year to do his spring cleaning. Wendy would have preferred a more permanent arrangement; and it seemed to her that spring would be long in coming; but this promise sent Peter away quite gay again. He had no sense of time, and was so full of adventures that all I have told you about him is only a halfpenny-worth of them. I suppose it was because Wendy knew this that her last words to him were these rather plaintive ones:

"You won't forget me, Peter, will you, before spring cleaning time comes?"

Of course Peter promised; and then he flew away. He took Mrs. Darling's kiss with him. The kiss that had been for no one else, Peter took quite easily. Funny. But she seemed satisfied.

Of course all the boys went to school; and most of them got into Class III, but Slightly was put first into Class IV and then into Class V. Class I is the top class. Before they had attended school a week they saw what goats they had been not to remain on the island; but it was too late now, and soon they settled down to being as ordinary as you or me or Jenkins minor. It is sad to have to say that the power to fly gradually left them. At first Nana tied their feet to the bed-posts so that they should not fly away in the night; and one of their diversions by day was to pretend to fall off buses; but by and by they ceased to tug at their bonds in bed, and found that they hurt themselves when they let go of the bus. In time they could not even fly after their hats. Want of practice, they called it; but what it really meant was that they no longer believed.

Michael believed longer than the other boys, though they jeered at him; so he was with Wendy when Peter came for her at the end of the first year. She flew away with Peter in the frock she had woven from leaves and berries in the Neverland, and her one fear was that he might notice how short it had become; but he never noticed, he had so much to say about himself.

She had looked forward to thrilling talks with him about old times, but new adventures had crowded the old ones from his mind.

"Who is Captain Hook?" he asked with interest when she spoke of the arch enemy.

"Don't you remember," she asked, amazed, "how you killed him and saved all our lives?"

"I forget them after I kill them," he replied carelessly.

When she expressed a doubtful hope that Tinker Bell would be glad to see her he said, "Who is Tinker Bell?"

"O Peter," she said, shocked; but even when she explained he could not remember.

"There are such a lot of them," he said. "I expect she is no more."

I expect he was right, for fairies don't live long, but they are so little that a short time seems a good while to them.

Wendy was pained too to find that the past year was but as yesterday to Peter; it had seemed such a long year of waiting to her. But he was exactly as fascinating as ever, and they had a lovely spring cleaning in the little house on the tree tops.

Next year he did not come for her. She waited in a new frock because the old one simply would not meet; but he never came.

"Perhaps he is ill," Michael said.

"You know he is never ill."

Michael came close to her and whispered, with a shiver, "Perhaps there is no such person, Wendy!" and then Wendy would have cried if Michael had not been crying.

Peter came next spring cleaning; and the strange thing was that he never knew he had missed a year.

That was the last time the girl Wendy ever saw him. For a little longer she tried for his sake not to have growing pains; and she felt she was untrue to him when she got a prize for general knowledge. But the years came and went without bringing the careless boy; and when they met again Wendy was a married woman, and Peter was no more to her than a little dust in the box in which she had kept her toys. Wendy was grown up. You need not be sorry for her. She was one of the kind that likes to grow up. In the end she grew up of her own free will a day quicker than other girls.

All the boys were grown up and done for by this time; so it is scarcely worth while saying anything more about them. You may see the twins and Nibs and Curly any day going to an office, each carrying a little bag and an umbrella. Michael is an engine- driver. Slightly married a lady of title, and so he became a lord. You see that judge in a wig coming out at the iron door? That used to be Tootles. The bearded man who doesn't know any story to tell his children was once John.

Wendy was married in white with a pink sash. It is strange to think that Peter did not alight in the church and forbid the banns.

Years rolled on again, and Wendy had a daughter. This ought not to be written in ink but in a golden splash.

She was called Jane, and always had an odd inquiring look, as if from the moment she arrived on the mainland she wanted to ask questions. When she was old enough to ask them they were mostly about Peter Pan. She loved to hear of Peter, and Wendy told her all she could remember in the very nursery from which the famous flight had taken place. It was Jane's nursery now, for her father had bought it at the three per cents from Wendy's father, who was no longer fond of stairs. Mrs. Darling was now dead and forgotten.

There were only two beds in the nursery now, Jane's and her nurse's; and there was no kennel, for Nana also had passed away. She died of old age, and at the end she had been rather difficult to get on with; being very firmly convinced that no one knew how to look after children except herself.

Once a week Jane's nurse had her evening off; and then it was Wendy's part to put Jane to bed. That was the time for stories. It was Jane's invention to raise the sheet over her mother's head and her own, this making a tent, and in the awful darkness to whisper:

"What do we see now?"

"I don't think I see anything to-night," says Wendy, with a feeling that if Nana were here she would object to further conversation.

"Yes, you do," says Jane, "you see when you were a little girl."

"That is a long time ago, sweetheart," says Wendy. "Ah me, how time flies!"

"Does it fly," asks the artful child, "the way you flew when you were a little girl?"

"The way I flew? Do you know, Jane, I sometimes wonder whether I ever did really fly."

"Yes, you did."

"The dear old days when I could fly!"

"Why can't you fly now, mother?"

"Because I am grown up, dearest. When people grow up they forget the way."

"Why do they forget the way?"

"Because they are no longer gay and innocent and heartless. It is only the gay and innocent and heartless who can fly."

"What is gay and innocent and heartless? I do wish I were gay and innocent and heartless."

Or perhaps Wendy admits she does see something.

"I do believe," she says, "that it is this nursery."

"I do believe it is," says Jane. "Go on."

They are now embarked on the great adventure of the night when Peter flew in looking for his shadow.

"The foolish fellow," says Wendy, "tried to stick it on with soap, and when he could not he cried, and that woke me, and I sewed it on for him."

"You have missed a bit," interrupts Jane, who now knows the story better than her mother. "When you saw him sitting on the floor crying, what did you say?"

"I sat up in bed and I said, 'Boy, why are you crying?'"

"Yes, that was it," says Jane, with a big breath.

"And then he flew us all away to the Neverland and the fairies and the pirates and the redskins and the mermaid's lagoon, and the home under the ground, and the little house."

"Yes! which did you like best of all?"

"I think I liked the home under the ground best of all."

"Yes, so do I. What was the last thing Peter ever said to you?"

"The last thing he ever said to me was, 'Just always be waiting for me, and then some night you will hear me crowing.'"

"Yes."

"But, alas, he forgot all about me," Wendy said it with a smile. She was as grown up as that.

"What did his crow sound like?" Jane asked one evening.

"It was like this," Wendy said, trying to imitate Peter's crow.

"No, it wasn't," Jane said gravely, "it was like this"; and she did it ever so much better than her mother.

Wendy was a little startled. "My darling, how can you know?"

"I often hear it when I am sleeping," Jane said.

"Ah yes, many girls hear it when they are sleeping, but I was the only one who heard it awake."

"Lucky you," said Jane.

And then one night came the tragedy. It was the spring of the year, and the story had been told for the night, and Jane was now asleep in her bed. Wendy was sitting on the floor, very close to the fire, so as to see to darn, for there was no other light in the nursery; and while she sat darning she heard a crow. Then the window blew open as of old, and Peter dropped in on the floor.

He was exactly the same as ever, and Wendy saw at once that he still had all his first teeth.

He was a little boy, and she was grown up. She huddled by the fire not daring to move, helpless and guilty, a big woman.

"Hullo, Wendy," he said, not noticing any difference, for he was thinking chiefly of himself; and in the dim light her white dress might have been the nightgown in which he had seen her first.

"Hullo, Peter," she replied faintly, squeezing herself as small as possible. Something inside her was crying "Woman, Woman, let go of me."

"Hullo, where is John?" he asked, suddenly missing the third bed.

"John is not here now," she gasped.

"Is Michael asleep?" he asked, with a careless glance at Jane.

"Yes," she answered; and now she felt that she was untrue to Jane as well as to Peter.

"That is not Michael," she said quickly, lest a judgment should fall on her.

Peter looked. "Hullo, is it a new one?"

"Yes."

"Boy or girl?"

"Girl."

Now surely he would understand; but not a bit of it.

"Peter," she said, faltering, "are you expecting me to fly away with you?"

"Of course; that is why I have come." He added a little sternly, "Have you forgotten that this is spring cleaning time?"

She knew it was useless to say that he had let many spring cleaning times pass.

"I can't come," she said apologetically, "I have forgotten how to fly."

"I'll soon teach you again."

"O Peter, don't waste the fairy dust on me."

She had risen; and now at last a fear assailed him. "What is it?" he cried, shrinking.

"I will turn up the light," she said, "and then you can see for yourself."

For almost the only time in his life that I know of, Peter was afraid. "Don't turn up the light," he cried.

She let her hands play in the hair of the tragic boy. She was not a little girl heart-broken about him; she was a grown woman smiling at it all, but they were wet smiles.

Then she turned up the light, and Peter saw. He gave a cry of pain; and when the tall beautiful creature stooped to lift him in her arms he drew back sharply.

"What is it?" he cried again.

She had to tell him.

"I am old, Peter. I am ever so much more than twenty. I grew up long ago."

"You promised not to!"

"I couldn't help it. I am a married woman, Peter."

"No, you're not."

"Yes, and the little girl in the bed is my baby."

"No, she's not."

But he supposed she was; and he took a step towards the sleeping child with his dagger upraised. Of course he did not strike. He sat down on the floor and sobbed; and Wendy did not know how to comfort him, though she could have done it so easily once. She was only a woman now, and she ran out of the room to try to think.

Peter continued to cry, and soon his sobs woke Jane. She sat up in bed, and was interested at once.

"Boy," she said, "why are you crying?"

Peter rose and bowed to her, and she bowed to him from the bed.

"Hullo," he said.

"Hullo," said Jane.

"My name is Peter Pan," he told her.

"Yes, I know."

"I came back for my mother," he explained, "to take her to the Neverland."

"Yes, I know," Jane said, "I have been waiting for you."

When Wendy returned diffidently she found Peter sitting on the bed-post crowing gloriously, while Jane in her nighty was flying round the room in solemn ecstasy.

"She is my mother," Peter explained; and Jane descended and stood by his side, with the look in her face that he liked to see on ladies when they gazed at him.

"He does so need a mother," Jane said.

"Yes, I know." Wendy admitted rather forlornly; "no one knows it so well as I."

"Good-bye," said Peter to Wendy; and he rose in the air, and the shameless Jane rose with him; it was already her easiest way of moving about.

Wendy rushed to the window.

"No, no," she cried.

"It is just for spring cleaning time," Jane said, "he wants me always to do his spring cleaning."

"If only I could go with you," Wendy sighed.

"You see you can't fly," said Jane.

Of course in the end Wendy let them fly away together. Our last glimpse of her shows her at the window, watching them receding into the sky until they were as small as stars.

As you look at Wendy, you may see her hair becoming white, and her figure little again, for all this happened long ago. Jane is now a common grown-up, with a daughter called Margaret; and every spring cleaning time, except when he forgets, Peter comes for Margaret and takes her to the Neverland, where she tells him stories about himself, to which he listens eagerly. When Margaret grows up she will have a daughter, who is to be Peter's mother in turn; and thus it will go on, so long as children are gay and innocent and heartless.

Memo

Memo

Memo

Memo